Casa Braccio by F. Marion Crawford

Francis Marion Crawford was born on August 2nd, 1854 at Bagni di Lucca, Italy. An only son and a nephew to Julia Ward Howe, the American poet and writer of 'The Battle Hymn of the Republic'.

His education began at St Paul's School, Concord, New Hampshire, then to Cambridge University; University of Heidelberg; and the University of Rome.

In 1879 Crawford went to India, to study Sanskrit and then edited The Indian Herald. In 1881 he returned to America to continue his Sanskrit studies at Harvard University.

At this time in Boston he lived at his Aunt Julia house and in the company of his Uncle, Sam Ward. His family was concerned about his employment prospects. After a singing career as a baritone was ruled out, he was encouraged to write.

In December 1882 his first novel, 'Mr Isaacs', was an immediate hit which was amplified by 'Dr Claudius' in 1883.

In October 1884 he married Elizabeth Berdan. They went on to have two sons and two daughters.

Encouraged by his excellent start to a literary career he returned to Italy with Elizabeth to make a permanent home, principally in Sant' Agnello, where he bought the Villa Renzi that then became Villa Crawford.

In the late 1890s, he began to write his historical works: 'Ave Roma Immortalis' (1898), 'Rulers of the South' (1900) and 'Gleanings from Venetian History' (1905). The Saracinesca series is perhaps his best work. 'Saracinesca' was followed by 'Sant' Ilario' in 1889, 'Don Orsino' in 1892 and 'Corleone' in 1897, that being the first major treatment of the Mafia in literature.

Francis Marion Crawford died at Sorrento on Good Friday 1909 at Villa Crawford of a heart attack.

Index of Contents

PART I

SISTER MARIA ADDOLORATA

CHAPTER I

Subiaco lies beyond Tivoli, southeast from Rome, at the upper end of a wild gorge in the Samnite mountains. It is an archbishopric, and gives a title to a cardinal, which alone would make it a town of importance. It shares with Monte Cassino the honour of having been chosen by Saint Benedict and Saint Scholastica, his sister, as the site of a monastery and a convent; and in a cell in the rock a portrait of the holy man is still well preserved, which is believed, not without reason, to have been painted from life, although Saint Benedict died early in the fifth century. The town itself rises abruptly to a great height upon a mass of rock, almost conical in shape, crowned by the cardinal's palace, and surrounded on three sides by rugged mountains. On the third, it looks down the rapidly widening valley in the direction of Vicovaro, near which the Licenza runs into the Anio, in the neighbourhood of Horace's farm. It is a very ancient town, and in its general appearance it does not differ very much from many similar ones amongst the Italian mountains; but its position is exceptionally good, and its importance has been stamped upon it by the hands of those who have thought it worth holding since the days of ancient Rome. Of late it has, of course, acquired a certain modernness of aspect; it has planted acacia trees in its little piazza, and it has a gorgeously arrayed municipal band. But from a little distance one neither hears the band nor sees the trees, the grim mediæval fortifications frown upon the valley, and the time-stained dwellings, great and small, rise in rugged irregularity against the lighter brown of the rocky background and the green of scattered olive groves and chestnuts. Those features, at least, have not changed, and show no disposition to change during generations to come.

In the year 1844, modern civilization had not yet set in, and Subiaco was, within, what it still appears to be from without, a somewhat gloomy stronghold of the Middle Ages, rearing its battlements and towers in a shadowy gorge, above a mountain torrent, inhabited by primitive and passionate people, dominated by ecclesiastical institutions, and, though distinctly Roman, a couple of hundred years behind Rome itself in all matters ethic and æsthetic. It was still the scene of the Santacroce murder, which really decided Beatrice Cenci's fate; it was still the gathering place of highwaymen and outlaws, whose activity found an admirable field through all the region of hill and plain between the Samnite range and the sea, while the almost inaccessible fortresses of the higher mountains, towards Trevi and the Serra di Sant' Antonio, offered a safe refuge from the halfhearted pursuit of Pope Gregory's lazy soldiers.

Something of what one may call the life-and-death earnestness of earlier times, when passion was motive and prejudice was law, survived at that time and even much later; the ferocity of practical love and hatred dominated the theory and practice of justice in the public life of the smaller towns, while the patriarchal system subjected the family in almost absolute servitude to its head.

There was nothing very surprising in the fact that the head of the house of Braccio should have obliged one of his daughters to take the veil in the Convent of Carmelite nuns, just within the gate of Subiaco, as his sister had taken it many years earlier. Indeed, it was customary in the family of the Princes of Gerano that one of the women should be a Carmelite, and it was a tradition not unattended with worldly advantages to the sisterhood, that the Braccio nun, whenever there was one, should be the abbess of that particular convent.

Maria Teresa Braccio had therefore yielded, though very unwillingly, to her father's insistence, and having passed through her novitiate, had finally taken the veil as a Carmelite of Subiaco, in the year 1841, on the distinct understanding that when her aunt died she was to be abbess in the elder lady's stead. The abbess herself was, indeed, in excellent health and not yet fifty years old, so that Maria Teresa—in religion Maria Addolorata—might have a long time to wait before she was promoted to an honour which she regarded as hereditary; but the prospect of such promotion was almost her only compensation for all she had left behind her, and she lived upon it and concentrated her character upon it, and practised the part she was to play, when she was quite sure that she was not observed.

Nature had not made her for a recluse, least of all for a nun of such a rigid Order as the Carmelites. The short taste of a brilliant social life which she had been allowed to enjoy, in accordance with an ancient tradition, before finally taking the veil, had shown her clearly enough the value of what she was to abandon, and at the same time had altogether confirmed her father in his decision. Compared with the freedom of the present day, the restrictions imposed upon a young girl in the Roman society of those times were, of course, tyrannical in the extreme, and the average modern young lady would almost as willingly go into a convent as submit to them. But Maria Teresa had received an impression which nothing could efface. Her intuitive nature had divined the possible semi-emancipation of marriage, and her temperament had felt in a certain degree the extremes of joyous exaltation and of that entrancing sadness which is love's premonition, and which tells maidens what love is before they know him, by making them conscious of the breadth and depth of his yet vacant dwelling.

She had learned in that brief time that she was beautiful, and she had felt that she could love and that she should be loved in return. She had seen the world as a princess and had felt it as a woman, and she had understood all that she must give up in taking the veil. But she had been offered no choice, and though she had contemplated opposition, she had not dared to revolt. Being absolutely in the power of her parents, so far as she was aware, she had accepted the fatality of their will, and bent her fair head to be shorn of its glory and her broad forehead to be covered forever from the gaze of men. And having submitted, she had gone through it all bravely and proudly, as perhaps she would have gone through other things, even to death itself, being a daughter of an old race, accustomed to deify honour and to make its divinities of tradition. For the rest of her natural life she was to live on the memories of one short, magnificent year, forever to be contented with the grim rigidity of conventual life in an ancient cloister surrounded by gloomy mountains. She was to be a veiled shadow amongst veiled shades, a priestess of sorrow amongst sad virgins; and though, if she lived long enough, she was to be the chief of them and their ruler, her very superiority could only make her desolation more complete, until her own shadow, like the others, should be gathered into eternal darkness.

Sister Maria Addolorata had certain privileges for which her companions would have given much, but which were traditionally the right of such ladies of the Braccio family as took the veil. For instance, she had a cell which, though not larger than the other cells, was better situated, for it had a little balcony looking over the convent garden, and high enough to afford a view of the distant valley and of the hills which bounded it, beyond the garden wall. It was entered by the last door in the corridor within, and was near the abbess's apartment, which was entered from the corridor, through a small antechamber which also gave access to the vast linen-presses. The balcony, too, had a little staircase leading down into the garden. It had always been the custom to carry the linen to and from the laundry through Maria Addolorata's cell, and through a postern gate in the garden wall, the washing being done in the town. By this plan, the annoyance was avoided of carrying the huge baskets through the whole length of the convent, to and from the main entrance, which was also much further removed from the house of Sora Nanna, the chief laundress. Moreover, Maria Addolorata had charge of all the convent linen, and the employment thus afforded her was an undoubted privilege in itself, for occupation of any kind not devotional was excessively scarce in such an existence.

In the eyes of the other nuns, the constant society of the abbess herself was also a privilege, and one not by any means to be despised. After all, the abbess and her niece were nearly related, they could talk of the affairs of their family, and the abbess doubtless received many letters from Rome containing all the interesting news of the day, and all the social gossip—perfectly innocent, of course which was the chronicle of Roman life. These were valuable compensations, and the nuns envied them. The abbess, too, saw her brother, the archbishop and titular cardinal of Subiaco, when the princely prelate came out from Rome for the coolness of the mountains in August and September, and his conversation was said to be not only edifying, but fascinating. The cardinal was a very good man, like many of the Braccio family, but he was also a man of the world, who had been sent upon foreign missions of importance, and had acquired some worldly fame as well as much ecclesiastical dignity in the course of his long life. It must be delightful, the nuns thought, to be his own sister, to receive long visits from him, and to hear all he had to say about the busy world of Rome. To most of them, everything beyond Rome was outer darkness.

But though the nuns envied the abbess and Maria Addolorata, they did not venture to say so, and they hardly dared to think so, even when they were all alone, each in her cell; for the concentration of conventual life magnifies small spiritual sins in the absence of anything really sinful, and to admit that she even faintly wishes she might be some one else is to tarnish the brightness of the nun's scrupulously polished conscience. It would be as great a misdeed, perhaps, as to allow the attention to wander to worldly matters during times of especial devotion. Nevertheless, the envy showed itself, very perceptibly and much against the will of the sisters themselves, in a certain cold deference of manner towards the young and beautiful nun who was one day to be the superior of them all by force of circumstances for which she deserved no credit. She had the position among them, and something of the isolation, of a young royal princess amongst the ladies of her queen mother's court.

There was about her, too, an undefinable something, like the shadow of future fate, a something almost impossible to describe, and yet distinctly appreciable to all who saw her and lived with her. It came upon her especially when she was silent and abstracted, when she was kneeling in her place in the choir, or was alone upon her little balcony over the garden. At such times a luminous pallor gradually took the place of her fresh and healthy complexion, her eyes grew unnaturally dark, with a deep, fixed fire in them, and the regular features took upon them the white, set straightness of a death mask. Sometimes, at such moments, a shiver ran through her, even in summer, and she drew her breath sharply once or twice, as though she were hurt. The expression was not one of suffering or pain, but was rather that of a person conscious of some great danger which must be met without fear or flinching.

She would have found it very hard to explain what she felt just then. She might have said that it was a consciousness of something unknown. She could not have said more than that. It brought no vision with it, beatific or horrifying; it was not the consequence of methodical contemplation, as the trance state is; and it was followed by no reaction nor sense of uneasiness. It simply came and went as the dark shadow of a thundercloud passing between her and the sun, and leaving no trace behind.

There was nothing to account for it, unless it could be explained by heredity, and no one had ever suggested any such explanation to Maria. It was true that there had been more than one tragedy in the Braccio family since they had first lifted their heads above the level of their contemporaries to become Roman Barons, in the old days before such titles as prince and duke had come into use. But then, most of the old families could tell of deeds as cruel and lives as passionate as any remembered by Maria's race, and Italians, though superstitious in unexpected ways, have little of that belief in hereditary fate which is common enough in the gloomy north.

"Was Sister Maria Addolorata a great sinner, before she became a nun?" asked Annetta, Sora Nanna's daughter, of her mother, one day, as they came away from the convent.

"What are you saying!" exclaimed the washerwoman, in a tone of rebuke. "She is a great lady, and the niece of the abbess and of the cardinal. Sometimes certain ideas pass through your head, my daughter!"

And Sora Nanna gesticulated, unable to express herself.

"Then she sins in her throat," observed Annetta, calmly. "But you do not even look at her—so many sheets—so many pillow-cases—and good day! But while you count, I look."

"Why should I look at her?" inquired Nanna, shifting the big empty basket she carried on her head, hitching her broad shoulders and wrinkling her leathery forehead, as her small eyes turned upward. "Do you take me for a man, that I should make eyes at a nun?"

"And I? Am I a man? And yet I look at her. I see nothing but her face when we are there, and afterwards I think about it. What harm is there? She sins in her throat. I know it."

Sora Nanna hitched her shoulders impatiently again, and said nothing. The two women descended through the steep and narrow street, slippery and wet with slimy, coal black mud that glittered on the rough cobble-stones. Nanna walked first, and Annetta followed close behind her, keeping step, and setting her feet exactly where her mother had trod, with the instinctive certainty of the born mountaineer. With heads erect and shoulders square, each with one hand on her hip and the other hanging down, they carried their burdens swiftly and safely, with a swinging, undulating gait as though it were a pleasure to them to move, and would require an effort to stop rather than to walk on forever. They wore shoes because they were well-to-do people, and chose to show that they were when they went up to the convent. But for the rest they were clad in the costume of the neighbourhood,—the coarse white shift, close at the throat, the scarlet bodice, the short, dark, gathered skirt, and the dark blue carpet apron, with flowers woven on a white stripe across the lower end. Both wore heavy gold earrings, and Sora Nanna had eight or ten strings of large coral beads around her throat.

Annetta was barely fifteen years old, brown, slim, and active as a lizard. She was one of those utterly unruly and untamable girls of whom there are two or three in every Italian village, in mountain or plain, a creature in whom a living consciousness of living nature took the place of thought, and with whom to be conscious was to speak, without reason or hesitation. The small, keen, black eyes were set under immense and arched black eyebrows which made the eyes themselves seem larger than they were, and the projecting temples cast shadows to the cheek which hid the rudimentary modelling of the coarse lower lids. The ears were flat and ill-developed, but close to the head and not large; the teeth very short, though perfectly regular and exceedingly white; the lips long, mobile, brown rather than red, and generally parted like those of a wild animal. The girl's smoothly sinewy throat moved with every step, showing the quick play of the elastic cords and muscles. Her blue-black hair was plaited, though far from neatly, and the braids were twisted into an irregular flat coil, generally hidden by the flap of the white embroidered cloth cross-folded upon her head and hanging down behind.

For some minutes the mother and daughter continued to pick their way down the winding lanes between the dark houses of the upper village. Then Sora Nanna put out her right hand as a signal to Annetta that she meant to stop, and she stood still on the steep descent and turned deliberately till she could see the girl.

"What are you saying?" she began, as though there had been no pause in the conversation. "That Sister Maria Addolorata sins in her throat! But how can she sin in her throat, since she sees no man but the gardener and the priest? Indeed, you say foolish things!"

"And what has that to do with it?" inquired Annetta. "She must have seen enough of men in Rome, every one of them a great lord. And who tells you that she did not love one of them and does not wish that she were married to him? And if that is not a sin in the throat, I do not know what to say. There is my answer."

"You say foolish things," repeated Sora Nanna.

Then she turned deliberately away and began to descend once more, with an occasional dissatisfied movement of the shoulders.

"For the rest," observed Annetta, "it is not my business. I would rather look at the Englishman when he is eating meat than at Sister Maria when she is counting clothes! I do not know whether he is a wolf or a man."

"Eh! The Englishman!" exclaimed Sora Nanna. "You will look so much at the Englishman that you will make blood with Gigetto, who wishes you well, and when Gigetto has waited for the Englishman at the corner of the forest, what shall we all have? The galleys. What do you see in the Englishman? He has red hair and long, long teeth. Yes—just like a wolf. You are right. And if he pays for meat, why should he not eat it? If he did not pay, it would be different. It would soon be finished. Heaven send us a little money without any Englishman! Besides, Gigetto said the other day that he would wait for him at the corner of the forest. And Gigetto, when he says a thing, he does it."

"And why should we go to the galleys if Gigetto waits for the Englishman?" inquired Annetta.

"Silly!" cried the older woman. "Because Gigetto would take your father's gun, since he has none of his own. That would be enough. We should have done it!"

Annetta shrugged her shoulders and said nothing.

"But take care," continued Sora Nanna. "Your father sleeps with one eye open. He sees you, and he sees also the Englishman every day. He says nothing, because he is good. But he has a fist like a paving-stone. I tell you nothing more."

They reached Sora Nanna's house and disappeared under the dark archway. For Sora Nanna and Stefanone, her husband, were rich people for their station, and their house was large and was built with an arch wide enough and high enough for a loaded beast of burden to pass through with a man on its back. And, within, everything was clean and well kept, excepting all that belonged to Annetta. There were airy upper rooms, with well-swept floors of red brick or of beaten cement, furnished with high beds on iron trestles, and wooden stools of well-worn brown oak, and tables painted a vivid green, and primitive lithographs of Saint Benedict and Santa Scholastica and the Addolorata. And there were lofts in which the rich autumn grapes were hung up to dry on strings, and where chestnuts lay in heaps, and figs were spread in symmetrical order on great sheets of the coarse grey paper made in Subiaco. There were apples, too, though poor ones, and there were bins of maize and wheat, waiting to be picked over before being ground in the primeval household mill. And there were hams and sides of bacon, and red peppers, and bundles of dried herbs, and great mountain cheeses on shelves. There was also a guest room, better than the rest, which Stefanone and his wife occasionally let to respectable travellers or to the merchants who came from Rome on business to stay a few days in Subiaco. At the present time the room was rented by the Englishman concerning whom the discussion had arisen between Annetta and her mother.

Angus Dalrymple, M.D., was not an Englishman, as he had tried to explain to Sora Nanna, though without the least success. He was, as his name proclaimed, a Scotchman of the Scotch, and a doctor of medicine. It was true that he had red hair, and an abundance of it, and long white teeth, but Sora Nanna's description was otherwise libellously incomplete and wholly omitted all mention of the good points in his appearance. In the first place, he possessed the characteristic national build in a superior degree of development, with all the lean, bony energy which has done so much hard work in the world. He was broad-shouldered, long-armed, long-legged, deep-chested, and straight, with sinewy hands and singularly well-shaped fingers. His healthy skin had that mottled look produced by countless freckles upon an almost childlike complexion. The large, grave mouth generally concealed the long teeth objected to by Sora Nanna, and the lips, though even and narrow, were strong rather than thin, and their rare smile was both genial and gentle. There were lines—as yet very faint—about the corners of the mouth, which told of a nervous and passionate disposition and of the strong Scotch temper, as well as of a certain sensitiveness which belongs especially to northern races. The pale but very bright blue eyes under shaggy auburn brows were fiery with courage and keen with shrewd enterprise. Dalrymple was assuredly not a man to be despised under any circumstances, intellectually or physically.

His presence in such a place as Subiaco, at a time when hardly any foreigners except painters visited the place, requires some explanation; for he was not an artist, but a doctor, and had never been even tempted to amuse himself with sketching. In the first place, he was a younger son of a good family, and received a moderate allowance, quite sufficient in those days to allow him considerable latitude of expenditure in old-fashioned Italy. Secondly, he had entirely refused to follow any of the professions known as 'liberal.' He had no taste for the law, and he had not the companionable character which alone can make life in the army pleasant in time of peace. His beliefs, or his lack of belief, together with an honourable conscience, made him naturally opposed to all churches. On the other hand, he had been attracted almost from his childhood by scientific subjects, at a period when the discoveries of the last fifty years appeared as misty but beatific visions to men of science. To the disappointment and, to some extent, to the humiliation of his family, he insisted upon studying medicine, at the University of St. Andrew's, as soon as he had obtained his ordinary degree at Cambridge. And having once insisted, nothing could turn him from his purpose, for he possessed English tenacity grafted upon Scotch originality, with a good deal of the strength of both races.

While still a student he had once made a tour in Italy, and like many northerners had fallen under the mysterious spell of the South from the very first. Having a sufficient allowance for all his needs, as has been said, and being attracted by the purely scientific side of his profession rather than by any desire to become a successful practitioner, it was natural enough that on finding himself free to go whither he pleased in pursuit of knowledge, he should have visited Italy again. A third visit had convinced him that he should do well to spend some years in the country; for by that time he had become deeply interested in the study of malarious fevers, which in those days were completely misunderstood. It would be far too much to say that young Dalrymple had at that time formed any complete theory in regard to malaria; but his naturally lonely and concentrated intellect had contemptuously discarded all explanations of malarious phenomena, and, communicating his own ideas to no one, until he should be in possession of proofs for his opinions, he had in reality got hold of the beginning of the truth about germs which has since then revolutionized medicine.

The only object of this short digression has been to show that Angus Dalrymple was not a careless idler and tourist in Italy, only half responsible for what he did, and not at all for what he thought. On the contrary, he was a man of very unusual gifts, of superior education, and of rare enterprise; a strong, silent, thoughtful man, about eight-and-twenty years of age, and just beginning to feel his power as something greater than he had suspected, when he came to spend the autumn months in Subiaco, and hired Sora Nanna's guest room, with a little room leading off it, which he kept locked, and in which he had a table, a chair, a microscope, some books, a few chemicals and some simple apparatus.

His presence had at first roused certain jealous misgivings in the heart of the town physician, Sor Tommaso Taddei, commonly spoken of simply as 'the Doctor,' because there was no other. But Dalrymple was not without tact and knowledge of human nature. He explained that he came as a foreigner to learn from native physicians how malarious fevers were treated in Italy; and he listened with patient intelligence to Sor Tommaso's antiquated theories, and silently watched his still more antiquated practice. And Sor Tommaso, like all people who think that they know a vast deal, highly approved of Dalrymple's submissive silence, and said that the young man was a marvel of modesty, and that if he could stay about ten years in Subiaco and learn something from Sor Tommaso himself, he might really some day be a fairly good doctor,—which were extraordinarily liberal admissions on the part of the old practitioner, and contributed largely towards reassuring Stefanone concerning his lodger's character.

For Stefanone and his wife had their doubts and suspicions. Of course they knew that all foreigners except Frenchmen and Austrians were Protestants, and ate meat on fast days, and were under the most especial protection of the devil, who fattened them in this world that they might burn the better in the next. But Stefanone had never seen the real foreigner at close quarters, and had not conceived it possible that any living human being could devour so much half-cooked flesh in a day as Dalrymple desired for his daily portion, paid for, and consumed. Moreover, there was no man in Subiaco who could and did swallow such portentous draughts of the strong mountain wine, without suffering any apparent effects from his potations. Furthermore, also, Dalrymple did strange things by day and night in the small laboratory he had arranged next to his bedroom, and unholy and evil smells issued at times through the cracks of the door, and penetrated from the bedroom to the stairs outside, and were distinctly perceptible all over the house. Therefore Stefanone maintained for a long time that his lodger was in league with the powers of darkness, and that it was not safe to keep him in the house, though he paid his bill so very regularly, every Saturday, and never quarrelled about the price of his food and drink. On the whole, however, Stefanone abstained from interfering, as he had at first been inclined to do, and entering the laboratory, with the support of the parish priest, a basin of holy water, and a loaded gun— all three of which he considered necessary for an exorcism; and little by little, Sor Tommaso, the doctor, persuaded him that Dalrymple was a worthy young man, deeply engaged in profound studies, and should be respected rather than exorcised.

"Of course," admitted the doctor, "he is a Protestant. But then he has a passport. Let us therefore let him alone."

The existence of the passport—indispensable in those days—was a strong argument in the eyes of the simple Stefanone. He could not conceive that a magician whose soul was sold to the devil could possibly have a passport and be under the protection of the law. So the matter was settled.

CHAPTER II

Sister Maria Addolorata sat by the open door of her cell, looking across the stone parapet of her little balcony, and watching the changing richness of the western sky, as the sun went down far out of sight behind the mountains. Though the month was October, the afternoon was warm; it was very still, and the air had been close in the choir during the Benediction service, which was just over. She leaned back in her chair, and her lips parted as she breathed, with a perceptible desire for refreshment in the breath. She held a piece of needlework in her heavy white hands; the needle had been thrust through the linen, but the stitch had remained unfinished, and one pointed finger pressed the doubled edge against the other, lest the material should slip before she made up her mind to draw the needle through. Deep in the garden under the balcony the late flowers were taking strangely vivid colours out of the bright sky above, and some bits of broken glass, stuck in the mortar on the top of the opposite wall as a protection against thieving boys, glowed like a line of rough rubies against the misty distance. Even the white walls of the bare cell and the coarse grey blanket lying across the foot of the small bed drank in a little of the colour, and looked less grey and less grim.

From the eaves, high above the open door, the swallows shot down into the golden light, striking great circles and reflecting the red gold of the sky from their breasts as they wheeled just beyond the wall, with steady wings wide-stretched, up and down; and each one, turning at full speed, struck upwards again and was out of sight in an instant, above the lintel. The nun watched them, her eyes trying to follow each of them in turn and to recognize them separately as they flashed into sight again and again.

Her lips were parted, and as she sat there she began to sing very softly and quite unconsciously. She could not have told what the song was. The words were strange and oddly divided, and there was a deadly sadness in a certain interval that came back almost with every stave. But the voice itself was beautiful beyond all comparison with ordinary voices, full of deep and touching vibrations and far harmonics, though she sang so softly, all to herself. Notes like hers haunt the ears—and sometimes the heart—when she who sang them has been long dead, and many would give much to hear but a breath of them again.

It was hard for Maria Addolorata not to sing sometimes, when she was all alone in her cell, though it was so strictly forbidden. Singing is a gift of expression, when it is a really natural gift, as much as speech and gesture and the smile on the lips, with the one difference that it is a keener pleasure to him or her that sings than gesture or speech can possibly be. Music, and especially singing, are a physical as well as an intellectual expression, a pleasure of the body as well as a 'delectation' of the soul. To sing naturally and spontaneously is most generally an endowment of natures physically strong and rich by the senses, independently of the mind, though melody may sometimes be the audible translation of a silent thought as well as the unconscious speech of wordless passion.

And in Maria's song there was a strain of that something unknown and fatal, which the nuns sometimes saw in her face and which was in her eyes now, as she sang; for they no longer followed the circling of the swallows, but grew fixed and dark, with fiery reflexions from the sunset sky, and the regular features grew white and straight and square against the deepening shadows within the narrow room. The deep voice trembled a little, and the shoulders had a short, shivering movement under the heavy folds of the dark veil, as the sensation of a presence ran through her and made her shudder. But the voice did not break, and she sang on, louder, now, than she realized, the full notes swelling in her throat, and vibrating between the narrow walls, and floating out through the open door to join the flight of the swallows.

The door of the cell opened gently, but she did not hear, and sang on, leaning back in her chair and gazing still at the pink clouds above the mountains.

"Death is my love, dark-eyed death—"

she sang.

"Maria!"

The abbess was standing in the doorway and speaking to her, but she did not hear.

"His hands are sweetly cold and gentle—
Flowers of leek, and firefly—
Holy Saint John!"

"Maria!" cried the abbess, impatiently. "What follies are you singing? I could hear you in my room!"

Maria Addolorata started and rose from her seat, still holding her needlework, and turning half round towards her superior, with suddenly downcast eyes. The elder lady came forward with slow dignity and walked as far as the door of the balcony, where she stood still for a moment, gazing at the beautiful sky. She was not a stately woman, for she was too short and stout, but she had that calm air of assured superiority which takes the place of stateliness, and which seems to belong especially to those who occupy important positions in the Church. Her large features, though too heavy, were imposing in their excessive pallor, while the broad, dark brown shadows all around and beneath the large black eyes gave the face a depth of expression which did not, perhaps, wholly correspond with the original character. It was a striking face, and considering the wide interval between the ages of the abbess and her niece, and the natural difference of colouring, there was a strong family resemblance in the two women.

The abbess sat down upon the only chair, and Maria remained standing before her, her sewing in her hands.

"I have often told you that you must not sing in your cell," said the abbess, in a coldly severe tone.

Maria's shoulders shook her veil a little, but she still looked at the floor.

"I cannot help it," she answered in a constrained voice. "I did not know that I was singing—"

"That is ridiculous! How can one sing, and not know it? You are not deaf. At least, you do not sing as though you were. I will not have it. I could hear you as far away as my own room—a love-song, too!"

"The love of death," suggested Maria.

"It makes no difference," answered the elder lady. "You disturb the peace of the sisters with your singing. You know the rule, and you must obey it, like the rest. If you must sing, then sing in church."

"I do."

"Very well, that ought to be enough. Must you sing all the time? Suppose that the Cardinal had been visiting me, as was quite possible, what impression would he have had of our discipline?"

"Oh, Uncle Cardinal has often heard me sing."

"You must not call him 'Uncle Cardinal.' It is like the common people who say 'Uncle Priest.' I have told you that a hundred times at least. And if the Cardinal has heard you singing, so much the worse."

"He once told me that I had a good voice," observed Maria, still standing before her aunt.

"A good voice is a gift of God and to be used in church, but not in such a way as to attract attention or admiration. The devil is everywhere, my daughter, and makes use of our best gifts as a means of temptation. The Cardinal certainly did not hear you singing that witch's love-song which I heard just now. He would have rebuked you as I do."

"It was not a love-song. It is about death—and Saint John's eve."

"Well, then it is about witches. Do not argue with me. There is a rule, and you must not break it."

Maria Addolorata said nothing, but moved a step and leaned against the door-post, looking out into the evening light. The stout abbess sat motionless in her straight chair, looking past her niece at the distant hills. She had evidently said all she meant to say about the singing, and it did not occur to her to talk of anything else. A long silence followed. Maria was not timid, but she had been accustomed from her childhood to look upon her aunt as an immensely superior person, moving in a higher sphere, and five years spent in the convent as novice and nun had rather increased than diminished the feeling of awe which the abbess inspired in the young girl. There was, indeed, no other sister in the community who would have dared to answer the abbess's rebuke at all, and Maria's very humble protest really represented an extraordinary degree of individuality and courage. Conventual institutions can only exist on a basis of absolute submission.

The abbess was neither harsh nor unkind, and was certainly not a very terrifying figure, but she possessed undeniable force of character, strengthened by the inborn sense of hereditary right and power, and her kindness was as imposing as her displeasure was lofty and solemn. She had very little sympathy for any weakness in others, but she was always ready to dispense the mercy of Heaven, vicariously, so to say, and with a certain royally suppressed surprise that Heaven should be merciful. On the whole, considering the circumstances, she admitted that Maria Addolorata had accepted the veil with sufficient outward grace, though without any vocation, and she took it for granted that with such opportunities the girl must slowly develop into an abbess not unlike her predecessors. She prayed regularly, of course, and with especial intention, for her niece, as for the welfare of the order, and assumed as an unquestionable result that her prayers were answered with perfect regularity, since her own conscience did not reproach her with negligence of her young relative's spiritual education.

To the abbess, religion, the order and its duties, presented themselves as a vast machine controlled for the glory of God by the Pope. She and her nuns were parts of the great engine which must work with perfect regularity in order that God might be glorified. Her mind was naturally religious, but was at the same time essentially of the material order. There is a material imagination, and there is a spiritual imagination. There are very good and devout men and women who take the world, present and to come, quite literally, as a mere fulfilment of their own limitations; who look upon what they know as being all that need be known, and upon what they believe of God and Heaven as the mechanical consequence of what they know rather than as the cause and goal, respectively, of existence and action; to whom the letter of the law is the arbitrary expression of a despotic power, which, somehow, must be looked upon as merciful; who answer all questions concerning God's logic with the tremendous assertion of God's will; whose God is a magnified man, and whose devil is a malignant animal, second only to God in understanding, while extreme from God in disposition. There are good men and women who, to use a natural but not flippant simile, take it for granted that the soul is cast into the troubled waters of life without the power to swim, or even the possibility of learning to float, dependent upon the bare chance that some one may throw it the life-buoy of ritual religion as its only conceivable means of salvation. And the opponents of each particular form of faith invariably take just such good men and women, with all their limitations, as the only true exponents of that especial creed, which they then proceed to tear in pieces with all the ease such an undue advantage of false premise gives them. None of them have thought of intellectual mercy as being, perhaps, an integral part of Christian charity. Faith they have in abundance, and hope also not a little; but charity, though it be for men's earthly ills and, theoretically, if not always practically, for men's spiritual shortcomings, is rigidly forbidden for the errors of men's minds. Why? No thinking man can help asking the little question which grows great in the unanswering silence that follows it.

All this is not intended as an apology for what the young nun, Maria Addolorata, afterwards did, though much of it is necessary in explanation of her deeds, which, however they may be regarded, brought upon her and others their inevitable logical consequences. Still less is it meant, in any sense, as an attack upon the conventual system of the cloistered orders, which system was itself a consequence of spiritual, intellectual and political history, and has a prime right to be judged upon the evidence of its causes, and not by the shortcomings of its results in changed times. What has been said merely makes clear the fact that the characters, minds, and dispositions of Maria Addolorata and of her aunt, the abbess, were wholly unsuited to one another. And this one fact became a source of life and death, of happiness and misery, of comedy and tragedy, to many individuals, even to the present day.

The nun remained motionless, pressing her cheek against the door-post and looking out. Her aunt had not quite shut the door by which she had entered, and a cool stream of air blew outward from the corridor and through the cell, bringing with it that peculiar odour which belongs to all large and old buildings inhabited by religious communities. It is made up of the cold exhalations from stone walls and paved floors in which there is always some dampness, of the acrid smell of the heavy, leathern, wadded curtains which shut off the main drafts of air, as the swinging doors do in a mine, of a faint but perceptible suggestion of incense which penetrates the whole building from the church or the chapel, and, not least, of the fumes from the cookery of the great quantities of vegetables which are the staple food of the brethren or the sisters. It is as imperceptible to the monks and nuns themselves as the smell of tobacco to the smoker.

It had been very close in the little cell, and Maria was glad of the coolness that came in through the open door. Her eyes were fixed on the sky with a longing look. Again the words of her song rose to her lips, but she checked them, remembering her aunt's presence, and with the effort to be silent came the strong wish to be free, to be over there upon those purple hills at evening, to look beyond and watch the sun sinking into the distant sea, to breathe her fill of the mountain air, to run along the crests of the hills till she should be tired, to sleep under the open sky, to see, in dreams, to-morrow's sun rising through the trees, to be waked by the song of birds and to find that the dream was true.

Instead of that, and instead of all it meant to her, there was to be the silent evening meal, the close, lighted chapel, the wearily nasal chant of the sisters, her lonely cell, with its close darkness, the unrefreshing sleep, broken by the bell calling her to another office in the chapel; then, at last, the dawn, and the day that would seem as much a prisoner as herself within the convent walls, and the praying and nasal chanting, and the counting of sheets and pillow-cases, and doing a little sewing, and singing to herself, perhaps, and then the being reproved for it—the whole varied by meals of coarse food, and periodical stations in her seat in the choir. The day! The very sun seemed imprisoned in his corner of the garden wall, dragging slowly at his chain, in a short half-circle, from morning till evening, like a watch-dog tied up in a yard beside his kennel. The night was better. Sometimes she could see the moon-rays through the cracks of the balcony door, as she lay in her bed. She could see them against the darkness, and the ends of them were straight white lines and round white spots on the floor and on the walls. Her thoughts played in them, and her maiden fancies caught them and followed them lightly out into the white night and far away to the third world, which is dreamland. And in her dreams she sang to the midnight stars, and clasped her bare arms round the moon's white throat, kissing the moon-lady's pale and passionate cheek, till she lost herself in the mysterious eyes, and found herself once more, bathed in cool star-showers, the queen of a tender dream.

There sat the abbess, in the only chair, stolid, righteous, imposing. The incarnation and representative of the ninety and nine who need no forgiveness, exasperatingly and mathematically virtuous as a dogma, a woman against whom no sort of reproach could be brought, and at the mere sight of whom false witnesses would shrivel up and die, like jelly-fish in the sun. She not only approved of the convent life, but she liked it. She was at liberty to do a thousand things which were not permitted to the nuns, but she had not the slightest inclination to do any of them, any more than she was inclined to admit that any of them could possibly be unhappy if they would only pray, sing, sleep, and eat boiled cabbage at the appointed hours. What had she in common with Maria Addolorata, except that she was born a princess and a Braccio?

Of what use was it to be a princess by birth, like a dozen or more of the sisters, or even a noble, like all the others? Of what use or advantage could anything be, where liberty was not? An even plainer and more desperate question rose in the young nun's heart, as she leaned her cheek against the door-post, still warm with the afternoon sun. Of what use was life, if it was to be lived in the tomb with the accompaniment of a lifelong funeral service? Why should not God be as well pleased with suicide as with self-burial? Why should not death all at once, by the sudden dash of cleanly steel, be as noble and acceptable a sacrifice as death by sordid degrees of orderly suffering, systematic starvation, and rigidly regulated misery? Was not life, life—and blood, blood—whether drawn by drops, or shed from a quick wound in the splendid redness of one heroic instant? Surely it would be as grand a thing, if a mere sacrifice were the object, to be laid down stark dead, with the death-thrust in the heart, at the foot of the altar, in all her radiant youth and full young beauty, untempted and unsullied, as to fast and pray through forty querulous years of misery in prison.

But then, there was the virtue of patience. Therein, doubtless, lay the difference. It was not the death alone that was to please God, but the long manner of it, the summed-up account of suffering, the interest paid on the capital of life after it was invested in death. God was to be pleased with items, and the sum of them. Item, a sleepless night. Item, a bad cold, caught by kneeling on the damp stones. Item, a dish of sweets refused on a feast-day. Item, the resolution not to laugh when a fly settled on the abbess's nose. Item, the resolution not to wish that her hair had never been cut off. Item, being stifled in summer and frozen in winter, in her cell. Item, appreciating that it was the best cell, and that she was better off than the other sisters.

Repeat the items for half a century, sum them up, and offer them to God as a meet and fitting sacrifice—the destruction, by fine degrees of petty suffering, of one woman's whole life, almost from the beginning, and quite to the end, with the total annihilation of all its human possibilities, of love, of motherhood, of reasonable enjoyment and legitimate happiness. That was the formula for salvation which Maria Addolorata had received with the veil.

And not only had she received it. It had been thrust upon her, because she chanced to be the only available daughter of the ancient house of Braccio, to fill the hereditary seat beneath the wooden canopy, as abbess of the Subiaco Carmelites. If there had been another sister, less fair, more religiously disposed, that sister would have been chosen in Maria's stead. But there was no other; and there must be a young Braccio nun, to take the place of the elder one, when the latter should have filled her account to overflowing with little items to be paid for with the gold of certain salvation.

That a sinful woman, full of sorrows, and weary of the world, might silently bow her head under the nun's veil, and wear out with prayerful austerity the deep-cut letters of her sin's story, that, at least, was a thing Maria could understand. There were faces amongst the sisters that haunted her in her solitude, lips that could have told much, but which said only 'Miserere'; eyes that had looked on love, and that fixed themselves now only on the Cross; cheeks blanched with grief and hollowed as the marble of an ancient fountain by often flowing tears; hearts that had given all, and had been beaten and bruised and rejected. The convent was for them; the life was a life for them; for them there was no freedom beyond these walls, in the living world, nor anywhere on this side of death. They had done right in coming, and they did right in staying; they were reasonable when they prayed that they might have time, before they died, to be sorry for their sins and to touch again the hem of the garment of innocence.

But even they, if they were told that it would be right, would they not rather shorten their time to a day, even to one instant, of aggregated pain, and offer up their sacrifice all at once? And why should it not be right? Did God delight in pain and suffering for its own sake? The passionate girl's heart revolted angrily against a Being that could enjoy the sufferings of helpless creatures.

But then, there was that virtue of patience again, which was beyond her comprehension. At last she spoke, her face still to the sunset.

"What difference can it make to God how we die?" she asked, scarcely conscious that she was speaking.

The abbess must have started a little, for the chair creaked suddenly, several seconds before she answered. Her face did not relax, however, nor were her hands unclasped from one another as they lay folded on her knees.

"That is a foolish question, my daughter," she said at last. "Do you think that God was not pleased by the sufferings of the holy martyrs, and did not reward them for what they bore?"

"No, I did not mean that," answered Maria, quickly. "But why should we not all be martyrs? It would be much quicker."

"Heaven preserve us!" exclaimed the abbess. "What are you thinking of, child?"

"It would be so much quicker," repeated Maria. "What are we here for? To sacrifice our lives to God. We wish to make this sacrifice, and God promises to accept it. Why would it be less complete if we were led to the altar as soon as we have finished our novitiate and quickly killed? It would be the same, and it would be much quicker. What difference can it make how we die, since we are to die in the end, without accomplishing anything except dying?"

By this time the abbess's pale hands were unclasped, and one of them pressed each knee, as she leaned far forward in her seat, with an expression of surprise and horror, her dark lips parted and all the lines of her colourless face drawn down.

"Are you mad, Maria?" she asked in a low voice.

"Mad? No. Why should you think me mad?" The nun turned and looked down at her aunt. "After all, it is the great question. Our lives are but a preparation for death. Why need the preparation be so long? Why should the death be so slow? Why should it be right to kill ourselves for the glory of God by degrees, and wrong to do it all at once, if one has the courage? I think it is a very reasonable question."

"Indeed, you are beside yourself! The devil suggests such things to you and blinds you to the truth, my child. Penance and prayer, prayer and penance—by the grace of Heaven it will pass."

"Penance and prayer!" exclaimed Maria, sadly. "That is it—a slow death, but a sure one!"

"I am more than sixty years old," replied the abbess. "I have done penance and prayed prayers all my life, and you see—I am well. I am stout."

"For charity's sake, do not say so!" cried Maria, making the sign of the horns with her fingers, to ward off the evil eye. "You will certainly fall ill."

"Our lives are of God. It is our own eyes that are evil. You must not make horns with your fingers. It is a heathen superstition, as I have often told you. But many of you do it. Maria, I wish to speak to you seriously."

"Speak, mother," answered the young nun, the strong habit of submission returning instantly with the other's grave tone.

"These thoughts of yours are very wicked. We are placed in the world, and we must continue to live in it, as long as God wills that we should. When God is pleased to deliver us, He will take us in good time. You and I and the sisters should be thankful that during our brief stay on earth this sanctuary has fallen to our lot, and this possibility of a holy life. We must take every advantage of it, thanking Heaven if our stay be long enough for us to repent of our sins and obtain indulgence for our venial shortcomings. It is wicked to desire to shorten our lives. It is wicked to desire anything which is not the will of God. We are here to live, to watch and to pray—not to complain and to rebel."

The abbess was stout, as she herself admitted, and between her sudden surprise at her niece's wholly unorthodox, not to say blasphemous, suggestion of suicide as a means of grace, and her own attempt at eloquence, she grew rapidly warm, in spite of the comparatively cool draft which was passing out from the interior of the building. She caught the end of her loose over-sleeve and fanned herself slowly when she had finished speaking.

But Maria Addolorata did not consider that she was answered. There in the cell of a Carmelite convent, in the heart of a young girl who had perhaps never heard of Shakespeare and who certainly knew nothing of Hamlet, the question of all questions found itself, and she found for it such speech as she could command. It broke out passionately and impatiently.

"What are we? And why are we what we are? Yes, mother—I know that you are good, and that all you say is true. But it is not all. There is all the world beyond it. To live, or not to live—but you know that this is not living! It is not meant to be living, as the people outside understand what living means. What does it all signify but death, when we take the veil, and lie before the altar, and are covered with a funeral pall? It means dying—then why not altogether dying? Has not God angels, in thousands, to praise Him and worship Him, and pray for sinners on earth? And they sing and pray gladly, because they are blessed and do not suffer, as we do. Why should God want us, poor little nuns, to live half dead, and to praise Him with voices that crack with the cold in winter, and to kneel till we faint with the heat in summer, and to wear out our bodies with fasting and prayer and penance, till it is all we can do to crawl to our places in the choir? Not I—I am young and strong still—nor you, perhaps, for you are strong still, though you are not young. But many of the sisters—yes, they are the best ones, I know—they are killing themselves by inches before our eyes. You know it—I know it—they know it themselves. Why should they not find some shorter way of death for God's glory? Or if not, why should they not live happily, since many of them could? Why should God, who made us, wish us to destroy ourselves—or if He does, then why may we not do it in our own way? Ah—it would be so short—a knife-thrust, and then the great peace forever!"

The abbess had risen and was standing before Maria, one hand resting on the back of the rush-bottomed chair.

"Blasphemy!" she cried, finding breath at last. "It is blasphemy, or madness, or both! It is the evil one's own doing! Forgive her, good God! She does not know what she is saying! Almighty and most merciful God, forgive her!"

For a moment Maria Addolorata was silent, realizing how far she had forgotten herself, and startled by the abbess's terrified eyes and excited tone. But she was naturally a far more daring woman than she herself knew. Though her face was pale, her lips smiled at her good aunt's fright.

"But that is not an answer—just to cry 'blasphemy!'" she said. "The question is clear—"

She did not finish the sentence. The abbess was really beside herself with religious terror. With almost violent hands she dragged and thrust her niece down till Maria fell upon her knees.

"Pray, child! Pray, before it is too late!" she cried. "Pray on your knees that this possession may pass, before your soul is lost forever!"

She herself knelt beside the girl upon the stones, still clasping her and pressing her down. And she prayed aloud, long, fervently, almost wildly, appealing to God for protection against a bodily tempting devil, who by his will, and with evil strength, was luring and driving a human soul to utter damnation.

CHAPTER III

"It is well," said Stefanone. "The world is come to an end. I will not say anything more."

He finished his tumbler of wine, leaned back on the wooden bench against the brown wall, played with the broad silver buttons of his dark blue jacket, and stared hard at Sor Tommaso, the doctor, who sat opposite to him. The doctor returned his glance rather unsteadily and betook himself to his snuffbox. It was of worn black ebony, adorned in the middle of the lid with a small view of Saint Peter's and the colonnades in mosaic, with a very blue sky. From long use, each tiny fragment of the mosaic was surrounded by a minute black line, which indeed lent some tone to the intensely clear atmosphere of the little picture, but gave the architecture represented therein a dirty and neglected appearance. The snuff itself, however, was of the superior quality known as Sicilian in those days, and was of a beautiful light brown colour.

"And why?" asked the doctor very slowly, between the operations of pinching, stuffing, snuffing, and dusting. "Why is the world come to an end?"

Stefanone's eyes grew sullen, with a sort of dull glare in their unwinking gaze. He looked dangerous just then, but the doctor did not seem to be in the least afraid of him.

"You, who have made it end, should know why," answered the peasant, after a short pause.

Stefanone was a man of the Roman type, of medium height, thick set and naturally melancholic, with thin, straight lips that were clean shaven, straight black hair, a small but aggressively aquiline nose and heavy hands, hairy on the backs of the fingers, between the knuckles. His wife, Sora Nanna, said that he had a fist like a paving-stone. He also looked as though he might have the constitution of a mule. He was at that time about five-and-thirty years of age, and there were a few strong lines in his face, notably those curved ones drawn from the beginning of the nostrils to the corners of the mouth, which are said to denote an uncertain temper.

He wore the dress of the richer peasants of that day, a coarse but spotless white shirt, very open at the throat, a jacket and waistcoat of stout dark blue cloth, with large and smooth silver buttons, knee-breeches, white stockings, and heavy low shoes with steel buckles. He combined the occupations of farmer, wine-seller, and carrier. When he was on the road between Subiaco and Rome, Gigetto, already mentioned, was supposed to represent him. It was understood that Gigetto was to marry Annetta—if he could be prevailed upon to do so, for he was the younger son of a peasant family which held its head even higher than Stefanone, and the young man as well as his people looked upon Annetta's wild ways with disapproval, though her fortune, as the only child of Stefanone and Sora Nanna, was a very strong attraction. In the meantime, Gigetto acted as though he were the older man's partner in the wine-shop, and as he was a particularly honest, but also a particularly idle, young man with a taste for singing and playing on the guitar, the position suited him admirably.

As for Sor Tommaso, with whom Stefanone seemed inclined to quarrel on this particular evening, he was a highly respectable personage in a narrow-shouldered, high-collared black coat with broad skirts, and a snuff-coloured waistcoat. He wore a stock which was decidedly shabby, but decent, and the thin cuffs of his shirt were turned back over the tight sleeves of his coat, in the old fashion. He also wore amazingly tight black trousers, strapped closely over his well-blacked boots. To tell the truth, these nether garments, though of great natural resistance, had lived so long at a high tension, so to say, that they were no longer equally tight at all points, and there were, undoubtedly, certain perceptible spots on them; but, on the whole, the general effect of the doctor's appearance was fashionable, in the fashion of several years earlier and judged by the standard of Subiaco. He wore his hair rather long, in a handsome iron-grey confusion, his face was close-shaven, and, though he was thin, his complexion was somewhat apoplectic.

Having duly and solemnly finished the operation of taking snuff, the doctor looked at the peasant.

"I do not wish to have said anything," he observed, by way of a general retraction. "These are probably follies."

"And for not having meant to say anything, you have planted this knife in my heart!" retorted Stefanone, the veins swelling at his temples. "Thank you. I wish to die, if I forget it. You tell me that this daughter of mine is making love with the Englishman. And then you say that you do not wish to have said anything! May he die, the Englishman, he, and whoever made him, with the whole family! An evil death on him and all his house!"

"So long as you do not make me die, too!" exclaimed Sor Tommaso, with rather a pitying smile.

"Eh! To die—it is soon said! And yet, people do die. You, who are a doctor, should know that. And you do not wish to have said anything! Bravo, doctor! Words are words. And yet they can sting. And after a thousand years, they still sting. You—what can you understand? Are you perhaps a father? You have not even a wife. Oh, blessed be God! You do not even know what you are saying. You know nothing. You think, perhaps, because you are a doctor, that you know more than I do. I will tell you that you are an ignorant!"

"Oh, beautiful!" cried the doctor, angrily, stung by what is still almost a mortal insult. "You—to me— ignorant! Oh, beautiful, most beautiful, this! From a peasant to a man of science! Perhaps you too have a diploma from the University of the Sapienza—"

"If I had, I should wrap half a pound of sliced ham—fat ham, you know—in it, for the first customer. What should I do with your diplomas! I ask you, what do you know? Do you know at all what a daughter is? Blood of my blood, heart of my heart, hand of this hand. But I am a peasant, and you are a doctor. Therefore, I know nothing."

"And meanwhile you give me 'ignorant' in my face!" retorted Sor Tommaso.

"Yes—and I repeat it!" cried Stefanone, leaning forwards, his clenched hand on the table. "I say it twice, three times—ignorant, ignorant, ignorant! Have you understood?"

"Say it louder! In that way every one can hear you! Beast of a sheep-grazer!"

"And you—crow-feeder! Furnisher of grave-diggers. And then—ignorant! Oh—this time I have said it clearly!"

"And it seems to me that it is enough!" roared the doctor, across the table. "Ciociaro! Take that!"

"Ciociaro? I? Oh, your soul! If I get hold of you with my hands!"

A 'ciociaro' is a hill-man who wears 'cioce,' or rags, bound upon his feet with leathern sandals and thongs. He is generally a shepherd, and is held in contempt by the more respectable people of the larger mountain towns. To call a man a 'ciociaro' is a bitter insult.

Stefanone in his anger had half risen from his seat. But the wooden bench on which he had been sitting was close to the wall behind him, and the heavy oak table was pushed up within a few inches of his chest, so that his movements were considerably hampered as he stretched out his hands rather wildly towards his adversary. The latter, who possessed more moral than physical courage, moved his chair back and prepared to make his escape, if Stefanone showed signs of coming round the table.

At that moment a tall figure darkened the door that opened upon the street, and a quiet, dry voice spoke with a strong foreign accent. It was Angus Dalrymple, returning from a botanizing expedition in the hills, after being absent all day.

"That is a very uncomfortable way of fighting," he observed, as he stood still in the doorway. "You cannot hit a man across a table broader than your arm is long, Signor Stefano."

The effect of his words was instantaneous. Stefanone fell back into his seat. The doctor's anxious and excited expression resolved itself instantly into a polite smile.

"We were only playing," he said suavely. "A little discussion—a mere jest. Our friend Stefanone was explaining something."

"If the table had been narrower, he would have explained you away altogether," observed Dalrymple, coming forward.

He laid a tin box which he had with him upon the table, and shook hands with Sor Tommaso. Then he slipped behind the table and sat down close to his host, as a precautionary measure in case the play should be resumed. Stefanone would have had a bad chance of being dangerous, if the powerful Scotchman chose to hold him down. But the peasant seemed to have become as suddenly peaceful as the doctor.

"It was nothing," said Stefanone, quietly enough, though his eyes were bloodshot and glanced about the room in an unsettled way.

At that moment Annetta entered from a door leading to the staircase. Her eyes were fixed on Dalrymple's face as she came forward, carrying a polished brass lamp, with three burning wicks, which she placed upon the table. Dalrymple looked up at her, and seeing her expression of inquiry, slowly nodded. With a laugh which drew her long red-brown lips back from her short white teeth, the girl produced a small flask and a glass, which she had carried behind her and out of sight when she came in. She set them before Dalrymple.

"I saw you coming," she said, and laughed again. "And then—it is always the same. Half a 'foglietta' of the old, just for the appetite."

Sor Tommaso glanced at Stefanone in a meaning way, but the girl's father affected not to see him. Dalrymple nodded his thanks, poured a few drops of wine into the glass and scattered them upon the brick floor according to the ancient custom, both for rinsing the glass and as a libation, and then offered to fill the glasses of each of the two men, who smiled, shook their heads, and covered their tumblers with their right hands. At last Dalrymple helped himself, nodded politely to his companions, and slowly emptied the glass which held almost all the contents of the little flask. The 'foglietta,' or 'leaflet' of wine, is said to have been so called from the twisted and rolled vine leaf which generally serves it for a stopper. A whole 'foglietta' contained a scant pint.

"Will you eat now?" asked Annetta, still smiling.

"Presently," answered Dalrymple. "What is there to eat? I am hungry."

"It seems that you have to say so!" laughed the girl. "It is a new thing. There is beefsteak or mutton, if you wish to know. And ham—a fresh ham cut to-day. It is one of the Grape-eater's, and it seems good. You remember, Sor Tommaso, the—speaking with respect to your face—the pig we called the Grape-eater last year? Speaking with respect, he was a good pig. It is one of his hams that we have cut. There is also salad, and fresh bread, which you like. And wine, I will not speak of it. Eh, he likes wine, the Englishman! He comes in with a long, long face—and when he goes to bed, his face is wide, wide. That is the wine. But then, it does nothing else to him. It only changes his face. When I look at him, I seem to see the moon waxing."

"You talk too much," said Stefanone.

"Never mind, papa! Words are not pennies. The more one wastes, the more one has!"

Dalrymple said nothing; but he smiled as she turned lightly with a toss of her small dark head and left the room.

"Fine blood," observed the doctor, with a conciliatory glance at the girl's father.

"You will be wanted before long, Sor Tommaso," said Dalrymple, gravely. "I hear that the abbess is very ill."

The doctor looked up with sudden interest, and put on his professional expression.

"The abbess, you say? Dear me! She is not young! What has she? Who told you, Sor Angoscia?"

Now, 'Sor Angoscia' signifies in English 'Sir Anguish,' but the doctor in spite of really conscientious efforts could not get nearer to the pronunciation of Angus. Nevertheless, with northern persistency, Dalrymple corrected him for the hundredth time. The doctor's first attempt had resulted in his calling the Scotchman 'Sor Langusta,' which means 'Sir Crayfish'—and it must be admitted that 'Anguish' was an improvement.

"Angus," said Dalrymple. "My name is Angus. The abbess has caught a severe cold from sitting in a draught when she was overheated. It has immediately settled on her lungs, and you may be sent for at any moment. I passed by the back of the convent on my way down, and the gardener was just coming out of the postern. He told me."

"Dear me, dear me!" exclaimed Sor Tommaso, shaking his head. "Cold—bronchitis, pleurisy, pneumonia—it is soon done! One would be enough! Those nuns, what do they eat? A little grass, a little boiled paste, a little broth of meat on Sundays. What strength should they have? And then pray, pray, sing, sing! It needs a chest! Poor lungs! I will go to my home and get ready—blisters—mustard—a lancet—they will not allow a barber in the convent to bleed them. Well—I make myself the barber! What a life, what a life! If you wish to die young, be a doctor at Subiaco, Sor Angoscia. Good night, dear friend. Good night, Stefanone. I wish not to have said anything—you know—that little affair. Let us speak no more about it. I am more beast than you, because I said anything. Good night."

Sor Tommaso got his stick from a dark corner, pressed his broad catskin hat upon his head, and took his respectability away on its tightly encased black legs.

"And may the devil go with you," said Stefanone, under his breath, as the doctor disappeared.

"Why?" inquired Dalrymple, who had caught the words.

"I said nothing," answered the peasant, thoughtfully trimming one wick of the lamp with the bent brass wire which, with the snuffers, hung by a chain from the ring by which the lamp was carried.

"I thought you spoke," said the Scotchman. "Well—the abbess is very ill, and Sor Tommaso has a job."

"May he do it well! So that it need not be begun again."

"What do you mean?" Dalrymple slowly sipped the remains of his little measure of wine.

"Those nuns!" exclaimed Stefanone, instead of answering the question. "What are they here to do, in this world? Better make saints of them—and good night! There would be one misery less. Do you know what they do? They make wine. Good! But they do not drink it. They sell it for a farthing less by the foglietta than other people. The devil take them and their wine!"

Dalrymple glanced at the angry peasant with some amusement, but did not make any answer.

"Eh, Signore!" cried Stefanone. "You who are a foreigner and a Protestant, can you not say something, since it would be no sin for you?"

"I was thinking of something to say, Signor Stefanone. But as for that, who does the business for the convent? They cannot do it themselves, I suppose. Who determines the price of their wine for them? Or the price of their corn?"

"They are not so stupid as you think. Oh, no! They are not stupid, the nuns. They know the price of this, and the cost of that, just as well as you and I do. But Gigetto's father, Sor Agostino, is their steward, if that is what you wish to know. And his father was before him, and Gigetto will be after him, with his pumpkin-head. And the rest is sung by the organ, as we say when mass is over. For you know about Gigetto and Annetta."

"Yes. And as you cannot quarrel with Sor Agostino on that account, I do not see but that you will either have to bear it, or sell your wine a farthing cheaper than that of the nuns."

"Eh—that is soon said. A farthing cheaper than theirs! That means half a baiocco cheaper than I sell it now. And the best is only five baiocchi the foglietta, and the cheapest is two and a half. Good bye profit—a pleasant journey to Stefanone. But it is those nuns. They are to blame, and the devil will pay them."

"In that case you need not," observed Dalrymple, rising. "I am going to wash my hands before supper."

"At your pleasure, Signore," answered Stefanone, politely.

As Dalrymple went out, Annetta passed him at the door, bringing in plates and napkins, and knives and forks. The girl glanced at his face as he went by.

"Be quick, Signore," she said with a laugh. "The beefsteak of mutton is grilling."

He nodded, and went up the dark stairs, his heavy shoes sending back echoes as he trod. Stefanone still sat at the table, turning the glass wine measure upside down over his tumbler, to let the last drops run out. He watched them as they fell, one by one, without looking up at his daughter, who began to arrange the plates for Dalrymple's meal.

"I will teach you to make love with the Englishman," he said slowly, still watching the dropping wine.

"Me!" cried Annetta, with real or feigned astonishment, and she tossed a knife and fork angrily into a plate, with a loud, clattering noise.

"I am speaking with you," answered her father, without raising his eyes. "Do you know? You will come to a bad end."

"Thank you!" replied the girl, contemptuously. "If you say so, it must be true! Now, who has told you that the Englishman is making love to me? An apoplexy on him, whoever he may be!"

"Pretty words for a girl! Sor Tommaso told me. A little more, and I would have torn his tongue out. Just then, the Englishman came in. Sor Tommaso got off easily."

The girl's tone changed very much when she spoke again, and there was a dull and angry light in her eyes. Her long lips were still parted, and showed her gleaming teeth, but the smile was altogether gone.

"Yes. Too easily," she said, almost in a whisper, and there was a low hiss in the words.

"In the meanwhile, it is true—what he said," continued Stefanone. "You make eyes at him. You wait for him and watch for him when he comes back from the mountains—"

"Well? Is it not my place to serve him with his supper? If you are not satisfied, hire a servant to wait on him. You are rich. What do I care for the Englishman? Perhaps it is a pleasure to roast my face over the charcoal, cooking his meat for him. As for Sor Tommaso—"

She stopped short in her speech. Her father knew what the tone meant, and looked up for the first time.

"O-èl" he exclaimed, as one suddenly aware of a danger, and warning some one else.

"Nothing," answered Annetta, looking down and arranging the knives and forks symmetrically on the clean cloth she had laid.

"I might have killed him just now in hot blood, when the Englishman came in," said Stefanone, reflectively. "But now my blood has grown cold. I shall do nothing to him."

"So much the better for him." She still spoke in a low voice, as she turned away from the table.

"But I will kill you," said Stefanone, "if I see you making eyes at the Englishman."

He rose, and taking up his hat, which lay beside him, he edged his way out along the wooden bench, moving cautiously lest he should shake the table and upset the lamp or the bottles. Annetta had turned again, at the threat he had uttered, and stood still, waiting for him to get out into the room, her hands on her hips, and her eyes on fire.

"You will kill me?" she asked, just as he was opposite to her. "Well—kill me, then! Here I am. What are you waiting for? For the Englishman to interfere? He is washing his hands. He always takes a long time."

"Then it is true that you have fallen in love with him?" asked Stefanone, his anger returning.

"Him, or another. What does it matter to you? You remind me of the old woman who beat her cat, and then cried when it ran away. If you want me to stay at home, you had better find me a husband."

"Do you want anything better than Gigetto? Apoplexy! But you have ideas!"

"You are making a good business of it with Gigetto, in truth!" cried the girl, scornfully. "He eats, he drinks, and then he sings. But he does not marry. He will not even make love to me—not even with an eye. And then, because I love the Englishman, who is a great lord, though he says he is a doctor, I must die. Well, kill me!" She stared insolently at her father for a moment. "Oh, well," she added scornfully, "if you have not time now, it must be for to-morrow. I am busy."

She turned on her heel with a disdainful fling of her short, dark skirt. Stefanone was exasperated, and his anger had returned. Before she was out of reach, he struck her with his open hand. Instead of striking her cheek, the blow fell upon the back of her head and neck, and sent her stumbling forwards. She caught the back of a chair, steadied herself, and turned again instantly, at her full height, not deigning to raise her hand to the place that hurt her.

"Coward!" she exclaimed. "But I will pay you—and Sor Tommaso—for that blow."

"Whenever you like," answered her father gruffly, but already sorry for what he had done.

He turned his back, and went out into the night. It was now almost quite dark, and Annetta stood still by the chair, listening to his retreating footsteps. Then she slowly turned and gazed at the flaring wicks of the lamp. With a gesture that suggested the movement of a young animal, she rubbed the back of her neck with one hand and leisurely turned her head first to one side and then to the other. Her brown skin was unusually pale, but there was no moisture in her eyes as she stared at the lamp.

"But I will pay you, Sor Tommaso," she said thoughtfully and softly.

Then turning her eyes from the lamp at last, she took up one of the knives from the table, looked at it, felt the edge, and laid it down contemptuously. In those days all the respectable peasants in the Roman villages had solid silver forks and spoons, which have long since gone to the melting-pot to pay taxes. But they used the same blunt, pointless knives with wooden handles, which they use to-day.

Annetta started, as she heard Dalrymple's tread upon the stone steps of the staircase, but she recovered herself instantly, gave a finishing touch to the table, rubbed the back of her head quickly once more, and met him with a smile.

"Is the beefsteak of mutton ready?" inquired the Scotchman, cheerfully, with his extraordinary accent.

Annetta ran past him, and returned almost before he was seated, bringing the food. The girl sat down at the end of the table, opposite the street door, and watched him as he swallowed one mouthful of meat after another, now and then stopping to drink a tumbler of wine at a draught.

"You must be very strong, Signore," said Annetta, at last, her chin resting on her doubled hand.

"Why?" inquired Dalrymple, carelessly, between two mouthfuls.

"Because you eat so much. It must be a fine thing to eat so much meat. We eat very little of it."

"Why?" asked the Scotchman, again between his mouthfuls.

"Oh, who knows? It costs much. That must be the reason. Besides, it does not go down. I should not care for it."

"It is a habit." Dalrymple drank. "In my country most of the people eat oats," he said, as he set down his glass.

"Oats!" laughed the girl. "Like horses! But horses will eat meat, too, like you. As for me—good bread, fresh cheese, a little salad, a drink of wine and water—that is enough."

"Like the nuns," observed Dalrymple, attacking the ham of the 'Grape-eater.'

"Oh, the nuns! They live on boiled cabbage! You can smell it a mile away. But they make good cakes."

"You often go to the convent, do you not?" asked the Scotchman, filling his glass, for the first mouthful of ham made him thirsty again. "You take the linen up with your mother, I know."

"Sometimes, when I feel like going," answered the girl, willing to show that it was not her duty to carry baskets. "I only go when we have the small baskets that one can carry on one's head. I will tell you. They use the small baskets for the finer things, the abbess's linen, and the altar cloths, and the chaplain's lace, which belongs to the nuns. But the sheets and the table linen are taken up in baskets as long as a man. It takes four women to carry one of them."

"That must be very inconvenient," said Dalrymple. "I should think that smaller ones would always be better."

"Who knows? It has always been so. And when it has always been so, it will always be so—one knows that."

Annetta nodded her head rhythmically to convey an impression of the immutability of all ancient customs and of this one in particular.

Dalrymple, however, was not much interested in the question of the baskets.

"What do the nuns do all day?" he asked. "I suppose you see them, sometimes. There must be young ones amongst them."

Annetta glanced more keenly at the Scotchman's quiet face, and then laughed.

"There is one, if you could see her! The abbess's niece. Oh, that one is beautiful. She seems to me a painted angel!"

"The abbess's niece? What is she like? Let me see, the abbess is a princess, is she not?"

"Yes, a great princess of the Princes of Gerano, of Casa Braccio, you know. They are always abbesses. And the young one will be the next, when this one dies. She is Maria Addolorata, in religion, but I do not know her real name. She has a beautiful face and dark eyes. Once I saw her hair for a moment. It is fair, but not like yours. Yours is red as a tomato."

"Thank you," said Dalrymple, with something like a laugh. "Tell me more about the nun."

"If I tell you, you will fall in love with her," objected Annetta. "They say that men with red hair fall in love easily. Is it true? If it is, I will not tell you any more about the nun. But I think you are in love with the poor old Grape-eater. It is good ham, is it not? By Bacchus, I fed him on chestnuts with my own hands, and he was always stealing the grapes. Chestnuts fattened him and the grapes made him sweet. Speaking with respect, he was a pig for a pope."

"He will do for a Scotch doctor then," answered Dalrymple. "Tell me, what does this beautiful nun do all day long?"

"What does she do? What can a nun do? She eats cabbage and prays like the others. But she has charge of all the convent linen, so I see her when I go with my mother. That is because the Princes of Gerano first gave the linen to the convent after it was all stolen by the Turks in 1798. So, as they gave it, their abbesses take care of it."

Dalrymple laughed at the extraordinary historical allusion compounded of the very ancient traditions of the Saracens in the south, and of the more recent wars of Napoleon.

"So she takes care of the linen," he said. "That cannot be very amusing, I should think."

"They are nuns," answered the girl. "Do you suppose they go about seeking to amuse themselves? It is an ugly life. But Sister Maria Addolorata sings to herself, and that makes the abbess angry, because it is against the rules to sing except in church. I would not live in that convent—not if they would fill my apron with gold pieces."

"But why did this beautiful girl become a nun, then? Was she unhappy, or crossed in love?"

"She? They did not give her time! Before she could shut an eye and say, 'Little youth, you please me, and I wish you well,' they put her in. And that door, when it is shut, who shall open it? The Madonna, perhaps? But she was of the Princes of Gerano, and there must be one of them for an abbess, and the lot fell upon her. There is the whole history. You may hear her singing sometimes, if you stand under the garden wall, on the narrow path after the Benediction hour and before Ave Maria. But I am a fool to tell you, for you will go and listen, and when you have heard her voice you will be like a madman. You will fall in love with her. I was a fool to tell you."

"Well? And if I do fall in love with her, who cares?" Dalrymple slowly filled a glass of wine.

"If you do?" The young girl's eyes shot a quick, sharp glance at him. Then her face suddenly grew grave as she saw that some one was at the street door, looking in cautiously. "Come in, Sor Tommaso!" she called, down the table. "Papa is out, but we are here. Come in and drink a glass of wine!"

The doctor, wrapped in a long broadcloth cloak with a velvet collar, and having a case of instruments and medicines under his arm, glanced round the room and came in.

"Just a half-foglietta, my daughter," he said. "They have sent for me. The abbess is very ill, and I may be there a long time. If you think they would remember to offer a Christian a glass up there, you are very much mistaken."

"They are nuns," laughed Annetta. "What can they know?"

She rose to get the wine for the doctor. There had not been a trace of displeasure in her voice nor in her manner as she spoke.

CHAPTER IV

Sor Tommaso was rarely called to the convent. In fact, he could not remember that he had been wanted more than half a dozen times in the long course of his practice in Subiaco. Either the nuns were hardly ever ill, or else they must have doctored themselves with such simple remedies as had been handed down to them from former ages. Possibly they had been as well off on the whole as though they had systematically submitted to the heroic treatment which passed for medicine in those days. As a matter of fact, they suffered chiefly from bad colds; and when they had bad colds, they either got well, or died, according to their several destinies. Sor Tommaso might have saved some of them; but on the other hand, he might have helped some others rather precipitately from their cells to that deep crypt, closed, in the middle of the little church, by a single square flag of marble, having two brass studs in it, and bearing the simple inscription: 'Here lie the bones of the Reverend Sisters of the order of the Blessed

Virgin Mary of Mount Carmel.' On the whole, it is doubtful whether the practice of not calling in the doctor on ordinary occasions had much influence upon the convent's statistics of mortality.

But though the abbess had more than once had a cold in her life, she had never suffered so seriously as this time, and she had made little objection to her niece's strong representations as to the necessity of medical aid. Therefore Sor Tommaso had been sent for in the evening and in great haste, and had taken with him a supply of appropriate material sufficient to kill, if not to cure, half the nuns in the convent. All the circumstances which he remembered from former occasions were accurately repeated. He rang at the main gate, waited long in the darkness, and heard at last the slapping and shuffling of shoes along the pavement within, as the portress and another nun came to let him in. Then there were faint rays of light from their little lamp, quivering through the cracks of the old weather-beaten door upon the cracked marble steps on which Sor Tommaso was standing. A thin voice asked who was there, and Sor Tommaso answered that he was the doctor. Then he heard a little colloquy in suppressed tones between the two nuns. The one said that the doctor was expected and must be let in without question. The other observed that it might be a thief. The first said that in that case they must look through the loophole. The second said that she did not know the doctor by sight. The first speaker remarked with some truth that one could tell a respectable person from a highwayman, and suddenly a small square porthole in the door was opened inwards, and a stream of light fell upon Sor Tommaso's face, as the nuns held up their little flaring lamp behind the grating. Behind the lamp he could distinguish a pair of shadowy eyes under an overhanging veil, which was also drawn across the lower part of the face.

"Are you really the doctor?" asked one of the voices, in a doubtful tone.

"He himself," answered the physician. "I am the Doctor Tommaso Taddei of the University of the Sapienza, and I have been called to render assistance to the very reverend the Mother Abbess."

The light disappeared, and the porthole was shut, while a second colloquy began. On the whole, the two nuns decided to let him in, and then there was a jingling of keys and a clanking of iron bars and a grinding of locks, and presently a small door, cut and hung in one leaf of the great, iron-studded, wooden gate, was swung back. Sor Tommaso stooped and held his case before him, for the entrance was low and narrow.

"God be praised!" he exclaimed, when he was fairly inside.

"And praised be His holy name," answered both the sisters, promptly.

Both had dropped their veils, and proceeded to bolt and bar the little door again, having set down the lamp upon the pavement. The rays made the unctuous dampness of the stone flags glisten, and Sor Tommaso shivered in his broadcloth cloak. Then, as before, he was conducted in silence through arched ways, and up many steps, and along labyrinthine corridors, his strong shoes rousing sharp, metallic echoes, while the nuns' slippers slapped and shuffled as one walked on each side of him, the one on the left carrying the lamp, according to the ancient rules of politeness. At last they reached the door of the antechamber at the end of the corridor, through which the way led to the abbess's private apartment, consisting of three rooms. The last door on the left, as Sor Tommaso faced that which opened into the antechamber, was that of Maria Addolorata's cell. The linen presses were entered from within the anteroom by a door on the right, so that they were actually in the abbess's apartment, an old-fashioned and somewhat inconvenient arrangement. Maria Addolorata, her veil drawn down, so that she could not see the doctor, but only his feet, and the folds of it drawn across her chin and mouth, received him at the door, which she closed behind him. The other two nuns set down their lamp on the floor of the corridor, slipped their hands up their sleeves, and stood waiting outside.

The abbess was very ill, but had insisted upon sitting up in her parlour to receive the doctor, dressed and veiled, being propped up in her great easy-chair with a pillow which was of green silk, but was covered with a white pillow-case finely embroidered with open work at each end, through which the vivid colour was visible—that high green which cannot look blue even by lamplight. Both in the anteroom and in the parlour there were polished silver lamps of precisely the same pattern as the brass ones used by the richer peasants, excepting that each had a fan-like shield of silver to be used as a shade on one side, bearing the arms of the Braccio family in high boss, and attached to the oil vessel by a movable curved arm. The furniture of the room was very simple, but there was nevertheless a certain ecclesiastical solemnity about the high-backed, carved, and gilt chairs, the black and white marble pavement, the great portrait of his Holiness, Gregory the Sixteenth, in its massive gilt frame, the superb silver crucifix which stood on the writing-table, and, altogether, in the solidity of everything which met the eye.

It was no easy matter to ascertain the good lady's condition, muffled up and veiled as she was. It was only as an enormous concession to necessity that Sor Tommaso was allowed to feel her pulse, and it needed all Maria Addolorata's eloquent persuasion and sensible argument to induce her to lift her veil a little, and open her mouth.

"Your most reverend excellency must be cured by proxy," said Sor Tommaso, at his wit's end. "If this reverend mother," he added, turning to the young nun, "will carry out my directions, something may be done. Your most reverend excellency's life is in danger. Your most reverend excellency ought to be in bed."

"It is the will of Heaven," said the abbess, in a very weak and hoarse voice.

"Tell me what to do," said Maria Addolorata. "It shall be done as though you yourself did it."

Sor Tommaso was encouraged by the tone of assurance in which the words were spoken, and proceeded to give his directions, which were many, and his recommendations, which were almost endless.

"But if your most reverend excellency would allow me to assist you in person, the remedies would be more efficacious," he suggested, as he laid out the greater part of the contents of his case upon the huge writing-table.

"You seem to forget that this is a religious house," replied the abbess, and she might have said more, but was interrupted by a violent attack of coughing, during which Maria Addolorata supported her and tried to ease her.

"It will be better if you go away," said the nun, at last. "I will do all you have ordered, and your presence irritates her. Come back to-morrow morning, and I will tell you how she is progressing."

The abbess nodded slowly, confirming her niece's words. Sor Tommaso very reluctantly closed his case, placed it under his arm, gathered up his broadcloth cloak with his hat, and made a low obeisance before the sick lady.

"I wish your most reverend excellency a good rest and speedy recovery," he said. "I am your most reverend excellency's most humble servant."

Maria Addolorata led him out into the antechamber. There she paused, and they were alone together for a moment, all the doors being closed. The doctor stood still beside her, waiting for her to speak.

"What do you think?" she asked.

"I do not wish to say anything," he answered.

"What do you wish me to say? A stroke of air, a cold, a bronchitis, a pleurisy, a pneumonia. Thanks be to Heaven, there is little fever. What do you wish me to say? For the stroke of air, a little good wine; for the cold, warm covering; for the bronchitis, the tea of marshmallows; for the pleurisy, severe blistering; for the pneumonia, a good mustard plaster; for the general system, the black draught; above all, nothing to eat. Frictions with hot oil will also do good. It is the practice of medicine by proxy, my lady mother. What do you wish me to say? I am disposed. I am her most reverend excellency's very humble servant. But I cannot perform miracles. Pray to the Madonna to perform them. I have not even seen the tip of her most reverend excellency's most wise tongue. What can I do?"

"Well, then, come back to-morrow morning, and I will see you here," said Maria Addolorata.

Sor Tommaso found the nuns waiting for him with their little lamp in the corridor, and they led him back through the vaulted passages and staircases and let him out into the night without a word.

The night was dark and cloudy. It had grown much darker since he had come up, as the last lingering light of evening had faded altogether from the sky. The October wind drew down in gusts from the mountains above Subiaco, and blew the doctor's long cloak about so that it flapped softly now and then like the wings of a night bird. After descending some distance, he carefully set down his case upon the stones and fumbled in his pockets for his snuffbox, which he found with some difficulty. A gust blew up a grain of snuff into his right eye, and he stamped angrily with the pain, hurting his foot against a rolling stone as he did so. But he succeeded in getting his snuff to his nose at last. Then he bent down in the dark to take up his case, which was close to his feet, though he could hardly see it. The gusty south wind blew the long skirts of his cloak over his head and made them flap about his ears. He groped for the box.

Just then the doctor heard light footsteps coming down the path behind him. He called out, warning that he was in the way.

"O-è, gently, you know!" he cried. "An apoplexy on the wind!" he added vehemently, as his head and hands became entangled more and more in the folds of his cloak.

"And another on you!" answered a woman's voice, speaking low through clenched teeth.

In the darkness a hand rose and fell with something in it, three times in quick succession. A man's low cry of pain was stifled in folds of broadcloth. The same light footsteps were heard for a moment again in the narrow, winding way, and Sor Tommaso was lying motionless on his face across his box, with his cloak over his head. The gusty south wind blew up and down between the dark walls, bearing now and then a few withered vine leaves and wisps of straw with it; and the night grew darker still, and no one passed that way for a long time.

CHAPTER V

When Angus Dalrymple had finished his supper, he produced a book and sat reading by the light of the wicks of the three brass lamps. Annetta had taken away the things and had not come back again. Gigetto strolled in and took his guitar from the peg on the wall, and idled about the room, tuning it and humming to himself. He was a tall young fellow with a woman's face and beautiful velvet-like eyes, as handsome and idle a youth as you might meet in Subiaco on a summer's feast-day. He exchanged a word of greeting with Dalrymple, and, seeing that the place was otherwise deserted, he at last slung his guitar over his shoulder, pulled his broad black felt hat over his eyes, and strolled out through the half-open door, presumably in search of amusement. Gigetto's chief virtue was his perfectly childlike and unaffected taste for amusing himself, on the whole very innocently, whenever he got a chance. It was natural that he and the Scotchman should not care for one another's society. Dalrymple looked after him for a moment and then went back to his book. A big glass measure of wine stood beside him not half empty, and his glass was full.

He was making a strong effort to concentrate his attention upon the learned treatise, which formed a part of the little library he had brought with him. But Annetta's idle talk about the nuns, and especially about Maria Addolorata and her singing, kept running through his head in spite of his determination to be serious. He had been living the life of a hermit for months, and had almost forgotten the sound of an educated woman's voice. To him Annetta was nothing more than a rather pretty wild animal. It did not enter his head that she might be in love with him. Sora Nanna was simply an older and uglier animal of the same species. To a man of Dalrymple's temperament, and really devoted to the pursuit of a serious object, a woman quite incapable of even understanding what that object is can hardly seem to be a woman at all.

But the young Scotchman was not wanting in that passionate and fantastic imagination which so often underlies and even directs the hardy northern nature, and the young girl's carelessly spoken words had roused it to sudden activity. In spite of himself, he was already forming plans for listening under the convent wall, if perchance he might catch the sound of the nun's wonderful voice, and from that to the wildest schemes for catching a momentary glimpse of the singer was only a step. At the same time, he was quite aware that such schemes were dangerous if not impracticable, and his reasonable self laughed down his unreasoning romance, only to be confronted by it again as soon as he tried to turn his attention to his book.

He looked up and saw that he had not finished his wine, though at that hour the measure was usually empty, and he wondered why he was less thirsty than usual. By force of habit he emptied the full glass and poured more into it,—by force of that old northern habit of drinking a certain allowance as a sort of duty, more common in those days than it is now. Then he began to read again, never dreaming that his strong head and solid nerves could be in any way affected by his potations. But his imagination this evening worked faster and faster, and his sober reason was recalcitrant and abhorred work.

The nun had fair hair and dark eyes and a beautiful face. Those were much more interesting facts than he could find in his work. She had a wonderful voice. He tried to recall all the extraordinary voices he had heard in his life, but none of them had ever affected him very much, though he had a good ear and some taste for music. He wondered what sort of voice this could be, and he longed to hear it. He shut up his book impatiently, drank more wine, rose and went to the open door. The gusty south wind fanned his face pleasantly, and he wished he were to sleep out of doors.

The Sora Nanna, who had been spending the evening with a friend in the neighbourhood, came in, her thin black overskirt drawn over her head to keep the embroidered head-cloth in its place. By and by, as Dalrymple still stood by the door, Stefanone appeared, having been to play a game of cards at a friendly wine-shop. He sat down by Sora Nanna at the table. She was mixing some salad in a big earthenware bowl adorned with green and brown stripes. They talked together in low tones. Dalrymple had nodded to each in turn, but the gusty air pleased him, and he remained standing by the door, letting it blow into his face.

It was growing late. Italian peasants are not great sleepers, and it is their custom to have supper at a late hour, just before going to bed. By this time it was nearly ten o'clock as we reckon the hours, or about 'four of the night' in October, according to old Italian custom, which reckons from a theoretical moment of darkness, supposed to begin at Ave Maria, half an hour after sunset.

Suddenly Dalrymple heard Annetta's voice in the room behind him, speaking to her mother. He had no particular reason for supposing that she had been out of the house since she had cleared the table and left him, but unconsciously he had the impression that she had been away, and was surprised to hear her in the room, after expecting that she should pass him, coming in from the street, as the others had done. He turned and walked slowly towards his place at the table.

"I thought you had gone out," he said carelessly, to Annetta.

The girl turned her head quickly.

"I?" she cried. "And alone? Without even Gigetto? When do I ever go out alone at night? Will you have some supper, Signore?"

"I have just eaten, thank you," answered Dalrymple, seating himself.

"Three hours ago. It was not yet an hour of the night when you ate. Well—at your pleasure. Do not complain afterwards that we make you die of hunger."

"Bread, Annetta!" said Stefanone, gruffly but good-naturedly. "And cheese, and salt—wine, too! A thousand things! Quickly, my daughter."

"Quicker than this?" inquired the girl, who had already placed most of the things he asked for upon the table.

"I say it to say it," answered her father. "'Hunger makes long jumps,' and I am hungry."

"Did you win anything?" asked Sora Nanna, with both her elbows on the table.

"Five baiocchi."

"It was worth while to pay ten baiocchi for another man's bad wine, for the sake of winning so much!" replied Sora Nanna, who was a careful soul. "Of course you paid for the wine?"

"Eh—of course. They pay for wine when they come here. One takes a little and one gives a little. This is life."

Annetta busied herself with the simple preparations for supper, while they talked. Dalrymple watched her idly, and he thought she was pale, and that her eyes were very bright. She had set a plate for herself, but had forgotten her glass.

"And you? Do you not drink?" asked Stefanone. "You have no glass."

"What does it matter?" She sat down between her father and mother.

"Drink out of mine, my little daughter," said Stefanone, holding his glass to her lips with a laugh, as though she had been a little child.

She looked quietly into his eyes for a moment, before she touched the wine with her lips.

"Yes," she answered, with a little emphasis. "I will drink out of your glass now."

"Better so," laughed Stefanone, who was glad to be reconciled, for he loved the girl, in spite of his occasional violence of temper.

"What does it mean?" asked Sora Nanna, her cunning peasant's eyes looking from one to the other, and seeming to belie her stupid face.

"Nothing," answered Stefanone. "We were playing together. Signor Englishman," he said, turning to Dalrymple, "you must sometimes wish that you were married, and had a wife like Nanna, and a daughter like Annetta."

"Of course I do," said Dalrymple, with a smile.

Before very long, he took his book and went upstairs to bed, being tired and sleepy after a long day spent on the hillside in a fruitless search for certain plants which, according to his books, were to be found in that part of Italy, but which he had not yet seen. He fell asleep, thinking of Maria Addolorata's lovely face and fair hair, on which he had never laid eyes. In his dreams he heard a rare voice ringing true, that touched him strangely. The gusty wind made the panes of his bedroom window rattle, and in the dream he was tapping on Maria Addolorata's casement and calling softly to her, to open it and speak to him, or calling her by name, with his extraordinary foreign accent. And he thought he was tapping louder and louder, upon the glass and upon the wooden frame, louder and louder still. Then he heard his name called out, and his heart jumped as though it would have turned upside down in its place, and then seemed to sink again like a heavy stone falling into deep water; for he was awake, and the voice that was calling him was certainly not that of the beautiful nun, but gruff and manly; also the tapping was not tapping any more upon a casement, but was a vigorous pounding against his own bolted door.

Dalrymple sat up suddenly and listened, wide awake at once. The square of his window was faintly visible in the darkness, as though the dawn were breaking. He called out, asking who was outside.

"Get up, Signore! Get up! You are wanted quickly!" It was Stefanone.

Dalrymple struck a light, for he had a supply of matches with him, a convenience of modern life not at that time known in Subiaco, except as an expensive toy, though already in use in Rome. As he was, he opened the door. Stefanone came in, dressed in his shirt and breeches, pale with excitement.

"You must dress yourself, Signore," he said briefly, as he glanced at the Scotchman, and then set down the small tin and glass lantern he carried.

"What is the matter?" inquired Dalrymple, yawning, and stretching his great white arms over his head, till his knuckles struck the low ceiling; for he was a tall man.

"The matter is that they have killed Sor Tommaso," answered the peasant.

Dalrymple uttered an exclamation of surprise and incredulity.

"It is as I say," continued Stefanone. "They found him lying across the way, in the street, with knife-wounds in him, as many as you please."

"That is horrible!" exclaimed Dalrymple, turning, and calmly trimming his lamp, which burned badly at first.

"Then dress yourself, Signore!" said Stefanone, impatiently. "You must come!"

"Why? If he is dead, what can I do?" asked the northern man, coolly. "I am sorry. What more can I say?"

"But he is not dead yet!" Stefanone was growing excited. "They have taken him—"

"Oh! he is alive, is he?" interrupted the Scotchman, dashing at his clothes, as though he were suddenly galvanized into life himself. "Then why did you tell me they had killed him?" he asked, with a curious, dry calmness of voice, as he instantly began to dress himself. "Get some clean linen, Signor Stefano. Tear it up into strips as broad as your hand, for bandages, and set the women to make a little lint of old linen—cotton is not good. Where have they taken Sor Tommaso?"

"To his own house," answered the peasant.

"So much the better. Go and make the bandages."

Dalrymple pushed Stefanone towards the door with one hand, while he continued to fasten his clothes with the other.

Stefanone was not without some experience of similar cases, so he picked up his lantern and went off. In less than a quarter of an hour, he and Dalrymple were on their way to Sor Tommaso's house, which was in the piazza of Subiaco, not far from the principal church. Half a dozen peasants, who had met the muleteers bringing the wounded doctor home from the spot where he had been found, followed the two men, talking excitedly in low voices and broken sentences. The dawn was grey above the houses, and the autumn mists had floated up to the parapet on the side where the little piazza looked down to the valley, and hung motionless in the still air, like a stage sea in a theatre. In the distance was heard the clattering of mules' shoes, and occasionally the deep clanking of the goats' bells. Just as the little party reached the small, dark green door of the doctor's house the distant convent bells tolled one, then two quick strokes, then three again, and then five, and then rang out the peal for the morning Angelus. The door of the dirty little coffee shop in the piazza was already open, and a faint light burned within. The air was damp, quiet and strangely resonant, as it often is in mountain towns at early dawn. The gusty October wind had gone down, after blowing almost all night.

The case was far from being as serious as Dalrymple had expected, and he soon convinced himself that Sor Tommaso was not in any great danger. He had fainted from fright and some loss of blood, but neither of the two thrusts which had wounded him had penetrated to his lungs, and the third was little more than a scratch. Doubtless he owed his safety in part to the fact that the wind had blown his cloak in folds over his shoulders and head. But it was also clear that his assailant had possessed no experience in the use of the knife as a weapon. When the group of men at the door were told that Sor Tommaso was not mortally wounded, they went away somewhat disappointed at the insignificant ending of the affair, though the doctor was not an unpopular man in the town.

"It is some woman," said one of them, contemptuously. "What can a woman do with a knife? Worse than a cat—she scratches, and runs away."

"Some little jealousy," observed another. "Eh! Sor Tommaso—who knows where he makes love? But meanwhile he is growing old, to be so gay."

"The old are the worst," replied the first speaker. "Since it is nothing, let us have a baiocco's worth of acquavita, and let us go away."

So they turned into the dirty little coffee shop to get their pennyworth of spirits. Meanwhile Dalrymple was washing and binding up his friend's wounds. Sor Tommaso groaned and winced under every touch, and the Scotchman, with dry gentleness, did his best to reassure him. Stefanone looked on in silence for some time, helping Dalrymple when he was needed. The doctor's servant-woman, a somewhat grimy peasant, was sitting on the stairs, sobbing loudly.

"It is useless," moaned Sor Tommaso. "I am dead."

"I may be mistaken," answered Dalrymple, "but I think not."

And he continued his operations with a sure hand, greatly to the admiration of Stefanone, who had often seen knife-wounds dressed. Gradually Sor Tommaso became more calm. His face, from having been normally of a bright red, was now very pale, and his watery blue eyes blinked at the light helplessly like a kitten's, as he lay still on his pillow. Stefanone went away to his occupations at last, and Dalrymple, having cleared away the litter of unused bandages and lint, and set things in order, sat down by the bedside to keep his patient company for a while. He was really somewhat anxious lest the wounds should have taken cold.

"If I get well, it will be a miracle," said Sor Tommaso, feebly. "I must think of my soul."

"By all means," answered the Scotchman. "It can do your soul no harm, and contemplation rests the body."

"You Protestants have not human sentiment," observed the Italian, moving his head slowly on the pillow. "But I also think of the abbess. I was to have gone there early this morning. She will also die. We shall both die."

Dalrymple crossed one leg over the other, and looked quietly at the doctor.

"Sor Tommaso," he said, "there is no other physician in Subiaco. I am a doctor, properly licensed to practise. It is evidently my duty to take care of your patients while you are ill."

"Mercy!" cried Sor Tommaso, with sudden energy, and opening his eyes very wide.

"Are you afraid that I shall kill them," asked Dalrymple, with a smile.

"Who knows? A foreigner! And the people say that you have converse with the devil. But the common people are ignorant."

"Very."

"And as for the convent—a Protestant—for the abbess! They would rather die. Figure to yourself what sort of a scandal there would be! A Protestant in a convent, and then, in that convent, too! The abbess would much rather die in peace."

"At all events, I will go and offer my services. If the abbess prefers to die in peace, she can answer to that effect. I will ask her what she thinks about it."

"Ask her!" repeated Sor Tommaso. "Do you imagine that you could see her? But what can you know? I tell you that last night she was muffled up in her chair, and her face covered. It needed the grace of Heaven, that I might feel her pulse! As for her tongue, God knows what it is like! I have not seen it. Not so much as the tip of it! Not even her eyes did I see. And to-day I was not to be admitted at all, because the abbess would be in bed. Imagine to yourself, with blisters and sinapisms, and a hundred things. I was only to speak with Sister Maria Addolorata, who is her niece, you know, in the anteroom of the abbess's apartment. They would not let you in. They would give you a bath of holy water through the loophole of the convent door and say, 'Go away, sinner; this is a religious house!' You know them very little."

"You are talking too much," observed Dalrymple, who had listened attentively. "It is not good for you. Besides, since you are able to speak, it would be better if you told me who stabbed you last night, that I may go to the police, and have the person arrested, if possible."

"You do not know what you are saying," answered Sor Tommaso, with sudden gravity. "The woman has relations—who could handle a knife better than she."

And he turned his face away.

CHAPTER VI

The sun was high when Dalrymple left Sor Tommaso in charge of the old woman-servant and went back to Stefanone's house to dress himself with more care than he had bestowed upon his hasty toilet at dawn. And now that he had plenty of time, he was even more careful of his appearance than usual; for he had fully determined to attempt to take Sor Tommaso's place in attendance upon the abbess. He therefore put on a coat of a sober colour and brushed his straight red hair smoothly back from his forehead, giving himself easily that extremely grave and trust-inspiring air which distinguishes many Scotchmen, and supports their solid qualities, while it seems to deny the possibility of any adventurous and romantic tendency.

At that hour nobody was about the house, and Dalrymple, stick in hand, sallied forth upon his expedition, looking for all the world as though he were going to church in Edinburgh instead of meditating an entrance into an Italian convent. He had said nothing more to the doctor on the subject. The people in the streets had most of them seen him often and knew him by name, and it did not occur to any one to wonder why a foreigner should wear one sort of coat rather than another, when he took his walks abroad. He walked leisurely; for the sky had cleared, and the sun was hot. Moreover, he followed the longer road in order to keep his shoes clean, instead of climbing up the narrow and muddy lane in which Sor Tommaso had been attacked. He reached the convent door at last, brushed a few specks of dust from his coat, settled his high collar and the broad black cravat which was then taking the place of the stock, and rang the bell with one steady pull. There was, perhaps, no occasion for nervousness. At all events, Dalrymple was as deliberate in his movements and as calm in all respects as he had ever been in his life. Only, just after he had pulled the weather-beaten bell-chain, a half-humorous smile bent his even lips and was gone again in a moment.

There was the usual slapping and shuffling of slippers in the vaulted archway within, but as it was now day, the loophole was opened immediately, and the portress came alone. Dalrymple explained in strangely accented but good Italian that Sor Tommaso had met with an accident in the night; that he, Angus Dalrymple, was a friend of the doctor's and a doctor himself, and had undertaken all of Sor Tommaso's duties, and, finally, that he begged the portress to find Sister Maria Addolorata, to repeat his story, and to offer his humble services in the cause of the abbess's recovery. All of which the veiled nun within heard patiently to the end.

"I will speak to Sister Maria Addolorata," she said. "Have the goodness to wait."

"Outside?" inquired Dalrymple, as the little shutter of the loophole was almost closed.

"Of course," answered the nun, opening it again, and shutting it as soon as she had spoken.

Dalrymple waited a long time in the blazing sun. The main entrance of the convent faced to the southeast, and it was not yet midday. He grew hot, after his walk, and softly wiped his forehead, and carefully folded his handkerchief again before returning it to his pocket. At last he heard the sound of steps again, and in a few seconds the loophole was once more opened.

"Sister Maria Addolorata will speak with you," said the portress's voice, as he approached his face to the little grating.

He felt an odd little thrill of pleasant surprise. But so far as seeing anything was concerned, he was disappointed. Instead of one veiled nun, there were now two veiled nuns.

"Madam," he began, "my friend Doctor Tommaso Taddei has met with an accident which prevents him from leaving his bed." And he went on to repeat all that he had told the portress, with such further explanations as he deemed necessary and persuasive.

While he spoke, Maria Addolorata drew back a little into the deeper shadow away from the loophole. Her veil hung over her eyes, and the folds were drawn across her mouth, but she gradually raised her head, throwing it back until she could see Dalrymple's face from beneath the edge of the black material. In so doing she unconsciously uncovered her mouth. The Scotchman saw a good part of her features, and gazed intently at what he saw, rightly judging that as the sun was behind him, she could hardly be sure whether he were looking at her or not.

As for her, she was doubtless inspired by a natural curiosity, but at the same time she understood the gravity of the case and wished to form an opinion as to the advisability of admitting the stranger. A glance told her that Dalrymple was a gentleman, and she was reassured by the gravity of his voice and by the fact that he was evidently acquainted with the abbess's condition, and must, therefore, be a friend of Sor Tommaso. When he had finished speaking, she immediately looked down again, and seemed to be hesitating.

"Open the door, Sister Filomena," she said at last.

The portress shook her head almost imperceptibly as she obeyed, but she said nothing. The whole affair was in her eyes exceedingly irregular. Maria Addolorata should have retired to the little room adjoining the convent parlour, and separated from it by a double grating, and Dalrymple should have been admitted to the parlour itself, and they should have said what they had to say to one another through the bars, in the presence of the portress. But Maria Addolorata was the abbess's niece. The abbess was too ill to give orders—too ill even to speak, it was rumoured. In a few days Maria Addolorata might be 'Her most Reverend Excellency.' Meanwhile she was mistress of the situation, and it was safer to obey her. Moreover, the portress was only a lay sister, an old and ignorant creature, accustomed to do what she was told to do by the ladies of the convent.

Dalrymple took off his hat and stooped low to enter through the small side-door. As soon as he had passed the threshold, he stood up to his height and then made a low bow to Maria Addolorata, whose veil now quite covered her eyes and prevented her from seeing him,—a fact which he realized immediately.

"Give warning to the sisters, Sister Filomena," said Maria Addolorata to the portress, who nodded respectfully and walked away into the gloom under the arches, leaving the nun and Dalrymple together by the door.

"It is necessary to give warning," she explained, "lest you should meet any of the sisters unveiled in the corridors, and they should be scandalized."

Dalrymple again bowed gravely and stood still, his eyes fixed upon Maria Addolorata's veiled head, but wandering now and then to her heavy but beautifully shaped white hands, which she held carelessly clasped before her and holding the end of the great rosary of brown beads which hung from her side. He thought he had never seen such hands before. They were high-bred, and yet at the same time there was a strongly material attraction about them.

He did not know what to say, and as nothing seemed to be expected of him, he kept silence for some time. At last Maria Addolorata, as though impatient at the long absence of the portress, tapped the pavement softly with her sandal slipper, and turned her head in the direction of the arches as though to listen for approaching footsteps.

"I hope that the abbess is no worse than when Doctor Taddei saw her last night," observed Dalrymple.

"Her most reverend excellency," answered Maria Addolorata, with a little emphasis, as though to teach him the proper mode of addressing the abbess, "is suffering. She has had a bad night."

"I shall hope to be allowed to give some advice to her most reverend excellency," said Dalrymple, to show that he had understood the hint.

"She will not allow you to see her. But you shall come with me to the antechamber, and I will speak with her and tell you what she says."

"I shall be greatly obliged, and will do my best to give good advice without seeing the patient."

Another pause followed, during which neither moved. Then Maria Addolorata spoke again, further reassured, perhaps, by Dalrymple's quiet and professional tone. She had too lately left the world to have lost the habit of making conversation to break an awkward silence. Years of seclusion, too, instead of making her shy and silent, had given her something of the ease and coolness of a married woman. This was natural enough, considering that she was born of worldly people and had acquired the manners of the world in her own home, in childhood.

"You are an Englishman, I presume, Signor Doctor?" she observed, in a tone of interrogation.

"A Scotchman, Madam," answered Dalrymple, correcting her and drawing himself up a little. "My name is Angus Dalrymple."

"It is the same—an Englishman or a Scotchman," said the nun.

"Pardon me, Madam, we consider that there is a great difference. The Scotch are chiefly Celts. Englishmen are Anglo-Saxons."

"But you are all Protestants. It is therefore the same for us."

Dalrymple feared a discussion of the question of religion. He did not answer the nun's last remark, but bowed politely. She, of course, could not see the inclination he made.

"You say nothing," she said presently. "Are you a Protestant?"

"Yes, Madam."

"It is a pity!" said Maria Addolorata. "May God send you light."

"Thank you, Madam."

Maria Addolorata smiled under her veil at the polite simplicity of the reply. She had met Englishmen in Rome.

"It is no longer customary to address us as 'Madam,'" she answered, a moment later. "It is more usual to speak to us as 'Sister' or 'Reverend Sister'—or 'Sister Maria.' I am Sister Maria Addolorata. But you know it, for you sent your message to me."

"Doctor Taddei told me."

At this point the portress appeared in the distance, and Maria Addolorata, hearing footsteps, turned her head from Dalrymple, raising her veil a little, so that she could recognize the lay sister without showing her face to the young man.

"Let us go," she said, dropping her veil again, and beginning to walk on. "The sisters are warned."

Dalrymple followed her in silence and at a respectful distance, congratulating himself upon his extraordinary good fortune in having got so far on the first attempt, and inwardly praying that Sor Tommaso's wounds might take a considerable time in healing. It had all come about so naturally that he had lost the sensation of doing something adventurous which had at first taken possession of him, and he now regarded everything as possible, even to being invited to a friendly cup of tea in Sister Maria Addolorata's sitting-room; for he imagined her as having a sitting-room and as drinking tea there in a semi-luxurious privacy. The idea would have amused an Italian of those days, when tea was looked upon as medicine.

They reached the end of the last corridor. Dalrymple, like Sor Tommaso, was admitted to the antechamber, while the portress waited outside to conduct him back again. But Maria did not take him into the abbess's parlour, into which she went at once, closing the door behind her. Dalrymple sat down upon a carved wooden box-bench, and waited. The nun was gone a long time.

"I have kept you waiting," she said, as she entered the little room again.

"My time is altogether at your service, Sister Maria Addolorata," he answered, rising quickly. "How is her most reverend excellency?"

"Very ill. I do not know what to say. She will not hear of seeing you. I fear she will not live long, for she can hardly breathe."

"Does she cough?"

"Not much. Not so much as last night. She complains that she cannot draw her breath and that her lungs feel full of something."

The case was evidently serious, and Dalrymple, who was a physician by nature, proceeded to extract as much information as he could from the nun, who did her best to answer all his questions clearly. The long conversation, with its little restraints and its many attempts at a mutual understanding, did more to accustom Maria Addolorata to Dalrymple's presence and personality than any number of polite speeches on his part could have done. There is an unavoidable tendency to intimacy between any two people who are together engaged in taking care of a sick person.

"I can give you directions and good advice," said Dalrymple, at last. "But it can never be the same as though I could see the patient myself. Is there no possible means of obtaining her consent? She may die for the want of just such advice as I can only give after seeing her. Would not her brother, his Eminence the Cardinal, perhaps recommend her to let me visit her once?"

"That is an idea," answered the nun, quickly. "My uncle is a man of broad views. I have heard it said in Rome. I could write to him that Doctor Taddei is unable to come, and that a celebrated foreign physician is here—"

"Not celebrated," interrupted Dalrymple, with his literal Scotch veracity.

"What difference can it make?" uttered Maria Addolorata, moving her shoulders a little impatiently. "He will be the more ready to use his influence, for he is much attached to my aunt. Then, if he can persuade her, I can send down the gardener to the town for you this afternoon. It may not be too late."

"I see that you have some confidence in me," said Dalrymple. "I am of a newer school than Doctor Taddei. If you will follow my directions, I will almost promise that her most reverend excellency shall not die before to-morrow."

He smiled now, as he gave the abbess her full title, for he began to feel as though he had known Maria Addolorata for a long time, though he had only had one glimpse of her eyes, just when she had raised her head to get a look at him through the loophole of the gate. But he had not forgotten them, and he felt that he knew them.

"I will do all you tell me," she answered quietly.

Dalrymple had some English medicines with him on his travels, and not knowing what might be required of him at the convent, he had brought with him a couple of tiny bottles.

"This when she coughs—ten drops," he said, handing the bottles to the nun. "And five drops of this once an hour, until her chest feels freer."

He gave her minute directions, as far as he could, about the general treatment of the patient, which Maria repeated and got by heart.

"I will let you know before twenty-three o'clock what the cardinal says to the plan," she said. "In this way you will be able to come up by daylight."

As Dalrymple took his leave, he held out his hand, forgetting that he was in Italy.

"It is not our custom," said Maria Addolorata, thrusting each of her own hands into the opposite sleeve.

But there was nothing cold in her tone. On the contrary, Dalrymple fancied that she was almost on the point of laughing at that moment, and he blushed at his awkwardness. But she could not see his face.

"Your most humble servant," he said, bowing to her.

"Good day, Signor Doctor," she answered, through the open door, as the portress jingled her keys and prepared to follow Dalrymple.

So he took his departure, not without much satisfaction at the result of his first attempt.

CHAPTER VII

Sor Tommaso recovered but slowly, though his injuries were of themselves not dangerous. His complexion was apoplectic and gouty, he was no longer young, and before forty-eight hours had gone by his wounds were decidedly inflamed and he had a little fever. At the same time he was by no means a courageous man, and he was ready to cry out that he was dead, whenever he felt himself worse. Besides this, he lost his temper several times daily with Dalrymple, who resolutely refused to bleed him, and he insisted upon eating and drinking more than was good for him, at a time when if he had been his own patient he would have enforced starvation as necessary to recovery.

Meanwhile the cardinal had exerted his influence with his sister, the abbess, and had so far succeeded that Dalrymple, who went every day to the convent, was now made to stand with his back to the abbess's open door, in order that he might at least ask her questions and hear her own answers. Many an old Italian doctor can tell of even stranger and more absurd precautions observed by the nuns of those days. As soon as the oral examination was over, Maria Addolorata shut the door and came out into the parlour, where Dalrymple finished his visit, prolonging it in conversation with her by every means he could devise.

Though encumbered with a little of the northern shyness, Dalrymple was not diffident. There is a great difference between shyness and diffidence. Diffidence distrusts itself; shyness distrusts the mere outward impression made on others. At this time Dalrymple had no object beyond enjoying the pleasure of talking with Maria Addolorata, and no hope beyond that of some day seeing her face without the veil. As for her voice, his present position as doctor to the convent made it foolish for him to run the risk of being caught listening for her songs behind the garden wall. But he had not forgotten what Annetta had told him, and Maria Addolorata's soft intonations and liquid depths of tone in speaking led him to believe that the peasant girl had not exaggerated the nun's gift of singing.

One day, after he had seen her and talked with her more than half a dozen times, he approached the subject, merely for the sake of conversation, saying that he had been told of her beautiful voice by people who had heard her across the garden.

"It is true," she answered simply. "I have a good voice. But it is forbidden here to sing except in church," she added with a sigh. "And now that my aunt is ill, I would not displease her for anything."

"That is natural," said Dalrymple. "But I would give anything in the world to hear you."

"In church you can hear me. The church is open on Sundays at the Benediction service. We are behind the altar in the choir, of course. But perhaps you would know my voice from the rest because it is deeper."

"I should know it in a hundred thousand," asseverated the Scotchman, with warmth.

"That would be a great many—a whole choir of angels!" And the nun laughed softly, as she sometimes did, now that she knew him so much better.

There was something warm and caressing in her laughter, short and low as it was, that made Dalrymple look at those full white hands of hers and wonder whether they might not be warm and caressing too.

"Will you sing a little louder than the rest next Sunday afternoon, Sister Maria?" he asked. "I will be in the church."

"That would be a great sin," she answered, but not very gravely.

"Why?"

"Because I should have to be thinking about you instead of about the holy service. Do you not know that? But nothing is sinful according to you Protestants, I suppose. At all events, come to the church."

"Do you think we are all devils, Sister Maria?" asked Dalrymple, with a smile.

"More or less." She laughed again. "They say in the town that you have a compact with the devil."

"Do you hear what is said in the town?"

"Sometimes. The gardener brings the gossip and tells it to the cook. Or Sora Nanna tells it to me when she brings the linen. There are a thousand ways. The people think we know nothing because they never see us. But we hear all that goes on."

Dalrymple said nothing in answer for some time. Then he spoke suddenly and rather hoarsely.

"Shall I never see you, Sister Maria?" he asked.

"Me? But you see me every day—"

"Yes,—but your face, without the veil."

Maria Addolorata shook her head.

"It is against all rules," she answered.

"Is it not against all rules that we should sit here and make conversation every day for half an hour?"

"Yes—I suppose it is. But you are here as a doctor to take care of my aunt," she added quickly. "That makes it right. You are not a man. You are a doctor."

"Oh,—I understand." Dalrymple laughed a little. "Then I am never to see your beautiful face?"

"How do you know it is beautiful, since you have never seen it?"

"From your beautiful hands," answered the young man, promptly.

"Oh!" Maria Addolorata glanced at her hands and then, with a movement which might have been quicker, concealed them in her sleeves.

"It is a sin to hide what God has made beautiful," said Dalrymple.

"If I have anything about me that is beautiful, it is for God's glory that I hide it," answered Maria, with real gravity this time.

Dalrymple understood that he had gone a little too far, though he did not exactly regret it, for the next words she spoke showed him that she was not really offended. Nevertheless, in order to exhibit a proper amount of contrition he took his leave with a little more formality than usual on this particular occasion. Possibly she was willing to show that she forgave him, for she hesitated a moment just before opening the door, and then, to his great surprise, held out her hand to him.

"It is your custom," she said, just touching his eagerly outstretched fingers. "But you must not look at it," she added, drawing it back quickly and hiding it in her sleeve with another low laugh. And she began to shut the door almost before he had quite gone through.

Dalrymple walked more slowly on that day, as he descended through the steep and narrow streets, and though he was surefooted by nature and habit, he almost stumbled once or twice on his way down, because, somehow, though his eyes looked towards his feet, he did not see exactly where he was going.

There is no necessity for analyzing his sensations. It is enough to say at once that he was beginning to be really in love with Maria Addolorata, and that he denied the fact to himself stoutly, though it forced itself upon him with every step which took him further from the convent. He felt on that day a strong premonitory symptom in the shape of a logical objection, as it were, to his returning again to see the nun. The objection was the evident and total futility of the almost intimate intercourse into which the two were gliding. The day must soon come when the abbess would no longer need his assistance. In all probability she would recover, for the more alarming symptoms had disappeared, and she showed signs of regaining her strength by slow degrees. It was quite clear to Dalrymple that, after her ultimate recovery, his chance of seeing and talking with Maria Addolorata would be gone forever. Sor Tommaso, indeed, recovered but slowly. Of the two his case was the worse, for fever had set in on the third day and had not left him yet, so that he assured Dalrymple almost hourly that his last moment was at hand. But he also was sure to get well, in the Scotchman's opinion, and the latter knew well enough that his own temporary privileges as physician to the convent would be withdrawn from him as soon as the Subiaco doctor should be able to climb the hill.

It was all, therefore, but a brief incident in his life, which could not possibly have any continuation hereafter. He tried in vain to form plans and create reasons for seeing Maria Addolorata even once a month for some time to come, but his ingenuity failed him altogether, and he grew angry with himself for desiring what was manifestly impossible.

With true masculine inconsequence, so soon as he was displeased with himself he visited his displeasure upon the object that attracted him, and on the earliest possible occasion, on their very next meeting. He assumed an air of coldness and reserve such as he had certainly not thought necessary to put on at his first visit. Almost without any preliminary words of courtesy, and without any attempt to prolong the short conversation which always took place before he was made to stand with his back to the abbess's open door, he coldly inquired about the good lady's condition during the past night, and made one or two observations thereon with a brevity almost amounting to curtness.

Maria Addolorata was surprised; but as her face was covered, and her hands were quietly folded before her, Dalrymple could not see that his behaviour had any effect upon her. She did not answer his last remark at all, but quietly bowed her head.

Then followed the usual serio-comic scene, during which Dalrymple stood turned away from the open door, asking questions of the sick woman, and listening attentively for her low-spoken answers. To tell the truth, he judged of her condition more from the sound of her voice than from anything else. He had also taught Maria Addolorata how to feel the pulse; and she counted the beats while he looked at his watch. His chief anxiety was now for the action of the heart, which had been weakened by a lifetime of unhealthy living, by food inadequate in quality, even when sufficient in quantity, by confinement within doors, and lack of life-giving sunshine, and by all those many causes which tend to reduce the vitality of a cloistered nun.

When the comedy was over, Maria Addolorata shut the door as usual; and she and Dalrymple were alone together in the abbess's parlour, as they were every day. The abbess herself could hear that they were talking, but she naturally supposed that they were discussing the details of her condition; and as she felt that she was really recovering, so far as she could judge, and as almost every day, after Dalrymple had gone, Maria Addolorata had some new direction of his to carry out, the elder lady's suspicions were not aroused. On the contrary, her confidence in the Scotch doctor grew from day to day; and in the long hours during which she lay thinking over her state and its circumstances, she made plans for his conversion, in which her brother, the cardinal, bore a principal part. She was grateful to Dalrymple, and it seemed to her that the most proper way of showing her gratitude would be to save his soul, a point of view unusual in the ordinary relations of life.

On this particular day, Maria Addolorata shut the door, and came forward into the parlour as usual. As usual, too, she sat down in the abbess's own big easy-chair, expecting that Dalrymple would seat himself opposite to her. But he remained standing, with the evident intention of going away in a few moments. He said a few words about the patient, gave one or two directions, and then stood still in silence for a moment.

Maria Addolorata lifted her head a little, but not enough to show him more than an inch of her face.

"Have I displeased you, Signor Doctor?" she asked, in her deep, warm voice. "Have I not carried out your orders?"

"On the contrary," answered Dalrymple, with a stiffness which he resented in himself. "It is impossible to be more conscientious than you always are."

Seeing that he still remained standing, the nun rose to her feet, and waited for him to go. She believed that she was far too proud to detain him, if he wished to shorten the meeting. But something hurt her, which she could not understand.

Dalrymple hesitated a moment, and his lips parted as though he were about to speak. The silence was prolonged only for a moment or two.

"Good morning, Sister Maria Addolorata," he said suddenly, and bowed.

"Good morning, Signor Doctor," answered the nun.

She bent her head very slightly, but a keener observer than Dalrymple was, just then, would have noticed that as she did so, her shoulders moved forward a little, as though her breast were contracted by some sudden little pain. Dalrymple did not see it. He bowed again, let himself out, and closed the door softly behind him.

When he was gone, Maria Addolorata sat down in the big easy-chair again, and uncovered her face, doubling her veil back upon her head, and withdrawing the thick folds from her chin and mouth. Her features were very pale, as she sat staring at the sky through the window, and her eyes fixed themselves in that look which was peculiar to her. Her full white hands strained upon each other a little, bringing the colour to the tips of her fingers. During some minutes she did not move. Then she heard her aunt's voice calling to her hoarsely. She rose at once, and went into the bedroom. The abbess's pale face was very thin and yellow now, as it lay upon the white pillow; the coverlet was drawn up to her chin, and a grimly carved black crucifix hung directly above her head.

"The doctor did not stay long to-day," she said, in a hollow tone.

"No, mother," answered the young nun. "He thinks you are doing very well. He wishes you to eat a wing of roast chicken."

"If I could have a little salad," said the abbess. "Maria," she added suddenly, "you are careful to keep your face covered when you are in the next room, are you not?"

"Always."

"You generally do not raise your veil until you come into this room, after the doctor is gone," said the elder lady.

"He went so soon, to-day," answered Maria Addolorata, with perfectly innocent truth. "I stayed a moment in the parlour, thinking over his directions, and I lifted my veil when I was alone. It is close to-day."

"Go into the garden, and walk a little," said the abbess. "It will do you good. You are pale."

If she had felt even a faint uneasiness about her niece's conduct, it was removed by the latter's manner.

CHAPTER VIII

Once more Dalrymple was sitting over his supper at the table in the vaulted room on the ground floor which Stefanone used as a wine shop. To tell the truth, it was very superior to the ordinary wine shops of Subiaco and had an exceptional reputation. The common people never came there, because Stefanone did not sell his cheap wine at retail, but sent it all to Rome, or took it thither himself for the sake of getting a higher price for it. He always said that he did not keep an inn, and perhaps as much on account of his relations with Gigetto's family, he assumed as far as possible the position of a wine-dealer rather than that of a wine-seller. The distinction, in Italian mountain towns, is very marked.

"They can have a measure of the best, if they care to pay for it," he said. "If they wish a mouthful of food, there is what there is. But I am not the village host, and Nanna is not a wine-shop cook, to fry tripe and peel onions for Titius and Caius."

The old Roman expression, denoting generally the average public, survives still in polite society, and Stefanone had caught it from Sor Tommaso.

Dalrymple was sitting as usual over his supper, by the light of the triple-beaked brass lamp, his measure of wine beside him, and a beefsteak, which on this occasion was really of beef, before him. Stefanone was absent in Rome, with a load of wine. Sora Nanna sat on Dalrymple's right, industriously knitting in Italian fashion, one of the needles stuck into and supported by a wooden sheath thrust into her waist-band, while she worked off the stitches with the others. Annetta sat opposite the Scotchman, but a little on one side of the lamp, so that she could see his face.

"Mother," she said suddenly, without lifting her chin from the hand in which it rested, "you do not know anything! This Signor Englishman is making love with a nun in the convent! Eh—what do you think of it? Only this was wanting. A little more and the lightning will fall upon the convent! These Protestants! Oh, these blessed Protestants! They respect nothing, not even the saints!"

"My daughter! what are you saying?"

Sora Nanna's fingers did not pause in their work, nor did her eyes look up, but the deep furrow showed itself in her thick peasant's forehead, and her coarse, hard lips twitched clumsily with the beginning of a smile.

"What am I saying? The truth. Ask rather of the Signore whether it is not true."

"It is silly," said Dalrymple, growing unnaturally red, and looking up sharply at Annetta, before he took his next mouthful.

"Look at him, mother!" laughed the girl. "He is red, red—he seems to me a boiled shrimp. Eh, this time I have guessed it! And as for Sister Maria Addolorata, she no longer sees with her eyes! To-day, when you were carrying in the baskets, you and the other women who went with us, I asked her whether the abbess was satisfied with the new doctor, and she answered that he was a very wise man, much wiser than Sor Tommaso. So I told her that it was a pity, because Sor Tommaso was getting well and would not allow the English doctor to come instead of him much longer. Then she looked at me. By Bacchus, I was afraid. Certain eyes! Not even a cat when you take away her kittens! A little more and she would have eaten me. And then her face made itself of marble—like that face of a woman that is built into the fountain in the piazza. Arch-priest! What a face!"

The girl stared hard at Dalrymple, and her mouth laughed wickedly at his evident embarrassment, while there was something very different from laughter in her eyes. During the long speech, Sora Nanna had stopped knitting, and she looked from her daughter to the Scotchman with a sort of half-stupid, half-cunning curiosity.

"But these are sins!" she exclaimed at last.

"And what does it matter?" asked the girl. "Does he go to confession? So what does it matter? He keeps the account himself, of his sins. I should not like to have them on my shoulders. But as for Sister Maria Addolorata—oh, she! I told you that she sinned in her throat. Well, the sin is ready, now. What is she waiting for? For the abbess to die? Or for Sor Tommaso to get well? Then she will not see the Signor Englishman any more. It would be better for her. When she does not see him any more, she will knead her pillow with tears, and make her bread of it, to bite and eat. Good appetite, Sister Maria!"

"You talk, you talk, and you conclude nothing," observed Sora Nanna. "You have certain thoughts in your head! And you do not let the Signore say even a word."

"What can he say? He will say that it is not true. But then, who will believe him? I should like to see them a little together. I am sure that she shows him her face, and that it is 'Signor Doctor' here, and 'Dear Signor Doctor' there, and a thousand gentlenesses. Tell the truth, Signore. She shows you her face."

"No," said Dalrymple, who had regained his self-possession. "She never shows me her face."

"What a shame for a Carmelite nun to show her face to a man!" cried the girl.

"But I tell you she is always veiled to her chin," insisted Dalrymple, with perfect truth.

"Eh! It is you who say so!" retorted Annetta. "But then, what can it matter to me? Make love with a nun, if it goes, Signore. Youth is a flower—when it is withered, it is hay, and the beasts eat it."

"This is true," said Sora Nanna, returning to her knitting. "But do not pay attention to her, Signore. She is stupid. She does not know what she says. Eat, drink, and manage your own affairs. It is better. What can a child understand? It is like a little dog that sees and barks, without understanding. But you are a much instructed man and have been round the whole world. Therefore you know many things. It seems natural."

Though Dalrymple was not diffident, as has been said, he was far from vain, on the whole, and in particular he had none of that contemptible vanity which makes a man readily believe that every woman he meets is in love with him. He had not the slightest idea at that time that Annetta, the peasant girl, looked upon him with anything more than the curiosity and vague interest usually bestowed on a foreigner in Italy.

He was annoyed, however, by what she said this evening, though he was also secretly surprised and delighted. The contradiction is a common one. The miser is half mad with joy on discovering that he has much more than he supposed, and bitterly resents, at the same time, any notice which may be taken of the fact by others.

Annetta did not enjoy his discomfiture and evident embarrassment, for she was far more deeply hurt herself than she realized, and every word she had spoken about Maria Addolorata had hurt her, though she had taken a sort of vague delight in teasing Dalrymple. She relapsed into silence now, alternately wishing that he loved her, and then, that she might kill him. If she could not have his heart, she would be satisfied with his blood. There was a passionate animal longing in the instinct to have him for herself, even dead, rather than that any other woman should get his love.

Dalrymple was aware only that the girl's words had annoyed him, while inwardly conscious that if what she said were true, the truth would make a difference in his life. He showed no inclination to talk any more, and finished his supper in a rather morose silence, turning to his book as soon as he had done. Then Gigetto came in with his guitar and sang and talked with the two women.

But he was restless that night, and did not fall asleep until the moon had set and his window grew dark. And even in his dreams he was restless still, so that when he awoke in the morning he said to himself that he had been foolish in his behaviour towards Maria Addolorata on the previous day. He felt tired, too, and his colour was less brilliant than usual. It was Sunday, and he remembered that if he chose he could go in the afternoon to the Benediction in the convent church and hear Maria's voice perhaps. But at the usual hour, just before noon, he went to make his visit to the abbess.

It was his intention to forget his stiff manner, and to behave as he had always behaved until yesterday. Strange to say, however, he felt a constraint coming upon him as soon as he was in the nun's presence. She received him as usual, there was the usual comic scene at the abbess's door, and, as every day, the two were alone together after her door was shut.

"Are you ill?" asked Maria Addolorata, after a moment's silence which, short as it was, both felt to be awkward.

Dalrymple was taken by surprise. The tone in which she had spoken was cold and distant rather than expressive of any concern for his welfare, but he did not think of that. He only realized that his manner must seem to her very unusual, since she asked such a question. An Italian would have observed that his own face was pale, and would have told her that he was dying of love.

"No, I am not ill," answered the Scotchman, simply, and in his most natural tone of voice.

"Then what is the matter with you since yesterday?" asked Maria Addolorata, less coldly, and as though she were secretly amused.

"There is nothing the matter—at least, nothing that I could explain to you."

She sat down in the big easy-chair and, as formerly, he took his seat opposite to her.

"There is something," she insisted, speaking thoughtfully. "You cannot deceive a woman, Signor Doctor."

Dalrymple smiled and looked at her veiled head.

"You said the other day that I was not a man, but a doctor," he answered. "I suppose I might answer that you are not a woman, but a nun."

"And is not a nun a woman?" asked Maria Addolorata, and he knew that she was smiling, too.

"You would not forgive me if I answered you," he said.

"Who knows? I might be obliged to, since I am obliged to meet you every day. It may be a sin, but I am curious."

"Shall I tell you?"

As though instinctively, Maria was silent for a moment, and turned her veiled face towards the abbess's door. But Dalrymple needed no such warning to lower his voice.

"Tell me," she said, and under her veil she could feel that her eyes were growing deep and the pupils wide and dark, and she knew that she had done wrong.

"How should I know whether you are a saint or only a woman, since I have never seen your face?" he asked. "I shall never know—for in a few days Doctor Taddei will be well again, and you will not need my services."

He saw the quick tightening of one hand upon the other, and the slight start of the head, and in a flash he knew that all Annetta had told him was true. The silence that followed seemed longer than the awkward pause which had preceded the conversation.

"It cannot be so soon," she said in a very low tone.

"It may be to-morrow," he answered, and to his own astonishment his voice almost broke in his throat, and he felt that his own hands were twisting each other, as though he were in pain. "I shall die without seeing you," he added almost roughly.

Again there was a short silence in the still room.

Suddenly, with quick movements of both hands at once, Maria Addolorata threw back the veil from her face, and drew away the folds that covered her mouth.

"There, see me!" she exclaimed. "Look at me well this once!"

Her face was as white as marble, and her dark eyes had a wild and startled look in them, as though she saw the world for the first time. A ringlet of red-gold hair had escaped from the bands of white that crossed her forehead in an even line and were drawn down straight on either side, for in the quick movement she had made she had loosened the pin that held them together under her chin, and had freed the dazzling throat down to the high collar.

Dalrymple's pale, bright blue eyes caught fire, and he looked at her with all his being, at her face, her throat, her eyes, the ringlet of her hair. He breathed audibly, with parted lips, between his clenched teeth.

Gradually, as he looked, he saw the red blush rise from the throat to the cheeks, from the cheeks to the forehead, and the marble grew more beautiful with womanly life. Then, all at once, he saw the hot tears welling up in her eyes, and in an instant the vision was gone. With a passionate movement she had covered her face with the veil, and throwing herself sideways against the high back of the chair, she pressed the dark stuff still closer to her eyes and mouth and cheeks. Her whole body shook convulsively, and a moment later she was sobbing, not audibly, but visibly, as though her heart were breaking.

Dalrymple was again taken by surprise. He had been so completely lost in the utterly selfish contemplation of her beauty that he had been very far from realizing what she herself must have felt as soon as she appreciated what she had done. He at once accused himself of having looked too rudely at her, but at the same time he was himself too much disturbed to argue the matter. Quite instinctively he rose to his feet and tried to take one of her hands from her veil, touching it comfortingly. But she made a wild gesture, as though to drive him away.

"Go!" she cried in a low and broken voice, between her sobs. "Go! Go quickly!"

She could not say more for her sobbing, but he did not obey her. He only drew back a little and watched her, all his blood on fire from the touch of her soft white hand.

She stifled her sobs in her veil, and gradually grew more calm. She even arranged the veil itself a little better, her face still turned away towards the back of the chair.

"Maria! Maria!" The abbess's voice was calling her, hoarsely and almost desperately, from the next room.

She started and sat up straight, listening. Then the cry was heard again, more desperate, less loud. With a quick skill which seemed marvellous in Dalrymple's eyes, Maria adjusted her veil almost before she had sprung to her feet.

"Wait!" she said. "Something is the matter!"

She was at the bedroom door in an instant, and in an instant more she was at her aunt's bedside.

"Maria—I am dying," said the abbess's voice faintly, as she felt the nun's arm under her head.

Dalrymple heard the words, and did not hesitate as he hastily felt for something in his pocket.

"Come!" cried Maria Addolorata.

But he was already there, on the other side of the bed, pouring something between the sick lady's lips.

It was fortunate that he was there at that moment. He had indeed anticipated the possibility of a sudden failure in the action of the heart, and he never came to the convent without a small supply of a powerful stimulant of his own invention. The liquid, however, was of such a nature that he did not like to leave the use of it to Maria Addolorata's discretion, for he was aware that she might easily be mistaken in the symptoms of the collapse which would really require its use.

The abbess swallowed a sufficient quantity of it, and Dalrymple allowed her head to lie again upon the pillow. She looked almost as though she were dead. Her eyes were turned up, and her jaw had dropped. Maria Addolorata believed that all was over.

"She is dead," she said. "Let us leave her in peace."

It is a very ancient custom among Italians to withdraw as soon as a dying person is unconscious, if not even before the supreme moment.

"She will probably live through this," answered Dalrymple, shaking his head.

Neither he nor the nun spoke again for a long time. Little by little, the abbess revived under the influence of the stimulant, the heart beat less faintly, and the mouth slowly closed, while the eyelids shut themselves tightly over the upturned eyes. The normal regular breathing began again, and the crisis was over.

"It is passed," said Dalrymple. "It will not come again to-day. We can leave her now, for she will sleep."

"Yes," said the abbess herself. "Let me sleep." Her voice was faint, but the words were distinctly articulated.

Then she opened her eyes and looked about her quite naturally. Her glance rested on Dalrymple's face. Suddenly realizing that she was not veiled, she drew the coverlet up over her face. It is a peculiarity of such cases, that the patient returns almost immediately to ordinary consciousness when the moment of danger is past.

"Go!" she said, with more energy than might have been expected. "This is a religious house. You must not be here."

Dalrymple retired into the parlour again, shutting the door behind him, and waited for Maria Addolorata, for it was now indispensable that he should give her directions for the night. During the few minutes which passed while he was alone, he stood looking out of the window. The excitement of the last half-hour had cut off from his present state of mind the emotion he had felt before the abbess's cry for help, but had not decreased the impression it had left. While he was helping the sick lady there had not been one instant in which he had not felt that there was more than the life of a half-saintly old woman in the balance, and that her death meant the end of his meetings with Maria Addolorata. Annetta's words came back to him, 'she will knead her pillow with tears and make her bread of it.'

Several minutes passed, and the door opened softly and closed again. Maria Addolorata came up to him, where he stood by the window. She did not speak for a moment, but he saw that her hand was pressed to her side.

"I have spent a bad half-hour," she said at last, with something like a gasp.

"It is the worst half-hour I ever spent in my life," answered Dalrymple. "I thought it was all over," he added.

"Yes," she said, "I thought it was all over."

He could hear his heart beating in his ears. He could almost hear hers. His hand went out toward her, cold and unsteady, but it fell to his side again almost instantly. But for the heart-beats, it seemed to him that there was an appalling stillness in the air of the quiet room. His manly face grew very pale. He slowly bit his lip and looked out of the window. An enormous temptation was upon him. He knew that if she moved to leave his side he should take her and hold her. There was a tiny drop of blood on his lip now. Something in him made him hope against himself that she would speak, that she would say some insignificant dry words. But every inch of his strong fibre and every ounce of his hot blood hoped that she would move, instead of speaking.

She sighed, and the sigh was broken by a quick-drawn breath. Slowly Dalrymple turned his white face and gleaming eyes to her veiled head. Still she neither spoke nor moved. He, in memory, saw her face, her mouth, and her eyes through the thick stuff that hid them. The silence became awful to him. His hands opened and shut convulsively.

She heard his breath and she saw the uncertain shadow of his hand, moving on the black and white squares of the pavement. She made a slight, short movement towards him and then stepped suddenly back, overcoming the temptation to go to him.

"No!"

He uttered the single word with a low, fierce cry. In an instant his arms were around her, pressing her, lifting her, straining her, almost bruising her. In an instant his lips were kissing a face whiter than his own, eyes that flamed like summer lightning between his kisses, lips crushed and hurt by his, but still not kissed enough, hands that were raised to resist, but lingered to be kissed in turn, lest anything should be lost.

A little splintering crash, the sound of a glass falling upon a stone floor in the next room, broke the stillness. Dalrymple's arms relaxed, and the two stood for one moment facing one another, pale, with fire in their eyes and hearts beating more loudly than before. Dalrymple raised his hand to his forehead, as though he were dazed, and made an uncertain step in the direction of the door. Maria raised her white hands towards him, and her eyelids drooped, even while she looked into his face.

He kissed her once more with a kiss in which all other kisses seemed to meet and live and die a lingering, sweet death. She sank into the deep old easy-chair, and when she looked up, he was gone.

CHAPTER IX

It rained during the afternoon, and Dalrymple sat in his small laboratory, among his books and the simple apparatus he used for his experiments. His little window was closed, and the southwest wind drove the shower against the clouded panes of glass, so that the rain came through the ill-fitted strips of lead which joined them, and ran down in small streams to the channel in the stone sill, whence the water found its way out through a hole running through the wall. He sat in his rush-bottomed chair, sideways by the deal table, one long leg crossed over the other. His hand lay on an open book, and his fingers occasionally tapped the page impatiently, while his eyes were fixed on the window, watching the driving rain.

He was not thinking, for he could not think. Over and over again the scene of the morning came back to him and sent the hot blood rushing to his throat. He tried to reflect, indeed, and to see whether what he had done was to have any consequences for him, or was to be left behind in his life, like a lovely view seen from a carriage window on a swift journey, gone before it is half seen, and never to be seen again, except in dreams. But he was utterly unable to look forward and reason about the future. Everything dragged him back, up the steep ascent to the convent, through the arched ways and vaulted corridors, to the room in which he had passed the supreme moments of his life. The only distinct impression of the future was the strong desire to feel again what he had felt that day; to feel it again and again, and always, as long as feeling could last; to stretch out his hands and take, to close them and hold, to make his, indubitably, what had been but questionably his for an instant, to get the one thing worth having, for himself, and only for himself. For the passion of a strong man is loving and taking, and the passion of a good woman is loving and giving. Dalrymple reasoned well enough, later,—too well, perhaps,—but during those hours he spent alone on that day, there was no power of reasoning in him. The world was the woman he loved, and the world's orbit was but the circle of his clasping arms. Beyond them was chaos, without form and void, clouded as the rain-streaked panes of his little window.

He looked at his watch more than once. At last he rose, threw a cloak over his shoulders and went out, locking the door of the little laboratory behind him as he always did, and thrusting the unwieldy key into his pocket.

He climbed the hill to the convent, taking the short cut through the narrow lanes. The rain had almost ceased, and the wet mist that blew round the corners of the dark houses was pleasant in his face. But he scarcely knew what he saw and felt on his way. He reached the convent church and went in, and stood by one of the pillars near the door.

It was a small church, built with a great choir for the nuns behind the high altar; from each side of the latter a high wooden screen extended to the walls, completely cutting off the space. It was dark, too, especially in such weather, and almost deserted, save for a number of old women who knelt on the damp marble pavement, some leaning against the backs of chairs, some resting one arm upon the plastered bases of the yellow marble columns. There were many lights on the high altar. Two acolytes, rough-headed boys of Subiaco, knelt within the altar rail, dressed in black cassocks and clean linen cottas. Two priests and a young deacon sat side by side on the right of the altar, with small black books in their hands. The nuns were chanting, unseen in the choir. No one noticed Dalrymple, wrapped in his cloak, as he leaned against the pillar near the door. His head was a little inclined, involuntarily respectful to ceremonies he neither believed in nor understood, but which had in them the imposing element of devout earnestness. Yet his eyes were raised and looked up from under his brows, steadily and watchfully, for he knew that Maria Addolorata was behind the screen, and from the first moment of entering the church it seemed to him that he could distinguish her voice from the rest.

He knew that it was hers, though he had never heard her sing. There was in all those sweet, colourless tones one tone that made ringing harmonies in his strong heart. Amongst all those mingling accents, there was one accent that touched his soul. Amidst the echoes that died softly away under the dim arches, there was one echo that died not, but rang on and on in his ears. There was a voice not like other voices there, nor like any he had ever heard. Many were strong and sweet; this one was not sweet and strong only, but alive with a divine life, winged with divine wings, essential of immortality, touching beyond tears, passionate as the living, breathing, sighing, dying world, grand as a flood of light, sad as the twilight of gods, full as a great water swinging to the tide of the summer's moon, fine-drawn as star-rays—a voice of gold.

As Dalrymple stood there in the shadow, he heard it singing to him and telling him all that he had not been told in words, all that he felt, and more also. For there was in it the passion of the woman, and the passionate remorse of the nun, the towering love of Maria Braccio, woman and princess, and the deep despair of Maria Addolorata, nun and sinner, unfaithful spouse of the Lord Christ, accused and self-accusing, self-wronged, self-judged, but condemned of God and foretasting the ultimate tragedy that is eternal—the tragedy of supreme hell.

The man who stood there knew that it was his doing, and the burden of his deeds bowed him bodily as he stood. But still he listened, and, as she sung, he watched her lips in the dark, inner mirror of sin's memory, and they drew him on.

Little by little, he heard only her voice, and the others chanted but faintly as from an infinite distance. And then, not in his thought, but in deed, she was singing alone, and the words of 'O Salutaris Hostia,' sounded in the dim church as they had never sounded before, nor could ever sound again, the appeal of a lost soul's agony to God, the glory of golden voice, the accent of transcendent genius, the passion, the strength, the despair, of an ancient race.

In the dark church the coarse, sad peasant women bowed themselves upon the pavement. One of them sobbed aloud and beat her breast. Angus Dalrymple kneeled upon one knee and pressed his brow against the foot of the pillar, kneeling neither to God, nor to the Sacred Host, nor to man's belief in Heaven or Hell, neither praying nor blaspheming, neither hoping nor dreading, but spell-bound upon a wrack of torture that was heart-breaking delight, his senses torn and strained to the utmost of his strong endurance, to the very scream of passion, his soul crucified upon the exquisite loveliness of his sin.

Then all was still for an instant. Again there was a sound of voices, as the nuns sang in chorus the 'Tantum Ergo.' But the voice of voices was silent among them. The solemn Benediction blessed the just and the unjust alike. The short verses and responses of the priests broke the air that still seemed alive and trembling.

Dalrymple rose slowly, and wrapped his cloak about him. Above the footsteps of the women going out of the church, he could hear the soft sound of all the nuns moving together as they left the choir. He knew that she was with them, and he stood motionless in his place till silence descended as a curtain between him and what had been. Then, with bent head, he went out into the rain that poured through the dim twilight.

CHAPTER X

They were together on the following day. The abbess was better, and as yet there had been no return of the syncope which Dalrymple dreaded.

Contrary to her habit, Maria Addolorata sat on a high chair by the table, her head veiled and turned away, her chin supported in her hand. Dalrymple was seated not far from her, leaning forward, and trying to see her face, silent, and in a dangerous mood. She had refused to let him come near her, and even to raise her veil. When she spoke, her voice was full of a profound sadness that irritated him instead of touching him, for his nerves were strung to passion and out of tune with regret.

"The sin of it; the deadly sin!" she said.

"There is no sin in it," he answered; but she shook her veiled head.

And there was silence again, as on the day before, but the stillness was of another kind. It was not the awful lull which goes before the bursting of the storm, when the very air seems to start at the fall of a leaf for fear lest it be already the thunder-clap. It was more like the noiseless rising of the hungry flood that creeps up round the doomed house, wherein is desperate, starving life, higher and higher, inch by inch—the flood of rising fate.

"You say that there is no sin in it," she said, after a time. "You say it, but you do not think it. You are a man—you have honour to lose—you understand that, at least—"

"You are a woman, and you have humanity's right to be free. It is an honourable right. You gave it up when you took that veil, not knowing what it was that you gave up. You have done no wrong. You have done nothing that any loving maiden need be ashamed of. I kissed you, for you could not help yourself. That is the monstrous crime which you say is to be punished with eternal damnation. It is monstrous that you should think so. It is blasphemy to say that God made woman to lead a life of suffering and daily misery, chained to a cross which it is agony to look at, and shame to break from."

"Go—leave me. You are tempting me again." She spoke away from him, not changing her position.

"If truth is temptation, I am tempting you, for I am showing you the truth. The truth is this. When you were almost a child they began to bend you and break you in the way they meant you to grow. You bent, but you were not broken. Your nature is too strong. There is a life of your own in you. It was against your will, and when you were just grown up, they buried you, your beauty, your youth, your fresh young heart, your voice and your genius—for it is nothing less. It was all done with deliberate intention for the glory of your family, blasphemously asserted to be the glory of God. It was pressed upon you, before you knew what you were doing, and made pleasant to you before you knew what it all meant. Your cross was cushioned for you and your crown of thorns was gilded. They made the seat under the canopy seem a seat in heaven. They even made you believe that the management of two or three score suffering women was government and power. It seemed a great thing to be abbess, did it not?"

Maria Addolorata bent her veiled head slowly twice or three times, in a heavy-hearted way.

"They made you believe all that," continued Dalrymple, with cold earnestness, "and much more besides—a great deal of which I know little, I suppose—the life to come, and saintship, and the glories of heaven. You have found out what it is all worth. We have found it out together. And they frightened you with hell. Do you know what hell is? A life without love, when one knows what love can mean. I am not eloquent; I wish I were. But I am plain, and I can tell you the truth."

"It is not the truth," answered the nun, slowly. "You tell me it is, to tempt me. I cannot drive you away by force. Will you not go? I cannot cry out for help—it would ruin me and you. Will you not leave me? But for God's grace, I am at your mercy, and there is little grace for me, a sinner."

"No, I will not go away," said Dalrymple, and it seemed to Maria that his voice was the voice of her fate.

"Then God have mercy!" she cried, in a low tone, and as her head sank forward, it was her forehead that rested in her right hand, instead of her chin.

"Love is more merciful than God," he answered.

There was a sudden softness in his voice which she had never heard, not even yesterday. Rising, he stole near to her, and standing, bent down and leaned upon the table by her side and spoke close to her ear. But he did not touch her. She could feel his breath through her veil when he spoke again. It was vital and fierce, and softly hot, like the breathing of a powerful wild beast.

"You are my God," he said. "I worship you, and adore you. But I must have you for mine always. I would rather kill you, and have no God, than lose you alive. Come with me. You are free. You can get through the garden at night—with good horses we can reach the sea to-morrow. There is an English ship of war at anchor in Civita Vecchia. The officers are my friends. Before to-morrow night we can be safe—married—happy. No one will know—no one will follow us. Maria—come—come—come!"

His voice sank to a vibrating whisper as he repeated the word again and again, closer and closer to her ear. Her hands had dropped from her forehead and lay upon the table. With bent head she listened.

"Come, my darling," he continued, fast and low. "I have a beautiful home, my father's home, my mother's—your laws and vows are nothing to them. You shall be honoured, loved—ah, dear! adored, worshipped—you do not know what we will do for you, to fill your life with sweet things. All your life, Maria, from to-morrow. Instead of pain and penance and everlasting suffering and weariness, you shall have all that the world holds of love and peace and flowers. And you shall sing your whole heart out when you will, and have music to play with from year's beginning to year's end and year's end again. Sweet, let me tell you how I love you—how you are alive in every drop of my blood, beating through me like living fire, through heart and soul and head and hand—"

With a quick movement she pressed her palms against her veil upon her ears to shut out the sound of his words. She rocked herself a little, as though the pain were almost greater than she could bear. But his hands moved too, stealthily, strongly, as a tiger's velvet feet, with a vibration all through them, to the very ends of his fingers. For he was in earnest. And the arm went softly round her, and closed gently upon her as her figure swayed in her chair; and the other sought hers, and found it cold as ice and trembling, and not strong to stop her hearing. And again she listened.

Wild and incoherent words fell from his lips, hot and low, with no reason in them but the overwhelming reason of love itself. For he was not an eloquent man, and now he took no thought of what he said. He was far too natural to be eloquent, and far too deeply stirred to care for the shape his love took in speech. There was in his words the strong rush of out-bursting truth which even the worst passion has when it is real to the roots. Words terrible and gentle, blasphemous and devout, wove themselves into a new language such as Maria Addolorata had never heard, nor dared to think of hearing. But he dared everything, to tell her, to hold her, against God and devil, heaven and earth, and all mankind. And he promised all he had, and all that was not his to promise nor to give, rending her beliefs to shreds, trampling on the broken fragments of all she had worshipped, tearing her chains link from link and scattering them like straw down the storm of passionate contempt. And then, again, pouring out love, and more love, and love again, as a stream of liquid fire let loose to flood all it meets with dazzling destruction and hot death.

It is not every woman that knows what it is to be so loved and to listen to such words, so spoken. Those who have heard and felt can understand, but not the rest. Gradually as he spoke, her veiled face was drawn toward his; gradually her hand raised the thick veil and drew it back; and again a little, and the hand that had struggled long and silently against his, lay still at last, and the face that had appealed in vain to Heaven, hid itself against the heart of the strong man.

"The Lord have mercy upon my sinful soul!" she softly prayed.

"I love you!" whispered Dalrymple, folding her to him with both his arms, and pressing his lips to her head. "That is all the world holds. That is all the Heaven there is, and we have it for our own."

But presently she drew back from him, clinging to him with her hands as though to hold him, and yet separating from him and looking up into his face.

"And to-morrow?" she said, with a despairing question in her tone.

"We will go away to-night," he answered, "and to-morrow will be ours, too, and all the to-morrows after that."

But she shook her head, and her hands loosened their hold upon his arms, still lingering on his sleeves.

"And leave her to die?" she asked, with a quick glance at the abbess's door.

Then she looked at him, with something of sudden fear as she met his eyes again. And almost instantly she turned from him, and threw herself forward upon the table as she sat.

"The sin, the deadly sin!" she moaned. "Oh, the horror of it all—the sin, the shame, the disgrace! That is the worst to bear—the shame! The undying shame of it!"

Dalrymple's brows bent themselves in a heavy frown, for he was in no temper to be thwarted, desperate as the risk might be. For himself, he knew that he was setting his life on the chances, if she consented, and that life would not be worth having if she refused. He knew well enough that they must almost certainly be pursued, and that there would be little hesitation about shooting him or cutting his throat if they were caught and if he resisted, as he knew that he should. He had been in love with her for days. The last twenty-four hours had made him desperate. And a desperate man is not to be played with, more especially if he chance to have any Highland blood in his veins.

"What do you believe in most?" he asked suddenly and almost brutally.

She turned, startled, and looked him in the face.

"Because, if you believe in God, as I suppose you do, I take God to witness that I shall be a dead man this night, unless you promise to go with me."

She stared, and turned white to the lips, as he had never seen her turn pale before. She leaned forward, gazing into his eyes and breathing hard.

"You do not mean that," she said, as though trying hard to convince herself.

"I mean it," he answered slowly, pale himself, and knowing what he said.

She leaned nearer to him and took his arms with her hands, for she could not speak. The terrible question was in his eyes.

"You would kill yourself, if I refused—if I would not go with you?" Still she could not believe him.

"Yes," he answered.

Once more the room was very still, as the two looked into one another's eyes. But Maria Addolorata said nothing. The frown deepened on Dalrymple's face, and his strong mouth was drawn, as a man draws in his lips at the moment of meeting death.

"Good-bye," he said, gently loosening himself from her hold.

Her hands dropped and she turned half round, following him as he went towards the door. His hand was almost on the latch. He did not turn. But as he heard her swift feet behind him, he bent his head a little. Her arms went round his throat, reaching up to his great height.

"No! No!" she cried, drawing his head down to her.

But he took her by the wrists and held her away from him at his arms' length.

"Are you in earnest?" he asked fiercely. "If you play with me any more, you shall die, too."

"But not to-day!" she answered imploringly. "Not to-night! Give me time—a day—a little while—"

"To lose you? No. I have been near losing you. I know what it means. Make up your mind. Yes, or no."

"To-night? But how? There is not time—these clothes I wear—"

She turned her head distractedly to one side and the other as she spoke, while he held her wrists. Dalrymple saw that there was reason in the objections she made. So dangerous a flight could not be undertaken without some preparation. He loosed her hands and began to pace the room, concentrating his mind upon the details. She watched him in silence, leaning against the back of the easy-chair. Then he stopped just before her.

"My cloak would come down to your feet," he said, measuring her height with his eyes. "I have a plaid which would cover your head. Once on horseback, no one would notice anything. Can you ride?"

"No. I never learned."

"That is unlucky. But we can manage it. The main thing would be to get a long start if possible—that you should not be missed—to get away just at the beginning of the longest time during which the nuns would not expect to see you. Where is your own room? Is it near this?"

Maria Addolorata told him, and explained the position of the balcony with the steps leading down into the garden. He asked her who kept the key of the postern. It was in the possession of the gardener, who took it away with him at night, but the lock was on the inside, and uncovered, as old Italian locks are. By raising the curved spring one could push back the bolt. There was a handle on the latter, for that purpose. There would be no difficulty about getting out, nor about letting Dalrymple in, provided that the night were dark.

"The moon is almost full," said Dalrymple, thoughtfully, and he began to walk up and down again. "Never mind. It must be to-morrow night. In your dark dress, when the sisters are asleep, if you keep in the shadow along the wall, there is not the slightest risk. I will be waiting for you on the other side of the gate with my cloak and plaid. I will have the horses ready, a little higher up. There is a good mule path which goes down into the valley on that side. You have only to reach the gate and let yourself out. It is very easy. Tell me at what time to be waiting."

Maria leaned heavily upon the chair, with bent head.

"I cannot do it—oh, I cannot!" she said despairingly. "The shame of it! To be the talk of Rome—the scandal of the day—a disgrace to my father and mother!"

Dalrymple frowned, and biting his lip, he struck his clenched fist softly with the palm of his hand, making a few quick steps backward and forward. He stopped suddenly and looked at her with dangerous eyes.

"I have told you," he said. "I will not repeat it. You must choose."

"Oh, you cannot be in earnest—"

"You shall see. It is plain enough," he added, with an accent of scorn. "You are more afraid of a little talk and gossip in Rome, than of being told to-morrow morning that I died in the night. That is Italian courage, I suppose."

She hung her head for a moment. Then, as she heard his footsteps, she threw her veil back and saw that he was going towards the door without a word.

"You are cruel," she said, half catching her breath. "You know that you make me suffer—that I cannot live without you."

"I shall certainly not live without you," he answered. "I mean to have you at any price, or I will die in the attempt to get you."

The words have a melodramatic look on paper. But he spoke them not only with his lips, but with his whole self. They were not out of keeping with his nature. There is no more desperate blood in the world's veins than that of the Celt when he is driven to bay or exasperated by passion. In him the reckless fatalism of the Asiatic is blended with the cool daring of the northerner.

Maria Addolorata had little experience of the world or of men, but she had the hereditary instincts of her sex, and as she looked at Dalrymple she recognized in him the man who would do what he said, or forfeit his life in trying to do it. There is no mistaking the truth about such men, at such moments.

"I believe you would," she said, and she felt pride in saying it.

Her own life was in the balance. She bent her head again. Her temples were throbbing, and it was hard to think at all connectedly.

"I want your answer," he said, still standing near the door. "Yes or no—for to-morrow night?"

"I cannot live without you," she answered slowly, and still looking down. "I must go."

But she did not meet his eyes, for she knew that she was wavering still, and almost as uncertain as before. All at once Dalrymple's manner changed. He came quietly to her side and took one of her hands, which hung idly over the back of the chair, in both of his.

"You must be in earnest, as I am, my dear," he said, very calmly and gently. "You must not play with a man's life and heart, as though they were worth nothing but play. You called me cruel, dear, a moment ago. But you are more cruel than I, for I do not hesitate."

"I must go," she repeated, still avoiding his look. "Yes, I must go. I should die without you."

"But to-morrow when I come, you will hesitate again," he said, still speaking very quietly. "I must be sure. You must give me some promise, something more than you have given me yet."

She looked up with startled eyes.

"You do not believe me?" she asked. "What shall I do? I—I promise! You yourself have never said that you promised."

"Does it need that?" He pressed the hand he held, with softly increasing strength, between his palms.

"No," she answered, looking at him. "I can see it. You will do what you say. I have promised, too."

He gazed incredulously into her face.

"Do you doubt me?" she asked.

"Have I not reason to doubt? You change your mind easily. I do not blame you. But how am I to believe?"

She grew impatient of his unbelief. Yet as he pressed her hand, the power he had over her increased with every second.

"But I will, I will!" she cried, in a low voice. "And still you doubt—I see it in your eyes. Have I not promised? What more can I do?"

"I do not know," he answered. "But you must make me believe you." The strength of his eyes seemed to be forcing something from her.

"I say it—I promise it—I swear it! Do I not love you? Am I not giving my soul for you? Have I not given it already? What more can I do or say?"

"I do not know," he answered a second time, holding her with his eyes. "I must believe you before I go."

He spoke honestly and earnestly, not meaning to exasperate her, searching in her look for what was unmistakably in his own. His hands shook, not weakly, as they held hers. His piercing eyes seemed to see through and through her. She trembled all over, and the colour rose to her face, more in despair of convincing him than in a blush of shame.

"Believe me!" she said, imperiously, and her eyelids contracted with the effort of her will.

But he said nothing. She felt that he was immeasurably stronger than she. But just then, he was not more desperate. There was a short, intense silence. Her face grew pale and was set with the fatal look she sometimes had.

"I pledge you with my blood!" she said suddenly.

Her eyes did not waver from his, but she wrenched her right hand from him, and before he could take it again, her even teeth had met in the flesh. The bright scarlet drops rose high and broke, and trickled in vivid stripes across her hand as she held it before his face. Her own was very white, but without a trace of pain. Something in the fierce action appealed strongly to the fiery Celtic nature of the man. His features relaxed instantly.

"I believe you," he said, and she knew it as his arms went round her; and the pain of the wound made his kisses sweeter.

CHAPTER XI

When Dalrymple left Maria on that day, he returned as usual to Stefanone's house. Sora Nanna was alone, for Stefanone was still absent in Rome, and Annetta had gone on the previous day with a number of women to the fair at Civitella San Sisto, which took place on Sunday. She was expected to return on Monday afternoon. It is usual enough for a party of women, with two or three men, to go to the fairs in neighbouring towns and to spend the night with the friends of some one of the company. It was more common still, in those days.

Sora Nanna gave Dalrymple his dinner and kept him company for a while. But he was gloomy and preoccupied, and before long she retired to the regions of the laundry, which was installed in a long low building that ran out into the vegetable garden at the back of the house. Monday was generally the day for ironing the heavy linen of the convent, which was taken up on Tuesdays in the huge baskets carried by four women, slung to a pole which rested on their shoulders in the old primitive fashion, just as litters are still carried in many parts of Asia. It had occurred more than once to Dalrymple, during the last two days, that he could hide almost anything he chose in one of these baskets, which were always delivered directly to Maria Addolorata and which she was at liberty to unpack in the privacy of the linen room if she chose.

He thought of this again as he sat over his dinner, and heard the endless song of the women, far off, at their work. He knew the habits of the house thoroughly and all the customs regarding the carrying up of the baskets, and he remembered that several of them would surely be taken to the convent on the morrow. He thought that if he could procure some more suitable clothes for Maria to wear, this would be a safe means of conveying them to her. She could put them on in her cell, just before the hour at which she was to expect him, so that there would be no time lost and the danger of detection during their flight would be greatly diminished. But there were all sorts of difficulties in the way, and he realized them one by one, until he almost abandoned the scheme in favour of the cloak and plaid which he had first proposed.

He pushed back his chair and went upstairs to his own room. The impression made upon him by Maria Addolorata, when she had bitten her hand, had been a strong one, but the man's nature, though not exactly distrustful, was melancholic and pessimistic. Two hours and more had passed since they had been together, and things had a different look. He realized more clearly the strength of the ties which bound Maria to her convent life, and the effort it must be to her to break them. He remembered the arguments he had used, and he saw that they had been those of passion rather than of reason. Their effect could not be lasting, when he himself was not there to lend them his words and the persuasion of his strength. Maria would repent of her promise, and there was nothing to bind her to it. Hitherto there had been no risk, no common danger. By a chain of natural circumstances he had made his way into a most extraordinary position, but it was in her power, in a moment of repentance, to force him from it. While the abbess was ill, Maria was virtually mistress of the convent. At a word from her the doors might be shut in his face. She might promise again, and bite her hand again, but when it came to his waiting outside the garden gate, she might be seized by a fit of repentance, and he might wait till morning.

As he sat in his room he realized all this, and more, for he knew that on calm reflexion he meant to do what he had that morning threatened in his haste. He had never been attached to life for its own sake. Melancholic men often are not. He had many times thought over the subject of suicide with a sort of grim interest in it, which indicated the direction his temper would take if he were ever absolutely defeated in a matter which he had at heart.

Nothing he had ever felt in his life had taken hold of him as his love for Maria Addolorata, for he had never really been in love before and he had completely abandoned himself to it, as such a man was sure to do in such surroundings. She was beautiful, but that was not all. Since he had heard her sing, he knew that her voice and her rare talent together were genius and nothing less. But that was far from being all. She was of his own class, and he had been seeing her daily, when the peasant women amongst whom he lived were little more than good-natured animals; but even that was not all. He was at that time of life when a man's character is apt to take a violent and sudden turn in its ultimate direction, when the forces that have been growing show themselves all at once, when passion, having appealed as yet but to the man, has climbed and is within reach of his soul, to take hold of it and twist it, or to be finally conquered, perhaps, in a holy life. But Dalrymple was very far from being the kind of man who could have taken refuge against himself in higher things. At a time when materialism was beginning to seem a great thing, he was a strong materialist in scientific questions. He grasped what he could see and held it, but what he could not see had no existence for him. Nothing transcendental attracted him beyond the sphere of mathematics. Yet he had not the materialist's temperament, for the Highland blood in his veins brought strong fancies and sudden passions to his head and heart, such as his chemistry could not explain; and when the brain burned and the heart beat fast, it meant doing or dying with him, as with many a Scotchman before and since. Life had never seemed to be worth much in his eyes, compared with a thing he wanted.

He sat still and thought the matter over, and considered the question of death, for a few short minutes. There was not a trace of philosophical speculation in his reflexions, or they would have lasted longer. He merely desired to be sure, with that curious Scotch caution, of his own intentions, in order not to be obliged to think the matter over again at the last minute.

He had drunk a measure of strong wine with his dinner, as usual. To-day it increased the gloom of his temper, and the pessimistic view he took. In less than a quarter of an hour he had made up his mind that if Maria Addolorata repented at a late hour and refused to leave the convent, he would make an attempt to carry her away by force. If he failed, and found himself shut off from all possibility of intercourse with her, life would not be worth living, and he would throw it away. When strong men are in that frame of mind, they generally accomplish what they have in view. Moreover, it is a great mistake to think that the people who think and talk of suicide will not take their own lives. On the contrary, statistics show that it is more often those who speak of it the most frequently, who ultimately make away with themselves. The mere fact of contemplating and discussing death familiarizes man with it till he does not even attribute to it its true value, which is little enough, as most of us know. Dalrymple was in earnest, and he knew it.

He rose from his chair and unlocked his little laboratory. Among many other things upon the long table there was a plain English oak box, filled with small stoppered bottles, each having a label upon it with the name of the contents written in his own hand. Some were merely medicines, which he carried with him in case his services should ever be required, as had happened at the present time. Others were chemicals which he used in his experiments, such as he could not easily have procured in Italy, outside of the great cities. One even contained the common spirits of camphor, of which he had once given Annetta a teaspoonful when she had complained of a chill and sickness. One, however, was more than half full of a solution of hydrocyanide of potassium, a liquid little less suddenly and surely fatal than the prussic acid which enters into its composition.

He took out this bottle and held it up to the light. The liquid was clear and transparent as water. He watched it curiously as he made it run up to the neck and back again. It might have been taken for pure alcohol, being absolutely colourless.

"It would not take much of that," he said to himself, with a grim smile.

His meditations were interrupted by the voice of Sora Nanna, who had opened his bedroom door without ceremony and stood calling to him. He came forward hastily from the laboratory and went up to her.

"You do not know!" she cried, laughing and holding up a letter. "Stefanone has written to me from Rome! To me! Who the devil knows what he says? I do not understand anything of it. Who should teach me to read? He takes me for a priest, that I should know how to read!"

Dalrymple laughed a little as he took the letter. He picked up his hat from a chair, for he meant to go out and spend the afternoon alone upon the hillside.

"We will read it downstairs," he said. "I am going for a walk."

He read it to her in the common room on the ground floor. It was a letter dictated by Stefanone to a public scribe, instructing his wife to tell Gigetto that she must send another load of wine to Rome as soon as possible, as the price was good in the market. Stefanone would remain in the city till it came, and sell it before returning.

"These husbands!" exclaimed Sora Nanna, with a grin. "What they will not do! They go, riding, riding, and they come back when it seems good to them. Who tells me what he does in Rome? Rome is great."

Dalrymple laughed, put on his hat and went off, leaving Sora Nanna to find Gigetto and give the necessary directions.

CHAPTER XII

Gigetto had refused to accompany Annetta and her party to the fair at Civitella San Sisto. He had been to Rome several times, and was far too fine a young gentleman to divert himself in such a very primitive place. He preferred to spend his leisure hours, which were very many, in elegant idleness, according to his lights, between the tobacconist's, the chemist's shop, which was the resort of all the superior men of the place after four o'clock in the afternoon, and the abundant, though not very refined table which was spread twice daily in his father's house. Civitella wine, Civitella fireworks, and especially Civitella girls, were quite beneath his notice. As for Annetta, he looked upon her with something like contempt, though he had a high respect for the fortune which must one day be hers. She was to be a necessary encumbrance of his future life, and for the present he meant to see as little of her as was conveniently possible without relinquishing his claims to her hand. She had admired him, in a way, until the arrival of Dalrymple, and he felt a little irritation at the Scotchman's presence in the house, so that he occasionally frightened Sora Nanna by talking of waiting for him with a gun at the corner of the forest. It produced a good impression, he thought, to show from time to time that he was not without jealousy. But as for going with her on such an expedition as a visit to a country fair, it was not to be expected of him.

Nevertheless, Annetta had enjoyed herself thoroughly with her companions, and was very glad that Gigetto had not been at her elbow with his city notions of propriety, which he applied to her, but made as elastic as he pleased for himself. She had been to high mass in the village church, crowded to suffocation, she had walked up and down the main street half the afternoon, arm in arm with the other girls, giggling and showing off her handsome costume to the poorer natives of the little place, and smiling wickedly at the handsome youths who stood idly in groups at the corners of the streets. She had dined sumptuously, and had made her eyes sparkle like rather vulgar little stars by drinking a glass of strong old white wine to the health and speedy marriage of all the other girls. She had gone out with them at dusk, and had watched the pretty fireworks in the small piazza, and had wandered on with them afterwards in the moonlight to the ruin of the Cyclopean fortress which overlooks the two valleys. Then back to the house of her friends, who kept the principal inn, and more tough chicken and tender salad and red wine for supper. And on the next day they had all gone down to the meagre vineyards, half way to San Vito and just below the thick chestnut woods which belong to the Marchese and feudal lord of that ancient town. And there amongst the showers of reddening vine leaves, she had helped to gather the last grapes of the year, with song and jest and laughter. At noon they climbed the hill again in the October sun, and dined upon the remains of the previous day's feast; then, singing still, they had started on their homeward downward way, happy and not half tired yet when they reached Subiaco in the evening glow.

They came trooping through the town to the little piazza in which the doctor's house was situated. They separated here, some to go up to the higher part, while others were to go down in the same direction as Annetta. The girl looked up at the doctor's windows, and her small eyes flashed viciously. It would be a pleasant ending to the two days' holiday to have a look at her work. Now that he was getting well, as Dalrymple told her, she was glad that she had not killed him. It was an even greater satisfaction to have almost frightened the old coward to death. She had been uneasy about the question of confession.

"By Bacchus," she laughed, "I will go and see Sor Tommaso. They say he is better."

So she took leave of her companions and entered the narrow door, and climbed the short flight of dark steps and knocked. The doctor's sleeping-room opened directly upon the staircase. He used the room on the ground floor as an office and dining-room, his old peasant woman-servant slept in the attic, and the other two rooms were let by the year. It was a very small house.

The old woman, whose name was Serafina, opened the bedroom door and thrust out her head, covered with a dark and threadbare shawl. There was a sibylline gloom about her withered face, as though she had lived a lifetime in the face of a horror to come.

"What do you want?" she croaked roughly, and not opening the door any wider.

"Eh! What do I want? I am the Annetta of Stefanone, and I have come to pay a visit to this dear doctor, because they say that he is better, God bless him."

"Oh! I did not recognize you," said the old woman. "I will ask."

Still holding the door almost closed, she drew in her head and spoke with Sor Tommaso. Annetta could hear his answer.

"Of course!" he said, in a voice still weak, but singularly oily with the politeness of his intention. "Let her favour us!"

The door was opened, and Annetta went in. Sor Tommaso was sitting up near the window, in a deep easy-chair covered with ragged green damask. The girl was surprised by his pallor, as compared with his formerly rubicund complexion. Peasant-like, she glanced about the room to judge of its contents before she spoke.

"How are you, dear Sor Tommaso?" she asked after the short pause. "Eh, what we have suffered for you, all of us! Who was this barbarian who wished to send you to Paradise?"

"Who knows?" returned Sor Tommaso, with amazing blandness. "I trust that he may be forgiven as I forgive him."

"What it is to be a wise man!" exclaimed Annetta, with affected admiration. "To have such sentiments! It is a beautiful thing. And how do you feel now, dear Sor Tommaso? Are you getting your strength again? They took your blood, those cowardly murderers! You must make it again."

Their eyes met, and each knew that the other knew and understood. Sor Tommaso smiled gently. The savage girl's mouth twitched as though she should have liked to laugh.

"Little by little; who goes slowly goes safely," answered the doctor. "I am an old man, you must know."

"Old!" Annetta was glad of the opportunity to laugh at last. "Old? Eh, on Sunday, when you have on those new black trousers of yours that are tight, tight—you seem to me a boy as young as Gigetto. For my part, I should prefer you. You are more serious. Gigetto! What must I say? He is handsome, he may be good, but he has not a head. There is nothing in that pumpkin."

"Blood of youth," answered Sor Tommaso. "It must boil. It must fling its chains about. Afterwards it begins to know the chains. Little by little it accustoms itself to them. Then it is quiet, quiet, as we old ones are. Sit down, my daughter. Serafina! A chair—the one that is not lame. These chairs remember the blessed soul of mamma," added Sor Tommaso, in explanation of their weakness.

"Requiesca'!" exclaimed Annetta, sitting down.

"Amen," responded Sor Tommaso. "You are so beautiful to-day," he continued, looking at her flowered bodice and new apron; "where have you been?"

"Where should I go? To Civitella. There was the fair. We ate certain chickens—tough! But the air of the mountain consumes. There were also fireworks."

"What? Have you walked?" asked Sor Tommaso.

"Even with two legs one can walk," laughed the girl. "But of course a beast is better with four. The beasts had all gone to Tivoli with wine for Rome. They had not come back yesterday morning. Therefore with these two feet I walked. I and many others, girls like me. It is true that I am half dead."

"You are fresher than lettuce," observed Sor Tommaso. "And then you have climbed up my stairs. This is a true Christian act. God return it to you. I am alone all day."

"But the Englishman comes to see you," said Annetta, indifferently.

"The Englishman, yes. He comes. More or less, he has almost cured me. But then, for his conversation, I say nothing!"

"Meanwhile he is also curing the abbess. He has a fortunate hand. There death, here death—he makes them all alive. Where is death, now? Here, perhaps? Hidden in some corner, or under the bed? He has certain medicines, that Englishman! Medicines that you do not even dream of. Strong! It is I that tell you. Sometimes, the whole house smells of them. Death could not resist them a moment. They drive even the flies out of the windows. The Englishman gave me some once. I had been in the sun and had drunk a gallon of cold water, foolish as I was. I was thirsty, as I am now. Well, he gave me a spoonful of something like water, mixed in water. I do not tell you anything. At first it burned me. Arch-priest, it burned! Then, not even a minute, and I had Paradise in my body. And so it passed."

"Who knows? A cordial, perhaps," observed Sor Tommaso, thoughtfully. "I have such cordials, too."

"I do not doubt it," answered the girl, suspiciously. "But I would rather not taste them. I feel quite well."

It crossed her mind that in return for three knife-thrusts, Sor Tommaso would probably not miss so good a chance of paying her with a glass of poison. She would certainly have done as much herself, had she been in his place.

"Who thought of offering you cordials!" replied the doctor, with a polite laugh. "I said it to say it. But if you are thirsty, command me. There is water and good wine. They are the best cordials."

"Eh, a little water. I do not refuse. As for the wine, no. I thank you the same. I am fasting and have walked. After supper, at home, I will drink."

"Serafina!" cried Sor Tommaso, and the old sibyl immediately appeared from the stairs, whither she had discreetly retired to wait during Annetta's visit. "Bring water, and that bottle of my wine from downstairs. You know, the bottle of old wine of Stefanone's that was opened."

"No, no. I want no wine," said Annetta, quickly.

"Bring it all the same. Perhaps she will do us the honour to drink it."

Serafina nodded, and her bare feet were heard on the stone steps as she descended.

"It is bad to drink pure water when one is very thirsty," said Sor Tommaso. "It cramps the stomach. A little wine gives the stomach strength. But it is best to eat. If you will eat, there are fresh jumbles. I also eat them."

"I thank you the same," answered Annetta. "I wish only water. It is a long way from Civitella, and there is no good spring. There is the brook that runs out of the pond at the foot of the last hill. But it is heavy water, full of stuff."

Serafina came back, bringing two heavy tumblers of pressed glass on a little black japanned tray, with a decanter of cold water. In her other hand she carried two bottles, one half full of wine, the other containing the white and sugary syrup of peach kernels of which Italians are so fond.

"I brought this also," she said, holding up the bottle as she set down the tray. "Perhaps it is better."

"Yes," said Sor Tommaso, nodding in approbation. "It is better."

"You will drink a little orgeat?" asked the old woman, in a tone of persuasion, and mixing it in the glass.

"Water, simply water," said Annetta, who was still suspicious. "Give me water in the other glass."

"But I have mixed already in both," answered Serafina. "Eh, you will drink it. You will not make an old woman like me go all the way down the stairs again. But then, it is good. It is I that tell you. I made it myself, yesterday morning, for the doctor, to refresh his blood a little."

Annetta had risen to her feet and was watching the glasses, as the old woman stirred the white syrup in the water with an old-fashioned, long-handled spoon. She did not wish to seem absurdly suspicious, and yet she distrusted her enemy. She took one of the glasses, went to his side, and held it to his lips as one gives an invalid drink.

"After you," he said, with a polite smile, but raising his hand to take the glass.

"Sick people first, well people afterwards," answered Annetta, smiling too, but watching him intently

He had satisfied himself that she really suspected foul play, for he knew the peasants well, and was only a degree removed from them himself. He at once dismissed her suspicions by drinking half the tumbler at a draught. She immediately took the other and emptied it eagerly, as she was really very thirsty.

"A little more?" suggested Serafina, in her croaking voice.

"No," interposed Sor Tommaso. "It might hurt her—so much at once."

But Annetta filled the tumbler with pure water, and emptied it again.

"At last!" she exclaimed with a sigh of satisfaction. "What thirst! I seemed to have eaten ashes! And now I thank you, Sor Tommaso, and I am going home; for it is Ave Maria, and I do not wish to make a bad meeting in the dark as happened to you. Ugly assassins! I will never forgive them, never! What am I to say at home? That you will come to supper one of these days?"

"Eh, if God wills," answered the doctor. "I will be accompanied by Serafina."

"I!" exclaimed the old woman. "I am afraid even of a cat! What could I do for you?"

"Company is always company," said Sor Tommaso, wisely. "Where one would not go, two go bravely. Good evening, my beautiful daughter," he added, looking up at Annetta. "The Madonna go with you."

"Thank you, and good evening," answered the girl, dropping half a courtsey, with a vicious twinkle in her little eyes.

She turned, and was out of the room in a moment. On the way home through the narrow streets in the evening glow, she sang snatches of song to herself, and thought of all she had said to Sor Tommaso, and of all he had said to her, and of how much afraid he was of her father's knife. For otherwise, as she knew, he would have had her arrested.

Suddenly, at the last turning she stopped and turned very pale, clasping both hands upon her bodice.

"Assassin!" she groaned, grinding her short white teeth. "He has poisoned me, after all! An evil death to him and all his house! Assassin!"

She forgot that she had experienced precisely the same sensations once before, when she had been overheated and had swallowed too much cold water.

CHAPTER XIII

With slow steps, and pressing her clasped hands to her bodice, the girl reached the door of her father's house at dusk. She knew that he was away, and that as she had not come home earlier her mother would be in the lower regions preparing Dalrymple's supper for him. The door which gave access to the staircase from the street was still open, and she was almost sure of being able to reach her own room unobserved, unless she chanced to come upon Dalrymple himself on the stairs. Just then she would rather have met him than her mother. She was in great pain, and it would have been hard to explain to Sora Nanna that she believed herself to have been deliberately poisoned.

She crept noiselessly up the stairs, which were almost dark, and she came to Dalrymple's door which faced the first landing. She paused and hesitated, leaning against the wall. He was a wise man in her opinion, and would of course understand her symptoms at once. But then, as she was poisoned, he could do nothing for her. If that were true, her next thought told her that Sor Tommaso must have poisoned himself. He would not do that. She had never heard of antidotes; for though poisoning was traditionally familiar to her and the people of her class, it was very uncommon. Yet her sharpened wit told her that if Sor Tommaso had swallowed the stuff, as he had done, with a smile, he had means at his disposal for counteracting it—some medicine which he had doubtless taken as soon as she had left him. But if he had medicine to save from poison, Dalrymple, who was a far wiser man, must have such medicines, too, and even better ones. This reflexion decided her. She was close to his door. It was probable that he would be in his room at that hour. She was in fear of her life, and she knocked.

But Dalrymple had not come back. He had gone for a long walk alone in the hills, had climbed higher as the sun sank lower, and was belated in steep paths along which even his mountain-trained feet trod with some caution. He was too familiar with the country to lose his way, but he by no means found the shortest way there was, nor was he especially anxious to do so. The hours would pass sooner in walking than in sitting over his books under the flaring little flames of the three brass beaks.

Annetta saw that there was no light in the room, for the hole through which the latch-string hung was worn wide with use. She felt dizzy, too, and the knife-like pain ran through her so that she bent herself. She knew that Dalrymple kept his medicines locked up in the laboratory, and that she could not get at them, though she would have had little hesitation in swallowing anything she found, in the simple certainty that all his medicines must be good in themselves, and therefore life-saving and good for her. But he was out, and she was sure that there could be nothing in the bedroom. She had herself too often looked into every corner when she watered and swept the brick floor each morning, and put things in order according to her primitive ideas.

She then and there lost her hold upon life. She was poisoned, and must die. She was as sure of it as the Chinaman who has seen an eagle, and who, recognizing that his hour is come, calmly lies down and breathes his last by the mere suspension of volition. In old countries the lower orders, as a rule, have but a low vitality. It may be truer to say that the vital volition is weak. Let the learned settle the definition. The fact is easily accounted for. During generations upon generations the majority of European agricultural populations live upon vegetable food, like the majority of Eastern Asiatics, and with the same result. Hard labour produces hard muscles, but vegetable food yields a low vital tension, so to say. Soldiers know it well enough. The pale-faced city clerk who eats meat twice a day will out-fight and out-last and out-starve the burly labourer whose big thews and sinews are mostly compounded of potatoes, corn, and water.

The girl crept up the stairs stealthily to her lonely little room, and lay down to die upon her bed, as though that were the only thing to be done under the circumstances. It never occurred to her to go to her mother and tell her what had happened and what she suspected, any more than it had suggested itself to Sor Tommaso to lay information against her for having stabbed him. If her father had been at home, she might perhaps have gone to him and told him with her dying breath that the doctor had killed her, and that Stefanone must avenge her. But he was away. She was stronger than her mother and had always dominated her. She knew also that if she complained, Sora Nanna would raise such a scream as would bring half Subiaco running to the house. The girl's animal instinct was to die alone, and quietly. So she made no sound, and lay upon her bed writhing in pain and holding her sides with all her might, but with close-set teeth and silent lips.

Looked at from the point of view of fact, it was all ridiculous enough. The girl had been all day in the hot autumn sun, had eaten a quantity of over-ripe figs and grapes, which might have upset the digestion of an ostrich, had tired even her strong limbs with the final walk home, and had then, at Sor Tommaso's house, swallowed nearly a quart of ice-cold water. It was not surprising that she should be very ill. It was not even strange that the theory of poison should suggest itself. To her it was tragedy, and meant nothing less than death, when she lay down upon her bed.

Between the spasms all sorts of things passed through her mind, when her head lay still upon the pillow. Chiefly and particularly her thoughts were filled with hatred of Sor Tommaso, and a sort of doglike longing to see Dalrymple's face before she died. She was still fascinated by the vision of his red hair and bright blue eyes which came back to her vividly, with the careless smile his hard face had for her half-childish, half-malicious sayings. And with the thought of him came also jealousy of Maria Addolorata, and another hatred which was deeper and stronger and more vengeful than any she owed Sor Tommaso. She felt, rather than understood, that Dalrymple loved the nun with all his heart. She had spoken of her to him and had watched his face, and had seen the quick, savage glare of his eyes, though his voice had only expressed his annoyance. As the vision of him rose before her, she saw him as he had been when the angry blush had overspread his face to the roots of his hair.

The image fixed itself. In the dim shadow behind it, she saw the face of Maria Addolorata like a death-mask, and those strange, deep eyes of the nun's looking scornfully at her over the man's shoulder, though she forgot him in the woman's deadly fascination. She stared, unable to close her lids, as it seemed to her, though she longed to shut out the sight. Then a dull noise seemed to be in her ears, a noise that was not a sound, but the stunning effect on her brain of a sound not heard but imagined. There were great circles of light around the nun's head, which cut through Dalrymple's face and then hid it. They were like glories, like the halos about the heads of saints. Annetta was angry with them, for she was sure that Maria Addolorata was bad, and sinned in her throat.

"An evil death on you and all your house!" cried the angry peasant girl, in a low voice.

"Death!" She could not tell whence the echo came back to her, in a tone strange to her ears—for it was her own, perhaps.

She was startled. The vision vanished, and she sat up on her bed with a quick movement, suddenly wide awake. The pain must have passed. No—it came again, but with far less keenness. She felt her face with her hands, and laughed softly, for she knew that she was alive. It was night, and she must have lain some time there all alone, for there was a silvery, misty something through the darkness, the white dawn of moonrise, which is not like the dawn of day, nor like the departing twilight. As she sat up she saw the outline of the hills, jagged against the crosses of the lead-joined panes in the window. There was the moon-dawn sending up its soft radiance to the sky. A little longer she watched, and a single bright point sent one level ray straight into her face. A moment more and the room was flooded with light so that she could see the smallest objects distinctly.

"But I am alive!" she exclaimed in a soft, glad tone. "The brigand only did me a spite. He was afraid to kill me."

The pain seized her again, less sharp than before, but keen enough to stir her anger. She still sat up, but bent forward, clasping her bodice. In the moonlight she could see her heavy shoes on her feet sticking up before her. Realizing that it was a disgraceful thing to lie down with them on, she sprang off the bed, and began to dust the coverlet with her hand. The pain passed.

After all, she reflected, she had swallowed a quantity of cold water at Sor Tommaso's, whether the first glass had contained any poison or not. She had not forgotten, either, that the same thing had once happened to her before, and that Dalrymple had made it pass with a spoonful of something that had stung her mouth and throat, but which had afterwards warmed her and cured her. She felt chilly now, and she wished that she had some of that same stinging, warming stuff.

Something moved, somewhere in the house. The girl listened intently for a moment. Probably Dalrymple had come back and was moving about in his room, washing his hands, as he always did before supper, and taking off his heavy boots. His room was immediately under hers, facing in the same direction. She went towards the door, intending to go down at once and ask him for some of his medicine. By this time she was persuaded that she was not in any danger, and her common-sense told her that she had merely made herself momentarily ill with too many grapes, too much cold water, and too long exposure to the sun. She did not care to let her mother know anything about it, for Sora Nanna would scold her. It would be a simple matter to catch the Scotchman at his door, to get what she wanted from him with an easily given promise of secrecy, and then to come downstairs as though nothing had happened.

Annetta only hesitated a moment, and then went out into the dark staircase, and crept down, as she had crept up, feeling her way at the turnings, by the wall. She reached the door, and was surprised to see that there was no light within—none of that yellow light which a lamp makes, but only the grey glimmer of the moonlight through the shadow, creeping out by the hole of the latch-string. Her ears had deceived her, and Dalrymple was not there. Nevertheless she believed that he was. The moonlight would be in his room as it was in hers, just overhead, and he might not have taken the trouble to light his lamp. It was very probable. She tapped softly, but there was no answer. She was afraid that her mother might come up the stairs and hear her speaking through the door, as though by stealth. She put her lips close to the hole of the latch and whistled softly. Her whistle was broken by her own smile as she fancied that Dalrymple might start at the unexpected sound.

But there was no response. Growing bolder, she called him gently.

"Signor! Are you there?"

There was no answer. Just then, as she stooped, the pain ran through her once more. She was so sure that she had heard him that she was convinced he must be within, very probably in his little laboratory beyond the bedroom. The pain hurt her, and he had the medicine. Very naturally she pulled the string and pushed the door open.

He was not there. The moonlight flooded everything, and the whitewashed walls reflected it, so that the place was as bright as day. The first object that met her eyes was a small bottle standing near the edge of the table in the middle of the room, where Dalrymple had carelessly set it down in the afternoon when Sora Nanna had called him to read her letter. It was directly in the line of the moon's rays, and the stopper gleamed like a little star.

Annetta started with joy as she saw it. It was the very bottle from which he had given her the camphor, less than a month ago—the same in size, in its transparent contents, in its label. It might have deceived a keener eye than hers.

The door of the laboratory stood open, as he had left it, being at the time preoccupied and careless. She only stopped a moment to assure herself that the bottle was the right one, reflecting that he had perhaps felt ill and had taken some of it himself. She went on and looked into the little room.

"Signore!" she called softly. But there was no answer.

It was clear that Dalrymple was either still out, or was downstairs at his supper, with her mother. He might be out, however. It was quite possible, on such a fine evening, for he was irregular in his hours. He would not like it if he came in suddenly and found her meddling with his belongings. She crossed the room again and softly shut the door. At least, if he came, she would not be found with the bottle in her hand. She could give an excuse.

It was all so natural. It was the same bottle. She knew the right quantity, for she had the peasant's memory for such detail. There was a glass and a decanter of water on a white plate on the table. She had no spoon, but that did not matter. She took out the stopper with her strong fingers, though it stuck a little. The pain ran through her again as she poured some of the contents into the tumbler, and it made her hand shake so that she poured out a little more than necessary. But it did not matter. She filled it up with water, held the glass up to the moonlight, and drank it at a draught, and set the empty tumbler upon the table again.

Instantly her features changed. She felt as though she were struck through head and heart and body with red-hot steel. Maria Addolorata's death-mask rose before her in the moonlight.

"An evil death on you and all your house!" she tried to say.

But the words were not out of her mouth before she shivered, caught herself by the table, sank down, and lay stone dead upon the brick floor.

There was no noise. Dying, she thought she screamed, but only the faintest moan had passed her lips.

The door was shut, and the quiet moonlight floated in and silvered her dark, dead face.

CHAPTER XIV

At moonrise on that evening, Maria Addolorata was standing at the open door of her cell, watching the dark clouds in the west, as they caught the light one by one, edge by edge. The black shadow of the convent covered all the garden still, and one passing could hardly have seen her as she stood there. Her veil was raised, and the cold mountain breeze chilled her cheeks. But she did not feel it, for she had been long by the abbess's bedside, and then long, again, in the close choir of the church, and her head was hot and aching.

To her, as she looked towards the western mountains and watched the piling clouds, and felt the cool, damp wind, it seemed as though there were something strangely tragic in the air that night. The wind whistled now and then through the cracks of the convent windows and over the crenellations of the old walls, as Death's scythe might whistle if he were mowing down men with a right good will, heaps upon heaps of slain. The old bell struck the hour, sullenly, with a dead thud in the air after each stroke, as a bell tolls for a burial. The very clouds were black and silver in the sky, like a funeral pall.

Maria Addolorata leaned against the door-post and looked out, her hand white in the shadow against the dark wood, her face whiter still. But on her hand there were two marks, visible even in the dimness. They would have been red in the day, and the place hurt her from time to time, for she had bitten it savagely. It was her pledge, and the pain of it reminded her of what she had promised to do.

She needed the reminder; for now that he was not near her, the enormous crime stood out, black and lofty as death itself. It was different when Dalrymple was at her side. His violent vitality dragged hers into action, dragged, drove it, and goaded it, as unwilling soldiers have been driven into battle in barbarous armies. Then the fatality seemed irresistible, then the dangers seemed small, and the burning red shame was pale and weak. Those bony young hands of his had strength in them for two, his gleaming eyes burnt out the resistance in hers, and lighted them with their own glow. The hearty recklessness of his unbelief drove through and through her composite faith, and riddled it with loopholes for her soul's escape. Then the reality of her passion made her nobler love mad to be free, and to break through the solid walls in which it had been born and had grown too strong. When his love was there, hers matched itself with his, to smite fortune in the face, to dare and out-dare heaven and hell for love's sake, with him, the bursting blood made iron of her hand, tingling to buffet coward fate's pale mouth. Then she was strong above women; then she was brave as brave men; then, having promised, to keep was but the natural hold of will, to die was but to dare one little adversary more.

But she was alone now, and thinking, as she looked out into the tragic night, and watched the blackness of the monumental clouds. She did not return to her former self, as some women do when the goad leaves the heart in peace for a moment. She did not say to herself that she would order the convent gate to be shut on Angus Dalrymple forever, and herself go back to the close choir, to sit in her seat amongst the rest, and sing holy songs with the others, restfully unhappy as many of them were. She knew far too well how strongly her heart could beat, and how icy cold her hands could grow when love was near her. Yet she shuddered with horror at what she had promised to do. She would struggle to the last, but she must yield when she heard his voice, and felt his hand, at the very last moment, when they should be at the garden gate, he drawing her on, she looking back.

It was perjury and sacrilege, and earthly shame, and eternal damnation. Nothing less. And the words had full and deadly meaning for her. It mattered little that he should think differently, being of another faith, or rather, of no faith at all. It was all true to her. It was not risk; it was certainty. What forgiveness had earth or heaven for a faithless nun? He talked of marriage, and he would marry her according to a rite that had a meaning in his eyes. Heaven would not divorce the sworn and plighted spouse of Christ to be the earthly wife of Angus Dalrymple.

Visions of eternal torment rose in her mind, a tangible searing hell alive with flame and devils, a sea of liquid fire, an ocean of boiling pitch, Satan commanding in the midst, and a myriad of fiends working his tormenting will.

Her pale lips curled scornfully in the dark. Those were not the terrors that frightened her, nor the horrors from which she shrank. There was a question which was not to be answered by her own soul in damnation or salvation, but by the lips of men hereafter—the question of the honour of her name. The traditions of the good old barons were not dead in that day, nor are they all dead yet. Many a Braccio had done evil deeds in his or her day, and one, at least, had evil deeds to do after Maria Addolorata had been laid in her grave. But sin was one thing, and dishonour was quite another, even in the eyes of the nun of Subiaco. For her sins she could and must answer with the weal or woe of her own soul. But her dishonour would be upon her father and her mother and upon all her race. Nor was there any dishonour deeper, more deadly, or more lasting than that brought upon a stainless name by a faithless nun. Maria Braccio hesitated at disgrace, while Maria Addolorata smiled at perdition. It was not the first time that honour had taken God's part against the devil in the history of her family.

That was the great obstacle of all, and she knew it now. She was able to face all consequences but that, terrible as they might be. The barrier was there, the traditional old belief in honour as first, and above every consideration. They had played upon that very belief, when, at the last, she had hesitated to take the veil. She had gone so far, they had told her, that it would be cowardly and dishonourable to turn back at the last minute. The same argument existed now. Then, she would at least have had human right and ecclesiastical law on her side, if she had refused to become a nun. Now, all was against her. Then, she would have had to face but the condemning opinion of a few who spoke of implied obligation. Now, she must stand up and be ashamed before the whole world. There would be a horrible publicity about it. She was too high born not to feel that all the world in which she should ever move was as one great family. Dalrymple might promise her honour and respect, and the affection of his own father and mother for the love of her parents, a home, respected wifehood, and all the rest. With his strength, he might impose her upon his family, and they might treat her as he should dictate, for he was a strong and dominant man. But in their hearts, Protestants, English people, foreigners as they were to her race, even they could not tell themselves honestly that it was not a shameful thing to break such vows as hers, shameful and nothing less. And if, for a moment, he were not there to hold them in his check, she should see it in their faces, and she must hang her head, for she could have nothing to answer. For him, she must not only sacrifice her soul, wrench out her faith, break her promise to God, and her vows to the Church. She must give herself to public, earthly shame, for his sake.

It was too much. She could bear anything but that. Rather than endure that, it was better to die.

The black clouds rose higher in the west, and the gloomy air blew upon her face. Her head was no longer hot, for a chilly horror had come upon her, like the shadow of something unspeakably awful, close at hand. Suddenly, she was afraid to be alone. A bat, lured by the second twilight of the moon's rising, whirled down from above, with softly flapping wings, and almost brushed her face. She drew back quickly into the doorway. It was a very tragic night, she thought. She shut the door, and groped her way out beyond her cell to the corridor, dimly illuminated by a single light hanging from the vault by a running cord. She entered the abbess's apartment. One of the sisters had taken her place, but Maria Addolorata sent her away by a gesture, and sat down by the bedside.

The old lady was either asleep, or did not notice her niece's coming. Her face was grey as ashes, and upturned in the shadow. Upon the stone floor stood the primitive Italian night-light, a wick supported in a triangular bit of tin by three little corks in oil floating on water in a tumbler. The light was very clear and steady, though there was little of it, and to Maria, who had been long in comparative darkness, the room seemed bright enough. There was little furniture besides the plain bed, a little table, a couple of chairs, and a tall, dark wardrobe. A grim crucifix hung above the abbess's head, on the white wall, the work of an age in which horror was familiar to the eye, and needed exaggeration to teach hardened humanity.

Maria was too much occupied with her own thoughts to notice the sick woman's condition at once. Besides, during the last two days there had been no return of the syncope, and the abbess had seemed to be improving steadily. She breathed rather heavily and seemed to be asleep.

Gradually, however, as the nun sat motionless beside her and as the storm of thought subsided, she became aware that all was not right. Her aunt's face was unnaturally grey, the breathing was unusually slow and heavy. When the breath was drawn in, the thin nostrils flattened themselves strangely on each side, and the features had a peaked look. Maria rose and felt the pulse. It was fluttering, and not always perceptible.

At first Maria's attention to these facts was only mechanical. Then, with a sudden sinking at her own heart, she realized what they might mean—another crisis like the one in which the abbess had so narrowly escaped death. It was true that on that occasion she had called for help more than once, showing that she had felt herself to be sinking. At present she seemed to be unconscious, which, if anything, was a worse feature.

Maria drew a long breath and held it, biting her lips, as people do in moments of suspense, doubt, and anxiety. It was as though fate had thrust the great decision onward at the last moment. The life that hung in the balance before her eyes meant the possibility of waiting, with the feeble consolation of being yet undecided.

She stood as still as a statue, her face like a mask, her hand on the unconscious woman's wrist. The stimulant which Dalrymple had shown her how to use was at hand—the glass with which to administer it. It would prolong life. It might save it.

Should she give it? The seconds ran to minutes, and the dreadful question was unanswered. If the abbess died, as die she almost certainly must within half an hour, if the medicine were not given to her—if she died, Maria would call the sisters, the portress would be instructed, and when Dalrymple came on the morrow, he would be told that all was over, and that he was no longer needed. Nothing could be more sure. He might do his utmost. He could not enter the convent again.

In a quick vision, as she stood stone-still, Maria saw herself alone in the chapel by night, prostrate, repentant, washing the altar steps with tears, forgiven of God, since God could still forgive her, honoured on earth as before, since none but the silent confessor could ever know what she had done, still less what she had meant to do. Her sorrow would be real, overwhelming, able to move Heaven to mercy, her penance true-hearted and severe as she deserved. Her name would be unspotted and unblemished.

It would be so easy, if she had not to see him again. How could she resist him, if he could so much as touch her hand? But if she were defended from him, she could bury his love and pray for him in the memory of the thing dead. All that, if she but let that heavy breathing go on a little longer, if she did not raise her hand and set a glass to those grey, parted lips.

They were parted now. The laboured breath was drawn through the teeth. The eyelids were a little raised, and showed but the white of the upturned eyes.

Maria stared fixedly into the pinched face, and a new horror came upon her.

It was murder she was doing. Nothing less. The power to save was there, and she would not use it. No—it could not be murder—it was not possible that she could do murder.

Still with wide eyes she stared. Surely the heavy breath had come more quickly a moment ago. It seemed an age between each rise and fall of the coverlet. There was a ghastly whistling sound of it between the teeth.

It was slower still. The eyelids were gradually opening—the blind white was horrible to see. Each breath was a convulsion that shook the frail body.

It was murder. Her hand shot out like lightning and seized the small bottle. Let anything come,—love, shame, heaven, damnation; it should not be murder.

She forced the unstoppered bottle into the dying woman's mouth with a desperate hand. The next breath was drawn with a choking effort. The whole body stirred. The thin hand appeared, grasped the coverlet with distorting energy, and then lay almost still, twitching convulsively second by second. Still Maria tried wildly to pour more of the stimulant between the set teeth. When they parted, no breath came, and the fingers only moved once more, for the very last time.

It was not murder, but it was death. The wasted old woman had outlived by two or three hours the strong, young peasant girl, and fate had laid her hand heavily upon the life of Maria Addolorata.

CHAPTER XV

When Dalrymple came home that evening, he found his supper already on the table and half cold. Sora Nanna was busier than her daughter, and less patient of the Scotchman's irregularities. If he could not come home at a reasonable hour, he must not expect her to keep everything waiting for him.

He sat down to the table without even going upstairs as usual to wash his hands, simply because the cooked meat would be cold and greasy if he let it stand five minutes longer. Being once seated in his place, he did not move for a long time. Sora Nanna came in more than once. She was very much preoccupied about the load of wine which her husband had ordered to be sent, and which, if possible, she meant to send off before morning, for she did not wish him to be absent in Rome with money in his pocket a day longer than necessary.

Gloomy and preoccupied, without even a book before him, Dalrymple sat with his back to the wall, drinking his wine in silence, and staring at the lamp. Sora Nanna asked him whether he had seen

Annetta. He shook his head without speaking. The woman observed that the girls were quite capable of spending a second night at Civitella to prolong the festivities. Dalrymple nodded, not caring at all.

Annetta being absent, Gigetto had not thought it necessary to put in an appearance. But Sora Nanna wished to see him again about the wine. With a grin, she asked Dalrymple whether he would keep house if she went out for half an hour. Again he nodded in silence. He heard her lock from the inside the door which opened from the staircase upon the street, for it was already late. Then she came through the common room again, with her overskirt over her head, went out, and left the door ajar. Dalrymple was alone in the house, unaware that Annetta was lying dead on the floor of his room upstairs.

Sora Nanna had not been gone a quarter of an hour when a boy came in from the street. Dalrymple knew him, for he was the son of the convent gardener.

The lad said that Dalrymple was wanted immediately, as the abbess was very ill. That was all he knew. He was rather a dull boy, and he repeated mechanically what he had been told. The Scotchman started and was about to speak, when he checked himself. He asked the boy two or three questions, in the hope of getting more accurate information, but could only elicit a repetition of the message. He was wanted immediately, as the abbess was very ill.

He covered his eyes with his hand for a few seconds. In a flash he saw that if he were ever to carry off Maria Addolorata, it must be to-night. The chances were a hundred to one that if there were another crisis, the abbess would be dead before he could reach the convent. Once dead, there was no knowing what might happen in the confusion that would ensue, and during the elaborate funeral ceremonies. The man had that daring temper that rises at obstacles as an eagle at a crag, without the slightest hesitation. When he dropped his hand upon the table he had made up his mind.

It was generally easy to get a good mule at any hour of the night in Subiaco. The mules were in their stables then. In the daytime it would have been very doubtful, when most of them were away in the vineyards, or carrying loads to the neighbouring towns. The convent gardener, who was well-to-do in the world, had a very good mule, as Dalrymple knew, and its stable was half-way up the ascent. The boy could saddle it with the pack-saddle without any difficulty, and meet him anywhere he chose. Dalrymple's reputation was excellent as a liberal foreigner who paid well, and the gardener would not blame the boy for saddling the mule without leave.

In a few words Dalrymple explained what he wanted, and to help the lad's understanding he gave him some coppers which filled the little fellow with energy and delight. The boy was to be at the top of the mule path leading down from above the convent to the valley in half an hour. Dalrymple told him that he wished to go to Tivoli, and that the boy could come with him if he chose, after the visit to the abbess was over. The boy ran away to saddle the mule.

Dalrymple rose quickly, and shut the street door in order to take the lamp with him to his room, and not to leave the house open with no light in it. The case was urgent. He went upstairs, carrying the lamp, and opened the door of his quarters. Instantly he recognized the faint, sickly odour of hydrocyanide of potassium, and remembered that he had left the bottle with the solution on his table that afternoon in his hurry. Then he looked down and saw a white face upon the floor, and the flowered bodice and smart skirt of the peasant girl.

He had solid nerves, and possessed that perfect indifference to death as a phenomenon which most medical men acquire in the dissecting-room. But he was shocked when, bending down, and setting the lamp upon the floor, he saw in a few seconds that Annetta had been dead some time. He even shook his head a little, very slowly, which meant a great deal for his hard nature. Glancing at the unstoppered bottle and at the empty glass, side by side on the table, he understood at once that the girl, intentionally or by mistake, had swallowed enough of the poison to kill half-a-dozen strong men. He remembered instantly how he had once given her spirits of camphor when she had felt ill, and he understood all the circumstances in a moment, almost as though he had seen them.

Scarcely thinking of what he was doing, though with an effort which any one who has attempted to lift a dead body from the ground will understand, he took up the lifeless girl, stiff and stark as she was, and laid her upon his own bed. It was a mere instinct of humanity. Then he went back and took the lamp and held it near her face, and shook his head again, thoughtfully. A word of pity escaped his lips, spoken very low.

He set the lamp down on the floor by the bedside, for there was no small table near. There never is, in peasants' houses. He began to walk up and down the room, thinking over the situation, which was grave enough.

Suddenly he smelt the acrid odour of burning cotton. He turned quickly, and saw that he had placed the three-beaked lamp so near to the bed that the overhanging coverlet was directly above one of the flames, and was already smouldering. He smothered it with the stuff itself between his hands, brought the lamp into the laboratory, and set it upon the table.

Then, realizing that his own case was urgent, he began to make his preparations. He took a clean bottle and poured thirty-five drops of laudanum into it, put in the stopper, and thrust it into his pocket. Unlocking another box, he took out some papers and a canvas bag of gold, such as bankers used to give travellers in those times when it was necessary to take a large supply of cash for a journey. He threw on his cloak, took his plaid over one arm and went back into his bedroom, carrying the lamp in the other hand. Then he hesitated, sniffing the air and the smell of the burnt cotton. Suddenly an idea seemed to cross his mind, for he put down the lamp and dropped his plaid upon a chair. He stood still a moment longer, looking at the dead girl as she lay on the bed, biting his lip thoughtfully, and nodding his head once or twice. He made a step towards the bed, then hesitated once more, and then made up his mind.

He went back to the bedside, and stooping a little lifted the body on his arms as though judging of its weight and of his power to carry it. His first instinct had been to lock the door of the room behind him, and to go up to the convent, leaving the dead girl where she was, whether he were destined to come back that night, or never. A moment's reflection had told him that if he did so he must certainly be accused of having poisoned her. He meant, if it were possible, to take Maria Addolorata on board of the English man-of-war at Civita Vecchia within twenty-four hours. So far as the carrying off of a nun was concerned, he would be safe on the ship; but if he were accused of murder, no matter how falsely, the captain would have a right to refuse his protection, even though he was Dalrymple's friend. A little chain of circumstances had led him to form a plan, in a flash, which, if successfully carried out, would account both for the disappearance of Annetta herself, and of Maria Addolorata as well.

His eyelids contracted slightly, and his great jaw set itself with the determination to overcome all obstacles. In a few seconds he had divested the dead girl of her heavy bodice and skirt and carpet apron and heavy shoes. He rolled the things into a bundle, tossed them into the laboratory, locked the door of the latter, and stuck the key into his pocket. He carefully stopped the bottle containing the remainder of the prussiate of potassium, and took that also. Then he rolled the body up carefully in his great plaid, mummy-like, and tied the ends of the shawl with shoe-laces which he had among his things. He drew his soft hat firmly down upon his forehead, and threw his cloak over his left shoulder. He lifted the body off the bed. It was so stark that it stood upright beside him. With his right arm round its waist, he raised it so high that he could walk freely, and he drew his wide cloak over it as well as he could, and freed his left hand. He grasped the lamp as he passed the table, listened at the door, though he knew that the house was locked below, and he cautiously and with difficulty descended the stairs.

Just inside the street door of the staircase there was a niche, as there is in almost all old Italian houses. He set the body in it, and went into the common room with the lamp. Taking the bottle with the laudanum in it from his pocket, he filled it more than half full of aniseed cordial, of which a decanter stood with other liquors upon a sideboard, as usual in such places. He returned it to his pocket, and listened again. Then he assured himself that he had all he needed—the bottle, money, his cloak, and a short, broad knife which he always took with him on his walks, more for the sake of cutting a loaf of bread if he stopped for refreshment than for any other purpose. His passport he had taken with his few other valuable papers from the box.

He left the lamp on the table, and unlocked the street door, though he did not pull it open. Brave as he was, his heart beat fast, for it was the first decisive moment. If Sora Nanna should come home within the next sixty seconds, there would be trouble. But there was no sound.

In the dark he went back to the door of the staircase, unlocked it, and opened it wide, looking out. The heavy clouds had so darkened the moonlight that he could hardly see. But the street was quiet, for it was late, and there were no watchmen in Subiaco at that time. A moment later, the door was closed behind him, and he was disappearing round the dark corner with Annetta's body in his arms, all wrapped with himself in his great cloak.

It was a long and terrible climb. A weaker man would have fainted or given it up long before Dalrymple set his foot firmly upon the narrow beaten path which ran along between the garden wall at the back of the convent, and the precipitous descent on his left. The sweat ran down over his hard, pale face in the dark, as he shook off his cloak and laid down his ghastly burden under the deep shadow of the low postern. He shook his big shoulders and wiped his brow, and stretched out his long arms, doubling them and stretching them again, for they were benumbed and asleep with the protracted effort. But so far it was done, and no one had met him. There had been little chance of that, but he was glad, all the same. And if, down at the house, any one went to his room, nothing would be found. He had the key of the little laboratory in his pocket. It would be long before they broke down the door and found Annetta's skirt and bodice and shoes wrapped together in a corner.

He went on up the ascent five minutes further, walking as though on air now that he carried no weight in his arms. At the top of the mule path the lad was already waiting for him with the mule. He told the little fellow that he might have to wait half an hour longer, as he must go into the convent to see the abbess before starting for Tivoli. He bid him tie the mule by the halter to the low branch of an overhanging fig-tree, and sit down to wait.

"It is a cool night," said Dalrymple, though he was hot enough himself. "Drink this, my boy."

He gave him the little bottle of aniseed, opening it as he did so. The boy smelt it and knew that it was good, for it is a common drink in the mountains. He drank half of it, pouring it into his mouth with a gurgling sound.

"Drink it all," said Dalrymple. "I brought it for you."

The boy did not hesitate, but drained it to the last drop, and handed the bottle back without a word. Dalrymple made him sit down near the mule's head, well aside from the path, in case any one should pass. He knew that between the unaccustomed dose of spirits and the thirty-five drops of opium, the lad would be sound asleep before long. For the rest, there was nothing to be done but to trust to luck. He had done the impossible already, so far as physical effort was concerned, but Fortune must not thwart him at the end. If she did, he had in his other pocket enough left of what had killed Annetta to settle his own affairs forever, and he might need it. At that moment he was absolutely desperate. It would be ill for any one who crossed his path that night.

CHAPTER XVI

Dalrymple wrapped his cloak about him once more, as he turned away, and retraced his steps by the garden wall. He glanced at the long dark thing that lay in the shadow of the postern, as he went by. It was not probable that it would be noticed, even if any one should pass that way, which was unlikely, between ten o'clock at night and three in the morning. He went on without stopping, and in three or four minutes he had gone round the convent to the main entrance, next to the church. He rang the bell. The portress was expecting him, and he was admitted without a word.

He found Maria Addolorata in the antechamber of the abbess's apartment, veiled, and standing with folded hands in the middle of the little hall. She must have heard the distant clang of the bell, for she was evidently waiting for him.

"Am I in time?" he asked in a tone of anxiety.

She shook her head slowly.

"Is she dead?"

"She was dead before I sent for you," answered Maria Addolorata, in a low and almost solemn tone. "No one knows it yet."

"I feared so," said Dalrymple.

He made a step towards the door of the parlour, naturally expecting that Maria would speak with him there, as usual. But she stepped back and placed herself in his way.

"No," she said briefly.

"Why not?" he asked in quick surprise.

She raised her finger to her veiled lips, and then pointed to the other door, to warn him that the portress was there and was almost within hearing. With quick suspicion he understood that she was keeping him in the antechamber to defend herself, that she had not been able to resist the desire to see him once more, and that she intended this to be their last meeting.

"Maria," he began, but he only pronounced her name, and stopped short, for a great fear took him by the throat.

"Yes," she answered, in her calm, low voice. "I have made up my mind. I will not go. God will perhaps forgive me what I have done. I will pray for forgiveness. But I will not do more evil. I will not bring shame upon my father's house, even for love of you."

Her voice trembled a little at the last words. Even veiled as she was, the vital magnetism of the man was creeping upon her already. She had resolved that she would see him once more, that she would tell him the plain truth that was right, that she would bid him farewell, and promise to pray for him, as she must pray for herself. But she had sworn to herself that she would not speak of love. Yet with the first words she spoke, the word and the vibration of love had come too. Her hands disappeared in her sleeves, and her nails pressed the flesh in the determination to be strong. She little guessed the tremendous argument he had in store.

"It is hard to speak here," he said. "Let us go into the parlour."

She shook her head, and again moved backwards a step, so that her shoulders were almost against the door.

"You must say what you have to say here," she answered after a moment's pause, and she felt strong again. "For my part, I have spoken. May God forget me in my utmost need if I go with you."

Dalrymple seemed little moved by the solemn invocation. It meant little enough to him.

"I must tell you a short story," he replied quietly. "Unless I tell you, you cannot understand. I have set my life upon your love, and I have gone so far that I cannot save my life except by you—my life and my honour. Will you listen to me?"

She nodded, and he heard her draw a quick breath. Then he began his story, putting it together clearly, from the facts he knew, in very few words. He told her how Annetta must have mistaken the bottle on his table for camphor, and how he had found her dead. Nothing would save him from the accusation of having murdered the girl but the absolute disappearance of her body. Maria shuddered and turned her head quickly when he told her that the body was lying under the postern arch behind the garden wall. He told her, too, that the boy was by this time asleep beside the mule on the path beyond. Then he told her of his plan, which was short, desperate, and masterly.

"You must tell no one that the abbess is dead," he said. "Go out through your cell into the garden, as soon as I am gone, and when I tap at the postern open the door. Leave a lamp in your cell. I will do the rest."

"What will you do?" asked Maria, in a low and wondering tone.

"You must lock the door of your cell on the inside and leave the lamp there," said Dalrymple. "You will wait for me in the garden by the gate. I will carry the poor girl's body in and lay it in your bed. Then I will set fire to the bed itself. Of course there is an under-mattress of maize leaves—there always is. I will leave the lamp standing on the floor by the bedside. I will shut the door and come out to you, and I can manage to slip the bolt of the garden gate from the outside by propping up the spring from within. You shall see."

"It is horrible!" gasped Maria. "And I do not see—"

"It is simple, and nothing else can save my life. Your cell is of course a mere stone vault, and the fire cannot spread. The sisters are asleep, except the portress, who will be far away. Long before they break down your door, the body will be charred by the fire beyond all recognition. They will see the lamp standing close by, and will suppose that you lay down to rest, leaving the lamp close to you—too close; that the abbess died while you were asleep, and that you had caught fire before you waked; that you were burned to death, in fact. The body will be buried as yours, and you will be legally dead. Consequently there will not be the slightest suspicion upon your good name. As for me, it will be supposed that I have procured other clothes for Annetta, thrown hers into the laboratory and carried her off. In due time I will send her father a large sum of money without comment. If you refuse, I must either be arrested, convicted, and sentenced to death for the murder of a girl who killed herself without my knowledge, or, as is probable, I shall go out now, sit down in a quiet place, and be found dead in the morning. It is certain death to me in either case. It would be absolutely impossible for me to get rid of the dead body without arousing suspicion. If it is wrong to save oneself by burning a dead body, it is not a great wrong, and I take it upon myself. It is the only wrong in the matter, unless it is wrong to love you and to be willing to die for you. Do you understand me?"

Leaning back against the door of the parlour, Maria Addolorata had almost unconsciously lifted her veil and was gazing into his eyes. The plan was horrible, but she could not help admiring the man's strength and daring. In his voice, even when he told her that he loved her, there was that quiet courage which imposes itself upon men and women alike. The whole situation was as clear as day to her in a moment, for all his calculations were absolutely correct,—the fire-proof vault of the cell, the certainty that the body would be taken for hers, above all, the assurance of her own supposed death, with the utter freedom from suspicion which it would mean for her ever afterwards. Was she not to be buried with Christian burial, mourned as dead, and freed in one hour from all the consequences of her life? It was masterly, though there was a horror in it.

She loved him more than her own soul. It was the fear of bringing shame upon her father and mother that had held her, far more than any spiritual dread. It was not strange that she should waver again when he had unfolded his scheme.

She turned, opened the door, and led him into the parlour, where the silver lamp was burning brightly.

"You must tell it all again," she said, still standing. "I must be quite sure that I understand."

He knew well enough that she had finally yielded, since she went so far. In his mind he quickly ran over the details of the plan once more, and mentally settled what still remained to be decided. But since she wished it, he went over all he had said already. Being able to speak in his natural voice without fear of being overheard by the portress, and feeling sure of the result, he spoke far more easily and more eloquently. Before he had finished he was holding her hand in his, and she was gazing intently into his eyes.

"It is life or death for me," he said, when he had told her everything. "Which shall it be?"

She was silent for a moment. Then her strong mouth smiled strangely.

"It shall be life for you, if I lose my soul for it," she said.

She felt the quick thrill and pressure of his hand, and all the man's tremendous energy was alive again.

"Then let us do it quickly," he answered. "I will go out with the portress. Go to your cell before we reach the end of the corridor, and shut the door with some noise. She will remember it afterwards. Wait at the garden gate till I tap softly, and leave the rest to me. There is no danger. Do not be afraid."

"Afraid!" she exclaimed proudly. "How little you know me! It never was fear that held me. Besides—with you!"

The two last words told him more than all she had ever said before, and for the first time he wholly trusted her. Besides, it was to be only for a few minutes, while he went out by the front gate and walked round to the back of the convent. The plan was so well conceived that it could not fail when put into execution.

They shook hands, as two people who have agreed to do a desperate deed, each for the other's sake. Then as their grasp loosened, Dalrymple turned towards the door, but turned again almost instantly and took her in his arms, and kissed her as men kiss women they love when their lives are in the balance. Then he went out, passed through the antechamber, and found the portress waiting for him as usual. She took up her little lamp and led the way in silence. A moment later he heard Maria come out and enter her cell, closing the door loudly behind her.

"Her most reverend excellency is in no danger now," he said to the portress, with Scotch veracity.

"Sister Maria Addolorata may then rest a little," answered the lay sister, who rarely spoke.

"Precisely so," said Dalrymple, drily.

Five minutes later he was at the garden gate, tapping softly. Immediately the door yielded to his gentle pressure, for Maria had already unfastened the lock within.

"Stand aside a little," said Dalrymple, in a whisper. "You need not see—it is not a pretty sight. Keep the door shut till I come back. Where is your cell?"

She pointed to a door that was open above the level of the garden. A little light came out. With womanly caution she had set the lamp in the corner behind the door when she had opened it, so as to show as little as possible from without.

She turned her head away as he passed her with his heavy burden, treading softly upon the hard, dry ground. But he was not half across the garden before she looked after him. She could not help it. The dark thing he carried in his arms attracted her, and a shudder ran through her. She closed the gate, and stood with her hand on the lock.

It seemed to her that he was gone an interminable time. Though the moon was now high, the clouds were so black that the garden was almost quite dark. Suddenly she heard his step, and he was nearer than she thought.

"It is burning well," he said with grim brevity.

He stooped and looked closely in the dimness at the old-fashioned lock. It was made as he supposed and could be easily slipped from without. He found a pebble under his foot, raised the spring, and placed the small stone under it, after examining the position of the cracks in the wood, which were many.

"There is plenty of time, now," he said, and he gently pushed her out upon the narrow walk, drawing the door after him.

With his big knife, working through the widest crack he teazed the bolt into the socket. Then with his shoulder he softly shook the whole door. He heard the spring fall into its place, as the pebble dropped upon the dry ground.

"No human being can suspect that the door has been opened," he said.

He wrapped her in his long cloak, standing beside her under the wall. Very gently he pushed the veil and bands away from her golden hair. She helped him, and he kissed the soft locks. Then about her head he laid his plaid in folds and drew it forward over her shoulders. She let him do it, not realizing what service the shawl had but lately done.

They walked forward. The boy was fast asleep and did not move. The mule stamped a little as they came up. Dalrymple lifted Maria upon the pack-saddle, sideways, and stretched the packing-cords behind her back.

"Hold on," he said. "I will lead the mule."

So it was all over, and the deed was done, for good or evil. But it was for evil, for it was a bad deed.

To the last, fortune favoured Dalrymple and Maria, and everything took place after their flight just as the strong man had anticipated. Not a trace of the truth was left behind. Early in the morning the abbess was found dead, and in the little cell near by, upon the still smouldering remains of the mattress, lay the charred and burned form of a woman. In Stefanone's house, the little bundle of clothes in the locked laboratory was all that was left of Annetta. All Subiaco said that the Englishman had carried off the peasant girl to his own country.

Up at the convent the nuns buried the abbess in great state, with catafalque and canopy, with hundreds of wax candles and endless funeral singing. They buried also another body with less magnificence, but with more pomp than would have been bestowed upon any of the other sisters, and not long afterwards a marble tablet in the wall of the church set forth in short good Latin sentences, how the Sister Maria Addolorata, of many virtues, had been burned to death in her bed on the eve of the feast of Saint Luke the Evangelist, and all good Christians were enjoined to pray for her soul—which indeed was in need of their prayers.

Stefanone returned from Rome, but it was a sad home-coming when he found that his daughter was gone, and unconsciously he repeated the very words she had last spoken when she was dying in Dalrymple's room all alone.

"An evil death on you and all your house!" he said, shaking his fist at the door of the room.

And Stefanone swore within himself solemnly that the Englishman should pay the price. And he and his paid it in full, and more also, after years had passed, even to generations then unborn.

This is the first act, as it were, of all the story, and between this one and the beginning of the next a few years must pass quickly, if not altogether in silence.

PART II

GLORIA DALRYMPLE

CHAPTER XVII

In the year 1861 Donna Francesca Campodonico was already a widow. Her husband, Don Girolamo Campodonico, had died within two years of their marriage, which had been one of interest and convenience so far as he had been concerned, for Donna Francesca was rich, whereas he had been but a younger son and poor. His elder brother was the Duca di Norba, the father of another Girolamo, who succeeded him many years later, of Gianforte Campodonico, and of the beautiful Bianca, in whose short, sad life Pietro Ghisleri afterwards held so large a part. But of these latter persons, some were then not yet born, and others were in their infancy, so that they play no part in this portion of the present history.

Donna Francesca was of the great Braccio family, the last of a collateral branch. She had inherited a very considerable estate, which, if she had no descendants, was to revert to the Princes of Gerano. She had married Don Girolamo in obedience to her guardians' advice, but not at all against her will, and she had become deeply attached to him during the short two years of their married life. He had never been strong, since his childhood, his constitution having been permanently injured by a violent attack of malarious fever when he had been a mere boy. A second fever, even more severe than the first, caught on a shooting expedition near Fiumicino, had killed him, and Donna Francesca was left a childless widow, in full possession of her own fortune and of a little more in the shape of a small jointure. It was thought that she would marry again before very long, but it was too soon to expect this as yet.

Among her possessions as the last of her branch of the Braccio family, of which the main line, however, was sufficiently well represented, was the small but beautiful palace in which she now lived alone. It was situated between the Capitoline Hill and the Tiber, surrounded on three sides by dark and narrow streets, but facing a small square in which there was an ancient church. When it is said that the palace was a small one, its dimensions are compared with the great Roman palaces, more than one of which could easily lodge a thousand persons. It was built on the same general plan as most of them, with a ground floor having heavily barred windows; a state apartment in the first story, with three stone balconies on the front; a very low second story above that, but not coextensive with it, because two of the great state rooms were higher than the rest and had clere-story windows; and last of all, a third story consisting of much higher rooms than the second, and having a spacious attic under the sloping roof, which was, of course, covered with red tiles in the old fashion. The palace, at that time known as the Palazzo, or 'Palazzetto,' Borgia, was externally a very good specimen of Renascence architecture of the period when the florid, 'barocco' style had not yet got the upper hand in Rome. The great arched entrance for carriages was well proportioned, the stone carvings were severe rather than graceful, the cornices had great nobility both of proportion and design. The lower story was built of rough-faced blocks of travertine stone, above which the masonry was smooth. The whole palace was of that warm, time-toned colour, which travertine takes with age, and which is, therefore, peculiar to old Roman buildings.

Within, though it could not be said that any part had exactly fallen to decay, there were many rooms which had been long disused, in which the old frescoes and architectural designs in grey and white, and bits of bold perspective painted in the vaults and embrasures, were almost obliterated by time, and in which such furniture as there was could not survive much longer. About one-half of the state apartment, comprising, perhaps, fifteen or twenty rooms, large and small, had been occupied by Donna Francesca and her husband, and she now lived in them alone. In that part of the palace there was a sort of quiet and stately luxury, the result of her own taste, which was strongly opposed to the gaudy fashions then introduced from Paris at the height of the Second Empire's importance. Girolamo Campodonico had been aware that his young wife's judgment was far better than his own in artistic matters, and had left all such questions entirely to her.

She had taken much pleasure in unearthing from attics and disused rooms all such objects as possessed any intrinsic artistic value, such as old carved furniture, tapestries, and the like. Whatever she found worth keeping she had caused to be restored just so far as to be useful, and she had known how to supply the deficiencies with modern material in such a way as not to destroy the harmony of the whole.

It should be sufficiently clear from these facts that Donna Francesca Campodonico was a woman of taste and culture, in the modern sense. Indeed, the satisfaction of her tastes occupied a much more important place in her existence than her social obligations, and had a far greater influence upon her subsequent life. Her favourite scheme was to make her palace at all points as complete within as its architect had made it outside, and she had it in her power to succeed in doing so. She was not, as some might think, a great exception in those days. Within the narrow limits of a certain class, in which the hereditary possession of masterpieces has established artistic intelligence as a stamp of caste, no people, until recently, have had a better taste than the Italians; as no people, beyond these limits, have ever had a worse. There was nothing very unusual in Donna Francesca's views, except her constant and industrious energy in carrying them out. Even this might be attributed to the fact that she had inherited a beautiful but dilapidated palace, which she was desirous of improving until, on a small scale, it should be like the houses of the great old families, such as the Saracinesca, the Savelli, the Frangipani, and her own near relatives, the Princes of Gerano.

She had an invaluable ally in her artistic enterprises in the person of an artist, who, in a sort of way, was considered as belonging to Casa Braccio, though his extraordinary talent had raised him far above the position of a dependent of the family, in which he had been born as the son of the steward of the ancient castle and estate of Gerano. As constantly happened in those days, the clever boy had been noticed by the Prince,—or, perhaps, thrust into notice by his father, who was reasonably proud of him. The lad had been taken out of his surroundings and thoroughly educated for the priesthood in Rome, but by the time he had attained to the age necessary for ordination, his artistic gifts had developed to such an extent that in spite of his father's disappointment, even the old Prince—the brother of Sister Maria Addolorata—advised Angelo Reanda to give up the Church, and to devote himself altogether to painting.

Young Reanda had been glad enough of the change in his prospects. Many eminent Italians have begun life in a similar way. Cardinal Antonelli was not the only one, for there have been Italian prime ministers as well as dignitaries of the Church, whose origin was as humble and who owed their subsequent distinction to the kindly interest bestowed on them by nobles on whose estates their parents were mere peasants, very far inferior in station to Angelo Reanda's father, a man of a certain education, occupying a position of trust and importance.

Nor was Reanda's priestly education anything but an advantage to him, so far as his career was concerned, however much it had raised him above the class in which he had been born. So far as latinity and rhetoric were to be counted he was better educated than his father's master; for with the same advantages he had greater talents, greater originality, and greater industry. As an artist, his mental culture made him the intellectual superior of most of his contemporaries. As a man, ten years of close association with the sons of gentlemen had easily enough made a gentleman of one whose instincts were naturally as refined as his character was sensitive and upright.

Donna Francesca, as the last of her branch of the family and an orphan at an early age, had of course been brought up in the house of her relatives of Gerano, and from her childhood had known Reanda's father, and Angelo himself, who was fully ten years older than she. Some of his first paintings had been done in the great Braccio palace, and many a time, as a mere girl, she had watched him at his work, perched upon a scaffolding, as he decorated the vault of the main hall. She could not remember the time when she had not heard him spoken of as a young genius, and she could distinctly recall the discussion which had taken place when his fate had been decided for him, and when he had been at last told that he might become an artist if he chose. At that time she had looked upon him with a sort of wondering admiration in which there was much real friendly feeling, and as she grew up and saw what he could do, and learned to appreciate it, she silently determined that he should one day help her to restore the dilapidated Palazzetto Borgia, where her father and mother had died in her infancy, and which she loved with that sort of tender attachment which children brought up by distant relations often feel for whatever has belonged to their own dimly remembered parents.

There was a natural intimacy between the young girl and the artist. Long ago she had played at ball with him in the great courtyard of the Gerano castle, when he had been at home for his holidays, wearing a black cassock and a three-cornered hat, like a young priest. Then, all at once, instead of a priest he had been a painter, dressed like other men and working in the house in which she lived. She had played with his colours, had scrawled with his charcoals upon the white plastered walls, had asked him questions, and had talked with him about the famous pictures in the Braccio gallery. And all this had happened not once, but many times in the course of years. Then she had unfolded to him her schemes about her own little palace, and he had promised to help her, by and bye, half jesting, half in earnest. She would give him rooms in the upper story to live in, she said, disposing of everything beforehand. He should be close to his work, and have it under his hand always until it was finished. And when there was no more to do, he might still live there and have his studio at the top of the old house, with an entrance of his own, leading by a narrow staircase to one of the dark streets at the back. She had noticed all sorts of peculiarities of the building in her occasional visits to it with the governess,—as, for instance, that there was a convenient interior staircase leading from the great hall to the upper story, by a door once painted like the wall, and hard to find, but now hanging on its hinges and hideously apparent. The great hall must all be painted again, and Angelo could live overhead and come down to his work by those steps. With childish pleasure she praised her own ingenuity in so arranging matters beforehand. Angelo was to help her in all she did, until the Palazzetto Borgia should be as beautiful as the Palazzo Braccio itself, though of course it was much smaller. Then she scrawled on the walls again, trying to explain to him, in childishly futile sketches, her ideas of decoration, and he would come down from his scaffold and do his best with a few broad lines to show her what she had really imagined, till she clapped her small, dusty hands with delight and was ultimately carried off by her governess to be made presentable for her daily drive in the Villa Borghese with the Princess of Gerano.

As a girl Francesca had the rare gift of seeing clearly in her mind what she wanted, and at last she had found herself possessed of the power to carry out her intentions. As a matter of course she had taken Reanda into her confidence as her chief helper, and the intimacy which dated from her childhood had continued on very much the same footing. His talent had grown and been consolidated by ten years of good work, and she, as a young married woman, had understood what she had meant when she had been a child. Reanda was now admittedly, in his department, the first painter in Rome, and that was fame in those days. His high education and general knowledge of all artistic matters made him an interesting companion in such work as Francesca had undertaken, and he had, moreover, a personal charm of manner and voice which had always attracted her.

No one, perhaps, would have called him a handsome man, and at this time he was no longer in his first youth. He was tall, thin, and very dark, though his black beard had touches of a deep gold-brown colour in it, which contrasted a little with his dusky complexion. He had a sad face, with deep, lustreless, thoughtful eyes, which seemed to peer inward rather than outward. In the olive skin there were heavy brown shadows, and the bony prominence of the brow left hollows at the temples, from which the fine black hair grew with a backward turn which gave something unusual to his expression. The aquiline nose which characterizes so many Roman faces, was thin and delicate, with sensitive nostrils that often moved when he was speaking. The eyebrows were irregular and thick, extending in a dark down beyond the lower angles of the forehead, and almost meeting between the eyes; but the somewhat gloomy expression which this gave him was modified by a certain sensitive grace of the mouth, little hidden by the thin black moustache or by the beard, which did not grow up to the lower lip, though it was thick and silky from the chin downwards.

It was a thoughtful face, but there was creative power in the high forehead, as there was direct energy in the long arms and lean, nervous hands. Donna Francesca liked to watch him at his work, as she had watched him when she was a little girl. Now and then, but very rarely, the lustreless eyes lighted up, just before he put in some steady, determining stroke which brought out the meaning of the design. There was a quick fire in them then, at the instant when the main idea was outwardly expressed, and if she spoke to him inadvertently at such a moment, he never answered her at once, and sometimes forgot to answer her at all. For his art was always first with him. She knew it, and she liked him the better for it.

The intimacy between the great lady and the artist was, indeed, founded upon this devotion of his to his painting, but it was sustained by a sort of community of interests extending far back into darker ages, when his forefathers had been bondsmen to her ancestors in the days of serfdom. He had grown up with the clearly defined sensation of belonging with, if not to, the house of Braccio. His father had been a trusty and trusted dependent of the family, and he had imbibed as a mere child its hereditary likes and dislikes, its traditions wise and foolish, together with an indomitable pride in its high fortunes and position in the world. And Francesca herself was a true Braccio, though she was descended from a collateral branch, and, next to the Prince of Gerano, had been to Reanda by far the most important person bearing the name. She had admired him when she had been a child, had encouraged him as she grew up, and now she provided his genius with employment, and gave him her friendship as a solace and delight both in work and idleness. It is said that only Italians can be admitted to such a position with the certainty that they will not under any circumstances presume upon it. To Angelo Reanda it meant much more than to most men who could have been placed as he was. His genius raised him far above the class in which he had been born, and his education, with his natural and acquired refinement, placed him on a higher level than the majority of other Roman artists, who, in the Rome of that day, inhabited a Bohemia of their own which has completely disappeared. Their ideas and conversation, when they were serious, interested him, but their manners were not his, and their gaiety was frankly distasteful to him. He associated with them as an artist, but not as a companion, and he particularly disliked their wives and daughters, who, in their turn, found him too 'serious' for their society, to use the time-honoured Italian expression. Nevertheless, his natural gentleness of disposition made him treat them all alike with quiet courtesy, and when, as often happened, he was obliged to be in their company, he honestly endeavoured to be one of them as far as he could.

On the other hand, he had no footing in the society to which Francesca belonged, but for which she cared so little. There were, indeed, one or two houses where he was received, as he was at Casa Braccio, in a manner which, for the very reason that it was familiar, proved his social inferiority—where he addressed the head of the house as 'Excellency' and was called 'Reanda' by everybody, elders and juniors alike, where he was appreciated as an artist, respected as a man, and welcomed occasionally as a guest when no other outsider was present, but where he was not looked upon as a personage to be invited even with the great throng on state occasions. He was as far from receiving such cold acknowledgments of social existence as those who received them and nothing else were distantly removed from intimacy on an equal footing.

He did not complain of such treatment, nor even inwardly resent it. The friendliness shown him was as real as the kindness he had received throughout his early youth from the Prince of Gerano, and he was not the man to undervalue it because he had not a drop of gentle blood in his veins. But his refined nature craved refined intercourse, and preferred solitude to what he could get in any lower sphere. The desire for the atmosphere of the uppermost class, rather than the mere wish to appear as one of its members, often belongs to the artistic temperament, and many artists are unjustly disliked by their fellows and pointed at as snobs because they prefer, as an atmosphere, inane elegance to inelegant intellectuality. It is often forgotten by those who calumniate them that hereditary elegance, no matter how empty-headed, is the result of an hereditary cultivation of what is thought beautiful, and that the vainest, silliest woman who dresses well by instinct is an artist in her way.

In Francesca Campodonico there was much more than such superficial taste, and in her Reanda found the only true companion he had ever known. He might have been for twenty years the intimate friend of all Roman society without meeting such another, and he knew it, and appreciated his good fortune. For he was not naturally a dissatisfied man, nor at all given to complain of his lot. Few men are, who have active, creative genius, and whose profession gives them all the scope they need. Of late years, too, Francesca had treated him with a sort of deference which he got from no one else in the world. He realized that she did, without attempting to account for the fact, which, indeed, depended on something past his comprehension.

He felt for her something like veneration. The word does not express exactly the attitude of his mind towards her, but no other defines his position so well. He was not in love with her in the Italian sense of the expression, for he did not conceive it possible that she should ever love him, whereas he told himself that he might possibly marry, if he found a wife to his taste, and be in love with his wife without in the least infringing upon his devotion to Donna Francesca.

That she was young and lovely, if not beautiful, he saw and knew. He even admitted unconsciously that if she had been an old woman he could not have 'venerated' her as he did, though veneration, as such, is the due of the old rather than of the young. Her spiritual eyes and virginal face were often before him in his dreams and waking thoughts. There was a maidenlike modesty, as it were, even about her graceful bodily self, which belonged, in his imagination, to a saint upon an altar, rather than to a statue upon a pedestal. There was something in the sweep of her soft dark brown hair which suggested that it would be sacrilege and violence for a man's hand to touch it. There was a dewy delicacy on her young lips, as though they could kiss nothing more earthly than a newly opened flower, already above the earth, but not yet touched by the sun. There was a thoughtful turn of modelling in the smooth, white forehead, which it was utterly beyond Reanda's art to reproduce, often as he had tried. He thought a great sculptor might succeed, and it was the one thing which made him sometimes wish that he had taken the chisel for his tool, instead of the brush.

She was never considered one of the great beauties of Rome. She had not the magnificent presence and colouring of her kinswoman, Maria Addolorata, whose tragic death in the convent of Subiaco—a fictitious tragedy accepted as real by all Roman society—had given her a special place in the history of the Braccio family. She had not the dark and queenly splendour of Corona d'Astradente, her contemporary and the most beautiful woman of her time. But she had, for those who loved her, something which was quite her own and which placed her beyond them in some ways and, in any case, out of competition for the homage received by the great beauties. No one recognized this more fully than Angelo Reanda, and he would as soon have thought of being in love with her, as men love women, as he would have imagined that his father, for instance, could have loved Maria Addolorata, the Carmelite nun.

The one human point in his devoted adoration lay in his terror lest Francesca Campodonico should die young and leave him to grow old without her. He sometimes told her so.

"You should marry," she answered one day, when they were together in the great hall which he was decorating.

She was still dressed in black, and as she spoke, he turned and saw the outline of her small pure face against the high back of the old chair in which she was sitting. It was so white just then that he fancied he saw in it that fatal look which belonged to some of the Braccio family, and which was always spoken of as having been one of Maria Addolorata's chief characteristics. He looked at her long and sadly, leaning against an upright of his scaffolding as he stood on the floor near her, holding his brushes in his hand.

"I do not think I shall ever marry," he answered at last, looking down and idly mixing two colours on his palette.

"Why not?" she asked quickly. "I have heard you say that you might, some day."

"Some day, some day—and then, all at once, the 'some day' is past, and is not any more in the future. Why should I marry? I am well enough as I am; there would only be unhappiness."

"Do you think that every one who marries must be unhappy?" she asked. "You are cynical. I did not know it."

"No. I am not cynical. I say it only of myself. There are many reasons. I could not marry such a woman as I should wish to have for my wife. You must surely understand that. It is very easy to understand."

He made as though he would go up the ladder to his little platform and continue his work. But she stopped him.

"What is the use of hurting your eyes?" she asked. "It is late, and the light is bad. Besides, I am not so sure that I understand what you mean, though you say that it is so easy. We have never talked about it much."

He laid his palette and brushes upon a ragged straw chair and sat down upon another, not far from her. There was no other furniture in the great vaulted hall, and the brick pavement was bare, and splashed in many places with white plaster. Fresco-painting can only be done upon stucco just laid on, while it is still moist, and a mason came early every day and prepared as much of the wall as Reanda could cover before night. If he did not paint over the whole surface, the remainder was chipped away and freshly laid over on the following morning.

The evening light already reddened the tall western windows, for it was autumn, and the days were shortening quickly. Reanda knew that he could not do much more, and sat down, to answer Francesca's question, if he could.

"I am not a gentleman, as you understand the word," he said slowly. "And yet I am certainly not of the class to which my father belonged. My position is not defined. I could not marry a woman of your class, and I should not care to marry one of any other. That is all. Is it not clear?"

"Yes," answered Francesca. "It is clear enough. But—"

She checked herself, and he looked into her face, expecting her to continue. But she said nothing more.

"You were going to find an objection to what I said," he observed.

"No; I was not. I will say it, for you will understand me. What you tell me is true enough, and I am sorry that it should be so. Is it not to some extent my fault?"

"Your fault?" cried Reanda, leaning forward and looking into her eyes. "How? I do not understand."

"I blame myself," answered Francesca, quietly. "I have kept you out of the world, perhaps, and in many ways. Here you live, day after day, as though nothing else existed for you. In the morning, long before I am awake, you come down your staircase through that door, and go up that ladder, and work, and work, and work, all day long, until it is dark, as you have worked to-day, and yesterday, and for months. And when you might and should be out of doors, or associating with other people, as just now, I sit and talk to you and take up all your leisure time. It is wrong. You ought to see more of other men and women. Do men of genius never marry? It seems to me absurd!"

"Genius!" exclaimed Reanda, shaking his head sadly. "Do not use the word of me."

"I will do as other people do," answered Francesca. "But that is not the question. The truth is that you live pent up in this old house, like a bird in a cage. I want you to spread your wings."

"To go away for a time?" asked Reanda, anxiously.

"I did not say that. Perhaps I should. Yes, if you could enjoy a journey, go away—for a time."

She spoke with some hesitation and rather nervously, for he had said more than she had meant to propose.

"Just to make a change," she added, after a moment's pause, as he said nothing. "You ought to see more of other people, as I said. You ought to mix with the world. You ought at least to offer yourself the chance of marrying, even if you think that you might not find a wife to your taste."

"If I do not find one here—" He did not complete the sentence, but smiled a little.

"Must you marry a Roman princess?" she asked. "What should you say to a foreigner? Is that impossible, too?"

"It would matter little where she came from, if I wished to marry her," he answered. "But I like my life as it is. Why should I try to change it? I am happy as I am. I work, and I enjoy working. I work for you, and you are satisfied. It seems to me that there is nothing more to be said. Why are you so anxious that I should marry?"

Donna Francesca laughed softly, but without much mirth.

"Because I think that in some way it is my fault if you have not married," she said. "And besides, I was thinking of a young girl whom I met, or rather, saw, the other day, and who might please you. She has the most beautiful voice in the world, I think. She could make her fortune as a singer, and I believe she wishes to try it. But her father objects. They are foreigners—English or Scotch—it is the same. She is a mere child, they say, but she seems to be quite grown up. There is something strange about them. He is a man of science, I am told, but I fancy he is one of those English enthusiasts about Italian liberty. His name is Dalrymple."

"What a name!" Reanda laughed. "I suppose they have come to spend the winter in Rome," he added.

"Not at all. I hear that they have lived here for years. But one never meets the foreigners, unless they wish to be in society. His wife died young, they say, and this girl is his only daughter. I wish you could hear her sing!"

"For that matter, I wish I might," said Reanda, who was passionately fond of music.

CHAPTER XVIII

Seventeen years had scored their account on Angus Dalrymple's hard face, and one great sorrow had set an even deeper mark upon him—a sorrow so deep and so overwhelming that none had ever dared to speak of it to him. And he was not the man to bear any affliction resignedly, to feed on memory, and find rest in the dreams of what had been. Sullenly and fiercely rebellious against his fate, he went down life, rather than through it, savage and silent, for the most part, Nero-like in his wish that he could end the world at a single blow, himself and all that lived. Yet it was characteristic of the man that he had not chosen suicide as a means of escape, as he would have done in his earlier years, if Maria Addolorata had failed him. It seemed cowardly now, and he had never done anything cowardly in his life. Through his grief the sense of responsibility had remained with him, and had kept him alive. He looked upon his existence not as a state from which he had a right to escape, but as a personal enemy to be fought with, to be despised, to be ill-treated barbarously, perhaps, but still as an enemy to murder whom in cold blood would be an act of cowardice.

There was little more than the mere sense of the responsibility, for he did little enough to fulfil his obligations. His wife had borne him a daughter, but it was not in Angus Dalrymple's nature to substitute one being in his heart for another. He could not love the girl simply because her mother was dead. He could only spoil her, with a rough idea that she should be spared all suffering as much as possible, but that if he gave her what she wanted, he had done all that could be expected of him. For the rest, he lived his own life.

He had a good intelligence and superior gifts, together with considerable powers of intellectual acquisition. He had believed in his youth that he was destined to make great discoveries, and his papers afterwards showed that he was really on the track of great and new things. But with his bereavement, all ambition as well as all curiosity disappeared in one day from his character. Since then he had never gone back to his studies, which disgusted him and seemed stale and flat. He grew rudely dogmatical when scientific matters were discussed before him, as he had become rough, tyrannical, and almost violent in his ordinary dealings with the world, whenever he found any opposition to his opinions or his will. The only exception he made was in his treatment of his daughter, whom he indulged in every way except in her desire to be a public singer. It seemed to him that to give her everything she wanted was to fulfil all his obligations to her; in the one question of appearing on the stage he was inflexible. He simply refused to hear of it, rarely giving her any reasons beyond the ordinary ones which present themselves in such cases, and which were far from answering the impulse of the girl's genius.

They had called her Gloria in the days of their passionate happiness. The sentimental name had meant a great deal to them, for Dalrymple had at that time developed that sort of uncouth sentimentality which is in strong men like a fungus on an oak, and disgusts them afterwards unless they are able to forget it. The two had felt that the glory of life was in the child, and they had named her for it, as it were.

Years afterwards Dalrymple brought the little girl to Rome, drawn back irresistibly to the place by that physical association of impressions which moves such men strongly. They had remained, keeping from year to year a lodging Dalrymple had hired, at first hired for a few months. He never went to Subiaco.

He gave Gloria teachers, the best that could be found, and there were good instructors in those days when people were willing to take time in learning. In music she had her mother's voice and talent. Her father gave her a musician's opportunities, and it was no wonder that she should dream of conquering Europe from behind the footlights as Grisi had done, and as Patti was just about to do in her turn.

She and her father spoke English together, but Gloria was bilingual, as children of mixed marriages often are, speaking English and Italian with equal ease. Dalrymple found a respectable middle-aged German governess who came daily and spent most of the day with Gloria, teaching her and walking with her—worshipping her, too, with that curious faculty for idealizing the very human, which belongs to German governesses when they like their pupils.

Dalrymple led his own life. Had he chosen to mix in Roman society, he would have been well received, as a member of a great Scotch family and not very far removed from the head of his house. No one of his relatives had ever known the truth about his wife except his father, who had died with the secret, and it was not likely that any one should ask questions. If any one did, he would certainly not satisfy such curiosity. But he cared little for society, and spent his time either alone with books and wine, or in occasional excursions into the artist world, where his eccentricities excited little remark, and where he met men who secretly sympathized with the Italian revolutionary movement, and dabbled in conspiracies which rather amused than disquieted the papal government.

Though Gloria was at that time but little more than sixteen years of age, her father took her with him to little informal parties at the studios or even at the houses of artists, where there was often good music, and clever if not serious conversation. The conventionalities of age were little regarded in such circles. Gloria appeared, too, much older than she really was, and her marvellous voice made her a centre of attraction at an age when most young girls are altogether in the background. Dalrymple never objected to her singing on such occasions, and he invariably listened with closed eyes and folded hands, as though he were assisting at a religious service. Her voice was like her mother's, excepting that it was pitched higher, and had all the compass and power necessary for a great soprano. Dalrymple's almost devout attitude when Gloria was singing was the only allusion, if one may call it so, which he ever made to his dead wife's existence, and no one who watched him knew what it meant. But he was often more silent than usual after she had sung, and he sometimes went off by himself afterwards and sat for hours in one of the old wine cellars near the Capitol, drinking gloomily of the oldest and strongest he could find. For he drank more or less perpetually in the evening, and wine made him melancholic and morose, though it did not seem to affect him otherwise. Little by little, however, it was dulling the early keenness of his intellect, though it hardly touched his constitution at all. He was lean and bony still, as in the old days, but paler in the face, and he had allowed his red beard to grow. It was streaked with grey, and there were small, nervous lines about his eyes, as well as deep furrows on his forehead and face.

Dalrymple had found in the artist world a man who was something of a companion to him at times,—a very young man, whom he could not understand, though his own dogmatic temper made him as a rule believe that he understood most things and most men. But this particular individual alternately puzzled, delighted, and irritated the nervous Scotchman.

They had made acquaintance at an artists' supper in the previous year, had afterwards met accidentally at the bookseller's in the Piazza di Spagna, where they both went from time to time to look at the English newspapers, and little by little they had fallen into the habit of meeting there of a morning, and of strolling in the direction of Dalrymple's lodging afterwards. At last Dalrymple had asked his companion to come in and look at a book, and so the acquaintance had grown. Gloria watched the young stranger, and at first she disliked him.

The aforesaid bookseller dealt, and deals still, in photographs and prints, as well as in foreign and Italian books. At the present time his establishment is distinctively a Roman Catholic one. In those days it was almost the only one of its kind, and was patronized alike by Romans and foreigners. Even Donna

Francesca Campodonico went there from time to time for a book on art or an engraving which she and Reanda needed for their work. They occasionally walked all the way from the Palazzetto Borgia to the Piazza di Spagna together in the morning. When they had found what they wanted, Donna Francesca generally drove home in a cab, and Reanda went to his midday meal before returning. For the line of his intimacy with her was drawn at this point. He had never sat down at the same table with her, and he never expected to do so. As the two stood to one another at present, though Francesca would willingly have asked him to breakfast, she would have hesitated to do so, merely because the first invitation would inevitably call attention to the fact that the line had been drawn somewhere, whereas both were willing to believe that it had never existed at all. Under any pressure of necessity she would have driven with him in a cab, but not in her own carriage. They both knew it, and by tacit consent never allowed such unknown possibilities to suggest themselves. But in the mornings, there was nothing to prevent their walking together as far as the Piazza di Spagna, or anywhere else.

They went to the bookseller's one day soon after the conversation which had led Francesca to mention the Dalrymples. As they walked along the east side of the great square, they saw two men before them.

"There goes the Gladiator," said Reanda to his companion, suddenly. "There is no mistaking his walk, even at this distance."

"What do you mean?" asked Francesca. "Unless I am mistaken, the man who is a little the taller, the one in the rough English clothes, is Mr. Dalrymple. I spoke of him the other day, you know."

"Oh! Is that he? The other has a still more extraordinary name. He is Paul Griggs. He is the son of an American consul who died in Civita Vecchia twenty years ago, and left him a sort of waif, for he had no money and apparently no relatives. Somehow he has grown up, Heaven knows how, and gets a living by journalism. I believe he was at sea for some years as a boy. He is really as much Italian as American. I have met him with artists and literary people."

"Why do you call him the Gladiator?" asked Francesca, with some interest.

"It is a nickname he has got. Cotogni, the sculptor, was in despair for a model last year. Griggs and two or three other men were in the studio, and somebody suggested that Griggs was very near the standard of the ancients in his proportions. They persuaded him to let them measure him. You know that in the 'Canons' of proportion, the Borghese Gladiator—the one in the Louvre—is given as the best example of an athlete. They measured Griggs then and there, and found that he was at all points the exact living image of the statue. The name has stuck to him. You see what a fellow he is, and how he walks."

"Yes, he looks strong," said Francesca, watching the man with natural curiosity.

The young American was a little shorter than Dalrymple, but evidently better proportioned. No one could fail to notice the vast breadth of shoulder, the firm, columnar throat, and the small athlete's head with close-set ears. He moved without any of that swinging motion of the upper part of the body which is natural to many strong men and was noticeable in Dalrymple, but there was something peculiar in his walk, almost undefinable, but conveying the idea of very great strength with very great elasticity.

"But he is an ugly man," observed Reanda, almost immediately. "Ugly, but not repulsive. You will see, if he turns his head. His face is like a mask. It is not the face you would expect with such a body."

"How curious!" exclaimed Francesca, rather idly, for her interest in Paul Griggs was almost exhausted.

They went on along the crowded pavement. When they reached the bookseller's and went in, they saw that the two men were there before them, looking over the foreign papers, which were neatly arranged on a little table apart. Dalrymple looked up and recognized Francesca, to whom he had been introduced at a small concert given for a charity in a private house, on which occasion Gloria had sung. He lifted his hat from his head and laid it down upon the newspapers, when Francesca rather unexpectedly held out her hand to him in English fashion. He had left a card at her house on the day after their meeting, but as she was alone in the world, she had no means of returning the civility.

"It would give me great pleasure if you would bring your daughter to see me," she said graciously.

"You are very kind," answered Dalrymple, his steely blue eyes scrutinizing her pure young features.

She only glanced at him, for she was suddenly conscious that his companion was looking at her. He, too, had laid down his hat, and she instantly understood what Reanda had meant by comparing his face to a mask. The features were certainly very far from handsome. If they were redeemed at all, it was by the very deep-set eyes, which gazed into hers in a strangely steady way, as though the lids never could droop from under the heavy overhanging brow, and then, still unwinking, turned in another direction. The man's complexion was of that perfectly even but almost sallow colour which often belongs to very strong melancholic temperaments. His face was clean-shaven and unnaturally square and expressionless, excepting for such life as there was in the deep eyes. Dark, straight, closely cut hair grew thick and smooth as a priest's skull-cap, low on the forehead and far forward at the temples. The level mouth, firmly closed, divided the lower part of the face like the scar of a straight sabre-cut. The nose was very thick between the eyes, relatively long, with unusually broad nostrils which ran upward from the point to the lean cheeks. The man wore very dark clothes of extreme simplicity, and at a time when pins and chains were much in fashion, he had not anything visible about him of gold or silver. He wore his watch on a short, doubled piece of black silk braid slipped through his buttonhole. He dressed almost as though he were in mourning.

Francesca unconsciously looked at him so intently for a moment that Dalrymple thought it natural to introduce him, fancying that she might have heard of him and might wish to know him out of curiosity.

"May I introduce Mr. Griggs?" he said, with the stiff inclination which was a part of his manner.

Griggs bowed, and Donna Francesca bent her head a little. Reanda came up and shook hands with the American, and Francesca introduced the artist to Dalrymple.

"I have long wished to have the pleasure of knowing you, Signor Reanda," said the latter. "We have many mutual acquaintances among the artists here. I may say that I am a great admirer of your work, and my daughter, too, for that matter."

Reanda said something civil as his hand parted from the Scotchman's. Francesca saw an opportunity of bringing Reanda and Gloria together.

"As you like Signor Reanda's painting so much," she said to Dalrymple, "will you not bring your daughter this afternoon to see the frescoes he is doing in my house? You know the Palazzetto? Of course—you left a card, but I had no one to return it," she added rather sadly. "Will you also come, Mr. Griggs?" she asked, turning to the American. "It will give me much pleasure, and I see you know Signor Reanda. This afternoon, if you like, at any time after four o'clock."

Both Dalrymple and Griggs secretly wondered a little at receiving such an invitation from a Roman lady whom the one had met but once before, and to whom the other had but just been introduced. But they bowed their thanks, and promised to come.

After a few more words they separated, Francesca and Reanda to pick out the engraving they wanted, and the other two men to return to their newspapers. By and bye Francesca passed them again, on her way out.

"I shall expect you after four o'clock," she said, nodding graciously as she went by.

Dalrymple looked after her, till she had left the shop.

"That woman is not like other women, I think," he said thoughtfully, to his companion.

The mask-like face turned itself deliberately towards him, with shadowy, unwinking eyes.

"No," answered Griggs, and he slowly took up his paper again.

CHAPTER XIX

Donna Francesca received her three guests in the drawing-room, on the side of the house which she inhabited. Reanda was at his work in the great hall.

Gloria entered first, followed closely by her father, and Francesca was dazzled by the young girl's brilliancy of colour and expression, though she had seen her once before. As she came in, the afternoon sun streamed upon her face and turned her auburn hair to red gold, and gleamed upon her small white teeth as her strong lips parted to speak the first words. She was tall and supple, graceful as a panther, and her voice rang and whispered and rang again in quick changes of tone, like a waterfall in the woods in summer. With much of her mother's beauty, she had inherited from her father the violent vitality of his youth. Yet she was not noisy, though her manners were not like Francesca's. Her voice rippled and rang, but she did not speak too loud. She moved swiftly and surely, but not with rude haste. Nevertheless, it seemed to Francesca that there must be some exaggeration somewhere. The elder woman at first set it down as a remnant of schoolgirl shyness, and then at once felt that she was mistaken, because there was not the smallest awkwardness nor lack of self-possession about it. The contrast between the young girl and Paul Griggs was so striking as to be almost violent. He was cold and funereal in his leonine strength, and his face was more like a mask than ever as he bowed and sat down in silence. When he did not remind her of a gladiator, he made her think of a black lion with a strange, human face, and eyes that were not exactly human, though they did not remind her of any animal's eyes which she had ever seen.

As for Dalrymple, she thought that he was singularly haggard and worn for a man apparently only in middle age. There was a certain imposing air about him, which she liked. Besides, she rarely met foreigners, and they interested her. She noticed that both men wore black coats and carried their tall hats in their hands. They were therefore not artists, nor to be classed with artists. She was still young enough to judge them to some extent by details, to which people attached a good deal more importance at that time than at present. She made up her mind in the course of the next few minutes that both Dalrymple and Griggs belonged to her own class, though she did not ask herself where the young American had got his manners. But somehow, though Gloria fascinated her eyes and her ears, she set down the girl as being inferior to her father. She wondered whether Gloria's mother had not been an actress; which was a curious reflexion, considering that the dead woman had been of her own house and name.

After exchanging a few words with her guests, Francesca suggested that they should cross to the other side and see the frescoes, adding that Reanda was probably still at work.

"You know him, Mr. Griggs?" she said, as they all rose to leave the room.

"Yes," he answered, "as one man knows another."

"What does that mean?" asked Francesca, moving towards the door to lead the way.

"It does not mean much," replied the young man, with curious ambiguity.

He was very gentle in his manner, and spoke in a low voice and rather diffidently. She looked at him as though mentally determining to renew the question at some other time. Her first impression was that of a sort of duality about the man, as she found the possibility of a double meaning in his answer. His magnificent frame seemed to belong to one person, his voice and manner to another. Both might be good in their way, but her curiosity was excited by the side which was the less apparent.

They all went through the house till they came to a door which divided the inhabited part from the hall in which Reanda was working. She knocked gently upon it with her knuckles, and then smiled as she saw Gloria looking at her.

"We keep it locked," she said. "The masons come in the morning to lay on the stucco. One never trusts those people. Signor Reanda keeps the key of this door."

The artist opened from within, and stood aside to let the party pass. He started perceptibly when he first saw Gloria. As a boy he had seen Maria Braccio more than once before she had entered the convent, and he was struck by the girl's strong resemblance to her. Francesca, following Gloria, saw his movement of surprise, and attributed it merely to admiration or astonishment such as she had felt herself a quarter of an hour earlier. She smiled a little as she went by, and Reanda knew that the smile was for him because he had shown surprise. He understood the misinterpretation, and resented it a little.

But she knew Reanda well, and before ten minutes had passed she had convinced herself that he was repelled rather than attracted by the young girl, in spite of the latter's undisguised admiration of his work. It was not mere unintelligent enthusiasm, either, and he might well have been pleased and flattered by her unaffected praise.

She was interested, too, in the technical mechanics of fresco-painting, which she had never before been able to see at close quarters. Everything interested Gloria, and especially everything connected with art.

As soon as they had all spoken their first words of compliment and appreciation, she entered into conversation with the painter, asking him all sorts of questions, and listening earnestly to what he said, until he realized that she was certainly not assuming an appearance of admiration for the sake of flattering him.

Meanwhile Francesca talked with Griggs, and Dalrymple, having gone slowly round the hall alone after all the others, came and stood beside the two and watched Francesca, occasionally offering a rather dry remark in a somewhat absent-minded way. It was all rather commonplace and decidedly quiet, and he was not much amused, though from time to time he seemed to become absorbed in studying Francesca's face, as though he saw something there which was past his comprehension. She noticed that he watched her, and felt a little uncomfortable under his steely blue eyes, so that she turned her head and talked more with Griggs than with him. Remembering what Reanda had told her of the young man's origin, she did not like to ask him the common questions about residence in Rome and his liking for Italy. She was self-possessed and ready enough at conversation, and she chose to talk of general subjects. They talked in Italian, of course. Dalrymple, as of old, spoke fluently, but with a strange accent. Any one would have taken Paul Griggs for a Roman. At last, almost in spite of herself, she made a remark about his speech.

"I was born here," answered Griggs. "It is much more remarkable that Miss Dalrymple should speak Italian as she does, having been born in Scotland."

"Are you talking about me?" asked the young girl, turning her head quickly, though she was standing with Reanda at some distance from the others.

"I was speaking of your accent in Italian," said Griggs.

"Is there anything wrong about it?" asked Gloria, with an anxiety that seemed exaggerated.

"On the contrary," answered Donna Francesca, "Mr. Griggs was telling me how perfectly you speak. But I had noticed it."

"Oh! I thought Mr. Griggs was finding fault," answered Gloria, turning to Reanda again.

Dalrymple looked at his daughter as though he were annoyed. The eyes of Francesca and Griggs met for a moment. All three were aware that they resented the young girl's quick question as one which they themselves would not have asked in her place, had they accidentally heard their names mentioned in a distant conversation. But Francesca instantly went on with the subject.

"To us Italians," she said, "it seems incredible that any one should speak our language and English equally well. It is as though you were two persons, Mr. Griggs," she added, smiling at the covered expression of her thought about him.

"I sometimes think so myself," answered Griggs, with one of his steady looks. "In a way, every one must have a sort of duality—a good and evil principle."

"God and the devil," suggested Francesca, simply.

"Body and soul would do, I suppose. The one is always in slavery to the other. The result is a sinner or a saint, as the case may be. One never can tell," he added more carelessly. "I am not sure that it matters. But one can see it. The battle is fought in the face."

"I do not understand. What battle?"

"The battle between body and soul. The face tells which way the fight is going."

She looked at his own, and she felt that she could not tell. But to a certain extent she understood him.

"Griggs is full of theories," observed Dalrymple. "Gloria, come down!" he cried in English, suddenly.

Gloria, intent upon understanding how fresco-painting was done, was boldly mounting the steps of the ladder towards the top of the little scaffolding, which might have been fourteen feet high. For the vault had long been finished, and Reanda was painting the walls.

"Nonsense, papa!" answered the young girl, also in English. "There's no danger at all."

"Well—don't break your neck," said Dalrymple. "I wish you would come down, though."

Francesca was surprised at his indifference, and at his daughter's calm disregard of his authority. Timid, too, as most Italian women of higher rank, she watched the girl nervously. Griggs raised his eyes without lifting his head.

"Gloria is rather wild," said Dalrymple, in a sort of apology. "I hope you will forgive her—she is so much interested."

"Oh—if she wishes to see, let her go, of course," answered Francesca, concealing a little nervous irritation she felt.

A moment later Gloria and Reanda were on the small platform, on one side of which only there was a hand rail. It had been made for him, and his head was steady even at a much greater elevation. He was pointing out to her the way in which the colours slowly changed as the stucco dried from day to day, and explaining how it was impossible to see the effect of what was done until all was completely dry. The others continued to talk below, but Griggs glanced up from time to time, and Francesca's eyes followed his. Dalrymple had become indifferent, allowing his daughter to do what she pleased, as usual.

When Gloria had seen all she wished to see, she turned with a quick movement to come down again, and on turning, she found herself much nearer to the edge than she had expected. She was bending forwards a little, and Griggs saw at once that she must lose her balance, unless Reanda caught her from behind. But she made no sound, and turned very white as she swayed a little, trying to throw herself back.

With a swift movement that was gentle but irresistible, Griggs pushed Francesca back, keeping his eyes on the girl above. It all happened in an instant.

"Jump!" he cried, in a voice of command.

She had felt that she must spring or fall, and her body was already overbalanced as she threw herself off, instinctively gathering her skirt with her hands. Dalrymple turned as pale as she. If she struck the bare brick floor, she could scarcely escape serious injury. But she did not reach it, for Paul Griggs caught her in his arms, swayed with her weight, then stood as steady as a rock, and set her gently upon her feet, beside her father.

"Maria Santissima!" cried Francesca, terrified, though instantly relieved, and dimly understanding the stupendous feat of bodily strength which had just been done before her eyes.

Above, Reanda leaned upon the single rail of the scaffolding with wide-staring eyes. Gloria was faint with the shock of fear, and grasped her father's arm.

"You ought to be ashamed of yourself!" he said roughly, in English, but in a low voice. "You probably owe your life to Mr. Griggs," he added, immediately regaining his self-possession.

Griggs alone seemed wholly unmoved by what had happened. Gloria had held one of her gloves loosely in her hand, and it had fallen to the ground as she sprang. He picked it up and handed it to her with a curious gentleness.

"It must be yours, Miss Dalrymple," he said.

CHAPTER XX

It was late before Reanda and Donna Francesca were alone together on that afternoon. When the first surprise and shock of Gloria's accident had passed, Francesca would not allow Dalrymple to take her away at once, as he seemed anxious to do. The girl was not in the least hurt, but she was still dazed and frightened. Francesca took them all back to the drawing-room and insisted upon giving them tea, because they were foreigners, and Gloria, she said, must naturally need something to restore her nerves. Roman tea, thirty years ago, was a strange and uncertain beverage, as both Gloria and her father knew, but they drank what Francesca gave them, and at last went away with many apologies for the disturbance they had made. To tell the truth, Francesca was glad when they were gone and she was at liberty to return to the hall where Reanda was still at work. She found him nervous and irritated. He came down from the scaffolding as soon as he heard her open the door. Neither spoke until she had seated herself in her accustomed chair, with a very frank sigh of relief.

"I am very grateful to you, Donna Francesca," said Reanda, twisting his beard round his long, thin fingers, as he glanced at her and then surveyed his work.

"It was your fault," she answered, tapping the worm-eaten arms of the old chair with both her white hands, for she herself was still annoyed and irritated. "Do not make me responsible for the girl's folly."

"Responsibility! May that never be!" exclaimed the artist, in the common Italian phrase, but with a little irony. "But as for the responsibility, I do not know whose it was. It was certainly not I who invited the young lady to go up the ladder."

"Well, it was her fault. Besides, the absent are always wrong. But she is handsome, is she not?"

Reanda shrugged his thin shoulders, and looked critically at his hands, which were smeared with paint.

"Very handsome," he said indifferently. "But it is a beauty that says nothing to me. One must be young to like that kind of beauty. She is a beautiful storm, that young lady. For one who seeks peace—" He shrugged his shoulders again. "And then, her manners! I do not understand English, but I know that her father was telling her to come down, and yet she went up. I do not know what education these foreigners have. Instruction, yes, as much as you please; but education, no. They have no more than barbarians. The father says, 'You must not do that.' And the daughter does it. What education is that? Of course, if they were friends of yours, I should not say it."

"Nevertheless that girl is very handsome," insisted Francesca. "She has the Venetian colouring. Titian would have painted her just as she is, without changing anything."

"Beauty, beauty!" exclaimed Reanda, impatiently. "Of course, it is beauty! Food for the brush, that says nothing to the heart. The devil can also take the shape of a beautiful woman. That is it. There is something in that young lady's face—how shall I say? It pleases me—little! You must forgive me, princess. My nerves are shaken. Divine goodness! To see a young girl flying through the air like Simon Magus! It was enough!"

Francesca laughed gently. Reanda shook his head with slow disapprobation, and frowned.

"I say the truth," he said. "There is something—I cannot explain. But I can show you," he added quickly.

He took up his palette and brushes from the chair on which they lay, and reached the white plastered wall in two steps.

"Paint her," said Francesca, to encourage him.

"Yes, I will show her to you—as I think she is," he answered.

He closed his eyes for a moment, calling up the image before him, then went back to the chair and took a quantity of colour from a tube which lay, with half-a-dozen others, in the hollow of the rush seat. They were not the colours he used for fresco-painting, but had been left there when he had made a sketch of a head two or three days previously. In a moment he was before the wall again. It was roughly plastered from the floor to the lower line of the frescoes. With a long, coarse brush he began to sketch a gigantic head of a woman. The oil paint lay well on the rough, dry surface. He worked in great strokes at the full length of his arm.

"Make her beautiful, at least," said Francesca, watching him.

"Oh, yes—very beautiful," he answered.

He worked rapidly for a few minutes, smiling, as his hand moved, but not pleasantly. Francesca thought there was an evil look in his face which she had never seen there before, and that his smile was wicked and spiteful.

"But you are painting a sunset!" she cried suddenly.

"A sunset? That is her hair. It is red, and she has much of it. Wait a little."

And he went on. It was certainly something like a sunset, the bright, waving streamers of the clouds flying far to right and left, and blending away to the neutral tint of the dry plaster as though to a grey sky.

"Yes, but it is still a sunset," said Francesca. "I have seen it like that from the Campagna in winter."

"She is not 'Gloria' for nothing," answered Reanda. "I am making her glorious. You shall see."

Suddenly, with another tone, he brought out the main features of the striking face, by throwing in strong shadows from the flaming hair. Francesca became more interested. The head was colossal, extraordinary, almost unearthly; the expression was strange.

"What a monster!" exclaimed Francesca at last, as he stood aside, still touching the enormous sketch here and there with his long brush, at arm's length. "It is terrible," she added, in a lower tone.

"Truth is always terrible," answered Reanda. "But you cannot say that it is not like her."

"Horribly like. It is diabolical!"

"And yet it is a beautiful head," said the artist. "Perhaps you are too near." He himself crossed the hall, and then turned round to look at his work. "It is better from here," he said. "Will you come?"

She went to his side. The huge face and wildly streaming hair stood out as though in three dimensions from the wall. The great, strong mouth smiled at her with a smile that was at once evil and sad and fatal. The strange eyes looked her through and through from beneath the vast brow.

"It is diabolical, satanical!" she responded, under her breath.

Reanda still smiled wickedly and watched her. The face seemed to grow and grow till it filled the whole range of vision. The dark eyes flashed; the lips trembled; the flaming hair quivered and waved and curled up like snakes that darted hither and thither. Yet it was horribly like Gloria, and the fresh, rich oil colours gave it her startling and vivid brilliancy.

It was the sudden and enormous expression of a man of genius, strung and stung, till irritation had to find its explosion through the one art of which he was absolute master—in a fearful caricature exaggerating beauty itself to the bounds of the devilish.

"I cannot bear it!" cried Francesca.

She snatched the big brush from his hand, and, running lightly across the room, dashed the colour left in it across the face in all directions, over the eyes and the mouth, and through the long red hair. In ten seconds nothing remained but confused daubs and splashes of brilliant paint.

"There!" cried Francesca. "And I wish I had never seen it!"

Still holding the brush in her hand, she turned her back to the obliterated sketch and faced Reanda, with a look of girlish defiance and satisfaction. His face was grave now, but he seemed pleased with what he had done.

"It makes no difference," he said. "You will never forget it."

He felt that he was revenged for the smile she had bestowed upon his apparent surprise at Gloria's beauty, when she had followed the girl into the hall, and had seen him start. He could not conceal his triumph.

"That is the young lady whom you thought I might wish to marry," he said. "You know me little after so many years, Donna Francesca. You have bestowed much kindness upon a man whom you do not know."

"My dear Reanda, who can understand you? But as for kindness, do not let me hear the word between you and me. It has no meaning. We are always good friends, as we were when I was a little girl and used to play with your paints. You have given me far more than I can ever repay you for, in your works. I do not flatter you, my friend. Cupid and Psyche, there in your frescoes, will outlive me and be famous when I am forgotten—yet they are mine, are they not? And you gave them to me."

The sweet young face turned to him with an unaffected, grateful smile. His sad features softened all at once.

"Ah, Donna Francesca," he said gently, "you have given me something better than Cupid and Psyche, for your gift will live forever in heaven."

She looked thoughtfully into his eyes, but with a sort of question in her own.

"Your dear friendship," he added, bending his head a little. Then he laughed suddenly. "Do not give me a wife," he concluded.

"And you, Reanda—do not make wicked caricatures of women you have only seen once! Besides, I go back to it again. I saw you start when she passed you at the door. You were surprised at her beauty. You must admit that. And then, because you are irritated with her, you take a brush and daub that monstrous thing upon the wall! It is a shame!"

"I started, yes. It was not because she struck me as beautiful. It was something much more strange. Do you know? She is the very portrait of Donna Maria, who was in the Carmelite convent at Subiaco, and who was burned to death. I have often told you that I remembered having seen her when I was a boy, both at Gerano and at the Palazzo Braccio, before she took the veil. There is a little difference in the colouring, I think, and much in the expression. But the rest—it is the image!"

Francesca, who could not remember her ill-fated kinswoman, was not much impressed by Reanda's statement.

"It makes your caricature all the worse," she answered, "since it was also a caricature of that holy woman. As for the resemblance, after all these years, it is a mere impression. Who knows? It may be. There is no portrait of Sister Maria Addolorata."

"Oh, but I remember well!" insisted Reanda.

"Well, it concludes nothing, after all," returned Francesca, with much logic. "It does not make a fiend of the poor nun, who is an angel by this time, and it does not make Miss Dalrymple less beautiful. And now, Signor Painter," she added, with another girlish laugh, "if we have quarrelled enough to restore your nerves, I am going out. It is almost dark, and I have to go to the Austrian Embassy before dinner, and the carriage has been waiting for an hour."

"You, princess!" exclaimed Reanda, in surprise; for she had not begun to go into the world yet since her husband's death.

"It is not a reception. We are to meet there about arranging another of those charity concerts for the deaf and dumb."

"I might have known," answered the painter. "As for me, I shall go to the theatre to-night. There is the Trovatore."

"That is a new thing for you, too. But I am glad. Amuse yourself, and tell me about the singing to-morrow. Remember to lock the door and take the key. I do not trust the masons in the morning."

"Do I ever forget?" asked Reanda. "But I will lock it now, as you go out; for it is late, and I shall go upstairs."

"Good night," said Francesca, as she turned to leave the room.

"And you forgive the caricature?" asked Reanda, holding the door open for her to pass.

"I would forgive you many things," she answered, smiling as she went by.

CHAPTER XXI

In those days the Trovatore was not an old-fashioned opera. It was not 'threshed-out,' to borrow the vigorous German phrase. Wagner had not eclipsed melody with 'tone-poetry,' nor made men feel more than they could hear. Many of the great things of this century-ending had not been done then, nor even dreamed of, and even musicians listened to the Trovatore with pleasure, not dreaming of the untried strength that lay waiting in Verdi's vast reserve. It was then the music of youth. To us it seems but the music of childhood. Many of us cannot listen to Manrico's death-song from the tower without hearing the grind-organ upon which its passion has grown so pathetically poor. But one could understand that music. The mere statement that it was comprehensible raises a smile to-day. It appealed to simple feelings. We are no longer satisfied with such simplicity, and even long for powers that do not appeal, but twist us with something stronger than our hardened selves, until we ourselves appeal to the unknown, in a sort of despairing ecstasy of unsatisfied delight, asking of possibility to stretch itself out to the impossible. We are in a strange phase of development. We see the elaborately artificial world-scape painted by Science on the curtain close before our eyes, but our restless hands are thrust through it and beyond, opening eagerly and shutting on nothing, though we know that something is there.

Angelo Reanda was passionately fond of what was called music in Italy more than thirty years ago. He had the true ear and the facile memory for melody common to Italians, who are a singing people, if not a musical race, and which constituted a talent for music when music was considered to be a succession of sounds rather than a series of sensuous impressions. He could listen to an opera, understand it without thought, enjoy it simply, and remember it without difficulty, like thousands of other Romans. Most of us would willingly go back to such childlike amusements if we could. A few possess the power even now, and are looked upon with friendly contempt by their more cultured, and therefore more tortured, musical acquaintances, whose dream it is to be torn to very rags in the delirium of orchestral passion.

Reanda went to the Apollo Theatre in search of merely pleasurable sensations, and he got exactly what he wanted. The old house was brilliant even in those days, less with light than with jewels, it is true, but perhaps that illumination was as good as any other. The Roman ladies and the ladies of the great embassies used then to sit through the whole evening in their boxes, and it was the privilege, as it is still in Rome, of the men in the stalls and pit to stand up between the acts and admire them and their diamonds as much as they pleased. The light was dim enough, compared with what we have nowadays; for gas was but just introduced in a few of the principal streets, and the lamps in the huge chandelier at the Apollo, and in the brackets around the house, were filled with the olive oil which to-day dresses the world's salad. But it was a soft warm light, with rich yellow in it, which penetrated the shadows and beautified all it touched.

Reanda, like the others, stood up and looked about him after the first act. His eyes were instantly arrested by Gloria's splendid hair, which caught the light from above. She was seated in the front of a box on the third tier, the second row of boxes being almost exclusively reserved in those days. Dalrymple was beside his daughter, and the dark, still face of Paul Griggs was just visible in the shadow.

Gloria saw the artist almost immediately, for he could not help looking at her curiously, comparing her face with the mad sketch he had made on the wall. She nodded to him, and then spoke to her father, evidently calling his attention to Reanda, for Dalrymple looked down at once, and also nodded, while Griggs leaned forward a little and stared vacantly into the pit.

"It is an obsession to-day," said Reanda to himself, reflecting that though the girl lived in Rome he had never noticed her before, and had now seen her twice on the same day.

He mentally added the reflexion that she must have good nerves, and that most young girls would be at home with a headache after such a narrow escape as hers. She was quite as handsome as he had thought, however, and even more so, now that he saw her in her girlish evening gown, which was just a little open at the throat, and without even the simplest of ornaments. The white material and the shadow around and behind her threw her head into strong relief.

The curtain went up again, and Reanda sat down and watched the performance and listened to the simple, stirring melodies. But he was uncomfortably conscious that Gloria was looking at the back of his head from her box. Nervous people know the unpleasant sensation which such a delusion can produce. Reanda moved uneasily in his seat, and looked round more than once, just far enough to catch sight of Gloria's hair without looking up into her eyes.

His thoughts were disturbed, and he recalled vividly the face of the dead nun, which he had seen long ago. The resemblance was certainly strong. Maria Addolorata had sometimes had a strange expression which was quite her own, and which he had not yet seen in Gloria. But he felt that he should see it some day. He was sure of it, so sure that he had thrown its full force into the sketch on the wall, knowing that it would startle Donna Francesca. It was not possible that two women should be so much alike and yet that one of them should never have that look. Perhaps Gloria had it now and was staring at the back of his head.

An unaccountable nervousness took possession of the sensitive man, and he suffered as he sat there. After the curtain dropped he rose and left the theatre without looking up, and crossed the narrow street to a little coffee shop familiar to him for many years. He drank a cup of coffee, broke off the end of a thin black Roman cigar, and smoked for a few minutes before he returned.

Gloria had not moved, but Griggs was either gone or had retired further back into the shadow. Dalrymple was leaning back in his chair, bony and haggard, one of his great hands hanging listlessly over the front of the box. Reanda sat down again, and determined that he would not turn round before the end of the act. But it was of no use. He irritated his neighbours on each side by his restlessness, and his forehead was moist as though he were suffering great pain. Again he faced about and stared upwards at the box. Gloria, to his surprise, was not looking at him, but in the shadow he met the inscrutable eyes of Paul Griggs, fixed upon him as though they would never look away. But he cared very little whether Griggs looked at him or not. He faced the stage again and was more quiet.

It was a good performance, and he began to be glad that he had come. The singers were young, the audience was inclined to applaud, and everything went smoothly. Reanda thought the soprano rather weak in the great tower scene.

"Calpesta il mio cadavere, ma salva il Trovator!"

—she sang in great ascending intervals.

Reanda sighed, for she made no impression on him, and he remembered that he had been deeply impressed, even thrilled, when he had first heard the phrase. He had realized the situation then and had felt with Leonora. Perhaps he had grown too old to feel that sort of young emotion any more. He sighed regretfully as he rose from his seat. Looking up once more, he saw that Gloria was putting on her cloak, her back turned to the theatre. He waited a moment and then moved on with the crowd, to get his coat from the cloak-room.

He went out and walked slowly up the Via di Tordinona. It was a dark and narrow street in those days. The great old-fashioned lanterns were swung up with their oil lamps in them, by long levers held in place by chains locked to the wall. Here and there over a low door a red light showed that wine was sold in a basement which was almost a cellar. The crowd from the theatre hurried along close by the walls, in constant danger from the big coaches that dashed past, bringing the Roman ladies home, for all had to pass through that narrow street. Landaus were not yet invented, and the heavy carriages rumbled loudly through the darkness, over the small paving-stones. But the people on foot were used to them, and stood pressed against the walls as they went by, or grouped for a moment on the low doorsteps of the dark houses.

Reanda went with the rest. He might have gone the other way, by the Banchi Vecchi, from the bridge of Sant' Angelo, and it would have been nearer, but he had a curious fancy that the Dalrymples might walk home, and that he might see Gloria again. Though it was not yet winter, the night was bright and cold, and It was pleasant to walk. The regular season at the Apollo Theatre did not begin until Christmas, but there were often good companies there at other times of the year.

The artist walked on, glancing at the groups he passed in the dim street, but neither pausing nor hurrying. He meant to let fate have her own way with him that night.

Fate was not far off. He had gone on some distance, and the crowd had dispersed in various directions, till he was almost alone as he emerged into the open space where the Via del Clementino intersects the Ripetta. At that moment he heard a wild and thrilling burst of song.

"Calpesta il mio cadavere, ma salva il Trovator!"

The great soprano rang out upon the midnight silence, like the voice of a despairing archangel, and there was nothing more.

"Hush!" exclaimed a man's voice energetically.

Two or three windows were opened high up, for no one had ever heard such a woman's voice in the streets before. Reanda peered before him through the gloom, saw three people standing at the next corner, and hastened his long steps. An instinct he could not explain told him that Gloria had sung the short strain, which had left him cold and indifferent when he had heard it in the theatre. He was neither now, and he was possessed by the desire to be sure that it had been she.

He was not mistaken. Griggs had recognized him first, and they had waited for him at the corner.

"It is an unexpected pleasure to meet twice in the same day," said Reanda.

"The pleasure is ours," answered Dalrymple, in the correct phrase, but with his peculiar accent. "I suppose you heard my daughter's screams," he added drily. "She was explaining to us how a particular phrase should be sung."

"Was I not right?" asked Gloria, quickly appealing to Reanda with the certainty of support.

"A thousand times right," he answered. "How could one be wrong with such a voice?"

Gloria was pleased, and they all walked on together till they reached the door of Dalrymple's lodging.

"Come in and have supper with us," said the Scotchman, who seemed to be less gloomy than usual. "I suppose you live in our neighbourhood?"

"No. In the Palazzetto Borgia, where I work."

"This is not exactly on your way home, then," observed Gloria. "You may as well rest and refresh yourself."

Reanda accepted the invitation, wondering inwardly at the assurance of the foreign girl. With her Italian speech she should have had Italian manners, he thought. The three men all carried tapers, as was then customary, and they all lit them before they ascended the dark staircase.

"This is an illumination," said Dalrymple, looking back as he led the way.

Gloria stopped suddenly, and looked round. She was following her father, and Reanda came after her, Griggs being the last.

"One, two, three," she counted, and her eyes met Reanda's.

Without the slightest hesitation, she blew out the taper he held in his hand. But, for one instant, he had seen in her face the expression of the dead nun, distinct in the clear light, and close to his eyes.

"Why did you do that?" asked Dalrymple, who had turned his head again, as the taper was extinguished.

"Three lights mean death," said Gloria, promptly; and she laughed, as she went quickly up the steps.

"It is true," answered Reanda, in a low voice, as he followed her; and it occurred to him that in a flash he had seen death written in the brilliant young face.

Ten minutes later, they were seated around the table in the Dalrymples' small dining-room. Reanda noticed that everything he saw there evidently belonged to the hired lodging, from the old-fashioned Italian silver forks, battered and crooked at the prongs, to the heavy cut-glass decanters, stained with age and use, at the neck, and between the diamond-shaped cuttings. There was supper enough for half-a-dozen people, however, and an extraordinary quantity of wine. Dalrymple swallowed a big tumbler of it before he ate anything. Paul Griggs filled his glass to the brim, and looked at it. He had hardly spoken since Reanda had joined the party.

The artist made an effort to be agreeable, feeling that the invitation had been a very friendly one, considering the slight acquaintance he had with the Dalrymples, an acquaintance not yet twenty-four hours old. Presently he asked Gloria if she had felt no ill effects from her extraordinary accident in the afternoon.

"I had not thought about it again," she answered. "I have thought of nothing but your painting all the evening, until that woman sang that phrase as though she were asking the Conte di Luna for more strawberries and cream."

She laughed, but her eyes were fixed on his face.

"'Un altro po' di fravole, e dammi crema ancor,'"

—she sang softly, in the Roman dialect.

Then she laughed again, and Reanda smiled at the absurd words—"A few more strawberries, and give me some more cream." But even the few notes, a lazy parody of the prima donna's singing of the phrase, charmed his simple love of melody.

"Don't look so grim, papa," she said in English. "Nobody can hear me here, you know."

"I should not think anybody would wish to," answered the Scotchman; but he spoke in Italian, in consideration of his guest, who did not understand English.

"I do not know why you are always so angry if I sing anything foolish," said the young girl, going back to Italian. "One cannot be always serious. But I was talking about your frescoes, Signor Reanda. I have thought of nothing else."

Again her eyes met the artist's, but fell before his. He was too great a painter not to know the value of such flattering speeches in general, and in a way he was inclined to resent the girl's boldness. But at the same time, it was hard to believe that she was not really in earnest, for she had that power of sudden gravity which lends great weight to little speeches. In spite of himself, and perhaps rightly, he believed her. Paul Griggs did not, and he watched her curiously.

"Why do you look at me like that?" she asked, turning upon him with a little show of temper.

"If your father will allow me to say so, you are the object most worth looking at in the room," answered the young man, calmly.

"You will make her vain with your pretty speeches, Griggs," said Dalrymple.

"I doubt that," answered Griggs.

He relapsed into silence, and drained a big tumbler of wine. Reanda suspected, with a shrewd intuition, that the American admired Gloria, but that she did not like him much.

"Miss Dalrymple is doing her best to make me vain with her praise," said Reanda.

"I never flattered any one in my life," answered Gloria. "Signor Reanda is the greatest painter in Italy. Everybody says so. It would be foolish of me to even pretend that after seeing him at work I had thought of anything else. We have all said, this evening, that the frescoes were wonderful, and that no one, not even Raphael, who did the same thing, has ever had a more beautiful idea of the history of Cupid and Psyche. Why should we not tell the truth, just because he happens to be here? How illogical you are!"

"I believe I excepted Raphael," said Dalrymple, with his national accuracy. "But Signor Reanda will not quarrel with me on that account, I am sure."

"But I did not except Raphael, nor any one," persisted Gloria, before Reanda could speak.

"Really, Signorina, though I am mortal and susceptible, you go a little too far. Flattery is not appreciation, you know."

"It is not flattery," she answered, and the colour rose in her face. "I am quite in earnest. Nobody ever painted anything better than your Cupid and Psyche. Raphael's is dull and uninteresting compared with it."

"I blush, but I cannot accept so much," said the Italian, smiling politely, but still trying to discover whether she meant what she said or not.

In spite of himself, as before, he continued to believe her, though his judgment told him that hers could not be worth much. But he was pleased to have made such an impression, and by quick degrees his prejudice against her began to disappear. What had seemed like boldness in her no longer shocked him, and he described it to himself as the innocent frankness of a foreign girl. It was not possible that any one so like the dead Maria Braccio could be vulgar or bold. From that moment he began to rank Gloria as belonging to the higher sphere from which his birth excluded him. It was a curious and quick transition, and he would not have admitted that it was due to her exaggerated praise of his work. Strange as it must seem to those not familiar with the almost impassable barriers of old Italian society, Reanda had that evening, for the first time in his life, the sensation of being liked, admired, and talked with by a woman of Francesca Campodonico's class; stranger still, it was one of the most delicious sensations he had ever experienced. Yet the woman in question was but a girl not yet seventeen years old. Before he rose to go home, he unconsciously resented Griggs's silent admiration for Gloria. To the average Italian, such silence is a sign that a man is in love, and Reanda was the more attracted to Gloria because she treated Griggs with such perfect indifference.

It was nearly one o'clock when he lighted his taper to descend the stairs. Griggs was also ready to go. It was a relief to know that he was not going to stay behind and talk with Gloria. They went down in silence.

"I wanted to ask you a question," said the American, as they came out upon the street, and blew out their tapers. "We live in opposite directions, so I must ask it now. Should you mind, if I wrote an article on your frescoes for a London paper?"

"Mind!" exclaimed the artist, with a sudden revulsion of feeling in favour of the journalist. "I should be delighted—flattered."

"No," said Griggs, coldly. "I shall not write as Miss Dalrymple talks. But I shall try and do you justice, and that is a good deal, when one is a serious artist, as you are."

Reanda was struck by the cool moderation of the words, which expressed his own modest judgment of himself almost too exactly to be agreeable after Gloria's unlimited praise. He thanked Griggs warmly, however, and they shook hands before they parted.

CHAPTER XXII

Three months passed, and Reanda was intimate with the Dalrymples. It was natural enough, considering the circumstances. They lived much alone, and Reanda was like them in this respect, for he rarely went where he was obliged to talk. During the day he saw much of Donna Francesca, but when it grew dark in the early afternoons of midwinter, the artist was thrown upon his own resources. In former years he had now and then done as many of the other artists did, and had sometimes for a month or two spent most of his evenings at the eating-house where he dined, in company with half-a-dozen others who frequented the same establishment. Each dropped in, at any hour that chanced to suit him, ate his supper, pushed back his chair, and joined in the general conversation, smoking, and drinking coffee or a little wine, until it was time to go home. There were grey-headed painters who had hardly been absent more than a few days in five and twenty years from their accustomed tables at such places as the Falcone, the Gabbione, or the Genio. But Reanda had never joined in any of these little circles for longer than a month or two, by which time he had exhausted the stock of his companions' ideas, and returned to solitude and his own thoughts. For he had something which they had not, besides his greater talent, his broader intelligence, and his deeper artistic insight. Donna Francesca's refining influence exerted itself continually upon him, and made much of the common conversation tiresome or disagreeable to him. A man whose existence is penetrated by the presence of a rarely refined woman seldom cares much for the daily society of men. He prefers to be alone, when he cannot be with her.

Reanda believed that what he felt for Francesca was a devoted and almost devout friendship. The fact that before many weeks had passed after his first meeting with Gloria he was perceptibly in love with the girl, while he felt not the smallest change in his relations with Donna Francesca, satisfactorily proved to him that he was right. It would not have been like an Italian and a Latin to compare his feelings for the two women by imaginary tests, as, for instance, by asking himself for which of the two he would make the greater sacrifice. He took it for granted that the one sentiment was friendship and the other love, and he acted accordingly.

He was distrustful, indeed, and very suspicious, but not of himself. Gloria treated him too well. Her eyes told him more than he felt able to believe. It was not natural that a girl so young and fresh and beautiful, with the world before her, should fall in love with a man of his age. That, at least, was what he thought. But the fact that it was unnatural did not prevent it from taking place.

Reanda ignored certain points of great importance. In the first place, Gloria had not really the world before her. Her little sphere was closely limited by her father's morose selfishness, which led him to keep her in Rome because he liked the place himself, and to keep away from his countrymen, whom he detested as heartily as Britons living abroad sometimes do. On the other hand, a vague dread lest the story of his marriage might some day come to the light kept him away from Roman society. He had fallen back upon artistic Bohemia for such company as he wanted, which was little enough, and as his child grew up he had not understood that she was developing early and coming to womanhood while she was still under the care of the governess he had provided. He had not even made any plans for her future, for he did not love her, though he indulged her as a selfish and easy means of fulfilling his paternal obligations. It was to get rid of her importunity that he began to take her to the houses of some of the married artists when she was only sixteen years old, though she looked at least two years older.

But in such society as that, Reanda was easily first, apart from the talent which placed him at the head of the whole artistic profession. He had been brought up, taught, and educated among gentlemen, sons of one of the oldest and most fastidious aristocracies in Europe, and he had their manners, their speech, their quiet air of superiority, and especially that exterior gentleness and modesty of demeanour which most touches some women. In Gloria's opinion, he even had much of their appearance, being tall, thin, and dark. Accustomed as she was to living with her father, who was gloomy and morose, and to seeing much of Paul Griggs, whose powers of silence were phenomenal at that time, Reanda's easy grace of conversation charmed and flattered her. He was, by many degrees, the superior in talent, in charm, in learning, to any one she had ever met, and it must not be forgotten that although he was twenty years older than she, he was not yet forty, and that, as he had not a grey hair in his head, he could still pass for a young man, though his grave disposition made him feel older than he was. Of the three melancholic men in whose society she chiefly lived, her father was selfish and morose; Griggs was gentle, but silent and incomprehensible, though he exerted an undoubted influence over her; Reanda alone, though naturally melancholy, was at once gentle, companionable, and talkative with her.

Dalrymple accepted the intimacy with indifference and even with a certain satisfaction. In his reflexions, he characterized Reanda as a rare combination of the great artist and the gentleman. Since Gloria had known him she had grown more quiet. She admired him and imitated his manner. It was a good thing. He was glad, too, that Reanda was not married, for it would have been a nuisance, thought Dalrymple, to have the man's wife always about and expecting to be amused.

It began to occur to him that Reanda might be falling in love with Gloria, and he did not resent the idea. In fact, though at first sight it should have seemed strange to an Englishman, he looked upon the idea with favour. He wished to live out his life in Italy, for he had got that fierce affection for the country which has overcome and bound many northern men, from Sir John Hawkwood to Landor and Browning. Though he did not love Gloria, he was attached to her in his own way, and did not wish to lose sight of her altogether. But, in consequence of his own irregular marriage, he could not marry her to a man of his own rank in Rome, who would not fail to make inquiries about her mother. It was most natural that he should look upon such a man as Reanda with favour. Reanda had many good qualities. Dalrymple's judgment was generally keen enough about people, and he had understood that such a woman as Donna Francesca Campodonico would certainly not make a personal friend of a painter, and allow him to occupy rooms in her palace, unless his character were altogether above suspicion.

Gloria was, of course, too young to be married yet, though she seemed to be so entirely grown up and altogether a woman. In this respect Dalrymple was not prejudiced. His own mother had been married at the age of seventeen, and he had lived long in Italy, where early marriages were common enough. There could certainly be no serious objection to the match on that score, when another year should have passed.

Dalrymple's only anxiety about his daughter concerned her strong inclination to be a public singer. The prejudice was by no means extraordinary, and as a Scotchman, it had even more weight with him than it could have had, for instance, with an Italian. Reanda entirely agreed with him on this point, and when Gloria spoke of it, he never failed to draw a lively picture of the drawbacks attending stage life. The artist spoke very strongly, for one of Gloria's earliest and chiefest attractions in his eyes had been the certainty he felt that she belonged to Francesca's class. For that reason her flattering admiration had brought with it a peculiar savour, especially delightful to the taste of a man of humble origin. Dalrymple did not understand that, but he knew that if Gloria married the great painter, the latter would effectually keep her from the stage.

As for Griggs, the Scotchman was well aware that the poor young journalist might easily fall in love with the beautiful girl. But this did not deter him at all from having Griggs constantly at the house. Griggs was the only man he had ever met who did not bore him, who could be silent for an hour at a time, who could swallow as much strong wine as he without the slightest apparent effect upon his manner, who understood all he said, though sometimes saying things which he could not understand—in short, Griggs was a necessity to him. The young man was perhaps aware of the fact, and he found Dalrymple congenial to his own temper; but he was as excessively proud as he was extremely poor, at that time, and he managed to refuse the greater part of the hospitality offered to him, simply because he could not return it. It was very rarely that he accepted an invitation to a meal, though he now generally came in the evening, besides meeting Dalrymple almost every morning when they went to the bookseller's together.

He puzzled the Scotchman strangely. He was an odd combination of a thinker and an athlete, half literary man, half gladiator. The common phrase 'an old head on young shoulders' described him as well as any phrase could. The shoulders were perhaps the more remarkable, but the head was not to be despised. A man who could break a horseshoe and tear in two a pack of cards, and who spent his spare time in studying Hegel and Kant, when he was not writing political correspondence for newspapers, deserved to be considered an exception. He seemed to have no material wants, and yet he had the animal power of enjoying material things even in excess, which is rare. He had a couple of rooms in the Via della Frezza, between the Corso and the Ripetta, where he lived in a rather mysterious way, though he made no secret about it. Occasionally an acquaintance climbed the steep stairs, but no one ever got him to open the door nor to give any sign that he was at home, if he were within. A one-eyed cobbler acted as porter downstairs, from morning till night, astride upon his bench and ever at work, an ill-savoured old pipe in his mouth.

"You may try," he answered, when any one asked for Griggs. "Who knows? Perhaps Sor Paolo will open. Try a little, if you have patience."

Patience being exhausted, the visitor came down the five flights again, and remonstrated with the cobbler.

"I did not say anything," he would reply, in a cloud of smoke. "Many have tried. I told you to try. Am I to tell you that no one has ever got in? Why? To disoblige you? If you want anything of Sor Paolo, say it to me. Or come again."

"But he will not open," objected the visitor.

"Oh, that is true," returned the man of one eye. "But if you wish to try, I am not here to hinder you. This is the truth."

Now and then, some one more inquisitive suggested that there might be a lady in the question. The one eye then fixed itself in a vacant stare.

"Females?" the cobbler would exclaim. "Not even cats. What passes through your head? He is alone always. If you do not believe me, you can try. I do not say Sor Paolo will not open the door. A door is a door, to be opened."

"But since I have tried!"

"And I, what can I do? You have come, you have seen, you have knocked, and no one has opened. May the Madonna accompany you! I can do nothing."

So even the most importunate of visitors departed at last. But Griggs had taken Dalrymple up to his lodgings more than once, and they had sat there for an hour talking over books. Dalrymple observed, indeed, that Griggs was more inclined to talk in his own rooms than anywhere else, and that his manner then changed so much as to make him almost seem to be a different man. There was a look of interest in the stony mask, and there was a light in the deep-set eyes which neither wine nor wit could bring there at other times. The man wore his armour against the world, as it were, a tough shell made up of a poor man's pride, and solid with that sense of absolute physical superiority which is an element in the character of strong men, and which the Scotchman understood. He himself had been of the strong, but not always the strongest. Paul Griggs had never yet been matched by any man since he had first got his growth. He was the equal of many in intellect, but his bodily strength was not equalled by any in his youth and manhood. The secret of his one well-hidden vanity lay in that. His moral power showed itself in his assumed modesty about it, for it was almost impossible to prevail upon him to make exhibition of it. Gloria alone seemed able to induce him, for her especial amusement, to break a silver dollar with his fingers, or tear a pack of cards, and then only in the presence of her father or Reanda, but never before other people.

"You are the strongest man in the world, are you not?" she asked him once.

"Yes," he answered. "I probably am, if it is I. I am vain of it, but not proud of it. That makes me think sometimes that I am two men in one. That might account for it, you know."

"What nonsense!" Gloria laughed.

"Is it? I daresay it is." And he relapsed into indifference, so far as she could see.

"What is the other man like?" she asked. "Not the strong man of the two, but the other?"

"He is a good man. The strong man is bad. They fight, and the result is insignificance. Some day one of the two will get the better of the other."

"What will happen then?" she asked lightly, and still inclined to laugh.

"One or the other, or both, will die, I suppose," he answered.

"How very unpleasant!"

She did not at all understand what he meant. At the same time she could not help feeling that he was eminently a man to whom she would turn in danger or trouble. Girl though she was, she could not mistake his great admiration of her, and by degrees, as the winter wore on, she trusted him more, though he still repelled her a little, for his saturnine calm was opposed to her violent vitality, as a black rock to a tawny torrent. Griggs had neither the manner nor the temper which wins women's hearts as a rule. Such men are sometimes loved by women when their sorrow has chained them to the rock of horror, and grief insatiable tears out their broken hearts. But in their strength they are not loved. They cannot give themselves yet, for their strength hinders them, and women think them miserly of words and of love's little coin of change. If they get love at last, it is as the pity which the unhurt weak feel for the ruined strong.

Gloria was not above irritating Griggs occasionally, when the fancy took her to seek amusement in that way. She knew how to do it, and he rarely turned upon her, even in the most gentle way.

"We are good friends, are we not?" she asked one day, when it was raining and he was alone with her, waiting for her father to come in.

"I hope so," he answered, turning his impassive face slowly towards her.

"Then you ought to be much nicer to me," she said.

"I am as nice as I know how to be," replied Griggs, with fixed eyes. "What shall I do?"

"That is it. You ought to know. You could talk and say pleasant things, for instance. Don't you admit that you are very dull to-day?"

"I admit it. I regret it, and I wish I were not."

"You need not be. I am sure you can talk very well, when you please. You are not exactly funny at any time, but to-day you are funereal. You remind me of those big black horses they use for hearses, you know."

"Thank you, thank you," said Griggs, quietly, repeating the words without emphasis.

"I don't like you!" she exclaimed petulantly, but with a little laugh.

"I know that," he answered. "But I like you very much. We were probably meant to differ."

"Then you might amuse me. It's awfully dull when it rains. Pull the house down, or tear up silver scudi, or something."

"I am not Samson, and I am not a clown," observed Griggs, coldly.

"I shall never like you if you are so disagreeable," said Gloria, taking up a book, and settling herself to read.

"I am afraid you never will," answered Griggs, following her example.

A few minutes passed in silence. Then Gloria looked up suddenly.

"Mr. Griggs?"

"Yes?"

"I did not mean to be horrid."

"No, of course not."

"Because, if I were ever in trouble, you know—I should come straight to you."

"Thank you," he answered very gently. "But I hope you will never be in trouble. If you ever should be—" He stopped.

"Well?"

"I do not think you would find anybody who would try harder to help you," he said simply.

She wished that his voice would tremble, or that he would put out his hand towards her, or show something a little more like emotion. But she had to be satisfied.

"Would it be the good man or the bad man that would help me?" she asked, remembering the former conversation.

"Both," answered Griggs, without hesitation.

"I am not sure that I might not like the bad man better," said Gloria, almost to herself.

"Is Reanda a bad man?" inquired Griggs, slowly, and looking for the blush in her face.

"Why?" But she blushed, as he expected.

"Because you like him better than me."

"You are quite different. It is of no use to talk about it, and I want to read."

She turned from him and buried herself in her book, but she moved restlessly two or three times, and it was some minutes before the heightened colour disappeared from her face.

She was very girlish still, and when she had irritated Griggs as far as such a man was capable of irritation, she preferred to refuse battle rather than deal with the difficulty she had created. But Griggs understood, and amongst his still small sufferings he often felt the little, dull, hopeless pang which tells a man that he is unlovable.

CHAPTER XXIII

Very late, one night in the Carnival season, Paul Griggs was walking the streets alone. His sufferings were no longer so small as they had been, and the bitterness of solitude was congenial to him.

He had been at the house of a Spanish artist, where there had been dancing and music and supper and improvised tableaux. Gloria and her father and Reanda had all been there, too, and something had happened which had stirred the depths of the young man's slow temper. He hated to make an exhibition of himself, and much against his will he had been exhibited, as it were, to help the gaiety of the entertainment. Cotogni, the great sculptor, had suggested that Griggs should appear as Samson, asleep with his head on Delilah's knee, and bound by her with cords which he should seem to break as the Philistines rushed in. He had refused flatly, again and again, till all the noisy party caught the idea and forced him to it.

They had dressed him in silk draperies, his mighty arms bare almost to the shoulder, and they had given him a long, dark, theatrical wig. They had bound his arms and chest with cords, and had made him lie down and pretend to be asleep at the feet of the artist's beautiful wife. They had made slipping knots in the cords, so that he could easily wrench them loose. Then the curtain had been drawn aside, and there had been a pause as the tableau was shown. All at once a mob of artists, draped hastily in anything they could lay their hands upon, and with all manner of helmets on their heads from the Spaniard's collection, had rushed in.

"The Philistines are upon thee!" cried Delilah in a piercing voice.

He sprang to his feet, his legs being free, and he struggled with the cords. The knots would not slip as they were meant to do. The situation lasted several seconds, and was ridiculous enough.

People began to laugh.

"Cut off his hair!" cried one.

"Of what use was the wig?" laughed another, and every one tittered.

Griggs could hear Gloria's clear, high laugh above the rest. His blood slowly rose in his throat. But no one pulled the curtain across. The Philistines, young artists, mad with Carnival, improvised a very eccentric dance of triumph, and the laughter increased.

Griggs looked at the cords. Then his mask-like face turned slowly to the audience. Only the great veins swelled suddenly at his temples, while every one watched him in the general amusement. Suddenly his eyes flashed, and he drew a deep breath, for he was angry. In an instant there was dead silence in the room. A moment later one of the cords, drawn tight round his chest, over the silk robe, snapped like a thread, then another, and then a third. Then in a sort of frenzy of anger he savagely broke the whole cord into pieces with his hands, tossing the bits contemptuously upon the floor. His face was as white as a dead man's.

A roar of applause broke the silence when the guests realized what he had done. The artists seized him and carried him high in procession round the room, the women threw flowers at him, and some one struck up a triumphal march on the piano. It was an ovation. Half an hour later, dressed again in his ordinary clothes, he found himself next to Gloria.

"You told me the other day that you were not Samson," she said. "You see you can be when you choose."

"No," answered Griggs, coldly; "I am a clown."

What she had said was natural enough, but somehow the satisfaction of his bodily vanity had stung his moral pride beyond endurance. It seemed a despicable thing to be as vain as he was of a gift for which he had not paid any price. Deep down, too, he felt bitterly that he had never received the slightest praise for any thought of his which he had written down and sent to that cauldron of the English daily press in which all individual right to distinction disappears, with all claim to praise, from written matter, however good it be. He worked, he read, he studied, he wrote late, and rose early to observe. But his natural gift was to be a mountebank, a clown, a circus Hercules. By stiffening one of his senseless arms he could bring down roars of applause. By years of bitter labour with his pen he earned the barest living. The muscles that a porter might have, offered him opulence, because it was tougher by a few degrees than the flesh of other men. The knowledge he had striven for just kept him above absolute want.

He slipped away from the gay party as soon as he could. His last glance round the room showed him Angelo Reanda and Gloria, sitting in a corner apart. The girl's face was grave. There was a gentle and happy light in the artist's eyes which Griggs had never seen. That also was the strong man's portion.

Wrathfully he strode away from the house, under the dim oil lamps, an unlighted cigar between his teeth, his soft felt hat drawn over his eyes. He crossed the city towards the Pantheon and the Piazza Navona, his cigar still unlighted.

The streets were alive, though it was very late. There was more freedom to be gay and more hope of being simply happy in those days. Many men and women wandered about in bands of ten or a dozen, singing in soft voices, above which now and then rose a few ringing tenor notes. There was laughter everywhere in the air; tambourines drummed and thumped and jingled, guitars twanged, and mandolines tinkled and quavered. From a dark lane somewhere off the broader thoroughfare, a single voice sang out in serenade. The Corso was bright with unusual lights, and strewn with the birdseed and plaster-of-Paris 'confetti,' with yellow sand and sprigs of box leaves, and withering flowers, and there was about all the neighbourhood that peculiar smell of plaster and crushed flower-stalks which belonged then to the street carnival of Rome. Further on, in the dim quarters by the Tiber, the wine shops were all crowded, and men stood and drank outside on the pavement, and paid, and went laughing on, laughing and singing, singing and laughing, through the night.

Griggs felt the penetrating loneliness of him who cannot laugh amidst laughter, and it was congenial to him. He had always been alone, and he felt that the world held no companion for him. There was satisfaction in knowing that no one could ever guess what went on between his heart and his head.

He wandered on with the same even, untiring stride, for a long time, through the dark and winding ways, from the Pantheon through the old city, through Piazza Paganica and Costaguti to Piazza Montanara, where the carters and carriers congregate from the country. There, in the middle of the three-cornered open space, a flag in the paving marked the spot on which men used to be put to death. To-night even the carriers were making merry. Griggs was thirsty, and paused at the door of a wine shop. Though it was winter, men were sitting outside, for there was no more room within. A flaring torch of pitched rope was stuck in an iron ring, and shed an uncertain, smoky light upon the men's faces. A drawer in an apron brought Griggs a glass, and he drank standing.

"It makes no difference," said a rough voice in the little crowd. "They may cut off my head there on the paving-stone. They would do me a favour. If I find him, I kill him. An evil death on him and all his house!"

Griggs looked at the speaker without surprise, for he had often heard such things said. He saw an iron-grey man in good peasant's clothes of dark blue with broad silver buttons, a man with a true Roman face, a small aquiline nose, and keen, dark eyes. He turned away, and began to retrace his steps.

In half an hour he was at the door of the old Falcone inn, gone now like many relics of that day. It stood in the Piazza of Saint Eustace near the Pantheon, and in its time was the best of the old-fashioned eating-houses. Griggs felt suddenly hungry. He had walked seven or eight miles since he had left the party. He entered, and passed through the crowded rooms below and up the narrow steps to a small upper chamber, where he hoped to be alone. But there, also, every seat was taken.

To his surprise Dalrymple and Reanda were at the table furthest from him, in earnest conversation, with a measure of wine between them. Griggs had never seen the Italian there before, but the latter caught sight of him as he stood in the door, and rose to his feet, making a sign which meant that he was going away, and that the chair was vacant. Griggs came forward, and looked into his face as they met. There was the same gentle and happy light in Reanda's eyes which had been there when he was sitting with Gloria in the corner of the Spanish artist's drawing-room. Then Griggs understood and knew the truth, and guessed the meaning of the unaccustomed pressure of the hand as Reanda greeted him without speaking, and hurriedly went out.

Dalrymple had seen Griggs coming and was already calling to a man in a spotless white jacket for another glass and more wine. The Scotchman's bony face was haggard, but there was a little colour in his cheeks, and he seemed pleased.

"Sit down, Griggs," he said. "There are no more chairs, so we can keep the table to ourselves. I hope you are half as thirsty as I am."

"Rather more than half," answered the other, and he drank eagerly. "Give me some more, please," he said, holding out his glass.

"I see that you are in the right humour to hear good news," said the Scot. "Reanda is to marry my daughter in the summer."

"I congratulate you all three," said Griggs, slowly, for he had known what was coming. "Let us drink the health of the couple."

"By all means," answered Dalrymple, filling again. "By all means let us drink. I could not swallow that sweet stuff at Mendoza's. This is better. By all means let us drink as much as we can."

"That might mean a good deal," said Griggs, quickly, and he drained a third glass. "Were you ever drunk, Dalrymple?" he inquired gravely.

"No. I never was," answered the Scotchman.

"Nor I. This seems a fitting occasion for trying an experiment. We might try to get drunk."

"By all means, let us try," replied Dalrymple. "I have my doubts about the possibility of the thing, however."

"So have I."

They sat opposite to one another in silence for some minutes, each satisfied that the other was in earnest. Dalrymple solemnly filled the glasses and then leaned back in his chair.

"You did not seem much surprised by what I told you," he observed at last. "I suppose you expected it."

"Yes. It seemed natural enough, though it is not always the natural things that happen."

"I think they are suited to marry. Of course, Reanda is very much older, but he is comparatively a young man still."

"Comparatively. He will make a better husband for having had experience, I daresay."

"That depends on what experience he has had. When I first saw him I thought he was in love with Donna Francesca. It would have been like an artist. They are mostly fools. But I was mistaken. He worships at a distance."

"And she preserves the distance," Griggs remarked. "You are not drinking fair. My glass is empty."

Dalrymple finished his and refilled both.

"I have been here some time," he observed, half apologetically. "But as I was saying—or rather, as you were saying—Donna Francesca preserves the distance. These Italians do that admirably. They know the difference between intimacy and familiarity."

"That is a nice distinction," said Griggs. "I will use it in my next letter. No. Donna Francesca could never be familiar with any one. They learn it when they are young, I suppose, and it becomes a race-characteristic."

"What?" asked Dalrymple, abruptly.

"A certain graceful loftiness," answered the younger man.

The Scotchman's wrinkled eyelids contracted, and he was silent for a few moments.

"A certain graceful loftiness," he repeated slowly. "Yes, perhaps so. A certain graceful loftiness."

"You seem struck by the expression," said Griggs.

"I am. Drink, man, drink!" added Dalrymple, suddenly, in a different tone. "There's no time to be lost if we mean to drink enough to hurt us before those beggars go to bed."

"Never fear. They will be up all night. Not that it is a reason for wasting time, as you say."

He drank his glass and watched Dalrymple as the latter did likewise, with that deliberate intention which few but Scotchmen can maintain on such occasions. The wine might have been poured into a quicksand, for any effect it had as yet produced.

"Those race-characteristics of families are very curious," continued Griggs, thoughtfully.

"Are they?" Dalrymple looked at him suspiciously.

"Very. Especially voices. They run in families, like resemblance of features."

"So they do," answered the other, thoughtfully. "So they do."

He had of late years got into the habit of often repeating such short phrases, in an absent-minded way.

"Yes," said Griggs. "I noticed Donna Francesca's voice, the first time I ever heard it. It is one of those voices which must be inherited. I am sure that all her family have spoken as she does. It reminds me of something—of some one—"

Dalrymple raised his eyes suddenly again, as though he were irritated.

"I say," he began, interrupting his companion. "Do you feel anything? Anything queer in your head?"

"No. Why?"

"You are talking rather disconnectedly, that is all."

"Am I? It did not strike me that I was incoherent. Probably one half of me was asleep while the other was talking." He laughed drily, and drank again. "No," he said thoughtfully, as he set down his glass. "I feel nothing unusual in my head. It would be odd if I did, considering that we have only just begun."

"So I thought," answered Dalrymple.

He ordered more wine and relapsed into silence. Neither spoke again for a long time.

"There goes another bottle," said Dalrymple, at last, as he drained the last drops from the flagon measure. "Drink a little faster. This is slow work. We know the old road well enough."

"You are not inclined to give up the attempt, are you?" inquired Griggs, whose still face showed no change. "Is it fair to eat? I am hungry."

"Certainly. Eat as much as you like."

Griggs ordered something, which was brought after considerable delay, and he began to eat.

"We are not loquacious over our cups," remarked Dalrymple. "Should you mind telling me why you are anxious to get drunk to-night for the first time in your life?"

"I might ask you the same question," answered Griggs, cautiously.

"Merely because you proposed it. It struck me as a perfectly new idea. I have not much to amuse me, you know, and I shall have less when my daughter leaves me. It would be an amusement to lose one's head in some way."

"In such a way as to be able to get it back, you mean. I was walking this evening after the party, and I came to the Piazza Montanara. There is a big flagstone there on which people used to leave their heads for good."

"Yes. I have seen it. You cannot tell me much about Rome which I do not know."

"There were a lot of carriers drinking close by. It was rather grim, I thought. An old fellow there had a spite against somebody. You know how they talk. 'They may cut off my head there on the paving-stone,' the man said. 'If I find him, I kill him. An evil death on him and all his house!' You have heard that sort of thing. But the fellow seemed to be very much in earnest."

"He will probably kill his man," said Dalrymple.

Suddenly his big, loose shoulders shook a little, and he shivered. He glanced towards the window, suspecting that it might be open.

"Are you cold?" asked Griggs, carelessly.

"Cold? No. Some one was walking over my grave, as they say. If we varied the entertainment with something stronger, we should get on faster, though."

"No," said Griggs. "I refuse to mix things. This may be the longer way, but it is the safer."

And he drank again.

"He was a man from Tivoli, or Subiaco," he remarked presently. "He spoke with that accent."

"I daresay," answered Dalrymple, who looked down into his glass at that moment, so that his face was in shadow.

Just then four men who had occupied a table near the door rose and went out. It was late, even for a night in Carnival.

"I hope they are not going to leave us all to ourselves," said Dalrymple. "The place will be shut up, and we need at least two hours more."

"At least," assented Paul Griggs. "But they expect to be open all night. I think there is time."

The men at the other tables showed no signs of moving. They sat quietly in their places, drinking steadily, by sips. Some of them were eating roasted chestnuts, and all were talking more or less in low tones. Occasionally one voice or another rose above the rest in an exclamation, but instantly subsided again. Italians of that class are rarely noisy, for though the Romans drink deep, they generally have strong heads, and would be ashamed of growing excited over their wine.

The air was heavy, for several men were smoking strong cigars. The vaulted chamber was lighted by a single large oil lamp with a reflector, hung by a cord from the intersection of the cross-arches. The floor was of glazed white tiles, and the single window had curtains of Turkey red. It was all very clean and respectable and well kept, even at that crowded season, but the air was heavy with wine and tobacco, and the smell of cooked food,—a peculiar atmosphere in which the old-fashioned Roman delighted to sit for hours on holidays.

Dalrymple looked about him, moving his pale blue eyes without turning his head. The colour had deepened a little on his prominent cheek bones, and his eyes were less bright than usual. But his red hair, growing sandy with grey, was brushed smoothly back, and his evening dress was unruffled. He and Griggs were so evidently gentlemen, that some of the Italians at the other tables glanced at them occasionally in quiet surprise, not that they should be there, but that they should remain so long, and so constantly renew their order for another bottle of wine.

Giulio, the stout, dark drawer in a spotless jacket, moved about silently and quickly. One of the Italians glanced at Griggs and Dalrymple and then at the waiter, who also glanced at them quickly and then shrugged his shoulders almost perceptibly. Dalrymple saw both glances, and his eyes lighted up.

"I believe that fellow is laughing at us," he said to Griggs.

"There is nothing to laugh at," answered the latter, unmoved. "But of course, if you think so, throw him downstairs."

Dalrymple laughed drily.

"There is a certain calmness about the suggestion," he said. "It has a good, old-fashioned ring to it. You are not a very civilized young man, considering your intellectual attainments."

"I grew up at sea and before the mast. That may account for it."

"You seem to have crammed a good deal into a short life," observed Dalrymple. "It must have been a classic ship, where they taught Greek and Latin."

"The captain used to call her his Ship of Fools. As a matter of fact, it was rather classic, as you say. The old man taught us navigation and Greek verse by turns for five years. He was a university man with a passion for literature, but I never knew a better sailor. He put me ashore when I was seventeen with pretty nearly the whole of my five years' pay in my pocket, and he made me promise that I would go to college and stay as long as my money held out. I got through somehow, but I am not sure that I bless him. He is afloat still, and I write to him now and then."

"An Englishman, I suppose?"

"No. An American."

"What strange people you Americans are!" exclaimed Dalrymple, and he drank again. "You take up a profession, and you wear it for a bit, like a coat, and then change it for another," he added, setting down his empty glass.

"Very much like you Scotch," answered Griggs. "I have heard you say that you were a doctor once."

"A doctor—yes—in a way, for the sake of being a man of science, or believing myself to be one. My family was opposed to it," he continued thoughtfully. "My father told me it was his sincere belief that science did not stand in need of any help from me. He said I was more likely to need the help of science, like other lunatics. I will not say that he was not right."

He laughed a little and filled his glass.

"Poor Dalrymple!" he exclaimed softly, still smiling.

Paul Griggs raised his slow eyes to his companion's face.

"It never struck me that you were much to be pitied," he observed.

"No, no. Perhaps not. But I will venture to say that the point is debatable, and could be argued. 'To be, or not to be' is a question admirably calculated to draw out the resources of the intellect in argument, if you are inclined for that sort of diversion. It is a very good thing, a very good thing for a man to consider and weigh that question while he is young. Before he goes to sleep, you know, Griggs, before he goes to sleep."

"'For in that sleep of death, what dreams may come—'" Griggs quoted, and stopped.

"'When we have shuffled off this mortal coil.' You do not know your Shakespeare, young man."

"'Must give us pause,'" continued Griggs. "I was thinking of the dreams, not of the rest."

"Dreams? Yes. There will be dreams there. Dreams, and other things—'this ae night of all.' Not that my reason admits that they can be more than dreams, you know, Griggs. Reason says 'to sleep—no more.' And fancy says 'perchance to dream.' Well, well, it will be a long dream, that's all."

"Yes. We shall be dead a long time. Better drink now." And Griggs drank.

"'Fire and sleet and candle-light,
And Christ receive thy soul;'"

said Dalrymple, with a far-away look in his pale eyes. "Do you know the Lyke-Wake Dirge, Griggs? It is a grand dirge. Hark to the swing of it.

"'This ae night, this ae night,
Every night and all,
Fire and sleet and candle-light,
And Christ receive thy soul.'"

He repeated the strange words in a dull, matter-of-fact way, with a Scotch accent rarely perceptible in his conversation. Griggs listened. He had heard the dirge before, with all its many stanzas, and it had always had an odd fascination for him. He said nothing.

"It bodes no good to be singing a dirge at a betrothal," said the Scotchman, suddenly. "Drink, man, drink! Drink till the blue devils fly away. Drink—

"'Till a' the seas gang dry, my love,
Till a' the seas gang dry.'

Not that it is in the disposition of the Italian inn-keeper to give us time for that," he added drily. "As I was saying, I am of a melancholic temper. Not that I take you for a gay man yourself, Griggs. Drink a little more. It is my opinion that a little more will produce an agreeable impression upon you, my young friend. Drink a little more. You are too grave for so very young a man. I should not wish to be indiscreet, but I might almost take you for a man in love, if I did not know you better. Were you ever in love, Griggs?"

"Yes," answered Griggs, quietly. "And you, Dalrymple? Were you never in love?"

Dalrymple's loosely hung shoulders started suddenly, and his pale blue eyes set themselves steadily to look at Griggs. The red brows were shaggy, and there was a bright red spot on each cheek bone. He did not answer his companion's question, though his lips moved once or twice as though he were about to speak. They seemed unable to form words, and no sound came from them.

His anger was near, perhaps, and with another man it might have broken out. But the pale and stony face opposite him, and the deep, still eyes, exercised a quieting influence, and whatever words rose to his lips were never spoken. Griggs understood that he had touched the dead body of a great passion, sacred in its death as it must have been overwhelming in its life. He struck another subject immediately, and pretended not to have noticed Dalrymple's expression.

"I like your queer old Scotch ballads," he said, humouring the man's previous tendency to quote poetry.

"There's a lot of life in them still," answered Dalrymple, absently twisting his empty glass.

Griggs filled it for him, and they both drank. Little by little the Italians had begun to go away. Giulio, the fat, white-jacketed drawer, sat nodding in a corner, and the light from the high lamp gleamed on his smooth black hair as his head fell forward.

"There is a sincere vitality in our Scotch poets," said Dalrymple, as though not satisfied with the short answer he had given. "There is a very notable power of active living exhibited in their somewhat irregular versification, and in the concatenation of their ratiocinations regarding the three principal actions of the early Scottish life, which I take to have been birth, stealing, and a violent death."

"'But of these three charity is the greatest,'" observed Griggs, with something like a laugh, for he saw that Dalrymple was beginning to make long sentences, which is a bad sign for a Scotchman's sobriety.

"No," answered Dalrymple, with much gravity. "There I venture—indeed, I claim the right—to differ with you. For the Scotchman is hospitable, but not charitable. The process of the Scotch mind is unitary, if you will allow me to coin a word for which I will pay with my glass."

And he forthwith fulfilled the obligation in a deep draught. Setting down the tumbler, he leaned back in his chair and looked slowly round the room. His lips moved. Griggs could just distinguish the last lines of another old ballad.

"'Night and day on me she cries,
And I am weary of the skies
Since—'"

He broke off and shook himself nervously, and looked at Griggs, as though wondering whether the latter had heard.

"This wine is good," he said, rousing himself. "Let us have some more. Giulio!"

The fat waiter awoke instantly at the call, looked, nodded, went out, and returned immediately with another bottle.

"Is this the sixth or the seventh?" asked Dalrymple, slowly.

"Eight with Signor Reanda's," answered the man. "But Signor Reanda paid for his as he went out. You have therefore seven. It might be enough." Giulio smiled.

"Bring seven more, Giulio," said the Scotchman, gravely. "It will save you six journeys."

"Does the Signore speak in earnest?" asked the servant, and he glanced at Griggs, who was impassive as marble.

"You flatter yourself," said Dalrymple, impressively, to the man, "if you imagine that I would make even a bad joke to amuse you. Bring seven bottles." Giulio departed.

"That is a Homeric order," observed Griggs.

"I think—in fact, I am almost sure—that seven bottles more will produce an impression upon one of us. But I have a decidedly melancholic disposition, and I accustomed myself to Italian wine when I was very young. Melancholy people can drink more than others. Besides, what does such a bottle hold? I will show you. A tumbler to you, and one to me. Drink; you shall see."

He emptied his glass and poured the remainder of the bottle into it.

"Do you see? Half a tumbler. Two and a half are a bottle. Seven bottles are seventeen and a half glasses. What is that for you or me in a long evening? My blue devils are large. It would take an ocean to float them all. I insist upon going to bed in a good humour to-night, for once, in honour of my daughter's engagement. By the bye, Griggs, what do you think of Reanda?"

"He is a first-rate artist. I like him very well."

"A good man, eh? Well, well—from the point of view of discretion, Griggs, I am doing right. But then, as you may very wisely object, discretion is only a point of view. The important thing is the view, and not the point. Here comes Ganymede with the seven vials of wrath! Put them on the table, Giulio," he said, as the fat waiter came noiselessly up, carrying the bottles by the necks between his fingers, three in one hand and four in the other. "They make a fine show, all together," he observed thoughtfully, with his bony head a little on one side.

"And may God bless you!" said Giulio, solemnly. "If you do not die to-night, you will never die again."

"I regard it as improbable that we shall die more than once," answered Dalrymple. "I believe," he said, turning to Griggs, "that when men are drunk they make mistakes about money. We will pay now, while we are sober."

Griggs insisted on paying his share. They settled, and Giulio went away happy.

The two strong men sat opposite to each other, under the high lamp in the small room, drinking on and on. There was something terrifying in the Scotchman's determination to lose his senses—something grimly horrible in the younger man's marble impassiveness, as he swallowed glass for glass in time with his companion. His face grew paler still, and colder, but there was a far-off gleaming in the shadowy eyes, like the glimmer of a light over a lonely plain through the dark. Dalrymple's spirits did not rise, but he talked more and more, and his sentences became long and involved, and sometimes had no conclusion. The wine was telling on him at last. He had never been so strong as Griggs, at his best, and he was no match for him now. The younger man's strangely dual nature seemed to place his head beyond anything which could affect his senses.

Dalrymple talked on and on, rambling from one subject to another, and not waiting for any answer when he asked a question. He quoted long ballads and long passages from Shakespeare, and then turned suddenly off upon a scientific subject, until some word of his own suggested another quotation.

Griggs sat quietly in his seat, drinking as steadily, but paying little attention now to what the Scotchman said. Something had got hold of his heart, and was grinding it like grain between the millstones, grinding it to dust and ashes. He knew that he could not sleep that night. He might as well drink, for it could not hurt him. Nothing material had power to hurt him, it seemed. He felt the pain of longing for the utterly unattainable, knowing that it was beyond him forever. The widowhood of the unsatisfied is hell, compared with the bereavement of complete possession. He had not so much as told Gloria that he had loved her. How could he, being but one degree above a beggar? The unspoken words burned furrows in his heart, as molten metal scores smoking channels in living flesh. Gloria would laugh, if she knew. The torture made his face white. There was the scorn of himself with it, because a mere child could hurt him almost to death, and that made it worse. A mere child, barely out of the schoolroom, petulant, spoiled, selfish!

But she had the glory of heaven in her voice, and in her face the fatal beauty of her dead mother's deadly sin. He need not have despised himself for loving her. Her whole being appealed to that in man to which no woman ever appealed in vain since the first Adam sold heaven to Satan for woman's love.

Dalrymple, leaning on his elbow, one hand in his streaked beard, the other grasping his glass, talked on and quoted more and more.

"'The flame took fast upon her cheek,
Took fast upon her chin,
Took fast upon her fair body
Because of her deadly sin.'"

His voice dropped to a hoarse whisper at the last words, and suddenly, regardless of his companion, his hand covered his eyes, and his long fingers strained desperately on his bony forehead. Griggs watched him, thinking that he was drunk at last.

"Because of her deadly sin," he repeated slowly, and the tone changed. "There is no sin in it!" he cried suddenly, in a low voice, that had a distant, ghostly ring in it.

He looked up, and his eyes were changed, and Griggs knew that they no longer saw him.

"Stiff," he said softly. "Quite stiff. Dead two or three hours, I daresay. It stands up on its feet beside me—certainly dead two or three hours."

He nodded wisely to himself twice, and then spoke again in the same far-off tone, gazing past Griggs, at the wall.

"The clothes-basket is a silly idea. Besides, I should lose the night. Rather carry it myself—wrap it up in the plaid. She'll never know, when she has it on her head. Who cares?"

A long silence followed. One hand grasped the empty glass. The other lay motionless on the table. The blue eyes, with widely dilated pupils, stared at the wall, never blinking nor turning. But in the face there was the drawn expression of a bodily effort. Presently Griggs saw the fine beads of perspiration on the great forehead. Then the voice spoke again, but in Italian this time.

"You had better look away while I go by. It is not a pretty sight. No," he continued, changing to English, "not at all a pretty sight. Stiff as a board still."

The unwinking eyes dilated. The bright colour was gone from the cheek bones.

"It burns very well," he said again in Italian. The whole face quivered and the hard lips softened and kissed the air. "It is golden—I can see it in the dark—but I must cover it, darling. Quick—this way. At last! No—you cannot see the fire, but it is burning well, I am sure. Hold on! Hold the pommel of the saddle with both hands—so!"

The voice ceased. Griggs began to understand. He touched Dalrymple's sleeve, leaning across the table.

"I say!" he called softly. "Dalrymple!"

The Scotchman started violently, and the pupils of his eyes contracted. The empty glass in his right hand rattled on the hard wood. Then he smiled vaguely at Griggs.

"By Jove!" he exclaimed in his natural voice. "I think I must have been napping—'Sleep'ry Sim of the Lamb-hill, and snoring Jock of Suport-mill!' By Jove, Griggs, we have got near the point at last. One bottle left, eh? The seventh.

"'Then up and gat the seventh o' them,
And never a word spake he;
But he has striped his bright brown brand—'

The rest has no bearing upon the subject," he concluded, filling both glasses. "Griggs," he said, before he drank, "I am afraid this settles the matter."

"I am afraid it does," said Griggs.

"Yes. I had hopes a little while ago, which appeared well founded. But that unfortunate little nap has sent me back to the starting-point. I should have to begin all over again. It is very late, I fancy. Let us drink this last glass to our own two selves, and then give it up."

Something had certainly sobered the Scotchman again, or at least cleared his head, for he had not been drunk in the ordinary sense of the word.

"It cannot be said that we have not given the thing a fair trial," said Griggs, gloomily. "I shall certainly not take the trouble to try it again."

Nevertheless he looked at his companion curiously, as they both rose to their feet together. Dalrymple doubled his long arms as he stood up and stretched them out.

"It is curious," he said. "I feel as though I had been carrying a heavy weight in my arms. I did once, for some distance," he added thoughtfully, "and I remember the sensation."

"Very odd," said Griggs, lighting a cigar.

Giulio, sitting outside, half asleep, woke up as he heard the steady tread of the two strong men go by.

"If you do not die to-night, you will never die again!" he said, half aloud, as he rose to go in and clear the room where the guests had been sitting.

CHAPTER XXIV

During the first few months of their marriage Reanda and Gloria believed themselves happy, and really were, since there is no true criterion of man's happiness but his own belief in it. They took a small furnished apartment at the corner of the Macel de' Corvi, with an iron balcony overlooking the Forum of Trajan. They would have had no difficulty in obtaining other rooms adjoining the two Reanda had so long occupied in the Palazzetto Borgia, but Gloria was opposed to the arrangement, and Reanda did not insist upon it. The Forum of Trajan was within a convenient distance of the palace, and he went daily to his work.

"Besides," said Gloria, "you will not always be painting frescoes for Donna Francesca. I want you to paint a great picture, and send it to Paris and get a medal."

She was ambitious for him, and dreamed of his winning world-wide fame. She loved him, and she felt that Francesca had caged him, as Francesca herself had once felt. She wished to remove him altogether from the latter's influence, both because she was frankly jealous of his friendship for the older woman, and wished to have him quite to herself, and also in the belief that he could do greater things if he were altogether freed from the task of decorating the palace, which had kept him far too long in one limited sequence of production. There was, moreover, a selfish consideration of vanity in her view, closely linked with her unbounded admiration for her husband. She knew that she was beautiful, and she wished his greatest work to be a painting of herself.

Gloria, however, wished also to take a position in Roman society, and the only person who could help her and her husband to cross the line was Francesca Campodonico. It was therefore impossible for Gloria to break up the intimacy altogether, however much she might wish to do so. Meanwhile, too, Reanda had not finished his frescoes.

Soon after the marriage, which took place in the summer, Dalrymple left Rome, intending to be absent but a few months in Scotland, where his presence was necessary on account of certain family affairs and arrangements consequent upon the death of Lord Redin, the head of his branch of the Dalrymples, and of Lord Redin's son only a few weeks later, whereby the title went to an aged great-uncle of Angus Dalrymple's, who was unmarried, so that Dalrymple's only brother became the next heir.

Gloria was therefore quite alone with her husband. Paul Griggs had also left Rome for a time on business connected with his journalistic career. He had in reality been unwilling to expose himself to the unnecessary suffering of witnessing Gloria's happiness, and had taken the earliest opportunity of going away. Gloria herself was at first pleased by his departure. Later, however, she wished that he would come back. She had no one to whom she could turn when she was in need of any advice on matters which Reanda could not or would not decide.

Reanda himself was at first as absolutely happy as he had expected to be, and Francesca Campodonico congratulated herself on having brought about a perfectly successful match. While he continued to work at the Palazzetto Borgia, the two were often together for hours, as in former times. Gloria had at first come regularly in the course of the morning and sat in the hall while her husband was painting, but she had found it a monotonous affair after a while. Reanda could not talk perpetually. More than once, indeed, he introduced his wife's face amongst the many he painted, and she was pleased, though not satisfied. He could not make her one of the central figures which appeared throughout the series, because the greater part of the work was done already, and it was necessary to preserve the continuity of each resemblance. Gloria wished to be the first everywhere, though she did not say so.

Little by little, she came less regularly in the mornings. She either stayed at home and studied seriously the soprano parts of the great operas then fashionable, or invented small errands which kept her out of doors. She sometimes met Reanda when he left the palace, and they walked home together to their midday breakfast.

Little by little, also, Francesca fell into the habit of visiting Reanda in the great hall at hours when she was sure that Gloria would not be there. It was not that she disliked to see them together, but rather because she felt that Gloria was secretly antagonistic. There was a small, perpetual, unexpressed hostility in Gloria's manner which could not escape so sensitive a woman as Francesca. Reanda felt it, too, but said nothing. He was almost foolishly in love with his wife, and he was devotedly attached to Francesca herself. For the present he was very simple in his dealings with himself, and he quietly shut his eyes to the possibility of a disagreement between the two women, though he felt that it was in the air.

Instead of diminishing with his marriage, the obligations under which he was placed towards Donna Francesca were constantly increasing. She saw and understood his wife's social ambition, and gave herself trouble to satisfy it. Reanda felt this keenly, and while his gratitude increased, he inwardly wished that each kindness might be the last. But Gloria had the ambition and the right to be received in society on a footing of equality, and no one but Francesca Campodonico could then give her what she wanted.

She did not obtain what is commonly called social success, though many people received her and her husband during the following winter. She got admiration in plenty, and she herself believed that it was friendship. Of the two, Reanda, who had no social ambition at all, was by far the more popular. He was, as ever, quiet and unassuming, as became a man of his extraordinary talent. He so evidently preferred in society to talk with intelligent people rather than to make himself agreeable to the very great, that the very great tried to attract him to themselves, in order to appear intelligent in the eyes of others. They altogether forgot that he was the son of the steward of Gerano, though he sometimes spoke unaffectedly of his boyhood.

But Gloria reminded people too often that she had a right to be where she was, as the daughter of Angus Dalrymple, who might some day be Lord Redin. Fortunately for her, no one knew that Dalrymple had begun life as a doctor, and very far from such prospects as now seemed quite within the bounds of realization. But even as the possible Lord Redin, her father's existence did not interest the Romans at all. They were not accustomed to people who thought it necessary to justify their social position by allusions to their parentage, and since Francesca Campodonico had assured them that Dalrymple was a gentleman, they had no further questions to ask, and raised their eyebrows when Gloria volunteered information on the subject of her ancestors. They listened politely, and turned the subject as soon as they could, because it bored them.

But the admiration she got was genuine of its kind, as admiration and as nothing else. Her magnificent voice was useful to ancient and charitable princesses who wished to give concerts for the benefit of the deserving poor, but her face disturbed the hearts of those excellent ladies who had unmarried sons, and of other excellent ladies who had gay husbands. Her beauty and her voice together were a danger, and must be admired from a distance. Gloria and her husband were asked to many houses on important occasions. Gloria went to see the princesses and duchesses, and found them at home. Their cards appeared regularly at the small house in the Macel de' Corvi, but there was always a mystery as to how they got there, for the princesses and the duchesses themselves did not appear, except once or twice when Francesca Campodonico brought one of her friends with her, gently insisting that there should be a proper call. Gloria understood, and said bitter things about society when she was alone, and by degrees she began to say them to her husband.

"These Romans!" she exclaimed at last. "They believe that there is nobody like themselves!"

Angelo Reanda's face had a pained look, as he laid his long thin hand upon hers.

"My dear," he said gently. "You have married an artist. What would you have? I am sure, people have received us very well."

"Very well! Of course—as though we had not the right to be received well. But, Angelo—do not say such things—that I have married an artist—"

"It is quite true," he answered, with a smile. "I work with my hands. They do not. There is the difference."

"But you are the greatest artist in the world!" she cried enthusiastically, throwing her arms round his neck, and kissing him again and again. "It is ridiculous. In any other city, in London, in Paris, people would run after you, people would not be able to do enough for you. But it is not you; it is I. They do not like me, Angelo, I know that they do not like me! They want me at their big parties, and they want me to sing for them—but that is all. Not one of them wants me for a friend. I am so lonely, Angelo."

Her eyes filled with tears, and he tried to comfort her.

"What does it matter, my heart?" he asked, soothingly. "We have each other, have we not? I, who adore you, and you, who love me—"

"Love you? I worship you! That is why I wish you to have everything the world holds, everything at your feet."

"But I am quite satisfied," objected Reanda, with unwise truth. "Do not think of me."

She loved him, but she wished to put upon him some of her uncontrollable longing for social success, in order to justify herself. To please her, he should have joined in her complaint. Her tears dried suddenly, and her eyes flashed.

"I will think of you!" she cried. "I have nothing else to think of. You shall have it all, everything—they shall know what a man you are!"

"An artist, my dear, an artist. A little better than some, a little less good than others. What can society do for me?"

She sighed, and the colour deepened a little in her cheeks. But she hid her annoyance, for she loved him with a love at once passionate and intentional, compounded of reality and of a strong inborn desire for emotion, a desire closely connected with her longing for the life of the stage, but now suddenly thrown with full force into the channel of her actual life.

Reanda began to understand that his wife was not happy, and the certainty reacted strongly upon him. He became more sad and abstracted from day to day, when he was not with her. He longed, as only a man of such a nature can long, for a friend in whom he could confide, and of whom he could ask advice. He had such a friend, indeed, in Francesca Campodonico, but he was too proud to turn to her, and too deeply conscious that she had done all she could to give Gloria the social position the latter coveted.

Francesca, on her side, was not slow to notice that something was radically wrong. Reanda's manner had changed by degrees since his marriage. His pride made him more formal with the woman to whom he owed so much, and she felt that she could do nothing to break down the barrier which was slowly rising between them. She suffered, in her way, for she was far more sincerely attached to the man than she recognized, or perhaps would have been willing to recognize, when she allowed herself to look the situation fairly in the face. For months she struggled against anything which could make her regret the marriage she had made. But at last she admitted the fact that she regretted it, for it thrust itself upon her and embittered her own life. Then she became conscious in her heart of a silent and growing enmity for Gloria, and of a profound pity for Angelo Reanda. Being ashamed of the enmity, as something both sinful in her eyes, and beneath the nobility of her nature, she expressed it, if that were expression, by allowing her pity for the man to assert itself as it would. That, she told herself, was a form of charity, and could not be wrong, however she looked at it.

All mention of Gloria vanished from her conversation with Reanda when they were alone together. At such times she did her best to amuse him, to interest him, and to take him out of himself. At first she had little success. He answered her, and sometimes even entered into an argument with her, but as soon as the subject dropped, she saw the look of harassed preoccupation returning in his face. So far as his work was concerned, what he did was as good as ever. Francesca thought it was even better. But otherwise he was a changed man.

In the course of the winter Paul Griggs returned. One day Francesca was sitting in the hall with Reanda, when a servant announced that Griggs had asked to see her. She glanced at Reanda's face, and instantly decided to receive the American alone in the drawing-room, on the other side of the house.

"Why do you not receive him here?" asked Reanda, carelessly.

"Because—" she hesitated. "I should rather see him in the drawing-room," she added a moment later, without giving any further explanation.

Griggs told her that he had come back to stay through the year and perhaps longer. She took a kindly interest in the young man, and was glad to hear that he had improved his position and prospects during his absence. He rarely found sympathy anywhere, and indeed needed very little of it. But he was capable of impulse, and he had long ago decided that Francesca was good, discreet, and kind. He answered her questions readily enough, and his still face warmed a little while she talked with him. She, on her part, could not help being interested in the lonely, hard-working man who never seemed to need help of any kind, and was climbing through life by the strength of his own hands. There was about him at that time an air of reserved power which interested though it did not attract those who knew him.

Suddenly he asked about Gloria and her husband. There was an odd abruptness in the question, and a hard little laugh, quite unnecessary, accompanied it. Francesca noted the change of manner, and remembered how she had at first conceived the impression that Griggs admired Gloria, but that Gloria was repelled by him.

"I suppose they are radiantly happy," he said.

Francesca hesitated, being truthful by nature, as well as loyal. There was no reason why Griggs should not ask her the question, which was natural enough, but she had many reasons for not wishing to answer it.

"Are they not happy?" he asked quickly, as her silence roused his suspicions.

"I have never heard anything to the contrary," answered Francesca, dangerously accurate in the statement.

"Oh!" Griggs uttered the ejaculation in a thoughtful tone, but said no more.

"I hope I have not given you the impression that there is anything wrong," said Francesca, showing her anxiety too much.

"I saw Dalrymple in England," answered Griggs, with ready tact. "He seems very well satisfied with the match. By the bye, I daresay you have heard that Dalrymple stands a good chance of dying a peer, if he ever dies at all. With his constitution that is doubtful."

And he went on to explain to Francesca the matter of the Redin title, and that as Dalrymple's elder brother, though married, was childless, he himself would probably come into it some day. Then Griggs took his leave without mentioning Reanda or Gloria again. But Francesca was aware that she had betrayed Reanda's unhappiness to a man who had admired Gloria, and had probably loved her before her marriage. She afterwards blamed herself bitterly and very unjustly for what she had done.

Griggs went away, and called soon afterwards at the small house in the Macel de' Corvi. He found Gloria alone, and she was glad to see him. She told him that Reanda would also be delighted to hear of his return. Griggs, who wrote about everything which gave him an opportunity of using his very various knowledge, wrote also upon art, and besides the first article he had written about Reanda, more than a year previously, had, since then, frequently made allusion to the artist's great talent in his newspaper correspondence. Reanda was therefore under an obligation to the journalist, and Gloria herself was grateful. Moreover, Englishmen who came to Rome had frequently been to see Reanda's work in consequence of the articles. One old gentleman had tried to induce the artist to paint a picture for him, but had met with a refusal, on the ground that the work at the Palazzetto Borgia would occupy at least another year. The Englishman said he should come back and try again.

Between Griggs and Gloria there was the sort of friendly confidence which could not but exist under the circumstances. She had known him long, and he had been her father's only friend in Rome. She remembered him from the time when she had been a mere child, before her sudden transition to womanhood. She trusted him. She understood perfectly well that he loved her, but she believed that she had it in her power to keep his love as completely in the background as he himself had kept it hitherto. Her instinct told her also that Griggs might be a strong ally in a moment of difficulty. His reserved strength impressed her even more than it impressed Francesca Campodonico. She received him gladly, and told him to come again.

He came, and she asked him to dinner, feeling sure that Reanda would wish to see him. He accepted the first invitation and another which followed before long. By insensible degrees, during the winter, Griggs became very intimate at the house, as he had been formerly at Dalrymple's lodgings.

"That young man loves you, my dear," said Reanda, one day in the following spring, with a smile which showed how little anxiety he felt.

Gloria laughed gaily, and patted her husband's hand.

"What men like that call love!" she answered. "Besides—a journalist! And hideous as he is!"

"He certainly has not a handsome face," laughed Reanda. "I am not jealous," he added, with sudden gravity. "The man has done much for my reputation, too, and I know what I owe him. I have good reason for wishing to treat him well, and I am all the more pleased, if you find him agreeable."

He made the rather formal speech in a decidedly formal tone, and with the unconscious intention of justifying himself in some way, though he was far too simple by nature to suspect himself of any complicated motive. She looked at him, but did not quite understand.

"You surely do not suppose that I ever cared for him!" she said, readily suspecting that he suspected her.

He started perceptibly, and looked into her eyes. She was very truly in earnest, but her exaggerated self-consciousness had given her tone a colour which he did not recognize. Some seconds passed before he answered her. Then the gentle light came into his face as he realized how much he loved her.

"How foolish you are, love!" he exclaimed. "But Griggs is younger than I—it would not be so very unnatural if you had cared for him."

She broke out passionately.

"Younger than you! So am I, much younger than you! But you are young, too. I will not have you suggest that you are not young. Of course you are. You are unkind, besides. As though it could make the slightest difference to me, if you were a hundred years old! But you do not understand what my love for you is. You will never understand it. I wish I loved you less; I should be happier than I am."

He drew her to him, reluctant, and the pained look which Francesca knew so well came into his face.

"Are you unhappy, my heart?" he asked gently. "What is it, dear? Tell me!"

She was nervous, and the confession or complaint had been unintentional and the result of irritation more than of anything else. The fact that he had taken it up made matters much worse. She was in that state in which such a woman will make a mountain of a molehill rather than forego the sympathy which her constitution needs in a larger measure than her small sufferings can possibly claim.

"Oh, so unhappy!" she cried softly, hiding her face against his coat, and glad to feel the tears in her eyes.

"But what is it?" he asked very kindly, smoothing her auburn hair with one hand, while the other pressed her to him.

As he looked over her head at the wall, his face showed both pain and perplexity. He had not the least idea what to do, except to humour her as much as he could.

"I am so lonely, sometimes," she moaned. "The days are so long."

"And yet you do not come and sit with me in the mornings, as you used to do at first." There was an accent of regret in his voice.

"She is always there," said Gloria, pressing her face closer to his coat.

"Indeed she is not!" he cried, and she could feel the little breath of indignation he drew. "I am a great deal alone."

"Not half as much as I am."

"But what can I do?" he asked, in despair. "It is my work. It is her palace. You are free to come and go as you will, and if you will not come—"

"I know, I know," she answered, still clinging to him. "You will say it is my fault. It is just like a man. And yet I know that you are there, hour after hour, with her, and she is young and beautiful. And she loves you—oh, I know she loves you!"

Reanda began to lose patience.

"How absurd!" he exclaimed. "It is ridiculous. It is an insult to Donna Francesca to say that she is in love with me."

"It is true." Gloria suddenly raised her head and drew back from him a very little. "I am a woman," she said. "I know and I understand. She meant to sacrifice herself and make you happy, by marrying you to me, and now she regrets it. It is enough to see her. She follows you with her eyes as you move, and there is a look in them—"

Reanda laughed, with an effort.

"It is altogether too absurd!" he said. "I do not know what to say. I can only laugh."

"Because you know it is true," answered Gloria. "It is for your sake that she has done it all, that she makes such a pretence of being friendly to me, that she pushes us into society, and brings her friends here to see me. They never come unless she brings them," she added bitterly. "There is no fear of that. The Duchess of Astrardente would not have her black horses seen standing in the Macel de' Corvi, unless Donna Francesca made her do it and came with her."

"Why not?" asked Reanda, simply, for his Italian mind did not grasp the false shame which Gloria felt in living in a rather humble neighbourhood.

"She would not have people know that she had friends living in such a place," Gloria answered.

Unwittingly she had dealt Reanda a deadly thrust.

He had fallen in love with her and had married her on the understanding with himself, so to say, that she was in all respects as much a great lady as Donna Francesca herself, and he had taken it for granted that she must be above such pettiness. The lodging was extremely good and had the advantage of being very conveniently situated for his work. It had never struck him that because it was in an unfashionable position, Gloria could imagine that the people she knew would hesitate to come and see her. Since their marriage she had done and said many little things which had shaken his belief in the thoroughness of her refinement. She had suddenly destroyed that belief now, by a single foolish speech. It would be hard to build it up again.

Like many men of genius he could not forgive his own mistake, and Gloria was involved in this one. Moreover, as an Italian, he fancied that she secretly suspected him of meanness, and when Italians are not mean, there is nothing which they resent more than being thought to be so. He had plenty of money, for he had always lived very simply before his marriage, and Dalrymple gave Gloria an allowance.

His tone changed, when he answered her, but she was far from suspecting what she had done.

"We will get another apartment at once," he said quietly.

"No," she answered at once, protesting, "you must not do anything of the kind! What an idea! To change our home merely because it is not on the Corso or the Piazza di Venezia!"

"You would prefer the Corso?" inquired Angelo. "That is natural. It is more gay."

The reflexion that the view of the deserted Forum of Trajan was dull suggested itself to him as a Roman, knowing the predilection of Roman women of the middle class for looking out of the window.

"It is ridiculous!" cried Gloria. "You must not think of it. Besides—the expense—"

"The expense does not enter into the question, my dear," he answered, having fully made up his mind. "You shall not live in a place to which you think your friends may hesitate to come."

"Friends! They are not my friends, and they never mean to be," she replied more hotly. "Why should I care whether they will take the trouble to come and see me or not? Let them stay away, if I am not good enough for them. Tell Donna Francesca not to bring them—not to come herself any more. I hate to feel that she is thrusting me down the throat of a society that does not want me! She only does it to put me under an obligation to her. I am sure she talks about me behind my back and says horrid things—"

"You are very unjust," said Reanda, hurt by the vulgarity of the speech and deeply wounded in his own pride.

"You defend her! You see!" And the colour rose in Gloria's cheeks.

"She has done nothing that needs defence. She has acted always with the greatest kindness to me and to us. You have no right to suppose that she says unkind things of you when you are not present. I cannot imagine what has come over you to-day. It must be the weather. It is sirocco."

Gloria turned away angrily, thinking that he was laughing at her, whereas the suggestion about the weather was a perfectly natural one in Rome, where the southeast wind has an undoubted effect upon the human temper.

But the seeds of much discussion were sown on that close spring afternoon. Reanda was singularly tenacious of small purposes, as he was of great ideas where his art was concerned, and his nature though gentle was unforgiving, not out of hardness, but because he was so sensitive that his illusions were easy to destroy.

He went out and forthwith began to search for an apartment of which his wife should have no cause to complain. In the course of a week he found what he wanted. It was a part of the second floor of one of the palaces on the Corso, not far from the Piazza di Venezia. It was partially furnished, and without speaking to Gloria he had it made comfortable within a few days. When it was ready, he gave her short warning that they were to move immediately.

Strange to say, Gloria was very much displeased, and did not conceal her annoyance. She really liked the small house in the Macel de' Corvi, and resented the way in which her husband had taken her remarks about the situation. To tell the truth, Reanda had deceived himself with the idea that she would be delighted at the change, and had spent money rather lavishly, in the hope of giving her a pleasant surprise. He was proportionately disappointed by her unexpected displeasure.

"What was the use of spending so much money?" she asked, with a discontented face. "People will not come to see us because we live in a fine house."

"I did not take the house with that intention, my dear," said Reanda, gently, but wounded and repelled by the remark and the tone.

"Well then, we might have stayed where we were," she answered. "It was much cheaper, and there was more sun for the winter."

"But this is gayer," objected Reanda. "You have the Corso under the window."

"As though I looked out of the window!" exclaimed Gloria, scornfully. "It was so nice—our little place there."

"You are hard to please, my dear," said the artist, coldly.

Then she saw that she had hurt him, which she had not meant to do. Her own nature was self-conscious and greedy of emotion, but not sensitive. She threw her arms round him, and kissed him and thanked him.

But Reanda was not satisfied. Day by day when Francesca looked at him, she saw the harassed expression deepening in his face, and she felt that every furrow was scored in her own heart. And she, in her turn, grew very grave and thoughtful.

CHAPTER XXV

Paul Griggs was a man compounded of dominant qualities and dormant contradictions of them which threatened at any moment to become dominant in their turn for a time. He himself almost believed that he had two separate individualities, if not two distinct minds.

It may be doubted whether it can be good for any man to dwell long upon such an idea in connexion with himself, however distinctly he may see in others the foundation of truth on which it rests. To Griggs, however, it presented itself so clearly that he found it impossible not to take it into consideration in the more important actions of his life. The two men were very sharply distinguished in his thoughts. The one man would do what the other would not. The other could think thoughts above the comprehension of the first.

The one was material, keen, strong, passionate, and selfish; pre-eminently adapted for hard work; conscientious in the force of its instinct to carry out everything undertaken by it to the very end, and judging that whatever it undertook was good and worth finishing; having something of the nature of a strong piece of clockwork which being wound up must run to the utmost limit before stopping, whether regulated to move fast or slow, with a fateful certainty independent of will; possessed of such uncommon strength as to make it dangerous if opposed while moving, and at the same time having an extraordinary inertia when not wound up to do a certain piece of work; self-reliant to a fault, as the lion is self-reliant in the superiority of physical endowment; gentle when not opposed, because almost incapable of action without a determinate object and aim; but developing an irresistible momentum when the inertia was overcome; thorough, in the sense in which the tide is thorough, in rising evenly and all at the same time, and as ruthless as the tide because it was that part of the whole man which was a result, and which, therefore, when once set in motion was almost beyond his control; reasonable only because, as a result, it followed its causes logically, and required a real cause to move it at first.

The other man in him was very different, almost wholly independent of the first, and very generally in direct conflict with it, at that time. It was an imaginative and meditative personality, easily deceived into assuming a false premise, but logical beyond all liability to deception when reasoning from anything it had accepted. Its processes were intuitively correct and almost instantaneous, while its assumptions were arbitrary in the extreme. It might begin to act at any point whatsoever, and unlike the material man, which required a will to move it at first, it struck spontaneously with the directness of straight lightning from one point to another, never misled in its path, though often fatally mistaken in the value of the points themselves.

Most men who have thought much, wisely or foolishly, and who have seen much, good or bad, are more or less conscious of their two individualities. Idle and thoughtless people are not, as a rule. With Griggs, the two were singularly distinct and independent. Sometimes it seemed to him that he sat in judgment, as a third person, between them. At other moments he felt himself wholly identified with the one and painfully aware of the opposition of the other. The imaginative part of him despised the material part for its pride of life and lust of living. The material part laughed to scorn the imaginative one for its false assumptions and unfounded beliefs. When he could abstract himself from both, he looked upon the intuitive personality as being himself in every true sense of the word, and upon the material man as a monstrous overgrowth and encumbrance upon his more spiritual self.

When he began to love Gloria Dalrymple, she appealed to both sides of his nature. For once, the spiritual instinct coincided with the direction given to the material man by a very earthly passion.

The cause of this was plain enough and altogether simple. The spiritual instinct had taken the lead. He had known Gloria before she had been a woman to be loved. The maiden genius of the girl had spoken to the higher man from a sphere above material things, and had created in him one of those assumed premises for subsequent spiritual intuition from which he derived almost the only happiness he knew. Then, all at once, the woman had sprung into existence, and her young beauty had addressed itself to the young gladiator with overwhelming force. The woman fascinated him, and the angelic being his imagination had assumed in the child still enchanted him.

He was not like Reanda; for his sensitiveness was one-sided, and therefore only half vulnerable. Gloria's faults were insignificant accidents of a general perfectness, the result of having arbitrarily assumed a perfect personality. They could not make the path of his spiritual intuitive love waver, and they produced no effect at all against his direct material passion. To destroy the prime beautiful illusion, something must take place which would upset the mistaken assumption from a point beyond it, so to say. As for the earthly part of his love, it was so strong that it might well stand alone, even if the other should disappear altogether.

Then came honour, and the semi-religious morality of the man, defending the woman against him, for the sake of the angel he saw through her. Chief of all, in her defence, stood his own conviction that she did not love him, and never would, nor ever could. To all intents and purposes, too, he had been her father's friend, though between the two men there had been little but the similarity of their gloomy characters. It was the will of the material man to be governed, and as no outward influence set it in motion, it remained inert, in unstable equilibrium, as a vast boulder may lie for ages on the very edge of a precipice, ready but not inclined to fall. There was fatality in its stillness, and in the certainty that if moved it must crash through everything it met.

Gloria had not the least understanding of the real man. She thought about him often during the months which followed his return, and a week rarely passed in which she did not see him two or three times. Her thoughts of him were too ignorant to be confused. She was conscious, rather than aware, that he loved her, but it seemed quite natural to her, at her age, that he should never express his love by any word or deed.

But she compared him with her husband, innocently and unconsciously, in matters where comparison was almost unavoidable. His leonine strength of body impressed her strongly, and she felt his presence in the room, even when she was not looking at him. Reanda was physically a weak and nervous man. When he was painting, the movements of his hand seemed to be independent of his will and guided by a superior unseen power, rather than directed by his judgment and will. Paul Griggs never made the slightest movement which did not strike Gloria as the expression of his will to accomplish something. He was wonderfully skilful with his hands. Whatever he meant to do, his fingers did, forthwith, unhesitatingly. His mental processes were similar, so far as she could see. If she asked him a question, he answered it categorically and clearly, if he were able. If not, he said so, and relapsed into silence, studying the problem, or trying to force his memory to recall a lost item. Reanda, on the other hand, answered most questions with the expression of a vague opinion, often right, but apparently not founded on anything particular. The accuracy of Griggs sometimes irritated the artist perceptibly, in conversation; but he took an interest in what Griggs wrote, and made Gloria translate many of the articles to him, reading aloud in Italian from the English. Strange to say, they pleased him for the very qualities which he disliked in the man's talk. The Italian mind, when it has developed favourably, is inclined to specialism rather than to generalization, and Griggs wrote of many things as though he were a specialist. He had enormous industry and great mechanical power of handling language.

"I have no genius," he said one day to Gloria, when she had been admiring something he had written, and using the extravagant terms of praise which rose easily to her lips. "Your husband has genius, but I have none. Some day I shall astonish you all by doing something very remarkable. But it will not be a work of genius."

It was in the late autumn days, more than a year and a half after Gloria's marriage. The southeast wind was blowing down the Corso, and the pavements were yellow and sticky with the moistened sand-blast from the African desert. The grains of sand are really found in the air at such times. It is said that the undoubted effect of the sirocco on the temper of Southern Italy is due to the irritation caused by inhaling the fine particles with the breath. Something there is in that especial wind, which changes the tempers of men and women very suddenly and strangely.

Gloria and her companion were seated in the drawing-room that afternoon, and the window was open. The wind stirred the white curtains, and now and then blew them inward and twisted them round the inner ones, which were of a dark grey stuff with broad brown velvet bands, in a fashion then new. Gloria had been singing, and sat leaning sideways on the desk of the grand piano. A tall red Bohemian glass stood beside the music on one of the little sliding shelves meant for the candles, and there were a few flowers in it, fresh an hour ago, but now already half withered and drooping under the poisonous breath of the southeast. The warm damp breeze came in gusts, and stirred the fading leaves and Gloria's auburn hair, and the sheet of music upright on the desk. Griggs sat in a low chair not far from her, his still face turned towards her, his shadowy eyes fixed on her features, his sinewy hands clasped round his crossed knees. The nature of the great athlete showed itself even in repose—the broad dark throat set deep in the chest, the square solidity of the shoulders, the great curved lines along the straightened arms, the small, compact head, with its close, dark hair, bent somewhat forward in the general relaxation of the resting muscles. In his complete immobility there was the certainty of instant leaping and flash-like motion which one feels rather than sees in the sleeping lion.

Gloria looked at him thoughtfully with half-closed lids.

"I shall surprise you all," he repeated slowly, "but it will not be genius."

"You will not surprise me," Gloria answered, still meeting his eyes. "As for genius, what is it?"

"It is what you have when you sing," said Griggs. "It is what Reanda has when he paints."

"Then why not what you do when you write?"

"The difference is simple enough. Reanda does things well because he cannot help it. When I do a thing well it is because I work so hard at it that the thing cannot help being done by me. Do you understand?"

"I always understand what you tell me. You put things so clearly. Yes, I think I understand you better than you understand yourself."

Griggs looked down at his hands and was silent for a moment. Mechanically he moved his thumb from side to side and watched the knot of muscle between it and the forefinger, as it swelled and disappeared with each contraction.

"Perhaps you do understand me. Perhaps you do," he said at last. "I have known you a long time. It must be four years, at least—ever since I first came here to work. It has been a long piece of life."

"Indeed it has," Gloria answered, and a moment later she sighed.

The wind blew the sheet of music against her. She folded it impatiently, threw it aside and resumed her position, resting one elbow on the narrow desk. The silence lasted several seconds, and the white curtains flapped softly against the heavy ones.

"I wonder whether you understand my life at all," she said presently.

"I am not sure that I do. It is a strange life, in some ways—like yourself."

"Am I strange?"

"Very."

"What makes you think so?"

Again he was silent for a time. His face was very still. It would have been impossible to guess from it that he felt any emotion at the moment.

"Do you like compliments?" he asked abruptly.

"That depends upon whether I consider them compliments or not," she answered, with a little laugh.

"You are a very perfect woman in very imperfect surroundings," said Griggs.

"That is not a compliment to the surroundings, at all events. I do not know whether to laugh or not. Shall I?"

"If you will. I like to hear you laugh."

"You should hear me cry!" And she laughed again at herself.

"God forbid!" he said gravely.

"I do sometimes," she answered, and her face grew suddenly sad, as he watched her.

He felt a quick pain for her in his heart.

"I am sorry you have told me so," he said. "I do not like to think of it. Why should you cry? What have you to cry for?"

"What should you think?" she asked lightly, though no smile came with the words.

"I cannot guess. Tell me. Is it because you still wish to be a singer? Is that it?"

"No. That is not it."

"Then I cannot guess." He looked for the answer in her face. "Will you tell me?" he asked after a pause.

"Of what use could it be?" Her eyes met his for a moment, the lids fell, and she turned away. "Will you shut the window?" she said suddenly. "The wind blows the things about. Besides, it is getting late."

He rose and went to the window. She watched him as he shut it, turning his back to her, so that his figure stood out distinct and black against the light. She realized what a man he was. With those arms and those shoulders he could do anything, as he had once caught her in the air and saved her life, and then, again, as he had broken the cords that night at Mendoza's house. There was nothing physical which such a man could not do. He was something on which to rely in her limited life, an absolute contrast to her husband, whose vagueness irritated her, while his deadness of sensibility, where she had wrung his sensitiveness too far, humiliated her in her own eyes. She had kept her secret long, she thought, though she had kept it for the simple reason that she had no one in whom to confide.

Griggs came back from the window and sat down near her again in the low chair, looking up into her face.

"Mr. Griggs," she said, turning from his eyes and looking into the piano, "you asked me a question just now. I should like to answer it, if I were quite sure of you."

"Are you not sure of me?" he asked. "I think you might be, by this time. We were just saying that we had known each other so long."

"Yes. But—all sorts of things have happened in that time, you know. I am not the same as I was when I first knew you."

"No. You are married. That is one great difference."

"Too great," said she. "Honestly, do you think me improved since my marriage?"

"Improved? No. Why should you improve? You are just what you were meant to be, as you always were."

"I know. You called me a perfect woman a little while ago, and you said my surroundings were imperfect. You must have meant that they did not suit me, or that I did not suit them. Which was it?"

"They ought to suit you," said Griggs. "If they do not, it is not your fault."

"But I might have done something to make them suit me. I sometimes think that I have not treated them properly."

"Why should you blame yourself? You did not make them, and they cannot unmake you. You have a right to be yourself. Everybody has. It is the first right. Your surroundings owe you more than you owe to them, because you are what you are, and they are not what they ought to be. Let them bear the blame. As for not treating them properly, no one could accuse you of that."

"I do not know—some one might. People are so strange, sometimes."

She stopped, and he answered nothing. Looking down into the open piano, she idly watched the hammers move as she pressed the keys softly with one hand.

"Some people are just like this," she said, smiling, and repeating the action. "If you touch them in a certain way, they answer. If you press them gently, they do not understand. Do you see? The hammer comes just up to the string, and then falls back again without making any noise. I suppose those are my surroundings. Sometimes they answer me, and sometimes they do not. I like things I can be sure of."

"And by things you mean people," suggested Griggs.

"Of course."

"And by your surroundings you mean—what?"

"You know," she answered in a low voice, turning her face still further away from him.

"Reanda?"

She hesitated for a moment, knowing that her answer must have weight on the man.

"I suppose so," she said at last. "I ought not to say so—ought I? Tell me the truth."

"The truth is, you are unhappy," he answered slowly. "There is no reason why you should not tell me so. Perhaps I might help you, if you would let me."

He almost regretted that he had said so much, little as it was. But she had wished him to say it, and more, also. Still turning from him, she rested her chin in her hand. His face was still, but there was the beginning of an expression in it which she had never seen. Now that the window was shut it was very quiet in the room, and the air was strangely heavy and soft and dim. Now and then the panes rattled a little. Griggs looked at the graceful figure as Gloria sat thinking what she should say. He followed the lines till his eyes rested on what he could see of her averted face. Then he felt something like a sharp, quick blow at his temples, and the blood rose hot to his throat. At the same instant came the bitter little pang he had known long, telling him that she had never loved him and never could.

"Are you really my friend?" she asked softly.

"Yes." The word almost choked him, for there was not room for it and for the rest.

She turned quietly and surveyed the marble mask with curious inquiry.

"Why do you say it like that," she asked; "as though you would rather not? Do you grudge it?"

"No." He spoke barely above his breath.

"How you say it!" she exclaimed, with a little laugh that could not laugh itself out, for there was a strange tension in the air, and on her and on him. "You might say it better," she added, the pupils of her eyes dilating a little so that the room looked suddenly larger and less distinct.

She knew the sensation of coming emotion, and she loved it. She had never thought before that she could get it by talking with Paul Griggs. He did not answer her.

"Perhaps you meant it," she said presently. "I hardly know. Did you?"

"Please be reasonable," said Griggs, indistinctly, and his hands gripped each other on his knee.

"How oddly you talk!" she exclaimed. "What have I said that was unreasonable?"

She felt that the emotion she had expected was slipping from her, and her nerves unconsciously resented the disappointment. She was out of temper in an instant.

"You cannot understand," he answered. "There is no reason why you should. Forgive me. I am nervous to-day."

"You? Nervous?" She laughed again, with a little scorn. "You are not capable of being nervous."

She was dimly conscious that she was provoking him to something, she knew not what, and that he was resisting her. He did not answer her last words. She went back to the starting-point again, dropping her voice to a sadder key.

"Honestly, will you be my friend?" she asked, with a gentle smile.

"Heart and soul—and hand, too, if you want it," he said, for he had recovered his speech. "Tell me what the trouble is. If I can, I will take you out of it."

It was rather an odd speech, and she was struck by the turn of the phrase, which expressed more strength than doubt of power to do anything he undertook.

"I believe you could," she said, looking at him. "You are so strong. You could do anything."

"Things are never so hard as they look, if one is willing to risk everything," he answered. "And when one has nothing to lose," he added, as an after-thought.

She sighed, and turned away again, half satisfied.

"There is nothing to risk," she said. "It is not a case of danger. And you cannot take my trouble and tear it up like a pack of cards with those hands of yours. I wish you could. I am unhappy—yes, I have told you so. But what can you do to help me? You cannot make my surroundings what they are not, you know."

"No—I cannot change your husband," said Griggs.

She started a little, but still looked away.

"No. You cannot make him love me," she said, softly and sadly.

The big hands lost their hold on one another, and the deep eyes opened a little wider. But she was not watching him.

"Do you mean to say—" He stopped.

She slowly bent her head twice, but said nothing.

"Reanda does not love you?" he said, in wondering interrogation. "Why—I thought—" He hesitated.

"He cares no more for me than—that!" The hand that stretched towards him across the open piano tapped the polished wood once, and sharply.

"Are you in serious earnest?" asked Griggs, bending forward, as though to catch her first look when she should turn.

"Does any one jest about such things?" He could just see that her lips curled a little as she spoke.

"And you—you love him still?" he asked, with pressing voice.

"Yes—I love him. The more fool I."

The words did not grate on him, as they would have jarred on her husband's ear. The myth he had imagined made perfections of the woman's faults.

"It is a pity," he said, resting his forehead in his hand. "It is a deadly pity."

Then she turned at last and saw his attitude.

"You see," she said. "There is nothing to be done. Is there? You know my story now. I have married a man I worship, and he does not care for me. Take it and twist it as you may, it comes to that and nothing else. You can pity me, but you cannot help me. I must bear it as well as I can, and as long as I must. It will end some day—or I will make it end."

"For God's sake do not talk like that!"

"How should I talk? What should I say? Is it of any use to speak to him? Do you think I have not begged him, implored him, besought him, almost on my knees, to give up that work and do other things?"

Griggs looked straight into her eyes a moment and then almost understood what she meant.

"You mean that he—that when he is painting there—" He hesitated.

"Of course. All day long. All the bitter live-long day! They sit there together on pretence of talking about it. You know—you can guess at least—it is the old, old story, and I have to suffer for it. She could not marry him—because she is a princess and he an artist—good enough for me—God knows, I love him! Too good for her, ten thousand times too good! But yet not good enough for her to marry! He needed a wife, and she brought us together, and I suppose he told her that I should do very well for the purpose. I was a good subject. I fell in love with him—that was what they wanted. A wife for her favourite! O God! When I think of it—"

She stopped suddenly and buried her face in both her hands, as she leaned upon the piano.

"It is not to be believed!" The strong man's voice vibrated with the rising storm of anger.

She looked up again with flashing eyes and pale cheeks.

"No!" she cried. "It is not to be believed! But you see it now. You see what it all is, and how my life is wrecked and ruined before it is half begun. It would be bad enough if I had married him for his fame, for his face, for his money, for anything he has or could have. But I married him because I loved him with all my soul, and worshipped him and everything he did."

"I know. We all saw it."

"Of course—was it anything to hide? And I thought he loved me, too. Do you know?" She grew more calm. "At first I used to go and sit in the hall when he was at work. Then he grew silent, and I felt that he did not want me. I thought it was because he was such a great artist, and could not talk and work, and wanted to be alone. So I stayed away. Then, once, I went there, and she was there, sitting in that great chair—it shows off the innocence of her white face, you know! The innocence of it!" Gloria laughed bitterly. "They were talking when I came, and they stopped as soon as the door opened. I am sure they were talking about me. Then they seemed dreadfully uncomfortable, and she went away. After that I went several times. Once or twice she came in while I was there. Then she did not come any more. He must have told her, of course. He kept looking at the door, though, as if he expected her at any moment. But she never came again in those days. I could not bear it—his trying to talk to me, and evidently wishing all the time that she would come. I gave up going altogether at last. What could I do? It was unbearable. It was more than flesh and blood could stand."

"I do not wonder that you hate her," said Griggs. "I have often thought you did."

Gloria smiled sadly.

"Yes," she answered. "I hate her with all my heart. She has robbed me of the only thing I ever had worth having—if I ever had it. I sometimes wonder—or rather, no. I do not wonder, for I know the truth well enough. I have been over and over it again and again in the night. He never loved me. He never could love any one but her. He knew her long ago, and has loved her all his life. Why should he put me in her place? He admired me. I was a beautiful plaything—no, not beautiful—" She paused.

"You are the most beautiful woman in the world," said Paul Griggs, with deep conviction.

He saw the blush of pleasure in her face, saw the fluttering of the lids. But he neither knew that she had meant him to say it, nor did he judge of the vast gulf her mind must have instantaneously bridged, from the outpouring of her fancied injuries and of her hatred for Francesca Campodonico, to the unconcealable satisfaction his words gave her.

"I have heard him say that, too," she answered a moment later. "But he did not mean it. He never meant anything he said to me—not one word of it all. You do not know what that means," she went on, working herself back into a sort of despairing anger again. "You do not know. To have built one's whole life on one thing, as I did! To have believed only one thing, as I did! To find that it is all gone, all untrue, all a wretched piece of acting—oh, you do not know! That woman's face haunts me in the dark—she is always there, with him, wherever I look, as they are together now at her house. Do you understand? Do you know what I feel? You pity me—but do you know? Oh, I have longed for some one—I have wished I had a dog to listen to me—sometimes—it is so hard to be alone—so very hard—"

She broke off suddenly and hid her face again.

"You are not alone. You have me—if you will have me."

Before he had finished speaking the few words, the first sob broke, violent, real, uncontrollable. Then came the next, and then the storm of tears. Griggs rose instinctively and came to her side. He leaned heavily on the piano, bending down a little, helpless, as some men are at such moments. She did not notice him, and her sobs filled the still room. As he stood over her he could see the bright tears falling upon the black and white ivory keys. He laid his trembling hand upon her shoulder. He could hardly draw his breath for the sight of her suffering.

"Don't—don't," he said, almost pathetic in his lack of eloquence when he thought he most needed it.

One of her hot hands, all wet with tears, went suddenly to her shoulder, and grasped his that lay there, with a convulsive pressure, seeming to draw him down as she bowed herself almost to the keyboard in her agony of weeping. Then, without thought, his other hand, cold as ice, was under her throat, bringing her head gently back upon his arm, till the white face was turned up to his. Sob by sob, more distantly, the tempest subsided, but still the great tears swelled the heavy lids and ran down across her face upon his wrist. Then the wet, dark eyes opened and looked up to his, above her head.

"Be my friend!" she said softly, and her fingers pressed his very gently.

He looked down into her eyes for one moment, and then the passion in him got the mastery of his honourable soul.

"How can I?" he cried in a broken, choking voice. "I love you!"

In an instant he was standing up, lifting her high from the floor, and the lips that had perhaps never kissed for love before, were pressed upon hers. What chance had she, a woman, in those resistless arms of his? In her face was the still, fateful look of the dead nun, rising from the far grave of a buried tragedy.

In his uncontrollable passion he crushed her to him, holding her up like a child. She struggled and freed her hands and pressed them both upon his two eyes.

"Please—please!" she cried.

There was a pitiful ring in the tone, like the bleating of a frightened lamb. He hurt her too, for he was overstrong when he was thoughtless.

She cried out to him to let her go. But as she hung there, it was not all fear that she felt. There came with it an uncertain, half-delirious thrill of delight. To feel herself but a feather to his huge strength, swung, tossed, kissed, crushed, as he would. There was fear already, there was all her innocent maidenlike resistance, beating against him with might and anger, there was the feminine sense of injury by outrageous violence; but with it all there was also the natural woman's delight in the main strength of the natural man, that could kill her in an instant if he chose, but that could lift her to itself as a little child and surround her and protect her against the whole world.

"Please—please!" she cried again, covering his fierce eyes and white face with her hands and trying to push him away. The tone was pathetic in its appeal, and it touched him. His arms relaxed, tightened again with a sort of spasm, and then she found herself beside him on her feet. A long silence followed.

Gloria sank into a chair, glanced at him and saw that his face was turned away, looked down again and then watched him. His chest heaved once or twice, as though he had run a short sharp race. One hand grasped the back of a chair as he stood up. All at once, without looking at her, he went to the window and stood there, looking out, but seeing nothing. The soft damp wind made the panes of glass rattle. Still neither broke the silence. Then he came to her and stood before her, looking down, and she looked down, too, and would not see him. She was more afraid of him now than when he had lifted her from her feet, and her heart beat fast. She wondered what he would say, for she supposed that he meant to ask her forgiveness, and she was right.

"Gloria—forgive me," he said.

She looked up, a little fear of him still in her face.

"How can I?" she asked, but in her voice there was forgiveness already.

Her womanly instinct, though she was so young, told her that the fault was hers, and that considering the provocation it was not a great one—what were a few kisses, even such kisses as his, in a lifetime?

And she had tempted him beyond all bounds and repented of it. Before the storm she had raised in him, her fancied woes sank away and seemed infinitely small. She knew that she had worked herself up to emotion and tears, though not half sure of what she was saying, that she had exaggerated all she knew and suggested all she did not know, that she had almost been acting a part to satisfy something in her which she could not understand. And by her acting she had roused the savage truth in her very face and it had swept down everything before it. She had not guessed such possibilities. Before the tempest of his love all she had ever felt or dreamed of feeling seemed colourless and cold. She dreaded to rouse it again, and yet she could never forget the instant thrill that had quivered through her when he had lifted her from her feet.

When she had answered him with her question, he stood still in silence for a moment. She was too perfect in his eyes for him to cast the blame upon her, yet he knew that it had not been all his fault. And in the lower man was the mad triumph of having kissed her and of having told her, once for all, the whole meaning of his being. She looked down, and he could not see her eyes. There was no chair near. To see her face he dropped upon his knee and lightly touched her hands that lay idly in her lap. She started, fearing another outbreak.

"Please—please!" he said softly, using the very word she had used to him.

"Yes—but—" She hesitated and then raised her eyes.

The mask of his face was all softened, and his lips trembled a little. His hands quivered, too, as they touched hers.

"Please!" he repeated. "I promise. Indeed, I promise. Forgive me."

She smiled, all at once, dreamily. All his emotion, and her desire for it, were gone.

"I asked you to be my friend," she said. "I meant it, you know. How could you? It was not kind."

"No—but forgive me," he insisted in a pleading tone.

"I suppose I must," she said at last. "But I shall never feel sure of you again. How can I?"

"I promise. You will believe me, not to-day, perhaps, nor to-morrow, but soon. I will be just what I have always been. I will never do anything to offend you again."

"You promise me that? Solemnly?" She still smiled.

"Yes. It is a promise. I will keep it. I will be your friend always. Give me something to do for you. It will make it easier."

"What can I ask you to do? I shall never dare to speak to you about my life again."

"I think you will, when you see that I am just as I used to be. And you forgive me, quite?"

"Yes. I must. We must forget to-day. It must be as though it had never happened. Will you forget it?"

"I will try." But of that he knew the utter impossibility.

"If you try, you can succeed. Now get up. Be reasonable."

He took her hand in both of his. She made a movement to withdraw it, and then submitted. He barely touched it with his lips and rose to his feet instantly.

"Thank you," she said simply.

She had never had such a mastery of charm over him as at that moment. But his mood was changed, and there was no breaking out of the other man in him, though he felt again the quick sharp throb in the temples, and the rising blood at his throat. The higher self was dominant once more, and the features was as still as a statue's.

He took leave of her very quickly and went out into the damp street and faced the gusty southeast wind.

When he was gone, she rose and went to the window with a listless step, and gazed idly through the glass at the long row of windows in the palace opposite, and then went back and sank down, as though very weary, upon a sofa far from the light. There was a dazed, wondering look in her face and she sat very still for a long time, till it began to grow dark. In the dusk she rose and went to the piano and sang softly to herself. Her voice never swelled to a full note, and the chords which her fingers sought were low and gentle and dreamy.

While she was singing, the door opened noiselessly, and Reanda came in and stood beside her. She broke off and looked up, a little startled. The same wondering, half-dazed look was in her face. Her husband bent down and kissed her, and she kissed him silently.

CHAPTER XXVI

Donna Francesca had put off her mourning, and went into the world again during that winter. The world said that she might marry if she so pleased, and was somewhat inclined to wonder that she did not. She could have made a brilliant match if she had chosen. But instead, though she appeared everywhere where society was congregated together, she showed a tendency to religion which surprised her friends.

A tendency to religion existed in the Braccio family, together with various other tendencies not at all in harmony with it, nor otherwise edifying. Those other tendencies seemed to be absent in Francesca, and little by little her acquaintances began to speak of her as a devout person. The Prince of Gerano even hinted that she might some day be an abbess in the Carmelite Convent at Subiaco, as many a lady of the great house had been before her. But Francesca was not prepared to withdraw from the world altogether, though at the present time she was very unhappy.

She suspected herself of a great sin, besides reproaching herself bitterly with many of her deeds which deserved no blame at all. Yet she was by no means morbid, nor naturally inclined to perpetual self-examination. On the contrary, she had always been willing to accept life as a simple affair which could not offer any difficulties provided that one were what she meant by "good"—that is, honest in word and deed, and scrupulous in doing thoroughly and with right intention those things which her religion required of her, but in which only she herself could judge of her own sincerity.

Of late, however, she had felt that there was something very wrong in all her recent life. The certainty of it dawned by degrees, and then burst upon her suddenly one day when she was with Reanda.

She had long ago noticed the change in his manner, the harassed look, and the sad ring in his voice, and for a time his suffering was her sorrow, and there was a painful pleasure in being able to feel for him with all her heart. He had gone through a phase which had lasted many months, and the change was great between his former and his present self. He had suffered, but indifference was creeping upon him. It was clear enough. Nothing interested him but his art, and perhaps her own conversation, though even that seemed doubtful to her.

They were alone together on a winter's afternoon in the great hall. The work was almost done, and they had been talking of the more mechanical decorations, and of the style of the furniture.

"It is a big place," said Francesca, "but I mean to fill it. I like large rooms, and when it is finished, I will take up my quarters here, and call it my boudoir."

She smiled at the idea. The hall was at least fifty feet long by thirty wide.

"All the women I know have wretched little sitting-rooms in which they can hardly turn round," she said. "I will have all the space I like, and all the air and all the light. Besides, I shall always have the dear Cupid and Psyche, to remind me of you."

She spoke the last words with the simplicity of absolute innocence.

"And me?" he asked, as innocently and simply as she. "What will you do with me?"

"Whatever you like," she said, taking it quite for granted, as he did, that he was to work for her all his life. "You can have a studio in the house, just as it used to be, if you please. And you can paint the great canvas for the ceiling of the dining-room. Or shall I restore the old chapel? Which should you rather do—oil-painting, or fresco?"

"You would not want the altar piece which I should paint," he said, with sudden sadness.

"Santa Francesca?" she asked. "It would have to be Santa Francesca. The chapel is dedicated to her. You could make a beautiful picture of her—a portrait, perhaps—" she stopped.

"Of yourself? Yes, I could do that," he answered quickly.

"No," she said, and hesitated. "Of your wife," she added rather abruptly.

He started and looked at her, and she was sorry that she had spoken. Gloria's beautiful face had risen in her mind, and it had seemed generous to suggest the idea. Finding a difficulty in telling him, she had thought it her duty to be frank.

He laughed harshly before he answered her.

"No," he said. "Certainly not a portrait of my wife. Not even to please you. And that is saying much."

He spoke very bitterly. In the few words, he poured out the pent-up suffering of many months. Francesca turned pale.

"I know, and it is my fault," she said in a low voice.

"Your fault? No! But it is not mine."

His hands trembled violently as he took up his palette and brushes and began to mix some colours, not knowing what he was doing.

"It is my fault," said Francesca, still very white, and staring at the brick floor. "I have seen it. I could not speak of it. You are unhappy—miserable. Your life is ruined, and I have done it. I!"

She bit her lip almost before the last word was uttered; for it was stronger and louder than she had expected it to be, and the syllable rang with a despairing echo in the empty hall.

Reanda shook his head, and bent over his colours with shaking hands, but said nothing.

"I was so happy when you were married," said Francesca, forcing herself to speak calmly. "She seemed such a good wife for you—so young, so beautiful. And she loves you—"

"No." He shook his head energetically. "She does not love me. Do not say that, for it is not true. One does not love in that way—to-day a kiss, to-morrow a sting—to-day honey, to-morrow snake-poison. Do not say that it is love, for it is not true. The heart tells the truth, all alone in the breast. A thousand words cannot make it tell one lie. But for me—it is finished. Let us speak no more of love. Let us talk of our good friendship. It is better."

"Eh, let us speak of it, of this friendship! It has cost tears of blood!"

Francesca, in the sincerity of what she felt, relapsed into the Roman dialect. Almost all Romans do, under any emotion.

"Everything passes," answered Reanda, laying his palette aside, and beginning to walk up and down, his hands in his pockets. "This also will pass," he added, as he turned. "We are men. We shall forget."

"But not I. For I did it. Your sadness cuts my heart, because I did it. I—I alone. But for me, you would be free."

"Would to Heaven!" exclaimed the artist, almost under his breath. "But I will not have you say that it is your fault!" he cried, stopping before her. "I was the fool that believed. A man of my age—oh, a serious man—to marry a child! I should have known. At first, I do not say. I was the first. She thought she had paradise in her arms. A husband! They all want it, the husband. But I, who had lived and seen, I should have known. Fool, fool! Ignorant fool!"

The words came out vehemently in the strong dialect, and the nervous, heart-wrung man struck his breast with his clenched fist, and his eyes looked upward.

"Reanda, Reanda! What are you saying? When I tell you that I made you marry her! It was here,—I was in this very chair,—and I told you about her. And I asked her here with intention, that you might see how beautiful she was. And then, neither one nor two, she fell in love with you! It would have been a miracle if you had not married her. And her father, he was satisfied. May that day be accursed when I brought them here to torment you!"

She spoke excitedly, and her lip quivered. He began to walk again with rapid, uncertain strides.

"For that—yes!" he said. "Let the day bear the blame. But I was the madman. Who leaves the old way and follows the new knows what he leaves, but not what he may find. I might have been contented. I was so happy! God knows how happy I was!"

"And I!" exclaimed Francesca, involuntarily; but he did not hear her.

She felt a curious sense of elation, though she was so truly sorry for him, and it disturbed her strangely. She looked at him and smiled, and then wondered why the smile came. There is a ruthless cruelty in the half-unconscious impulses of the purest innocence, of which vice itself might be ashamed in its heart. It is simple humanity's assertion of its prior right to be happy. She smiled spontaneously because she knew that Reanda no longer loved Gloria, and she felt that he could not love her again; and for a while she was too simply natural to quarrel with herself for it, or to realize what it meant.

He was nervous, melancholy, and unstrung, and he began to talk about himself and his married life for the first time, pouring out his sufferings and thoughtless of what Francesca might think and feel. He, too, was natural. Unlike his wife, he detested emotion. To be angry was almost an illness to his over-finely organized temperament. In a way, Griggs had been right in saying that Reanda seemed to paint as an agent in the power of an unseen, directing influence. Beauty made him feel itself, and feel for it in his turn with his brush. The conception was before him, guiding his hand, before a stroke of the work was done. There was the lightning-like co-respondence and mutual reaction between thought and execution, which has been explained by some to be the simultaneous action of two minds in man, the subjective and the objective. In doing certain things he had the patience and the delicacy of one for whom time has no meaning. He could not have told whether his hand followed his eye, or his eye followed his hand. His whole being was of excessively sensitive construction, and emotion of any kind, even pleasure, jarred upon its hair-fine sensibilities. And yet, behind all this, there was the tenacity of the great artist and the phenomenal power of endurance, in certain directions, which is essential to prize-winning in the fight for fame. There was the quality of nerve which can endure great tension in one way, but can bear nothing in other ways.

He went on, giving vent to all he felt, talking to himself rather than to Francesca. He could not reproach his wife with any one action of importance. She was fond of Paul Griggs. But it was only Griggs! He smiled. In his eyes, the cold-faced man was no more than a stone. In their excursions into society she had met men whom he considered far more dangerous, men young, handsome, rich, having great names. They admired her and said so to her in the best language they had, which was no doubt often very eloquent. Had she ever looked twice at one of them? No. He could not reproach her with that. The Duchess of Astrardente was not more cold to her admirers than Gloria was. It was not that. There were little things, little nothings, but in thousands. He tried to please her with something, and she laughed in his face, or found fault. She had small hardnesses and little vulgarities of manner that drove him mad.

"I had thought her like you," he said suddenly, turning to Francesca. "She is not. She is coarse-grained. She has the soul of a peasant, with the face of a Madonna. What would you have? It is too much. Love is an illusion. I will have no more of it. Besides, love is dead. It would be easier to wake a corpse. I shall live. I may forget. Meanwhile there is our friendship. That is of gold."

Francesca listened in silence, thoughtful and with downcast eyes, as the short, disjointed sentences broke vehemently from his lips, each one accusing her in her own heart of having wrought the misery of two lives, one of which was very dear to her. Too dear, as she knew at last. The scarlet shame would have burned her face, if she had owned to herself that she loved this man, whom she had married to another, believing that she was making his happiness. She would not own it. Had she admitted it then, she would have been capable of leaving him within the hour, and of shutting herself up forever in the Convent at Subiaco to expiate the sin of the thought. It was monstrous in her eyes, and she would still refuse to see it.

But she owned that there was the suspicion, and that Angelo Reanda was far dearer to her than anything else on earth. Her innocence was so strong and spotless that it had a right to its one and only satisfaction. But what she felt for Reanda was either love, or it was blasphemy against the holy thing in whose place he stood in her temple. It must not be love, and therefore, as anything else, it was too much. And the strange joy she felt because Gloria was nothing to him, still filled her heart, though it began to torment her with the knowledge of evil which she had never understood.

There was much else against him, too, in her pride of race, and it helped her just then, for it told her how impossible it was that she, a princess of the house of Braccio, should love a mere artist, the son of a steward, whose forefathers had been bondsmen to her ancestors from time immemorial. It was out of the question, and she would not believe it of herself. Yet, as she looked into his delicate, spiritual face and watched the shades of expression that crossed it, she felt that it made little difference whence he came, since she understood him and he understood her.

She became confused by her own thoughts and grasped at the idea of a true and perfect friendship, with a somewhat desperate determination to see it and nothing else in it, for the rest of her life, rather than part with Angelo Reanda.

"Friends," she said thoughtfully. "Yes—always friends, you and I. But as a friend, Reanda, what can I do? I cannot help you."

"The time for help is past, if it ever came. You are a saint—pray for me. You can do that."

"But there is more than that to be done," she said, ready to sacrifice anything or everything just then. "Do not tell me it is hopeless. I will see your wife often and I will talk to her. I am older than she, and I can make her understand many things."

"Do not try it," said Reanda, in an altered tone. "I advise you not to try it. You can do no good there, and you might find trouble."

"Find trouble?" repeated Francesca, not understanding him. "What do you mean? Does she dislike me?"

"Have you not seen it?" he asked, with a bitter smile.

Francesca did not answer him at once, but bent her head again. Once or twice she looked up as though she were about to speak.

"It is as I tell you," said Reanda, nodding his head slowly.

Francesca made up her mind, but the scarlet blood rose in her face.

"It is better to be honest and frank," she said. "Is Gloria jealous of me?" She was so much ashamed that she could hardly look at him just then.

"Jealous! She would kill you!" he cried, and there was anger in his voice at the thought. "Do not go to her. Something might happen."

The blush in Francesca's face deepened and then subsided, and she grew very pale again.

"But if she is jealous, she loves you," she said earnestly and anxiously.

He shrugged his high thin shoulders, and the bitter smile came back to his face.

"It is a stage jealousy," he said cruelly. "How could she pass the time without something to divert her? She is always acting."

"But what is she jealous of?" asked Francesca. "How can she be jealous of me? Because you work here? She is free to come if she likes, and to stay all day. I do not understand."

"Who can understand her? God, who made her, understands her. I am only a man. I know only one thing, that I loved her and do not love her. And she makes a scene for every day. One day it is you, and another day it is the walls she does not like. You will forgive me, Princess. I speak frankly what comes to my mouth from my heart. The whole story is this. She makes my life intolerable. I am not an idle man, the first you may meet in society, to spend my time from morning to night in studying my wife's caprices. I am an artist. When I have worked I must have peace. I do not ask for intelligent conversation like yours. But I must have peace. One of these days I shall strangle her with my hands. The Lord will forgive me and understand. I am full of nerves. Is it my fault? She twists them as the women wring out clothes at the fountain. It is not a life; it is a hell."

"Poor Reanda! Poor Reanda!" repeated Francesca, softly.

"I do not pity myself," he said scornfully. "I have deserved it, and much more. But I am human. If it goes on a little longer, you may take me to Santo Spirito, for I am going mad. At least I should be there in holy peace. After her, the madmen would all seem doctors of wisdom. Do you know what will happen this evening? I go home. 'Where have you been?' she will ask. 'At the Palazzetto.' 'What have you been doing?' 'Painting—it is my trade.' 'Was Donna Francesca there?' 'Of course. She is mistress in her own house.' 'And what did you talk of?' 'How should I remember? We talked.' Then it will begin. It will be an inferno, as it always is. 'Leave hope behind, all ye that enter here!' I can say it, if ever man could! You are right to pity me. Before it is finished you will have reason to pity me still more. Let us hope it may finish soon. Either San Lorenzo, or Santo Spirito—with the mad or with the dead."

"Poor Reanda!"

"Yes—poor Reanda, if you like. People envy me, they say I am a great artist. If they think so, let them say it. It seems to them that I am somebody." He laughed, almost hysterically. "Somebody! Stuff for Santo Spirito! That is all she has left me in two years—not yet two years."

"Do not talk of Santo Spirito," said Francesca. "You shall not go mad. When you are unhappy, think of our friendship and of all the hours you have here every day." She hesitated and seemed to make an effort over herself. "But it is impossible that it should be all over, so hopelessly and so soon. She is nervous, perhaps. The climate does not suit her—"

Reanda laughed wildly, for he was rapidly losing all control of himself.

"Therefore I should take her away and go and live somewhere else!" he cried. "That would be the end! I should tear her to pieces with my hands—"

"Hush, hush! You are talking madly—"

"I know it. There is reason. It will end badly, one of these days, unless I end first, and that may happen also. Without you it would have happened long ago. You are the good angel in my life, the one friend God has sent me in my tormented existence, the one star in my black sky. Be my friend still, always, for ever and ever, and I shall live forever only to be your friend. As for love—the devil and his demons will know what to do with it—they will find their account in it. They have lent it, and they will take their payment in blood and tears of those who believe them."

"But there is love in the world, somewhere," said Francesca, gently.

"Yes—and in hell! But not in heaven—where you will be."

Francesca sighed unconsciously, and looked long away towards the great windows at the end of the hall. Reanda gathered up his palette and brushes with a steadier hand. His anger had not spent itself, but it made him suddenly strong, and the outburst had relieved him, though it was certain that it would be followed by a reaction of profound despondency.

All at once he came close to Francesca. She looked up, half startled by his sudden movement.

"At least it is true—this one thing," he said. "I can count upon you."

"Yes. You can count upon me," she answered, gazing into his eyes.

He did not move. The one hand held his palette, the other hung free by his side. All at once she took it in hers, still looking up into his eyes.

"I am very fond of you," she said earnestly. "You can count upon me as long as we two live."

"God bless you," he said, more quietly than he had spoken yet, and his hand pressed hers a little.

There could be no harm in saying as much as that, she thought, when it was so true and so simply said. It was all she could ever say to him, or to herself, and there was no reason why she should not say it. He would not misunderstand her. No man could have mistaken the innocence that was the life and light of her clear eyes. She was glad she had said it, and she was glad long afterwards that she had said it on that day, quietly, when no one could hear them in the great still hall.

CHAPTER XXVII

Reanda went home that evening in a very disturbed state of mind. He had been better so long as he had not given vent to what he felt; for, as with many southern men of excitable temper and weak nerves, his thoughts about himself, as distinguished from his pursuits, did not take positive shape in his mind until he had expressed them in words. Amongst the Latin races the phrase, 'he cannot think without speaking,' has more truth as applied to some individuals than the Anglo-Saxon can easily understand.

For many months the artist had been most unhappy. His silence concerning his grief had been almost exemplary, and had been broken only now and then by a hasty exclamation of annoyance when Gloria's behaviour had irritated him beyond measure. He was the gentlest of men; and even when he had lost his temper with her, he had never spoken roughly.

"You are hard to please, my dear," he had sometimes said.

But that had been almost the strongest expression of his displeasure. It was not, indeed, that he had exercised very great self-control in the matter, for he had little power of that sort over himself. If he was habitually mild and gentle in his manner with Gloria, it was rather because, like many Italians, he dreaded emotion as something like an illness, and could avoid it to some extent merely by not speaking freely of what he felt. Silence was generally easy to him; and he had not broken out more than two or three times in all his life, as he had done on that afternoon alone with Francesca.

The inevitable consequence followed immediately,—a consequence as much physical as mental, for when he went away from the Palazzetto, his clear dark eyes were bloodshot and yellow, and his hands had trembled so that he had hardly been able to find the armholes of his great-coat in putting it on. He walked with an uncertain and agitated step, glancing to right and left of him as he went, half-fiercely, half-timidly, as though he expected a new adversary to spring upon him from every corner. The straight line of the houses waned and shivered in the dusk, as he looked at them, and he saw flashes of light in the air. His head was hot and aching, and his hat hurt him. Altogether he was in a dangerous state, not unlike that which, with northern men, sometimes follows hard drinking.

He hated to go home that evening. So far as he was conscious, he had neither misrepresented nor in any way exaggerated the miseries of his domestic existence; and he felt that it was before him now, precisely as he had described it. There would be the same questions, to which he would give the same answers, at which Gloria would put on the same expression of injured hopelessness, unless she broke out and lost her temper, which happened often enough. The prospect was intolerable. Reanda thrust his hands deep into the pocket of his overcoat, and glared about him as he turned the corner of the Via degli Astalli, and saw the Corso in the distance. But he did not slacken his pace as he went along under the gloomy walls of the Austrian Embassy—the Palace of Venice—the most grim and fortress-like of all Roman palaces.

He felt as a poor man may feel when, hot and feverish from working by a furnace, he knows that he must face the winter storm of freezing sleet and piercing wind in his thin and ragged jacket to go home—a plunge, as it were, from molten iron into ice, with no protection from the cold. Every step of the homeward way was hateful to him. Yet he knew his own weakness well enough not to hesitate. Had he stopped, he might have been capable of turning in some other direction, and of spending the whole evening with some of his fellow-artists, going home late in the night, when Gloria would be asleep. The thought crossed his mind. If he did that, he was sure to be carried away into speaking of his troubles to men with whom he had no intimacy. He was too proud for that. He wished he could go back to Francesca, and pour out his woes again. He had not said half enough. He should like to have it out, to the very end, and then lie down and close his eyes, and hear Francesca's voice soothing him and speaking of their golden friendship. But that was impossible, so he went home to face his misery as best he could.

There was exaggeration in all he thought, but there was none in the effect of his thoughts upon himself. He had married a woman unsuited to him in every way, as he was unsuited to her. The whole trouble lay there. Possibly he was not a man to marry at all, and should have led his solitary life to the end, illuminated from the outside, as it were, by Francesca Campodonico's faithful friendship and sweet influence. All causes of disagreement, considered as forces in married life, are relative in their value to the comparative solidity of the characters on which they act—a truism which ought to be the foundation of social charity, but is not. Reanda could not be blamed for his brittle sensitivenesses, nor Gloria for a certain coarse-grained streak of cruelty, which she had inherited from her father, and which had combined strangely with the rare gifts and great faults of her dead mother—the love of emotion for its own sake, and the tendency to do everything which might produce it in herself and those about her. Emotion was poison to Reanda. It was his wife's favourite food.

He reached his home, and went up the well-lighted marble staircase, wishing that he were ascending the narrow stone steps at the back of the Palazzetto Borgia, taper in hand, to his old bachelor quarters, to light his lamp, to smoke in peace, and to spend the evening over a sketch, or with a book, or dreaming of work not yet done. He paused on the landing, before he rang the bell of his apartment. The polished door irritated him, with its brass fittings and all that it meant of married life and irksome social obligation. He never carried a key, because the Roman keys of those times were large and heavy; but he had been obliged to use one formerly, when he had lived by himself. The necessity of ringing the bell irritated him again, and he felt a nervous shock of unwillingness as he pulled the brass knob. He set his teeth against the tinkling and jangling that followed, and his eyelids quivered. Everything hurt him. He did not feel sure of his hands when he wanted to use them. He was inclined to strike the silent and respectful man-servant who opened the door, merely because he was silent and respectful. He went straight to his own dressing-room, and shut himself in. It would be a relief to change his clothes. He and Gloria were to go to a reception in the evening, and he would dress at once. In those days few Romans dressed for dinner every day.

He dropped a stud, for his hands were shaking so that he could hardly hold anything; and he groped for the thing on his knees. The blood went to his head, and hurt him violently, as though he had received a blow.

Gloria's room was next to his, and she heard him moving about. She knocked and tried the door, but it was locked; and she heard him utter an exclamation of annoyance, as he hunted for the stud. She thought it was meant for her, and turned angrily back from the door. On any other day he would have called her, for he had heard her trying to get in. But he shrugged his lean shoulders impatiently, glanced once towards her room, found his stud, and went on dressing.

He really made an effort to get control of himself while he was alone. But to all intents and purposes he was actually ill. His face was drawn and sallow; his eyes were yellow and bloodshot; and there were deep, twitching lines about his mouth. His nostrils moved spasmodically when he drew breath, and his long thin hands fumbled helplessly at the studs and buttons of his clothes. At last he was dressed, and went into the drawing-room. Gloria was already there, waiting by the fireside, with an injured and forbidding expression in her beautiful face.

Reanda came to the fireside, and stood there, spreading out his trembling hands to the blaze. He dreaded the first word, as a man lying ill of brain fever dreads each cracking explosion in a thunderstorm. Strained as their relations had been for a long time, he had never failed to kiss Gloria when he came home. This evening he barely glanced at her, and stood watching the dancing tongues of the wood fire, not daring to think of the sound of his wife's voice. It came at last cool and displeased.

"Are you ill?" she asked, looking steadily at him.

"No," he answered with an effort, and his outstretched hands shook before the fire.

"Then what is the matter with you?"

"Nothing." He did not even turn his eyes to her, as he spoke the single word.

A silence followed, during which he suffered. Nevertheless, the first dreaded shock of hearing her voice was over. Though he had barely glanced at her, he had known from her face what the sound of the voice would be.

Gloria leaned back in her chair and watched the fire, and sighed. Griggs had been with her in the afternoon, and she had been happy, quite innocently, as she thought. The man's dominating strength and profound earnestness, which would have been intolerably dull to many women, smoothed Gloria, as it were. She said that he ironed the creases out of her life for her. It was not a softening influence, but a calming one, bred of strength pressing heavily on caprice. She resisted it, but took pleasure in finding that it was irresistible. Now and then it was not merely a steady pressure. He had a sledge hammer amongst his intellectual weapons, and once in a while it fell upon one of her illusions. She laughed at the destruction, and had no pity for the fragments. They were not illusions integral with her vanity, for he thought her perfect, and he would not have struck at her faults if he had seen them. Her faults grew, for they had root in her vital nature, and drew nourishment from his enduring strength, which surrounded them and protected them in the blind, whole-heartedness of his love. For the rest, he had kept his word. She had seen him turn white and bite his lip, sometimes, and more than once he had left her abruptly, and had not come back again for several days. But he had never forgotten his promise, in any word or deed since he had given it.

It is a dangerous thing to pile up a mountain of massive reality from which to look out upon the fading beauty of a fleeting illusion. In his influence on Gloria's life, the strong man had overtopped the man of genius by head and shoulders. And she loved the strange mixture of attraction and repulsion she felt when she was with Griggs—the something that wounded her vanity because she could not understand it, and the protecting shield that overspread that same vanity, and gave it freedom to be vain beyond all bounds. She would not have admitted that she loved the man. It was her nature to play upon his pity with the wounds her love for her husband had suffered. Yet she knew that if she were free she should marry him, because she could not resist him, and there was pleasure in the idea that she controlled so irresistible a force. The contrast between him and Reanda was ever before her, and since she had learned how weak genius could be, the comparison was enormously in favour of the younger man.

As Reanda stood there before the fire that evening, she despised him, and her heart rebelled against his nature. His nervousness, his trembling hands, his almost evident fear of being questioned, were contemptible. He was like a hunted animal, she thought. Two hours earlier her friend had stood there, solid, leonine, gladiatorial, dominating her with his square white face, and still, shadowy eyes, quietly stretching to the flames two hands that could have torn her in pieces,—a man imposing in his stern young sadness, almost solemn in his splendid physical dignity.

She looked at Reanda, and her lip curled with scorn of herself for having loved such a thing. It was long since she had seen the gentle light in his face which had won her heart two years ago. She was familiar with his genius, and it no longer surprised her into overlooking his frailty. His fame no longer flattered her. His gentleness was gone, and had left, not hardness nor violence, in its place, but a sort of irritable palsy of discontent. That was what she called it as she watched him.

"You used to kiss me when you came home," she said suddenly, leaning far back in her chair.

Mechanically he turned his head. The habit was strong, and she had reminded him of it. He did not wish to quarrel, and he did not reason. He moved a step to her side and bent down to kiss her forehead. The automatic conjugality of the daily kiss might have a good effect. That was what he thought, if he thought at all.

But she put up her hands suddenly, and thrust him back rudely.

"No," she said. "That sort of thing is not worth much, if I have to remind you to do it."

Her lip curled again. His high shoulders went up, and he turned away.

"You are hard to please," he said, and the words were as mechanical as the action that had preceded them.

"It cannot be said that you have taken much pains to please me of late," she answered coldly.

The servant announced dinner at that moment, and Reanda made no answer, though he glanced at her nervously. They went into the dining-room and sat down.

The storm brewed during the silent meal. Reanda scarcely ate anything, and drank a little weak wine and water.

"You hardly seem well enough to go out this evening," said Gloria, at last, but there was no kindness in the tone.

"I am perfectly well," he answered impatiently. "I will go with you."

"There is not the slightest necessity," replied his wife. "I can go alone, and you can go to bed."

"I tell you I am perfectly well!" he said with unconcealed annoyance. "Let me alone."

"Certainly. Nothing is easier."

The voice was full of that injured dignity which most surely irritated him, as Gloria knew. But the servant was in the room, and he said nothing, though it was a real effort to be silent. His tongue had been free that day, and it was hard to be bound again.

They finished dinner almost in silence, and then went back to the drawing-room by force of habit. Gloria was still in her walking-dress, but there was no hurry, and she resumed her favourite seat by the fire for a time, before going to dress for the reception.

CHAPTER XXVIII

There was something exasperating in the renewal of the position exactly as it had been before dinner. To make up for having eaten nothing, Reanda drank two cups of coffee in silence.

"You might at least speak to me," observed Gloria, as he set down the second cup. "One would almost think that we had quarrelled!"

The hard laugh that followed the words jarred upon him more painfully than anything that had gone before. He laughed, too, after a moment's silence, half hysterically.

"Yes," he said; "one might almost think that we had quarrelled!" And he laughed again.

"The idea seems to amuse you," said Gloria, coldly.

"As it does you," he answered. "We both laughed. Indeed, it is very amusing."

"Donna Francesca has sent you home in a good humour. That is rare. I suppose I ought to be grateful."

"Yes. I am in a fine humour. It seems to me that we both are." He bit his cigar, and blew out short puffs.

"You need not include me. Please do not smoke into my face."

The smoke was not very near her, but she made a movement with her hands as though brushing it away.

"I beg your pardon," he said politely, and he moved to the other side of the fireplace.

"How nervous you are!" she exclaimed. "Why can you not sit down?"

"Because I wish to stand," he answered, with returning impatience. "Because I am nervous, if you choose."

"You told me that you were perfectly well."

"So I am."

"If you were perfectly well, you would not be nervous," she replied.

He felt as though she were driving a sharp nail into his brain.

"It does not make any difference to you whether I am nervous or not," he said, and his eye began to lighten, as he sat down.

"It certainly makes no difference to you whether you are rude or not."

He shrugged his shoulders, said nothing, and smoked in silence. One thin leg was crossed over the other and swung restlessly.

"Is this sort of thing to last forever?" she inquired coldly, after a silence which had lasted a full minute.

"I do not know what you mean," said Reanda.

"You know very well what I mean."

"This is insufferable!" he exclaimed, rising suddenly, with his cigar between his teeth.

"You might take your cigar out of your mouth to say so," retorted Gloria.

He turned on her, and an exclamation of anger was on his lips, but he did not utter it. There was a remnant of self-control. Gloria leaned back in her chair, and took up a carved ivory fan from amongst the knick-knacks on the little table beside her. She opened it, shut it, and opened it again, and pretended to fan herself, though the room was cool.

"I should really like to know," she said presently, as he walked up and down with uneven steps.

"What?" he asked sharply.

"Whether this is to last for the rest of our lives."

"What?"

"This peaceful existence," she said scornfully. "I should really like to know whether it is to last. Could you not tell me?"

"It will not last long, if you make it your principal business to torment me," he said, stopping in his walk.

"I?" she exclaimed, with an air of the utmost surprise. "When do I ever torment you?"

"Whenever I am with you, and you know it."

"Really! You must be ill, or out of your mind, or both. That would be some excuse for saying such a thing."

"It needs none. It is true." He was becoming exasperated at last. "You seem to spend your time in finding out how to make life intolerable. You are driving me mad. I cannot bear it much longer."

"If it comes to bearing, I think I have borne more than you," said Gloria. "It is not little. You leave me to myself. You neglect me. You abuse the friends I am obliged to find rather than be alone. You neglect me in every way—and you say that I am driving you mad. Do you realize at all how you have changed in this last year? You may have really gone mad, for all I know, but it is I who have to suffer and bear the consequences. You neglect me brutally. How do I know how you pass your time?"

Reanda stood still in the middle of the room, gazing at her. For a moment he was surprised by the outbreak. She did not give him time to answer.

"You leave me in the morning," she went on, working her coldness into anger. "You often go away before I am awake. You come back at midday, and sometimes you do not speak a word over your breakfast. If I speak, you either do not answer, or you find fault with what I say; and if I show the least enthusiasm for anything but your work, you preach me down with proverbs and maxims, as though I were a child. I am foolish, young, impatient, silly, not fit to take care of myself, you say! Have you taken care of me? Have you ever sacrificed one hour out of your long day to give me a little pleasure? Have you ever once, since we were married, stayed at home one morning and asked me what I would do— just to make one holiday for me? Never. Never once! You give me a fine house and enough money, and you think you have given me all that a woman wants."

"And what do you want?" asked Reanda, trying to speak calmly.

"A little kindness, a little love—the least thing of all you promised me and of all I was so sure of having! Is it so much to ask? Have you lied to me all this time? Did you never love me? Did you marry me for my face, or for my voice? Was it all a mere empty sham from the beginning? Have you deceived me from the first? You said you loved me. Was none of it true?"

"Yes. I loved you," he answered, and suddenly there was a dulness in his voice.

"You loved me—"

She sighed, and in the stillness that followed the little ivory fan rattled as she opened and shut it. To his ear, the tone in which she had spoken had rung false. If only he could have heard her voice speaking as it had once sounded, he must have been touched.

"Yes," she continued. "You loved me, or at least you made me think you did. I was young and I believed you. You do not even say it now. Perhaps because you know how hard it would be to make me believe you."

"No. That is not the reason."

She waited a moment, for it was not the answer she had expected.

"Angelo—" she began, and waited, but he said nothing, though he looked at her. "It is not true, it cannot be true!" she said, suddenly turning her face away, for there was a bitter humiliation in it.

"It is much better to say it at once," he said, with the supernaturally calm indifference which sometimes comes upon very sensitive people when they are irritated beyond endurance. "I did love you, or I should not have married you. But I do not love you any longer. I am sorry. I wish I did."

"And you dare to tell me so!" she cried, turning upon him suddenly.

A moment later she was leaning forward, covering her face with her hands, and speaking through them.

"You have the heart to tell me so, after all I have been to you—the devotion of years, the tenderness, the love no man ever had of any woman! Oh, God! It is too much!"

"It is said now. It is of no use to go back to a lie," observed Reanda, with an indifference that would have seemed diabolical even to himself, had he believed her outbreak to be quite genuine. "Of what use would it be to pretend again?"

"You admit that you have only pretended to love me?" She raised her flushed face and gleaming eyes.

"Of late—if you call it a pretence—"

"Oh, not that—not that! I have seen it—but at first. You did love me. Say that, at least."

"Certainly. Why should I have married you?"

"Yes—why? In spite of her, too—it is not to be believed."

"In spite of her? Of whom? Are you out of your mind?"

Gloria laughed in a despairing sort of way.

"Do not tell me that Donna Francesca ever wished you to be married!" she said.

"She brought us together. You know it. It is the only thing I could ever reproach her with."

"She made you marry me?"

"Made me? No! You are quite mad."

He stamped his foot impatiently, and turned away to walk up and down again. His cigar had gone out, but he gnawed at it angrily. He was amazed at what he could still bear, but he was fast losing his head. The mad desire to strangle her tingled in his hands, and the light of the lamp danced when he looked at it.

"She has made you do so many things!" said Gloria.

Her tone had changed again, growing hard and scornful, when she spoke of Donna Francesca.

"What has she made me do that you should speak of her in that way?" asked Reanda, angrily, re-crossing the room.

"She has made you hate me—for one thing," Gloria answered.

"That is not true!" Reanda could hardly breathe, and he felt his voice growing thick.

"Not true! Then, if not she, who else? You are with her there all day—she talks about me, she finds fault with me, and you come home and see the faults she finds for you—"

"There is not a word of truth in what you say—"

"Do not be so angry, then! If it were not true, why should you care? I have said it, and I will say it. She has robbed me of you. Oh, I will never forgive her! Never fear! One does not forget such things! She has got you, and she will keep you, I suppose. But you shall regret it! She shall pay me for it!"

Her voice shook, for her jealousy was real, as was all her emotion while it lasted.

"You shall not speak of her in that way," said Reanda, fiercely. "I owe her and her family all that I am, all that I have in the world—"

"Including me!" interrupted Gloria. "Pay her then—pay her with your love and yourself. You can satisfy your conscience in that way, and you can break my heart."

"There is not the slightest fear of that," answered Reanda, cruelly.

She rose suddenly to her feet and stood before him, blazing with anger.

"If I could find yours—if you had any—I would break it," she said. "You dare to say that I have no heart, when you can see that every word you say thrusts it through like a knife, when I have loved you as no woman ever loved man! I said it, and I repeat it—when I have given you everything, and would have given you the world if I had it! Indeed, you are utterly heartless and cruel and unkind—"

"At least, I am honest. I do not play a part as you do. I say plainly that I do not love you and that I am sorry for it. Yes—really sorry." His voice softened for an instant. "I would give a great deal to love you as I once did, and to believe that you loved me—"

"You will tell me that I do not—"

"Indeed, I will tell you so, and that you never did—"

"Angelo—take care! You will go too far!"

"I could never go far enough in telling you that truth. You never loved me. You may have thought you did. I do not care. You talk of devotion and tenderness and all the like! Of being left alone and neglected! Of going too far! What devotion have you ever shown to me, beyond extravagantly praising everything I painted, for a few months after we were married. Then you grew tired of my work. That is your affair. What is it to me whether you admire my pictures or Mendoza's, or any other man's? Do you think that is devotion? I know far better than you which are good and which are bad. But you call it devotion. And it was devotion that kept you away from me when I was working, when I was obliged to work—for it is my trade, after all—and when you might have been with me day after day! And it was devotion to meet me with your sour, severe look every day when I came home, as though I were a secret enemy, a conspirator, a creature to be guarded against like a thief—as though I had been staying away from you on purpose, and of my will—instead of working for you all day long. That was your way of showing your love. And to torment me with questions, everlastingly believing that I spend my time in talking against you to Donna Francesca—"

"You do!" cried Gloria, who had not been able to interrupt his incoherent speech. "You love her as you never loved me—as you hate me—as you both hate me!"

She grasped his sleeve in her anger, shaking his arm, and staring into his eyes.

"You make me hate you!" he answered, trying to shake her off.

"And you succeed, between you—You and your—"

In his turn he grasped her arm with his long, thin fingers, with nervous roughness.

"You shall not speak of her—"

"Shall not? It is the only right I have left—that and the right to hate you—you and that infamous woman you love—yes—you and your mistress—your pretty Francesca!" Her laugh was almost a scream.

His fury overflowed. After all, he was the son of a countryman, of the steward of Gerano. He snatched the ivory fan from her hand and struck her across the face with it. The fragile thing broke to shivers, and the fragments fell between them.

Gloria turned deadly white, but there was a bright red bar across her cheek. She looked at him a moment, and into her face there came that fateful look that was like her dead mother's.

Then without a word she turned and left the room.

CHAPTER XXIX

The daughter of Angus Dalrymple and Maria Braccio was not the woman to bear a blow tamely, or to hesitate long as to the surest way of resenting it. Before she had reached the door she had determined to leave the house at once, and ten minutes had not passed before she found herself walking down the Corso, veiled and muffled in a cloak, and having all the money she could call her own, in her pocket, together with a few jewels of little value, given her by her father.

Reanda had sunk into a chair when the door had closed behind her, half stunned by the explosion of his own anger. He looked at the bits of broken ivory on the carpet, and wondered vaguely what they meant. He felt as though he had been in a dream of which he could not remember the distorted incidents at all clearly. His breath came irregularly, his heart fluttered and stood still and fluttered again, and his hands twitched at the fringe on the arms of the chair. By and bye, the butler came in to take away the coffee cups and he saw that his master was ill. Under such circumstances nothing can equal the gentleness of an Italian servant. The man called some one to help him, and got Reanda to his dressing-room, and undressed him and laid him upon the long leathern sofa. Then they knocked at the bedroom door, but there was no answer.

"Do not disturb the signora," said Reanda, feebly. "She wishes to be alone. We shall not want the carriage."

Those were the only words he spoke that evening, and the servants understood well enough that something had happened between husband and wife, and that it was best to be silent and to obey. No one tried the door of the bedroom. If any one had turned the handle, it would have been found to be locked. The key lay on the table in the hall, amongst the visiting-cards. Dalrymple's daughter had inherited some of his quick instinct and presence of mind. She had felt sure that if she locked the door of her room when she left the house, her husband would naturally suppose that she had shut herself in, not wishing to be disturbed, and would respect her desire to be alone. It would save trouble, and give her time to get away. He could sleep on the sofa in his dressing-room, as he actually did, in the illness of his anger, treated as Italians know how to treat such common cases, of which the consequences are sometimes fatal. Many an Italian has died from a fit of rage. A single blood-vessel, in the brain, a little weaker than the rest, and all is over in an apoplexy. But Reanda was not of an apoplectic constitution. The calming treatment acted very soon, he fell asleep, and did not wake till daylight, quite unaware that Gloria was not in the next room, sleeping off her anger as he had done.

She had gone out in her first impulse to leave the house of the man who had so terribly insulted her. Under her veil the hot blood scorched her where the blow had left its red bar, and her rage and wounded pride chased one another from her heart to her head while with every beating of her pulse the longing for revenge grew wilder and stronger.

She had left the house with one first idea—to find Paul Griggs and tell him what had happened. No other thought crossed her mind, and her steps turned mechanically down the Corso, for he still lived in his two rooms in the Via della Frezza.

It was early still. People dined at six o'clock in those days, and it was not yet eight when Gloria found herself in the street. It was quiet, though there were many people moving about. During the hours between dinner and the theatre there were hardly any carriages out, and the sound of many footsteps and of many low voices filled the air. Gloria kept to the right and walked swiftly along, never turning her head. She had never been out in the streets alone at night in her life, and even in her anger she felt a sort of intoxication of freedom that was quite new to her, a beginning of satisfaction upon him who had injured her. There was Highland blood in her veins, as well as Italian passion.

The southeast wind was blowing down the street behind her, that same strange and tragic wind, tragic and passionate, that had blown so gustily down upon Subiaco from the mountains, on that night long ago when Maria Addolorata had stood aside by the garden gate to let Dalrymple pass, bearing something in his arms. Gloria knew it by its sad whisper and by the faint taste of it and smell of it, through her close-drawn veil.

On she went, down the Corso, till she came to the Piazza Colonna, and saw far on her left, beyond the huge black shaft of the column, the brilliant lights from the French officers' Club. She hesitated then, and slackened her speed a little. The sight of the Club reminded her of society, of what she was doing, and of what it might mean. As she walked more slowly, the wind gained upon her, as it were, from behind, and tried to drive her on. It seemed to be driving her from her husband's house with all its might, blowing her skirts before her and her thick veil. She passed the square, keeping close to the shutters of the shops under the Palazzo Piombino—gone now, to widen the open space. A gust, stronger than any she had felt yet, swept down the pavement. She paused a moment, leaning against the closed shutters of the clockmaker Ricci, whose shop used to be a sort of landmark in the Corso. Just then a clock within struck eight strokes. She heard them all distinctly through the shutters.

She hesitated an instant. It was eight o'clock. She had not realized what time it was. If she found the street door shut in the Via della Frezza, it would be hard to get at Griggs. She had passed the house more than once in her walks, and she knew that Griggs lived high up in the fifth story. It might be already too late. She hesitated and looked up and down the pavement. A young French officer of Zouaves was coming towards her; his high wrinkled and varnished boots gleamed in the gaslight. He had a black beard and bright young eyes, and was smoking a cigarette. He was looking at her and slackened his pace as he came near. She left her place and walked swiftly past him, down the Corso.

All at once she felt in the gust that drove her a cool drop of rain just behind her ear, and a moment later, passing a gas-lamp, she saw the dark round spots on the grey pavement. In her haste, she had brought no umbrella. She hurried on, and the wind blew her forward with all its might, so that she felt her steps lightened by its help. The Corso was darker and there were fewer people. The rain fell fast when she reached San Carlo, where the street widens, and she gathered her cloak about her as well as she could and crossed to the other side, hoping to find more shelter. She was nearing the Via della Frezza, and she knew some of the ins and outs of the narrow streets behind the tribune of the great church. It was very dark as she turned the semicircle of the apse, and the rain fell in torrents, but it was shorter to go that way, for Griggs lived nearer to the Ripetta than to the Corso, and she followed a sort of crooked diagonal, in the direction of his house. She thought the streets led by that way to the point she wished to reach, and she walked as fast as she could. The flare of an occasional oil lamp swung out high at the end of its lever showed her the way, and showed her, too, the rush of the yellow water down the middle channel of the street. She looked in vain for the turning she expected on her right. She had not lost her way, but she had not found the short cut she had looked for. Emerging upon the broad Ripetta, she paused an instant at the corner and looked about, though she knew which way to turn. Just then there were heavy splashing footsteps close to her.

"Permit me, Signora," said a voice that was rough and had an odd accent, though the tone was polite, and a huge umbrella was held over her head.

She shrank back against the wall quickly, in womanly fear of a strange man.

"No, thank you!" she exclaimed in answer.

"But yes!" said the man. "It rains. You are getting an illness, Signora."

The faint light showed her that she would be safe enough in accepting the offer. The man was evidently a peasant from the mountains, and he was certainly not young. His vast black cloak was turned back a little by his arm and showed the lining of green flannel and the blue clothes with broad silver buttons which he wore.

"Thank you," she said, for she was glad of the shelter, and she stood still under the enormous blue cotton umbrella, with its battered brass knob and its coloured stripes.

"But I will accompany you," said the man. "It is certainly not beginning to finish. Apoplexy! It rains in pieces!"

"Thank you. I am not going far," said Gloria. "You are very kind."

"It seems to be the act of a Christian," observed the peasant.

She began to move, and he walked beside her. He would have thought it bad manners to ask whither she was going. Through the torrents of rain they went on in silence. In less than five minutes she had found the door of Griggs's house. To her intense relief it was still open, and there was the glimmer of a tiny oil lamp from a lantern in the stairway. Gloria felt for the money in her pocket. The man did not wait, nor speak, and was already going away. She called him.

"I wish to give you something," said Gloria.

"To me?" exclaimed the man, in surprise. "No, Signora. It seems that you make a mistake."

"Excuse me," Gloria answered. "In the dark, I did not see. I am very grateful to you. You are from the country?"

She wished to repair the mistake she had made, by some little civility. The man stood on the doorstep, with his umbrella hanging backward over his shoulder, and she could see his face distinctly,—a typical Roman face with small aquiline features, keen dark eyes, a square jaw, and iron-grey hair.

"Yes, Signora. Stefanone of Subiaco, wine merchant, to serve you. If you wish wine of Subiaco, ask for me at Piazza Montanara. Signora, it rains columns. With permission, I go."

"Thank you again," she answered.

He disappeared into the torrent, and she was left alone at the foot of the gloomy stairs, under the feeble light of the little oil lamp. She had thrown back her veil, for it was soaked with water and stuck to her face. Little rivulets ran down upon the stones from her wet clothes, which felt intolerably heavy as she stood there, resting one gloved hand against the damp wall and staring at the lantern. Her thoughts had been disturbed by her brief interview with the peasant; the rain chilled her, and her face burned. She touched her cheek with her hand where Reanda had struck her. It felt bruised and sore, for the blow had not been a light one. The sensation of the wet leather disgusted her, and she drew off the glove with difficulty, turning it inside out over her full white hand. Then she touched the place again, and patted it, softly, and felt it. But her eyes did not move from the lantern.

There was one of those momentary lulling pauses in the rush of events which seem sent to confuse men's thoughts and unsettle their purposes. Had she reached the house five minutes earlier, she would not have hesitated a moment at the foot of the stairs. Suddenly she turned back to the door, and stood there looking out. It looked very black. She gathered her dripping skirt back as she bent forward a little and peered into the darkness. The rain fell in sheets, now, with the unquavering sound of a steadily rushing torrent. It would be madness to go out into it. A shiver ran through her, and another. She was very cold and miserable. No doubt Griggs had a fire upstairs, and a pleasant light in his study. He would be there, hard at work. She would knock, and he would open, and she would sit down by the fire and dry herself, and pour out her misery. The red bar was still across her face—she had seen it in the looking-glass when she had put on her hat.

To go back, to see her husband that night—it was impossible. Later, perhaps, when he should be asleep, Griggs would find a carriage and take her home. No one would ever know where she had been, and she would never tell any more than Griggs would. She felt that she must see him and tell him everything, and feel his strength beside her. After all, he was the only friend she had in the world, and it was natural that she should turn to him for help, in her father's absence. He was her father's friend, too.

She shivered again and again from head to foot, and she drew back from the door. For a moment she hesitated. Then with a womanly action she began to shake the rain out of her cloak and her skirts as well as she could, wetting her hands to the wrists. As she bent down, shaking the hem of the skirt, the blood rushed to her face again, and the place he had struck burned and smarted. It was quite a different sensation from what she had felt when she had touched it with her cool wet hand. She straightened herself with a spring and threw back her head, and her eyes flashed fiercely in the dark. The accidents of fate closed round her, and the hands of her destiny had her by the throat, choking her as she breathed.

There was no more hesitation. With quick steps she began to ascend the short, steep flights. It was dark, beyond the first turning, but she went on, touching the damp walls with her hands. Then there was a glimmer again, and a second lantern marked the first landing and shone feebly upon a green door with a thin little square of white marble screwed to it for a door-plate and a name in black. She glanced at it and went on, for she knew that Griggs lived on the fifth floor. She was surefooted, like her father, as she went firmly up, panting a little, for her drenched clothes weighed her down. There was one more light, and then there were no more. She counted the landings, feeling the doors with her hands as she went by, dizzy from the constant turning in the darkness. At last she thought she had got to the end, and groping with her hands she found a worsted string and pulled it, and a cracked little bell jangled and beat against the wood inside. She heard a pattering of feet, and a shrill, nasal child's voice called out the customary question, inquiring who was there. She asked for Griggs.

"He is not here," answered the child, and she heard the footsteps running away again, though she called loudly.

Her heart sank. But she groped her way on. The staircase ended, for it was the top of the house, and she found another door, and felt for a string like the one she had pulled, but there was none. Something told her that she was right, and with the sudden, desperate longing to be inside, with her strong protector, in the light and warmth, she beat upon the door with the palms of her hands, her face almost touching the cold painted wood studded with nails, that smelled of wet iron.

Then came the firm, regular footsteps of the strong man, and his clear, stern voice spoke from within, not in a question, but in a curt refusal to open.

"Go away," he said, in Italian. "You have mistaken the door."

But she beat with her hands upon the heavy wood.

"Let me in!" she cried in English. "Let me in!"

There was a deep exclamation of surprise, and the oiled bolt clanked back in its socket. The door opened inward, and Paul Griggs held up a lamp with a green shade, throwing the light into Gloria's face.

CHAPTER XXX

Gloria pushed past Griggs and stood beside him in the narrow entry. He shut the door mechanically, and turned slowly towards her, still holding up the lamp so that it shone upon her face.

"What has happened to you?" he asked, slowly and steadily, his shadowed eyes fixed upon her.

"He has beaten me, and I have come to you. Look at my face."

He saw the red bar across her cheek. He did not raise his voice, and there was little change in his features, but his eyes glowed suddenly, like the eyes of a wild beast, and he swore an oath so terrible that Gloria turned a little pale and shrank from him. Then he was silent, and they stood together. She could hear his breath. She could see him trying to swallow, for his throat was suddenly as dry as cinders. Very slowly his frown deepened to a scowl, and two straight furrows clove their way down between his eyes, his dark eyebrows were lifted evilly, upward and outward, and little by little the strong, clean shaven upper lip rose at the corners and showed two gleaming, wolfish teeth. The smooth, close hair bristled from the point where it descended upon his forehead.

Gloria shrank a little. She had seen such a look in an angry lion; just the look, without a motion of the limbs. Then it all disappeared, and the still face she knew so well was turned to hers.

"Will you come in?" he asked in a constrained tone. "It is my work-room. I will light a fire, and you must dry yourself. How did you get so wet? You did not come on foot?"

He opened the door while he was speaking, and led the way with the lamp. Gloria shivered as she followed, for there was a small window open in the entry, and her clothes clung to her in the cold draught. She closed the door behind her, as she went in. It was very little warmer within than without, and the small fireplace was black and cold. Instinctively she glanced at Griggs. He wore a rough pilot coat that had seen much service, buttoned to his throat. He set the little lamp with its green shade down upon the table amidst a mass of papers and books, and drew forward the only easy-chair there was, a dilapidated piece of furniture covered with faded yellow reps and ragged fringes that dragged on the floor. He took a great cloak from a clothes-horse in the corner and threw it over the chair, smoothing it carefully with his hands.

"If you will sit down, I will try and make a fire," he said quietly.

She sat down as he bade her, wondering a little at his calmness, but remembering the awful words that had escaped his lips when she had spoken, and the look of the wild beast and incarnate devil that had been one moment in his face. She looked about her while he began to make a fire, not hindering him, for she was shivering. The room was large, but very poorly furnished. There were two great tables, covered with books and papers; there was a deal bookcase along one wall and an antiquated cabinet between the two windows, one of its legs propped up with a dingy faded paper. The coarse green carpet was threadbare, but still whole. There were half-a-dozen plain chairs with green and white rush seats in various parts of the room. On the narrow white marble mantel-shelf stood two china candlesticks, in one of which there was a piece of candle that had guttered when last burning. In the middle a cheap American clock of white metal ticked loudly, and the hands pointed to twenty minutes before nine. In one corner was the clothes-horse, with two or three overcoats hanging on it, and two hats, one of which was hanging half over on one side. It looked as though two cloaked skeletons in hats were embracing. In another corner by the door a black stick and an umbrella stood side by side. But for the books the place would have had a desolate look. The air smelt of strong tobacco.

Gloria looked about her curiously, though her heart was beating fast. The man was familiar to her, dear to her in many ways, and over much in her life. The place where he lived contained a part of him which she did not know. Her breath came quickly in the anticipation of an emotion greater even than what she had felt already, but her eyes wandered in curiosity from one object to another. Suddenly she heard the loud cracking of breaking wood. There was a blaze of paper from the fireplace, illuminating all the room, and some light pieces he was throwing on kindled quickly. He was breaking them—she looked—it was one of the rush-bottomed chairs.

"What are you doing?" she cried, leaning suddenly far forward.

"Making a good fire," he answered. "There happened to be only one bit of wood in my box, so I am taking these things."

He broke the legs and the rails of the chair in his hands, as a child would break twigs, and heaped them up upon the blaze.

"There are five more," he observed. "They will make a good fire."

He arranged the burning mass to suit him, looked at it, and then turned.

"You ought to be a little nearer," he said, and he lifted the chair with her in it and set her before the fireplace.

It had all looked and felt desperately desolate half a minute earlier. It was changed now. He went to a corner and filled a small glass with wine from a straw-covered flask and brought it to her. She thanked him with her eyes and drank half of it eagerly. He knelt down before the fire again, for as the paper burned away underneath, the light sticks fell inward and might go out. When he had arranged it all again, he looked round and met her eyes, still kneeling.

"Is that better?" he asked quietly.

"You are so good," said Gloria, letting her eyelids droop as she looked from him to the pleasant flame.

He put out his hand and gently touched the hem of her cloth skirt.

"You are drenched," he said.

Then, before she realized what he was doing, he bent down and kissed the wet cloth, and without looking at her rose to his feet, got another chair and sat down near her. A soft blush of pleasure had risen in her cheeks. They were little things that he did, but they were like him, unaffected, strong, direct. Another man would have made apologies for having no wood and would have tried to make a fire of the single stick. Another man would have made excuses for the disorder of his room, or for the poverty of its furniture, perhaps. The other man she thought of was her husband, and possibly she had her father in her mind, too.

"When you are rested, tell me your story," he said, and his face hardened all at once.

She began to speak in a low and uncertain voice, reciting almost mechanically many things which she had often told him before. He listened without moving a muscle. Her voice was dear to him, whether she repeated the endless history of her woes for the tenth or the hundredth time. Where she was concerned he had no judgment, and he had no criterion, for he had never loved another woman with whom he could compare her. All that was of her was of paramount interest and weighty importance. He could not hear it too often. But to-night her first words had told him of the violent crisis in her life with Reanda, and he listened to all she said, before she reached that point, with an interest he had never felt before. But he would not look at her, for he must have taken her in his arms, as he had done once, months before now. She had come for protection and for help, and her need was the life spring of his honour.

As she went on, her voice took colour from her emotion, her hands moved now and then in short swift gestures, and her dark eyes burned. The marvellous dramatic power she possessed blazed out under the lash of her wrongs, and she found words she had only groped for until that moment. She described the miserably nervous feebleness of the man with scathing contempt, her tone made evil deeds of his shortcomings, her scorn made his weakness a black crime; her jealous anger fastened upon Francesca Campodonico and tore her honour to shreds and her virtues to rags of abomination; and her flaming pride blazed out in searing hatred and contempt for the coward who had struck her in the face.

"He broke my fan across my face!" she cried with the ascending intonation of a fury rising still, and still more fiercely beautiful. "He slashed my face with it and broke it and threw the bits down at my feet! There, look at it! That is his work—oh, give it back to him, kill him for me, tear him to pieces for me—make him feel what I have felt to-day!"

She had pushed her brown hat and veil back from her head, and her wet cloak had long ago fallen from her shoulders. One straight, white hand shot out and fastened upon her companion's arm, as he sat beside her, and she shook it in savage confidence of his iron strength.

A dead silence followed, but the fire made of the broken chairs roared and blazed on the low brick hearth. The man kept his eyes upon it fixedly, as though it were his salvation, for he felt that if he looked at her he was lost. She had come to him not for love, but for protection, of her own free will. Yet he felt that his honour was burning in him, with no longer life, if she stayed there, than the short, quick fire itself. His voice was thick when he answered, as though he were speaking through a velvet pall.

"I will kill him, if he will fight," he answered, with an effort. "I will not murder him, even for you."

She started, for she had not realized how he would take literally what she said. She had no experience of desperate men in her limited life.

"Murder him? No!" she said, snatching back her hand from his arm. "No, no! I never meant that."

"I am glad you did not. If you did, I should probably break down and do it to please you. But if he will fight like a man, I will kill him to please myself. Now I will go and get a carriage and take you home."

He rose to his feet and, turning, turned away from her, going toward the corner to get an overcoat. She followed him with her eyes, in silence.

"You are not afraid to be left alone for a quarter of an hour?" he asked, buttoning his coat, and looking toward his umbrella.

"Do not go just yet," she answered softly.

"I must. It is getting late. I shall not find a carriage if I wait any longer. I must go now."

"Do not go."

She heard him breathe hard once or twice. Then with quick strides he was beside her, and speaking to her.

"Gloria, I cannot stand it—I warn you. I love you in a way you cannot understand. You must not keep me here."

"Do not go," she said again, in the deep, soft tone of her golden voice.

"I must."

He turned from her and went towards the door. Soft and swift she followed him, but he was in the entry before her hand was on his arm. It was almost dusk out there. He stopped.

"I cannot go back to him," she said, and he could see the light in her eyes, and very faintly the red bar across the face he loved.

"You should—there is nowhere else for you to go," he said, and in the dark his hand was finding the bolt of the door to the stairs.

"No—there is nowhere else—I cannot go back to him," she answered, and the voice quavered uncertainly as the night breeze sighing amongst reeds.

"You must—you must," he tried to say.

Her weight was all upon his arm, but it was nothing to him. He steadily drew back the bolt. He turned up his face so that he could not see her.

With sudden strength her white hands went round his sinewy dark throat as he threw back his head.

"You are all I have in the world!" she half said, half whispered. "I will not let you go!"

"You?" His voice broke out as through a bursting shell.

"Yes. Come back!"

His arm fell like lead to his side. Gently she drew him back to the door of the study. The blaze of the fire shot into her face.

"Come," she said. "See how well it burns."

"Yes," he said, mechanically, "it is burning well."

He stood aside an instant at the door to let her pass. His eyelids closed and his face became rigid as a death mask of a man dead in passion. One moment only; then he followed her and softly shut the door.

CHAPTER XXXI

The brilliant winter morning had an intoxicating quality in it, after the heavy rain which had fallen in the night, and Paul Griggs felt that it was good to be alive as he threaded the narrow streets between his lodging and the Piazza Colonna. He avoided the Corso; for he did not know whom he might meet, and he had no desire to meet any one, except Angelo Reanda.

Naturally enough, his first honourable impulse was to go to the artist, to tell him something of the truth, and to give him an opportunity of demanding the common satisfaction of a hostile meeting. It did not occur to him that Reanda would not wish to exchange shots with him and have the chance of taking his life. Griggs was not the man to refuse such an encounter, and at that moment he felt so absolutely sure of himself that the idea of being killed was very far removed from his thoughts. It was without the slightest emotion that he enquired for Reanda at the latter's house, but he was very much surprised to hear that the painter had gone out as usual at his customary hour. He hesitated a moment and then decided not to leave a card, upon which he could not have written a message intelligible to Reanda which should not have been understood also by the servant who received it. Griggs made up his mind that he would write a formal note later in the day. He took it for granted that Reanda must be searching for his wife.

It was necessary to find a better lodging than the one in the Via della Frezza, and to provide as well as he could for Gloria's comfort. He was met by a difficulty upon which he had not reflected as yet, though he had been dimly aware of it more than once during the past twelve hours.

He was almost penniless, and he had no means of obtaining money at short notice. The payments he received from the newspapers for which he worked came regularly, but were not due for at least three weeks from that day. Alone in his bachelor existence he could have got through the time very well and without any greater privations than his capriciously ascetic nature had often imposed upon itself.

He was not an improvident man, but in his lonely existence he had no sense of future necessities, and the weakest point in his judgment was his undiscriminating generosity. Of the value of money as a store against possible needs, he had no appreciation at all, and he gave away what he earned beyond his most pressing requirements in secret and often ill-judged charities, whenever an occasion of doing so presented itself, though he never sought one. For himself, he was able to subsist on bread and water, and the meagre fare was scarcely a privation to his hardy constitution. If he chanced to have no money to spare for fuel, he bore the cold and buttoned up his old pea-jacket to the throat while he sat at work at his table. His self-respect made him wise and careful in regard to his dress, but in other matters many a handicraftsman was accustomed to more luxury than he. At the present juncture he had been taken unawares, and he found himself in great difficulty. He had left himself barely enough for subsistence until the arrival of the next remittance, and that meant but a very few scudi; and yet he knew that certain expenses must be met immediately, almost within the twenty-four hours. The very first thing was to get a lodging suitable for Gloria. It would be necessary to pay at least one month's rent in advance. Even if he were able to do that, he would be left without a penny for daily expenses. He had no bank account; for he cashed the drafts he received and kept the money in his room. He had never borrowed of an acquaintance, and the idea was repulsive to him and most humiliating. Had he possessed any bit of jewelry, or anything of value, he would have sold the object, but he had nothing of the kind. His books were practically valueless, consisting of such volumes as he absolutely needed for his daily use, chiefly cheap editions, poorly bound and well worn. He needed at least fifty scudi, and he did not possess quite ten. Three weeks earlier he had sent a hundred, anonymously, to free a starving artist from debt.

His position was only very partially enviable just then, but the bright north wind seemed to blow his troubles back from him as he faced it, walking home from his ineffectual attempt to meet Reanda. It was very unlike the man to return to his lodging without having accomplished anything, but he was hardly conscious of the fact. The face of the ancient city was suddenly changed, and it seemed as though nothing could go wrong if he would only allow fortune to play her own game without interference. He walked lightly, and there was a little colour in his face. He tried to think of what he should do to meet his present difficulties, but when he thought of them they were whirled away, shapeless and unrecognizable, and he felt a sense of irresistible power with each breath of the crisp dry air.

As he went along he glanced at the houses he passed, and on some of the doors were little notices scrawled in queer handwritings and telling that a lodging was to let. Occasionally he paused, looked up and hesitated, and then he went on. The difficulty was suddenly before him, and he knew that even if he looked at the rooms he could not hire them, as he had not enough money to cover the first month's rent. Immediately he attempted to devise some means of raising the sum he needed, but before he had reached the very next corner the clear north wind had blown the trouble away like a cobweb. With all his strength and industry and determination, he was still a very young man, and perplexity had no hold upon him since passion had taken its own way.

He reached the corner of his own street and stood still for a few moments. He could almost have smiled at himself as he paused. He had been out more than an hour and had done nothing, thought out nothing, made no definite plan for the future. His present poverty, which was desperate enough, had put on a carnival mask and laughed at him, as it were, and ran away when he tried to grapple with it and look it in the face. Gloria was there, upstairs in that tall house on which the morning sun was shining, and nothing else could possibly matter. But if anything mattered, it would be simple to talk it over together and to decide it in common.

Suddenly he felt ashamed of himself and of the confusion of his own intelligence. There was something meek and childish in standing still at the street corner, watching the people as they went by, listening to the regularly recurring yell of the man who was selling country vegetables from a hand-cart, and looking into the faces of people who went by, as though expecting to find there some solution of a difficulty which his disturbed powers of concentration did not clearly grasp. He could not think connectedly, much less could he reason sensibly. He made a few steps forward towards his house, and then stopped again, asking himself what he was going to do. He felt that he had no right to go back to Gloria until he had decided something for the future. He felt like a boy who has been sent on an errand, and who comes back having forgotten what he was to do. All at once he had lost his hold upon the logic of common-sense, and when he groped for a thread that might lead him, he was suddenly dazzled by the blaze of his happiness and deafened by the voice of his own joy.

He went on again and came to his own door. The one-eyed cobbler was at work, astride of his little bench with a brown pot of coals beside him. From time to time, when he had drawn the waxed yarn out through the leather on both sides, he blew into his black hands. Griggs stood still and looked at him in idle indetermination, and only struggling against the power that drew him towards the stairs.

"A fine north wind," observed Griggs, by way of salutation.

"It seems that it must be said," grunted the old man, punching a fresh hole in the sole he was cobbling. "To me, my fingers say it. It has always been a fine trade, this cobbling. It is a gentleman's trade because one is always sitting down."

"I am going to change my lodging," said Griggs.

The cobbler looked up, resting his dingy fists upon the bench on each side of the shoe, his awl in one hand, the other half encased in a leathern sheath, black with age.

"After so many years!" he exclaimed. "The world will also come to an end. I expected that it would. Now where will you take lodging?"

"Where I can find one. I want a little apartment—"

"It seems that your affairs go better," observed the old man, scrutinizing the other's face with his one eye.

"No. No better. That is the trouble. I want a little apartment, and I do not want to pay for it till the end of the first month."

"Then wait till the end of the month before you move to it, Signore."

"That is impossible."

"Then there is a female," said the cobbler, without the slightest hesitation. "I understand. Why did you not say so?"

Griggs hesitated. The man's guess had taken him by surprise. He reflected that it could make no difference whether the old cobbler knew of Gloria's coming or not.

"There is a signora—a relation of mine—who has come to Rome."

"A fair signora? Very beautiful? With a little eye of the devil? I have seen. Thanks be to heaven, one eye is still good. You are dark, and your family is fair. How can it interest me?"

"What? Has she gone out?" asked Griggs, in sudden anxiety. "When?"

"I had guessed!" exclaimed the cobbler, with a grunting laugh, and he ran the delicate bristles, which pointed the yarn, in opposite directions through the hole he had made, caught one yarn round the knot on the handle of the awl and the other round the leather sheath on his left hand. He drew the yarn tight to his arm's length with a vicious jerk.

"When did the signora go out?" enquired Griggs, repeating his question.

"It may be half an hour ago. Apoplexy! If your relations are all as beautiful as that!"

But Griggs was already moving towards the staircase. The cobbler called him back, and he stood still at the foot of the steps.

"There is the little apartment on the left, on the third floor," said the man. "The lodgers went away yesterday. I was going to ask you to write me a notice to put up on the door. As for paying, the padrone will not mind, seeing that you are an old lodger. It is good, do you know? There is sun. There is also a kitchen. There are five rooms with the entry."

"I will take it," said Griggs, instantly, and he ran up the stairs.

He was breathless with anxiety as he entered his work-room, and looked about him for something which should tell him where Gloria was gone. Almost instantly his eyes fell upon a sheet of paper lying before his accustomed seat. The writing on it was hers.

"I have gone to tell him. I shall be back soon."

That was all it said, but it was enough to blacken the sun that streamed through the windows upon the old carpet. Griggs sat down and rested his head in his hand. With the cloud that came between him and happiness, his powers of reason returned, and he saw quickly, in the pre-vision of logic, a scene of violence and anger between husband and wife, a possible reconciliation, and the instant wreck of his storm-driven love. It was impossible to know what Gloria would tell Reanda.

At the same instant the difficulties of his position rushed upon him and demanded an instant solution. He looked about him at the poor room, the miserable furniture, and the worn-out carpet, and the horror of poverty smote him in the face. He had allowed Gloria to come to him, and he knew that he could not support her decently. He had never found himself in so desperate a position in the course of his short and adventurous life. He could face anything when he alone was to suffer privation, but it was horrible to force misery upon the woman he loved.

Then, too, he asked himself what was to happen to Gloria if Reanda killed him, as was possible enough. And if he were not killed, there was Dalrymple, her father, who might return at any moment. No one could foretell what the Scotchman would do. It would be like him to do nothing except to refuse ever to see his daughter again. But he, also, might choose to fight, though his English traditions would be against it. In any case, Gloria ran the risk of being left alone, ruined and unprotected.

But the present problem was a meaner one, though not less desperate in its way. He reproached himself with having wasted even an hour when the case was so urgent. Without longer hesitation, he began to write letters to the editors for whom he worked, requesting them as a favour to advance the next remittance. Even then, he could scarcely expect to have money in less than ten days, and there was no one to whom he would willingly turn for help. Under ordinary circumstances he would have gone without food for days rather than have borrowed of an acquaintance, but he realized that he must overcome any such false pride within a day or two, at the risk of making Gloria suffer.

In those first hours he was not conscious of any question of right or wrong in what had taken place. Honour, in a rather worldly sense, had always supplied for him the place of all other moral considerations. The woman he loved had been ill-treated by her husband, and had come to him for protection. He had done his best, in spite of his love, to make her go back, and she had known how to refuse. Men, as men, would not blame him for what he was doing. Gloria, as a woman, could never reproach him with having tempted her. He might suffer for his deeds, but he could never blush for them.

CHAPTER XXXII

Meanwhile, Gloria had gone out alone, intending to find her husband and to tell him that the die was cast, that she had left him in haste and anger, but that she never would return to his house. She felt that she must live through the chain of emotions to the very last link, as it were, until she could feel no more. It was like her to go straight to Reanda and take up the battle where she had interrupted it. Her anger had been sudden, but it was not brief. She had left weakness, and had found strength to add to her own, and she wished the man who had hurt her to feel how strong she was, and how she was able to take her life out of his hands and to keep it for herself, and live it as she pleased in spite of him and every one. The wild blood that ran in her veins was free, now, and she meant that no one but herself should ever again have the right to thwart it, to tell her heart that it should beat so many times in each minute and no more. She was perfectly well aware that she was accepting social ruin with her freedom, but she had long nourished a rancorous hatred for the society which had seemed to accept her under protest, for Francesca's sake, and she was ready enough to turn her back on it before it should finally make up its polite mind to relegate her to the middle distance of indifferent toleration.

As for Reanda, on that first morning she hated him with all her soul, for himself, and for what he had done to her. She had words ready for him, and she turned and fitted them in her heart that they might cut him and stab him as long as he could feel. The selfishness with a tendency to cruelty which was a working spring of her father's character was strong in her, and craved the satisfaction of wounding. A part of the sudden joy in life which she felt as she walked towards what had been her home, lay in the certainty of dealing back fourfold hurt for every real and fancied injury she had ever suffered at Reanda's hands.

She felt quite sure of finding him. She did not imagine it possible that after what had happened he should go to the Palazzetto Borgia to work as usual. Besides, he must have discovered her absence by this time, and would in all probability be searching for her. She smiled at the idea, and she went swiftly on, keenly ready to give all the pain she could.

At her own door the servant seemed surprised to see her. Every one had supposed that she was still in her room, for it was not yet midday, and she sometimes slept very late. She glanced at the hall table and saw her key lying amongst the cards where she had thrown it when she had left the house. The servant did not see her take it, for she made a pretence of turning the cards over to find some particular one. She asked indifferently about her husband. The man said that Reanda had gone out as usual. Gloria started a little in surprise, and inquired whether he had left no message for her. On hearing that he had given none, she sent the servant away, went to her own room, and locked herself in.

With a curious Scotch caution very much at variance with her conduct, she reflected that as the servants were evidently not aware of what had taken place, they might as well be kept in the dark. In a few moments she gave the room the appearance which it usually had in the morning. With perfect calmness she dressed for the day, and then rang for her maid.

She told the woman that she had slept badly, had got up early, and had gone out for a long walk; that she now intended to leave Rome for a few days, for a change of air, and must have what she needed packed within an hour. She gave a few orders, clearly and concisely, and then went out again, leaving word that if Reanda returned he should be told that she was coming back very soon.

Clearly, she thought, he must have supposed that she was still sleeping, and he had gone to his painting without any further thought of her. Again she smiled, and a line of delicate cruelty was faintly shadowed about her lips. She left the house and walked in the direction of the Palazzetto. Reanda always came home to the midday breakfast, and it was nearly time for him to be on his way. Gloria knew every turning which he would take, and she hoped to meet him. Her eyes flashed in anticipation of the contest, and she felt that he would not be able to meet them. They would be too bright for him. There was a small mark on her cheek still, where one of the sharp edges of the ivory slats had scratched her fair skin, and there was a slight redness on that side, but the bright red bar was gone. She was glad of it, as she nodded to a passing acquaintance.

She wished to assure herself that her husband was really at the Palazzetto, and she inquired of the porter at the great gate whether Reanda had been seen that morning. The man said that he had come at the usual hour, and stood aside for her to pass, but she turned from him abruptly and went away without a word.

The blood rose in her cheeks, and her heart beat angrily. He had attached no more importance than this to what he had done, and had gone to his painting as though nothing had happened. He had not even tried to see her in the morning to beg her pardon for having struck her. Strange to say, in spite of what she herself had done, that was what most roused her anger. She demanded the satisfaction of his asking her forgiveness, as though she had no fault to find with herself. In comparison with his cowardly violence to her, her leaving him for Griggs was as nothing in her eyes.

She walked more slowly as she went homewards, and the unspoken bitterness of her heart choked her, and the sharp words she could not speak cut her cruelly. She compared the hand that had dared to hurt though it had not strength to kill, with that other, dearer, gentler, more terrible hand, which could have killed anything, but which would rather be burned to the wrist than let one of its fingers touch her roughly. She compared them, and she loved the one and she loathed the other, with all her heart. And with that same hand Reanda, at that same moment, was painting some goddess's face, and it had forgotten whose divinely lovely cheek it had struck. It was painting unless, perhaps, it lay in Francesca's. But Gloria had not forgotten, and she would repay before the day darkened.

Her husband, since he was calm enough to go to his work, would come home for his breakfast when he was hungry. Gloria went back to her room and superintended the packing of what she needed. But she was not so calm as she had been half an hour earlier, and she waited impatiently for her husband's return and for the last scene of the drama. When the things were packed, she had the box taken out to the hall and sent for a cab. As she foresaw the situation, she would leave the house forever as soon as the last word was spoken. Then she went into the drawing-room and waited, watching the clock.

There, on the mantelpiece, lay the broken fan, where the fragments had been placed by the servant. Gloria looked at them, handled them curiously, and felt her cheek softly with her hand. He must have struck her with all his might, she thought, to have hurt her as he had with so light a weapon; and the whole quarrel came back to her vividly, in every detail, and with every spoken word.

She could not regret what she had done. With an attempt at self-examination, which was only a self-justification, she tried to recall the early days when she had loved her husband, and to conjure up the face with the gentle light in it. She failed, of course, and the picture that came disgusted her and was unutterably contemptible and weak and full of cowardice. The face of Paul Griggs came in its place a moment later, and she heard in her ears the deep, stern voice, quavering with strength rather than with weakness, and she could feel the arms she loved about her, pressing her almost to pain, able to press her to death in their love-clasp.

The hands of the clock went on, and Reanda did not come. She was surprised to find how long she had waited, and with a revulsion of feeling she rose to her feet. If he would not come, she would not wait for him. She was hungry, too. It was absurd, perhaps, but she would not eat his bread nor sit at his table, not even alone. She went to her writing-table and wrote a note to him, short, cruel, and decisive. She wrote that if her father had been in Rome she would have gone to him for protection. As he was absent, she had gone to her father's best friend and her own—to Paul Griggs. She said nothing more. He might interpret the statement as he pleased. She sealed the note and addressed it, and before she went out of the house she gave it to the servant, to be given to Reanda as soon as he came home. The man-servant went downstairs with her, and stood looking after the little open cab; he saw Gloria speak to the coachman, who nodded and changed his direction before they were out of sight.

At the door in the Via della Frezza the cabman let down Gloria's luggage and drove away. She stood still a moment and looked at the one-eyed cobbler.

"You have given the signore a beautiful fright," observed the old man. "I told him you had gone out. With one jump he was upstairs. By this time he cries."

Gloria took a silver piece of two pauls from her purse.

"Can you carry up these things for me?" she inquired, concealing her annoyance at the man's speech.

"I am not a porter," said the cobbler, with his head on one side. "But one must live. With courage and money one makes war. There are three pieces. One at a time. But you must watch the door while I carry up the box. If any one should steal my tools, it would be a beautiful day's work. Without them I should be in the middle of the street. You will understand, Signora. It is not to do you a discourtesy, but my tools are my bread. Without them I cannot eat. There is also the left boot of Sor Ercole. If any one were to steal it, Sor Ercole would go upon one leg. Imagine the disgrace!"

"I will stay here," said Gloria. "Do not be afraid."

The cobbler, who was a strong old man, got hold of the trunk and shouldered it with ease. When he stood up, Gloria saw that he was bandy-legged and very short.

She turned and stood on the threshold of the street door as she had stood on the previous night. No one would have believed that a few hours earlier the rain had fallen in torrents, for the pavement was dry, and even under the arch there seemed to be no dampness. Looking up the street towards the Corso, she saw that there was a wine shop, a few doors higher on the opposite side. Two or three men were standing before it, under the brown bush which served for a sign, and amongst them she saw a peasant in blue cloth clothes with silver buttons and clean white stockings. She recognized him as the man who had held his umbrella over her in the storm. He also saw her, lifted his felt hat and came forwards, crossing the street. His look was fixed on her face with a stare of curiosity as he stood before her.

"I hope you have not caught cold, Signora," he said, with steady, unwinking eyes. "We passed a beautiful storm. Signora, I sell wine to that host. If you should need wine, I recommend him to you." He pointed to the shop.

"You told me to ask for you at the Piazza Montanara," said Gloria, smiling.

"With that water you could not see the shop," answered Stefanone. "Signora, you are very beautiful. With permission, I say that you should not walk alone at night."

"It was the first and last time," said Gloria. "Fortunately, I met a person of good manners. I thank you again."

"Signora, you are so beautiful that the Madonna and her angels always accompany you. With permission, I go. Good day."

To the last, until he turned, he kept his eyes steadily fixed on Gloria's face, as though searching for a resemblance in her features. She noticed his manner and remembered him very distinctly after the second meeting.

The cobbler came back again, closely followed by Griggs himself, who said nothing, but took possession of the small valise and bag which Gloria had brought in addition to her box. He led the way, and she followed him swiftly. Inside the door of his lodging he turned and looked at her.

"Please do not go away suddenly without telling me," he said in a low voice. "I am easily frightened about you."

"Really?"

Gloria held out her two hands to meet him. He nodded as he took them.

"That is better than anything you have ever said to me." She drew him to her.

It was natural, for she was thinking how Reanda had calmly gone back to his work that morning, without so much as asking for her. The contrast was too great and too strong, between love and indifference.

They went into the work-room together, and Gloria sat down on one of the rush chairs, and told Griggs what she had done. He walked slowly up and down while she was speaking, his eyes on the pattern of the old carpet.

"I might have stayed," she said at last. "The servants did not even know that I had been out of the house."

"You should have stayed," said Griggs. "I ought to say it, at least."

But as he spoke the mask softened and the rare smile beautified for one instant the still, stern face.

CHAPTER XXXIII

Reanda neither wished to see Gloria again, nor to take vengeance upon Paul Griggs. He was not a brave man, morally or physically, and he was glad that his wife had left him. She had put him in the right, and he had every reason for refusing ever to see her again. With a cynicism which would have been revolting if it had not been almost childlike in its simplicity, he discharged his servants, sold his furniture, gave up his apartment in the Corso, and moved back to his old quarters in the Palazzetto Borgia. But he did not acknowledge Gloria's note in any other way.

She had left him, and he wished to blot out her existence as though he had never known her, not even remembering the long two years of his married life. She was gone. There was no Gloria, and he wished that there never had been any woman with her name and face.

On the third day, he met Paul Griggs in the street. The younger man saw Reanda coming, and stood still on the narrow pavement, in order to show that he had no intention of avoiding him. As the artist came up, Griggs lifted his hat gravely. Reanda mechanically raised his hand to his own hat and passed the man who had injured him, without a word. Griggs saw a slight, nervous twitching in the delicate face, but that was all. He thought that Reanda looked better, less harassed and less thin, than for a long time. He had at once returned to his old peaceful life and enjoyed it, and had evidently not the smallest intention of ever demanding satisfaction of his former friend.

Francesca Campodonico had listened in nervous silence to Reanda's story.

"She has done me a kindness," he concluded. "It is the first. She has given me back my freedom. I shall not disturb her."

The colour was in Francesca's face, and her eyes looked down. Her delicate lips were a little drawn in, as though she were making an effort to restrain her words, for it was one of the hardest moments of her life. Being what she was, it was impossible for her to understand Gloria's conduct. But at the same time she felt that she was liberated from something which had oppressed her, and the colour in her cheeks was a flash of satisfaction and relief mingled with a certain displeasure at her own sensations and the certainty that she should be ashamed of them by and bye.

It was not in her nature to accept such a termination for Reanda's married life, however he himself might be disposed to look upon it.

"You are to blame almost as much as Gloria," she said, and she was sincerely in earnest.

She was too good and devout a woman to believe in duelling, but she was far too womanly to be pleased with Reanda's indifference. It was wicked to fight duels and unchristian to seek revenge. She knew that, and it was a conviction as well as an opinion. But a man who allowed another to take his wife from him and did not resent the injury could not command her respect. Something in her blood revolted against such tameness, though she would not for all the world have had Reanda take Gloria back. Between the two opposites of conviction and instinct, she did not know what to do. Moreover, Reanda had struck his wife. He admitted it, though apologetically and with every extenuating circumstance which he could remember.

"Yes," he answered. "I know that I did wrong. Am I infallible? Holy Saint Patience! I could bear no more. But it is clear that she was waiting for a reason for leaving me. I gave it to her, and she should be grateful. She also is free, as I am."

"It is horrible!" exclaimed Francesca, with sorrowful emphasis.

She blamed herself quite as much as Reanda or Gloria, because she had brought them together and had suggested the marriage. Reanda's thin shoulders went up, and he smiled incredulously.

"I do not see what is so horrible," he answered. "Two people think they are in love. They marry. They discover their mistake. They separate. Well? It is finished. Let us make the sign of the cross over it."

The common Roman phrase, signifying that a matter is ended and buried, as it were, jarred upon Francesca, for whom the smallest religious allusion had a real meaning.

"It is not the sign of the cross which should be made," she said sadly and gravely, and the colour was gone from her face now. "There are two lives wrecked, and a human soul in danger. We cannot say that it is finished, and pass on."

"What would you have me do?" asked Reanda, almost impatiently. "Take her back?"

"No!" exclaimed Francesca, with a sharp intonation as though she were hurt.

"Well, then, what? I do not see that anything is to be done. She herself can think of her soul. It is her property. She has made me suffer enough—let some one else suffer. I have enough of it."

"You will forgive her some day," said Francesca. "You are angry still, and you speak cruelly. You will forgive her."

"Never," answered Reanda, with emphasis. "I will not forgive her for what she made me bear, any more than I will forgive Griggs for receiving her when she left me. I will not touch them, but I will not forgive them. I am not angry. Why should I be?"

Francesca sighed, for she did not understand the man, though hitherto she had always understood him, or thought that she had, ever since she had been a mere child, playing with his colours and brushes in the Palazzo Braccio. She left the hall and went to her own sitting-room on the other side of the house. As soon as she was alone, the tears came to her eyes. She was hardly aware of them, and when she felt them on her cheeks she wondered why she was crying, for she did not often shed tears, and was a woman of singularly well balanced nature, able to control herself on the rare occasions when she felt any strong emotion.

In spite of Reanda's conduct, she determined not to leave matters as they were without attempting to improve them. She wrote a note to Paul Griggs, asking him to come and see her during the afternoon.

He could not refuse to answer the summons, knowing, as he did, that he must in honour respond to any demand for an explanation coming from Reanda's side. Gloria wished him to reply to the note, giving an excuse and hinting that no good could come of any meeting.

"It is a point of honour," he answered briefly, and she yielded, for he dominated her altogether.

Francesca received him in her own small sitting-room, which overlooked the square before the Palazzetto. It was very quiet, and there were roses in old Vienna vases. It was a very old-fashioned room, the air was sweet with the fresh flowers, and the afternoon sun streamed in through a single tall window. Francesca sat on a small sofa which stood crosswise between the window and the writing-table. She had a frame before her on which was stretched a broad band of deep red satin, a piece of embroidery in which she was working heraldic beasts and armorial bearings in coloured silks.

She did not rise, nor hold out her hand, but pointed to a chair near her, as she spoke.

"I asked you to come," she said, "because I wish to speak to you about Gloria."

Griggs bent his head, sat down, and waited with a perfectly impassive face. Possibly there was a rather unusual aggressiveness in the straight lines of his jaw and his even lips. There was a short silence before Francesca spoke again.

"Do you know what you have done?" she asked, finishing a stitch and looking quietly into the man's deep eyes.

He met her glance calmly, but said nothing, merely bending his head again, very slightly.

"It is very wicked," said she, and she began to make another stitch, looking down again.

"I have no doubt that you think so," answered Paul Griggs, slowly nodding a third time.

"It is not a question of opinion. It is a matter of fact. You have ruined the life of an innocent woman."

"If social position is the object of existence, you are right," he replied. "I have nothing to say."

"I am not speaking of social position," said Donna Francesca, continuing to make stitches.

"Then I am afraid that I do not understand you."

"Can you conceive of nothing more important to the welfare of men and women than social position?"

"It is precisely because I do, that I care so little what society thinks. I do not understand you."

"I have known you some time," said Francesca. "I had not supposed that you were a man without a sense of right and wrong. That is the question which is concerned now."

"It is a question which may be answered from more than one point of view. You look at it in one way, and I in another. With your permission, we will differ about it, since we can never agree."

"There is no such thing as differing about right and wrong," answered Donna Francesca, with a little impatience. "Right is right, and wrong is wrong. You cannot possibly believe that you have done right. Therefore you know that you have done wrong."

"That sort of logic assumes God at the expense of man," said Griggs, calmly.

Francesca looked up with a startled expression in her eyes, for she was shocked, though she did not understand him.

"God is good, and man is sinful," she answered, in the words of her simple faith.

"Why?" asked Griggs, gravely.

He waited for her answer to the most tremendous question which man can ask, and he knew that she could not answer him, though she might satisfy herself.

"I have never talked about religion with an atheist," she said at last, slowly pushing her needle through the heavy satin.

"I am not an atheist, Princess."

"A Protestant, then—"

"I am not a Protestant. I am a Catholic, as you are."

She looked up suddenly and faced him with earnest eyes.

"Then you are not a good Catholic," she said. "No good Catholic could speak as you do."

"Even the Apostles had doubts," answered Griggs. "But I do not pretend to be good. Since I am a man, I have a right to be a man, and to be treated as a man. If the right is not given me freely, I will take it. You cannot expect a body to behave as though it were a spirit. A man cannot imitate an invisible essence, any more than a sculptor can imitate sound with a shape of clay. When we are spirits, we shall act as spirits. Meanwhile we are men and women. As a man, I have not done wrong. You have no right to judge me as an angel. Is that clear?"

"Terribly clear!" Francesca slowly shook her head. "And terribly mistaken," she added.

"You see," answered the young man. "It is impossible to argue the point. We do not speak the same language. You, by your nature, believe that you can imitate a spirit. You are spiritual by intuition and good by instinct, according to the spiritual standard of good. I am, on the contrary, a normal man, and destined to act as men act. I cannot understand you and you, if you will allow me to say so, cannot possibly understand me. That is why I propose that we should agree to differ."

"And do you think you can sweep away all right and wrong, belief and unbelief, salvation and perdition, with such a statement as that?"

"Not at all," replied Griggs. "You tell me that I am wicked. That only means that I am not doing what you consider right. You deny my right of judgment, in favour of your own. You make witnesses of spirits against the doings of men. You judge my body and condemn my soul. And there is no possible appeal from your tribunal, because it is an imaginary one. But if you will return to the facts of the case, you will find it hard to prove that I have ruined the life of an innocent woman, as you told me that I had."

"You have! There is no denying it."

"Socially, and it is the fault of society. But society is nothing to me. I would be an outcast from society for a much less object than the love of a woman, provided that I had not to do anything dishonourable."

"Ah, that is it! You forget that a man's honour is his reputation at the club, while the honour of a woman is founded in religion, and maintained upon a single one of God's commandments—as you men demand that it shall be."

Griggs was silent for a moment. He had never heard a woman state the case so plainly and forcibly, and he was struck by what she said. He could have answered her quickly enough. But the answer would not have been satisfactory to himself.

"You see, you have nothing to say," she said. "But in one way you are right. We cannot argue this question. I did not ask you to come in order to discuss it. I sent for you to beg you to do what is right, as far as you can. And you could do much."

"What should you think right?" asked Griggs, curious to know what she thought.

"You should take Gloria to her father, as you are his friend. Since she has left her husband, she should live with her father."

"That is a very simple idea!" exclaimed the young man, with something almost like a laugh.

"Right is always simple," answered Francesca, quietly. "There is never any doubt about it."

She looked at him once, and then continued to work at her embroidery. His eyes rested on the pure outline of her maidenlike face, and he was silent for a moment. Somehow, he felt that her simplicity of goodness rebuked the simplicity of his sin.

"You forget one thing," said Griggs at last. "You make a spiritual engine of mankind, and you forget the mainspring of the world. You leave love out of the question."

"Perhaps—as you understand love. But you will not pretend to tell me that love is necessarily right, whatever it involves."

"Yes," answered the young man. "That is what I mean. Unless your God is a malignant and maleficent demon, the overwhelming passions which take hold of men, and against which no man can fight beyond a certain point, are right, because they exist and are irresistible. As for what you propose that I should do, I cannot do it."

"You could, if you would," said Francesca. "There is nothing to hinder you, if you will."

"There is love, and I cannot."

CHAPTER XXXIV

Paul Griggs left Francesca with the certainty in his own mind that she had produced no impression whatever upon him, but he was conscious that his opinion of her had undergone a change. He was suddenly convinced that she was the best woman he had ever known, and that Gloria's accusations were altogether unjust and unfounded. Recalling her face, her manner, and her words, he knew that whatever influence she might have had upon Reanda, there could be no ground for Gloria's jealousy. She certainly disturbed him strangely, for Gloria was perfect in his eyes, and he accepted all she said almost blindly. The fact that Reanda had struck her now stood in his mind as the sole reason for the separation of husband and wife.

Gloria was far from realizing what influence she had over the man she loved. It seemed to her, on the contrary, that she was completely dominated by him, and she was glad to feel his strength at every turn. Her enormous vanity was flattered by his care of her, and by his uncompromising admiration of her beauty as well as of her character, and she yielded to him purposely in small things that she might the better feel his strength, as she supposed. The truth, had she known it, was that he hardly asserted himself at all, and was ready to make any and every sacrifice for her comfort and happiness. He had sacrificed his pride to borrow money from a friend to meet the first necessities of their life together. He would have given his life as readily.

They led a strangely lonely existence in the little apartment in the Via della Frezza. The world had very soon heard of what had happened, and had behaved according to its lights. Walking alone one morning while Griggs was at work, Gloria had met Donna Tullia Meyer, whom she had known in society, and thoughtlessly enough had bowed as though nothing had happened. Donna Tullia had stared at her coldly, and then turned away. After that, Gloria had realized what she had already understood, and had either not gone out without Griggs, or, when she did, had kept to the more secluded streets, where she would not easily meet acquaintances.

Griggs worked perpetually, and she watched him, delighting at first in the difference between his way of working and that of Angelo Reanda; delighted, too, to be alone with him, and to feel that he was writing for her. She could sit almost in silence for hours, half busy with some bit of needlework, and yet busy with him in her thoughts. It seemed to her that she understood him—she told him so, and he believed her, for he felt that he could not be hard to understand.

He was as singularly methodical as Reanda was exceptionally intuitive. She felt that his work was second to her in his estimation of it, but that, since they both depended upon it for their livelihood, they had agreed together to put it first. With Reanda, art was above everything and beyond all other interests, and he had made her feel that he worked for art's sake rather than for hers. There was a vast difference in the value placed upon her by the two men, in relation to their two occupations.

"I have no genius," said Griggs to her one day. "I have no intuitions of underlying truth. But I have good brains, and few men are able to work as hard as I. By and bye, I shall succeed and make money, and it will be less dull for you."

"It is never dull for me when I can be with you," she answered.

As he looked, the sunshine caught her red auburn hair, and the love-lights played with the sunshine in her eyes. Griggs knew that life had no more dulness for him while she lived, and as for her, he believed what she said.

Without letting him know what she was doing, she wrote to her father. It was not an easy letter to write, and she thought that she knew the savage old Scotchman's temper. She told him everything. At such a distance, it was easy to throw herself upon his mercy, and it was safer to write him all while he was far away, so that there might be nothing left to rouse his anger if he returned. She had no lack of words with which to describe Reanda's treatment of her; but she was also willing to take all the blame of the mistake she had made in marrying him. She had ruined her life before it had begun, she said. She had taken the law into her own hands, to mend it as best she could. Her father knew that Paul Griggs was not like other men—that he was able to protect her against all comers, and that he could make the world fear him if he could not make it respect her. Her father must do as he thought right. He would be justified, from the world's point of view, in casting her off and never remembering her existence again, but she begged him to forgive her, and to think kindly of her. Meanwhile, she and Griggs were wretchedly poor, and she begged her father to continue her allowance.

If Paul Griggs had seen this letter, he would have been startled out of some of his belief in Gloria's perfection. There was a total absence of any moral sense of right or wrong in what she wrote, which would have made a more cynical man than Griggs was look grave. The request for the continuation of the allowance would have shocked him and perhaps disgusted him. The whole tone was too calm and business-like. It was too much as though she were fulfilling a duty and seeking to gain an object rather than appealing to Dalrymple to forgive her for yielding to the overwhelming mastery of a great passion. It was cold, it was calculating, and it was, in a measure, unwomanly.

When she had sent the letter, she told Griggs what she had done, but her account of its contents satisfied him with one of those brilliant false impressions which she knew so well how to convey. She told him rather what she should have said than what she had really written, and, as usual, he found that she had done right.

It was not that she would not have written a better letter if she had been able to compose one. She had done the best that she could. But the truth lay there, or the letter was composed as an expression of what she knew that she ought to feel, and was not the actual outpouring of an overfull heart. She could not be blamed for not feeling more deeply, nor for her inability to express what she did not feel. But when she spoke of it to the man she loved, she roused herself to emotion easily enough, and her words sounded well in her own ears and in his. To the last, he never understood that she loved such emotion for its own sake, and that he helped her to produce it in herself. In the comparatively simple view of human nature which he took in those days, it seemed to him that if a woman were willing to sacrifice everything, including social respectability itself, for any man, she must love him with all her heart. He could not have understood that any woman should give up everything, practically, in the attempt to feel something of which she was not capable.

In reply to her letter, Dalrymple sent a draft for a considerable sum of money, through his banker. The fact that it was addressed to her at Via della Frezza was the only indication that he had received her letter. In due time, Gloria wrote to thank him, but he took no notice of the communication.

"He never loved me," she said to Griggs as the days went by and brought her nothing from her father. "I used to think so, when I was a mere child, but I am sure of it now. You are the only human being that ever loved me."

She was pale that day, and her white hand sought his as she spoke, with a quiver of the lip.

"I am glad of it," he answered. "I shall not divide you with any one."

So their life went on, somewhat monotonously after the first few weeks. Griggs worked hard and earned more money than formerly, but he discovered very soon that it would be all he could do to support Gloria in bare comfort. He would not allow her to use her own money for anything which was to be in common, or in which he had any share whatever.

"You must spend it on yourself," he said. "I will not touch it. I will not accept anything you buy with it—not so much as a box of cigarettes. You must spend it on your clothes or on jewels."

"You are unkind," she answered. "You know how much pleasure it would give me to help you."

"Yes. I know. You cannot understand, but you must try. Men never do that sort of thing."

And, as usual, he dominated her, and she dropped the subject, inwardly pleased with him, and knowing that he was right.

His strength fascinated her, and she admired his manliness of heart and feeling as she had never admired any qualities in any one during her life. But he did not amuse her, even as much as she had been amused by Reanda. He was melancholic, earnest, hard working, not inclined to repeat lightly the words of love once spoken in moments of passion. He meant, perhaps, to show her how he loved her by what he would do for her sake, rather than tell her of it over and over again. And he worked as he had never worked before, hour after hour, day after day, sitting at his writing-table almost from morning till night. Besides his correspondence, he was now writing a book, from which he hoped great things—for her. It was a novel, and he read her day by day the pages he wrote. She talked over with him what he had written, and her imagination and dramatic intelligence, forever grasping at situations of emotion for herself and others, suggested many variations upon his plan.

"It is my book," she often said, when they had been talking all the evening.

It was her book, and it was a failure, because it was hers and not his. Her imagination was disorderly, to borrow a foreign phrase, and she was altogether without any sense of proportion in what she imagined. He did not, indeed, look upon her as intellectually perfect, though for him she was otherwise unapproachably superior to every other woman in the world. But he loved her so wholly and unselfishly that he could not bear to disappoint her by not making use of her suggestions. When she was telling him of some scene she had imagined, her voice and manner, too, were so thoroughly dramatic that he was persuaded of the real value of the matter. Divested of her individuality and transferred in his rather mechanically over-correct language to the black and white of pen and ink, the result was disappointing, even when he read it to her. He knew that it was, and wasted time in trying to improve what was bad from the beginning. She saw that he failed, and she felt that he was not a man of genius. Her vanity suffered because her ideas did not look well on his paper.

Before he had finished the manuscript, she had lost her interest in it. Feeling that she had, and seeing it in her face, he exerted his strength of will in the attempt to bring back the expression of surprise and delight which the earlier readings had called up, but he felt that he was working uphill and against heavy odds. Nevertheless he completed the work, and spent much time in fancied improvement of its details. At a later period in his life he wrote three successful books in the time he had bestowed upon his first failure, but he wrote them alone.

Gloria's face brightened when he told her that it was done. She took the manuscript and read over parts of it to herself, smiling a little from time to time, for she knew that he was watching her. She did not read it all.

"Dedicate it to me," she said, holding out one hand to find his, while she settled the pages on her knees with the other.

"Of course," he answered, and he wrote a few words of dedication to her on a sheet of paper.

He sent it to a publisher in London whom he knew. It was returned with some wholesome advice, and Gloria's vanity suffered another blow, both in the failure of the book which contained so many of her ideas and in the failure of the man to be successful, for in her previous life she had not been accustomed to failure of any sort.

"I am afraid I am only a newspaper man, after all," said Paul Griggs, quietly. "You will have to be satisfied with me as I am. But I will try again."

"No," answered Gloria, more coldly than she usually spoke. "When you find that you cannot do a thing naturally, leave it alone. It is of no use to force talent in one direction when it wants to go in another."

She sighed softly, and busied herself with some work. Griggs felt that he was a failure, and he felt lonely, too, for a moment, and went to his own room to put away the rejected manuscript in a safe place. It was not his nature to destroy it angrily, as some men might have done at his age.

When he came back to the door of the sitting-room he heard her singing, as she often did when she was alone. But to-day she was singing an old song which he had not heard for a long time, and which reminded him painfully of that other house in which she had lived and of that other man whom she never saw, but who was still her husband.

He entered the room rather suddenly, after having paused a moment outside, with his hand on the door.

"Please do not sing that song!" he said quickly, as he entered.

"Why not?" she asked, interrupting herself in the middle of a stave.

"It reminds me of unpleasant things."

"Does it? I am sorry. I will not sing it again."

But she knew what it meant, for it reminded her of Reanda. She was no longer so sure that the reminiscence was all painful.

CHAPTER XXXV

In spite of all that Griggs could do, and he did his utmost, it was hard to live in anything approaching to comfort on the meagre remuneration he received for his correspondence, and his pride altogether forbade him to allow Gloria to contribute anything to the slender resources of the small establishment. At first, it had amused her to practise little economies, even in the matter of their daily meals. Griggs denied himself everything which was not absolutely necessary, and it pleased Gloria to imitate him, for it made her feel that she was helping him. The housekeeping was a simple affair enough, and she undertook it readily. They had one woman servant as cook and maid-of-all-work, a strong young creature, not without common-sense, and plentifully gifted with that warm, superficial devotion which is common enough in Italian servants. Gloria had kept house for her father long enough to understand what she had undertaken, and it seemed easy at first to do the same thing for Griggs, though on a much more restricted scale.

But the restriction soon became irksome. In a more active and interesting existence, she would perhaps not have felt the constant pinching of such excessive economy. If there had been more means within her reach for satisfying her hungry vanity, she could have gone through the daily round of little domestic cares with a lighter heart or, at least, with more indifference. But she and Griggs led a very lonely life, and, as in all lonely lives, the smallest details became important.

It was not long before Gloria wished herself in her old home in the Corso, not indeed with Reanda, but with Paul Griggs. He had made her promise to use only the money he gave her himself for their housekeeping. She secretly deceived him and drew upon her own store, and listened in silence to his praise of her ingenuity in making the little he was able to give her go so far. He trusted her so completely that he suspected nothing.

She expected that at the end of three months her father would send her another draft, but the day passed, and she received nothing, so that she at last wrote to him again, asking for money. It came, as before, without any word of inquiry or greeting. Dalrymple evidently intended to take this means of knowing from time to time that his daughter was alive and well. She would be obliged to write to him whenever she needed assistance. It was a humiliation, and she felt it bitterly, for she had thought that she had freed herself altogether and she found herself still bound by the necessity of asking for help.

It seemed very hard to be thus shut off from the world in the prime of her youth, and beauty, and talent. To a woman who craved admiration for all she did and could do, it was almost unbearable. Paul Griggs worked and looked forward to success, and was satisfied in his aspirations, and more than happy in the companionship of the woman he so dearly loved.

"I shall succeed," he said quietly, but with perfect assurance. "Before long we shall be able to leave Rome, and begin life somewhere else, where nobody will know our story. It will not be so dull for you there."

"It is never dull when I am with you," said Gloria, but there was no conviction in the tone any more. "If you would let me go upon the stage," she added, with a change of voice, "things would be very different. I could earn a great deal of money."

But Paul Griggs was as much opposed to the project as Reanda had been, and in this one respect he really asserted his will. He was so confident of ultimately attaining to success and fortune by his pen that he would not hear of Gloria's singing in public.

"Besides," he said, after giving her many and excellent reasons, "if you earned millions, I would not touch the money."

She sighed for the lost opportunities of brilliant popularity, but she smiled at his words, knowing how she had used her own money for him, and in spite of him. But for her own part she had lost all belief in his talent since the failure of the book he had written.

The long summer days were hard to bear. He was not able to leave Rome, for he was altogether dependent upon his regular correspondence for what he earned, and he did not succeed in persuading his editors to employ him anywhere else, for the very reason that he did so well what was required of him where he was.

The weather grew excessively hot, and it was terribly dreary and dull in the little apartment in the Via della Frezza. All day long the windows were tightly closed to keep out the fiery air, both the old green blinds and the glass within them. Griggs had moved his writing-table to the feeble light, and worked away as hard as ever. Gloria spent most of the hot hours in reading and dreaming. They went out together early in the morning and in the evening, when there was some coolness, but during the greater part of the day they were practically imprisoned by the heat.

Gloria watched the strong man and wondered at his power of working under any circumstances. He was laborious as well as industrious. He often wrote a page over two and three times, in the hope of improving it, and he was capable of spending an hour in finding a quotation from a great writer, not for the sake of quoting it, but in order to satisfy himself that he had authority for using some particular construction of phrase. He kept notebooks in which he made long indexed lists of words which in common language were improperly used, with examples showing how they should be rightly employed.

"I am constructing a superiority for myself," he said once. "No one living takes so much pains as I do."

But Gloria had no faith in his painstaking ways, though she wondered at his unflagging perseverance. Her own single great talent lay in her singing, and she had never given herself any trouble about it. Reanda, too, though he worked carefully and often slowly, worked without effort. It was true that Griggs never showed fatigue, but that was due to his amazing bodily strength. The intellectual labour was apparent, however, and he always seemed to be painfully overcoming some almost unyielding difficulty by sheer force of steady application, though nothing came of it, so far as she could see.

"I cannot understand why you take so much trouble," she said. "They are only newspaper articles, after all, to be read to-day and forgotten to-morrow."

"I am learning to write," he answered. "It takes a long time to learn anything unless one has a great gift, as you have for singing. I have failed with one book, but I will not fail with another. The next will not be an extraordinary book, but it will succeed."

Nothing could disturb him, and he sat at his table day after day. He was moved by the strongest incentives which can act upon a man, at the time when he himself is strongest; namely, necessity and love. Even Gloria could never discover whether he had what she would have called ambition. He himself said that he had none, and she compared him with Reanda, who believed in the divinity of art, the temple of fame, and the reality of glory.

In the young man's nature, Gloria had taken the place of all other divinities, real and imaginary. His enduring nature could no more be wearied in its worship of her than it could be tired in toiling for her. He only resented the necessity of cutting out such a main part of the day for work as left him but little time to be at leisure with her.

She complained of his industry, for she was tired of spending her life with novels, and the hours hung like leaden weights upon her, dragging with her as she went through the day.

"Give yourself a rest," she said, not because she thought he needed it, but because she wished him to amuse her.

"I am never tired of working for you," he answered, and the rare smile came to his face.

With any other man in the world she might have told the truth and might have said frankly that her life was growing almost unbearable, buried from the world as she was, and cut off from society. But she was conscious that she should never dare to say as much to Paul Griggs. She was realizing, little by little, that his love for her was greater than she had dreamed of, and immeasurably stronger than what she felt for him.

Then she knew the pain of receiving more than she had to give. It was a genuine pain of its kind, and in it, as in many other things, she suffered a constant humiliation. She had taken herself for a heroic character in the great moment when she had resolved to leave her husband, intuitively sure that she loved Paul Griggs with all her heart, and that she should continue to love him to the end in spite of the world. She knew now that there was no endurance in the passion.

The very efforts she made to sustain it contributed to its destruction; but she continued to play her part. Her strong dramatic instinct told her when to speak and when to be silent, and how to modulate her voice to a tender appeal, to a touching sadness, to the strength of suppressed emotion. It was for a good object, she told herself, and therefore it must be right. He was giving his life for her, day by day, and he must never know that she no longer loved him. It would kill him, she thought; for with him it was all real. She grew melancholy and thought of death. If she died young, he should never guess that she had not loved him to the very last.

In her lonely thoughts she dwelt upon the possibility, for it was a possibility now. There was that before her which, when it came, might turn life into death very suddenly. She had moments of tenderness when she thought of her own dead face lying on the white pillow, and the picture was so real that her eyes filled with tears. She would be very beautiful when she was dead.

The idea took root in her mind; for it afforded her an inward emotion which touched her strangely and cost her nothing. It gained in fascination as she allowed it to come back when it would, and the details of death came vividly before her imagination, as she had read of them in books,—her own white face, the darkened room, the candles, Paul Griggs standing motionless beside her body.

One day he looked from his work and saw tears on her cheeks. He dropped his pen as though something had struck him unawares; and he was beside her in a moment, looking anxiously into her eyes.

"What is it?" he asked, and his hands were on hers and pressed them.

"It is nothing," she answered. "It is natural, I suppose—"

"No. It is not natural. You are unhappy. Tell me what is the matter."

"It is foolish," she said, turning her face from him. "I see you working so hard day after day. I am a burden to you—it would be better if I were out of the way. You are working yourself to death. If you could see your face sometimes!" And more tears trickled down.

His strong hands shook suddenly.

"I am not working too hard—for me," he answered, but his voice trembled a little. "One of your tears hurts me more than a hundred years of hard work. Even if it were true—I would rather die for you than live to be the greatest man that ever breathed—without you."

She threw her arms about his neck, and hid her face upon his shoulder.

"Tell me you love me!" she cried. "You are all I have in the world!"

"Does it need telling?" he asked, soothing her.

Then all at once his arms tightened so that she could hardly draw breath for a moment, and his head was bent down and rested for an instant upon her neck as though he himself sought rest and refuge.

"I think you know, dear," he said.

She knew far better than he could tell her, for the truth of his passion shook the dramatic and artificial fabric of her own to its foundations; and even as she pressed him to her, she felt that secret repugnance which those who do not love feel for those who love them overmuch. It was mingled with a sense of shame which made her hate herself, and she began to suffer acutely.

When she thought of Reanda, as she now often did, she longed for what she had felt for him, rather than for anything she had ever felt for Paul Griggs. In the pitiful reaching after something real, she groped for memories of true tenderness, and now and then they came back to her from beyond the chaos which lay between, as memories of home come to a man cast after many storms upon a desert island. She dwelt upon them and tried to construct an under-life out of the past, made up only of sweet things amongst which all that had not been good should be forgotten. She went for comfort to the days when she had loved Reanda, before their marriage—or when she had loved his genius as though it were himself, believing that it was all for her.

Beside her always, with even, untiring strength, Paul Griggs toiled on, his whole life based and founded in hers, every penstroke for her, every dream of her, every aspiration and hope for her alone. He was splendidly unconscious of his own utter loneliness, blankly unaware of the life-comedy—or tragedy— which Gloria was acting for him out of pity for the heart she could break, and out of shame at finding out what her own heart was. Had he known the truth, the end would have come quickly and terribly. But he did not know it. The woman's gifts were great, and her beauty was greater. Greater than all was his whole-souled belief in her. He had never conceived it possible, in his ignorance of women, that a woman should really love him. She, whom he had first loved so hopelessly, had given him all she had to give, which was herself, frankly and freely. And after she had come to him, she loved him for a time, beyond even self-deception. But when she no longer loved him, she hid her secret and kept it long and well; for she feared him. He was not like Reanda. He would not strike only; he would kill and make an end of both.

But she might have gone much nearer to the truth without danger. It was not his nature to ask anything nor to expect much, and he had taken all there was to take, and knew it, and was satisfied.

CHAPTER XXXVI

The summer passed, with its monotonous heat. Rain fell in August and poisoned the campagna with fever for six weeks, and the clear October breezes blew from the hills, and the second greenness of the late season was over everything for a brief month of vintage and laughter. Then came November with its pestilent sirocco gales and its dampness, pierced and cut through now and then by the first northerly winds of winter.

And then, one day, there was a new life in the little apartment in the Via della Frezza. Fate, relentless, had brought to the light a little child, to be the grandson of that fated Maria Braccio who had died long ago, to have his day of happiness and his night of suffering in his turn and to be a living bond between Gloria and the man who loved her.

They called the boy Walter Crowdie for a relative of Angus Dalrymple, who had been the last of the name. It was convenient, and he would never need any other, nor any third name after the two given to him in baptism.

For a few days after the child's birth, Griggs left his writing-table. He was almost too happy to work, and he spent many hours by Gloria's side, not talking, for he knew that she must be kept quiet, but often holding her hand and always looking at her face, with the strong, dumb devotion of a faithful bloodhound.

Often she pretended to be sleeping when he was there, though she was wide awake and could have talked well enough. But it was easier to seem to be asleep than to play the comedy now, while she was so weak and helpless. With the simplicity of a little child Griggs watched her, and when her eyes were closed believed that she was sleeping. As soon as she opened them he spoke to her. She understood and sometimes smiled in spite of herself, with close-shut lids. He thought she was dreaming of him, or of the child, and was smiling in her sleep.

As she lay there and thought over all that had happened, she knew that she hated him as she had never loved him, even in the first days. And she hated the child, for its life was the last bond, linking her to Paul Griggs and barring her from the world forever. Until it had been there she had vaguely felt that if she had the courage and really wished it, she might in some way get back to her old life. She knew that all hope of that was gone from her now.

In the deep perspective of her loosened intelligence the endless years to come rolled away, grey and monotonous, to their vanishing point. She had made her choice and had not found heart to give it up, after she had made it, while there was yet time. Time itself took shape before her closed eyes, as many succeeding steps, and she saw herself toiling up them, a bent, veiled figure of great weariness. It was terrible to look forward to such truth, and the present was no better. She grasped at the past and dragged it up to her and looked at its faded prettiness, and would have kissed it, as though it had been a living thing. But she knew that it was dead and that what lived was horrible to her.

She wished that she might die, as she had often thought she might during the long summer months. In those days her eyes had filled with tears of pity for herself. They were dry now, for the suffering was real and the pain was in her bodily heart. Yet she was so strong, and she feared Paul Griggs with such an abject fear, that she played the comedy when she could not make him think that she was asleep.

"My only thought is for you," she said. "It is another burden on you."

He was utterly happy, and he laughed aloud.

"It is another reason for working," he said.

And even as he said it she saw the writing-table, the poor room, his stern, determined face and busy hand, and herself seated in her own chair, with a half-read novel on her lap, staring at the grey future of mediocrity and mean struggling that loomed like a leaden figure above his bent head. Year after year, perhaps, she was to sit in that chair and watch the same silent battle for bare existence. It was too horrible to be borne. If only he were a man of genius, she could have suffered it all, she thought, and more also. But he himself said that he had no genius. His terrible mechanics of mind killed the little originality he had. His gloomy sobriety over his work made her desperate. But she feared him. The belief grew on her that if he ever found out that she did not love him, he would end life then, for them both—perhaps for them all three.

Surely, hell had no tortures worse than hers, she thought. Yet she bore them, in terror of him. And he was perfectly happy and suspected nothing. She could not understand how with his melancholy nature and his constant assertion that he had but a little talent and much industry for all his stock in trade, he could believe in his own future as he did. It was an anomaly, a contradiction of terms, a weak point in the low level of his unimaginative, dogged strength. She thought often of the poor book he had written. She had heard that talent was stirred to music by a great passion that strung it and struck it, till its heartstrings rang wild changes and breathed deep chords, and burst into rushing harmonies of eloquence. But his love was dumb and dull, though it might be deadly. There had been neither eloquence nor music in his book. It had been an old story, badly told. He had said that he was only fit to be a newspaper man, and it was true, so far as she could see. His letters to the paper were excellent in their way, but that was all he could do. And she had given him, in the child, another reason for being what he was, hard-working, silent—dull.

She looked at him and wondered; for there was a mystery in his shadowy eyes and still face, which had promised much more than she had ever found in him. There was something mysterious and dreadful, too, in his unnatural strength. The fear of him grew upon her, and sometimes when he kissed her she burst into tears out of sheer terror at his touch.

"They are tears of happiness," she said, trembling and drying her eyes quickly.

She smiled, and he believed her, happier every day in her and in the child.

Then came the realization of the grey dream of misery. Again she was seated by the window in her accustomed chair, and he was in his place, pen in hand, eyes on paper, thoughts fixed like steel in that obstinate effort to do better, while she had the certainty of his failure before her. And between them, in a straw cradle with a hood, all gauze and lace and blue ribbons, lay the thing that bound her to him and cut her off forever from the world,—little Walter Crowdie, the child without a name, as she called him in her thoughts. And above the child, between her and Paul Griggs, floated the little imaginary stage on which she was to go on acting her play over and over again till all was done. She had not even the right to shed tears for herself without telling him that they were for the happiness he expected of her.

He would not leave her. He had scarcely been out of the house for weeks, though the only perceptible effect of remaining indoors so long was that he had grown a little paler. She implored him to go out. In a few days she would be able to go with him, and meanwhile there was no reason why he should be perpetually at her side. He yielded to her importunity at last, and she was left alone with the child.

It was a relief even greater than she had anticipated. She could cry, she could laugh, she could sing, and he was not there to ask questions. For one moment after she had heard the outer door close behind him she almost hesitated as to which she should do, for she was half hysterical with the long outward restraint of herself while, inwardly, she had allowed her thoughts to run wild as they would. She stood for a moment, and there was a vague, uncertain look in her face. Then her breast heaved, and she burst into tears, weeping as never before in her short life, passionately, angrily, violently, without thought of control, or indeed of anything definite.

Before an hour had passed Griggs came back. She was seated quietly in her chair, as when he had left her. The light was all behind her, and he could not see the slight redness of her eyes. Pale as she was, he thought she had never been more beautiful. There was a gentleness in her manner, too, beyond what he was accustomed to. He believed that perhaps she might be the better for being left to herself for an hour or two every day, until she should be quite strong again. On the following day she again suggested that he should go out for a walk, and he made no objection.

Again, as soon as he was gone, she burst into tears, almost in spite of herself, though she unconsciously longed for the relief they had brought her the first time. But to-day the fit of weeping did not pass so soon. The spasms of sobbing lasted long after her eyes were dry, and she had less time to compose herself before Griggs returned. Still, he noticed nothing. The tears had refreshed her, and he found that same gentleness which had touched him on the previous day.

Several times, after that, he went out and left her alone in the afternoon. Then, one day, while he was walking, a heavy shower came on, and he made his way home as fast as he could. He opened the door quickly and came upon her to find her sobbing as though her heart would break.

He turned very pale and stood still for a moment. There was terror in her face when she saw him, but in an instant he was holding her in his arms and kissing her hair, asking her what was the matter.

"I am a millstone around your neck!" she sobbed. "It is breaking my heart—I shall die, if I see you working so!"

He tried to comfort her, soothing her and laughing at her fears for him, but believing her, as he always did. Little by little, her sobs subsided, and she was herself again, as far as he could see. He tried to argue the case fairly on its merits.

She listened to him, and listening was a new torture, knowing as she did what her tears were shed for. But she had to play the comedy again, at short notice, not having had the time to compose herself and enjoy the relief she found in crying alone.

It was a relief which she sought again and again. When she thought of it afterwards, it was as an indescribable, half-painful, half-pleasant emotion through which she passed every day. When she felt that it was before her, as soon as Griggs was out of the house, she made a slight effort to resist it, for she was sensible enough to understand that it was becoming a habit which she could not easily break.

Even after she was quite strong again, Griggs often left her to herself for an hour, and he did not again come in accidentally and find her in tears. He thought it natural that she should sometimes wish to be alone.

One day, when she had dried her eyes, she took a sheet of paper from his table and began to write. She had no distinct intention, but she knew that she was going to write about herself and her sufferings. It gave her a strange and unhealthy pleasure to set down in black and white all that she suffered. She could look at it, turn it, change it, and look at it again. Constantly, as the pen ran on, the tears came to her eyes afresh, and she brushed them away with a smile.

Then, all at once, she looked at the clock—the same cheap little American clock which had ticked so long on the mantelpiece in Griggs's old lodging upstairs. She knew that he would be back before long, and she tore the sheets she had covered into tiny strips and threw them into the waste-paper basket. When Griggs returned, she was singing softly to herself over her needlework.

But she had enjoyed a rare delight in writing down the story of her troubles. The utter loneliness of her existence, when Griggs was not with her, made it natural enough. Then a strange thought crossed her mind. She would write to Reanda and tell him that she had forgiven him, and had expiated the wrong she had done him. She craved the excitement of confession, and it could do no harm. He might, perhaps, answer her. Griggs would never know, for she always received the letters and sorted them for him, merely to save him trouble. The correspondence of a newspaper man is necessarily large, covering many sources of his information.

It was rather a wild idea, she thought, but it attracted her, or rather it distracted her thoughts by taking her out of the daily comedy she was obliged to keep up. There was in it, too, a very slight suggestion of danger; for it was conceivable, though almost impossible, that some letter of hers or her husband's might fall into Griggs's hands. There was a perverseness about it which was seductive to her tortuous mind.

At the first opportunity she wrote a very long letter. It was the letter of a penitent. She told him all that she had told herself a hundred times, and it was a very different production from the one she had sent to her father nearly a year earlier. There were tears in the phrases, there were sobs in the broken sentences. And there were tears in her own eyes when she sealed it.

She was going to ring for the woman servant to take it, and her hand was on the bell. She paused, looked at the addressed envelope, glanced furtively round the room, and then kissed it passionately. Then she rang.

Griggs came home later than usual, but he thought she was preoccupied and absent-minded.

"Has anything gone wrong?" he asked anxiously.

"Wrong?" she repeated. "Oh no!" She sighed. "It is the same thing. I am always anxious about you. You were a little pale before you went out and you had hardly eaten anything at breakfast."

"There is nothing the matter with me," laughed Griggs. "I am indestructible. I defy fate."

She started perceptibly, for she was too much of an Italian not to be a little superstitious.

CHAPTER XXXVII

Stephanone was often seen in the Via della Frezza, for the host of the little wine shop was one of his good customers. The neighbourhood was very quiet and respectable, and the existence of the wine shop was a matter of convenience and almost of necessity to the respectable citizens who dwelt there. They sent their women servants or came themselves at regular hours, bringing their own bottles and vessels of all shapes and of many materials for the daily allowance of wine; they invariably paid in cash, and they never went away in the summer. The business was a very good one; for the Romans, though they rarely drink too much and are on the whole a sober people, consume an amount of strong wine which would produce a curious effect upon any other race, in any other climate. Stefanone, though his wife had formerly thought him extravagant, had ultimately turned out to be a very prudent person, and in the course of a thirty years' acquaintance with Rome had selected his customers with care, judgment, and foresight. Whenever he was in Rome and had time to spare he came to the little shop in the Via della Frezza. He had stood godfather for one of the host's children, which in those days constituted a real tie between parents and god-parents.

But he had another reason for his frequent visits since that night on which he had accompanied Gloria and had shielded her from the rain with his gigantic brass-tipped umbrella. He took an interest in her, and would wait a long time in the hope of seeing her, sitting on a rush-bottomed stool outside the wine shop, and generally chewing the end of a wisp of broom. He had the faculty of sitting motionless for an hour at a time, his sturdy white-stockinged legs crossed one over the other, his square peasant's hands crossed upon his knee,—the sharp angles of the thumb-bones marked the labouring race,—his soft black hat tilted a little forward over his eyes, his jacket buttoned up when the weather was cool, thrown back and showing the loosened shirt open far below the throat when the day was warm.

Gloria reminded him of Dalrymple. The process of mind was a very simple one and needs no analysis. He had sought Dalrymple for years, but in vain, and Gloria had something in her face which recalled her father, though the latter's features were rough and harshly accentuated. Stefanone had made the acquaintance of the one-eyed cobbler without difficulty and had ascertained that there was a mystery about Gloria, whom the cobbler had first seen on the morning after Stefanone had met her in the storm. It was of course very improbable that she should be the daughter of Dalrymple and Annetta, but even the faint possibility of being on the track of his enemy had a strong effect upon the unforgiving peasant. If he ever found Dalrymple, he intended to kill him. In the meanwhile he had found a simple plan for finding out whether Gloria was the Scotchman's daughter or not. He waited patiently for the spring, and he came to Rome now every month for a week at a time.

More than once during the past year he had brought small presents of fruit and wine and country cakes for Gloria, and both she and Griggs knew all about him, and got their wine from the little shop which he supplied. Gloria was pleased by the decent, elderly peasant's admiration of her beauty, which he never failed to express when he got a chance of speaking to her. When little Walter Crowdie was first carried out into the sun, Stefanone was in the street, and he looked long and earnestly into the baby's face.

"There is the same thing in the eyes," he muttered, as he turned away, after presenting the nurse with a beautiful jumble, which looked as though it had been varnished, and was adorned with small drops of hard pink sugar. "If it is he—an evil death on him and all his house."

And he strolled slowly back to the wine shop, his hand fumbling with the big, curved, brass-handled knife which he carried in the pocket of his blue cloth breeches.

He was certainly mistaken about the baby's eyes, which were remarkably beautiful and of a very soft brown; whereas Dalrymple's were hard, blue, and steely, and it was not possible that anything like an hereditary expression should be recognizable in the face of a child three weeks old. But his growing conviction made his imagination complete every link which chanced to be missing in the chain.

One day, in the spring, he met Griggs when the latter was going out alone.

"A word, Signore, if you permit," he said politely.

"Twenty," replied Griggs, giving the common Roman answer.

"Signore, Subiaco is a beautiful place," said the peasant. "In spring it is an enchantment. In summer, I tell you nothing. It is as fresh as Paradise. There is water, water, as much as you please. Wine is not wanting, and it seems that you know that. The butcher kills calves twice a week, and sometimes an ox when there is an old one, or one lame. Eh, in Subiaco, one is well."

"I do not doubt it when I look at you," answered Griggs, without a smile.

"Thanks be to Heaven, my health still assists me. But I am thinking of you and of your beautiful lady and of that little angel, whom God preserve. In truth, you appear to me as the Holy Family. I should not say it to every one, but the air of Subiaco is thin, the water is light, and, for a house, mine is of the better ones. One knows that we are country people, but we are clean people; there are neither chickens nor children. If you find a flea, I will have him set in gold. You shall say, 'This is the flea that was found in Stefanone's house.' In that way every one will know. I do not speak of the beds. The pope could sleep in the one in the large room at the head of the staircase, the pope with all his cardinals. They would say, 'Now we know that this is indeed a bed.' Do you wish better than this? I do not know. But if you will bring your lady and the baby, you will see. Eyes tell no lies."

"And the price?" inquired Griggs, struck by the good sense of the suggestion.

"Whatever you choose to give. If you give nothing, we shall have had your company. In general, we take three pauls a day, and we give the wine. You shall make the price as you like it. Who thinks of these things? We are Christians."

When Griggs spoke of the project to Gloria, she embraced it eagerly. He said that he should be obliged to come to Rome every week on account of his correspondence. But Subiaco was no longer as inaccessible as formerly, and there was now a good carriage road all the way and a daily public conveyance. He should be absent three days, and would spend the other four with her.

It was a sacrifice on his part, as she guessed from the way in which he spoke, but it was clearly necessary that Gloria and the child should have country air during the coming summer. He had often reproached himself with not having made some such arrangement for the preceding hot season, but he had seen that she did not suffer from the heat, and his presence in the capital had been very necessary for his work. Now, however, it looked possible enough, and before Stefanone went back to the country for his next trip a preliminary agreement had been made.

Gloria looked forward with impatience to the liberty she was to gain by his regular absences, for her life was becoming unbearable. She felt that she could not much longer sustain the perpetual comedy she was acting, unless she could get an interval of rest from time to time. At first, the hour he gave her daily when he went out alone had been a relief and had sufficed. The tears she shed, the letters she wrote to Reanda, rested her and refreshed her. For she had written others since that first one, though he had never answered any of them. But the small daily interruption of her acting was no longer enough. The taste of liberty had bred an intense craving for more of it, and she dreamed of being alone for days together.

She wrote to Reanda now without the slightest hope of receiving any reply, as madmen sometimes write endless letters to women they love, though they have never exchanged a word with them. It was a vent for her pent-up suffering. It could make no difference, and Griggs could never know. Her strange position put the point of faithfulness out of the question. She was in love with her husband, and the man who loved her held her to her play of love by the terror she felt of what lay behind his gentleness. She dreamed once that he had found out the truth, and was tearing her head from her body with those hands of his, slowly, almost gently, with mysterious eyes and still face. She woke, and found that the heavy tress of her hair was twisted round her throat and was choking her; but the impression remained, and her dread of Griggs increased, and it became harder and harder to act her part.

At the same time the attraction of secretly writing to her husband grew stronger, day by day. She did not send him all she wrote, nor a tenth part of all, and the greater portion of her outpourings went into the fire, or they were torn to infinitesimal bits and thrown into the waste-paper basket. She was critical, in a strangely morbid way, of what she wrote. The fact that she was acting for Griggs, and knew it, made her dread to write anything to Reanda which could possibly seem insincere. No aspiring young author ever took greater pains over his work than she sometimes bestowed upon the composition of these letters, or judged his work more conscientiously and severely than she. And the result was that she told of her life with wonderful sincerity and truth. Truth was her only luxury in the midst of the great lie she had to sustain. She revelled in it, and yet, fearing to lose it, she used it with a conscientiousness which she had never exhibited in anything she had done before. It was her single delight, and she treasured it with scrupulous and miserly care. In her letters, at least, she could be really herself.

But the strain was telling upon her visibly, and Griggs was very anxious about her, and hastened their departure for Subiaco as soon as the weather began to grow warm, hoping that the mountain air would bring the colour back to her pale cheeks. For her beauty's sake, he could almost have deprecated the prospect, strange to say, for she had never seemed more perfectly beautiful than now. She was thinner than she had formerly been, and her pallor had refined her by softening the look of hard and brilliant vitality which had characterized her before she had left Reanda. There is perhaps no beauty which is not beautified by a touch of sadness. Griggs saw it, and while his eyes rejoiced, his heart sank.

He knew what an utterly lonely life she was leading, even as he judged her existence, and the tender string was touched in his deep nature. She had sacrificed everything for him, as he told himself many a time in his solitary walks. All the love he had given and had to give could never repay her for what she had given him. Marriage, he reflected, was often a bargain, but such devotion as hers was a gift for which there could be no return. She had ruined herself in the eyes of the world for him, but the world would never accuse him, nor shut its doors upon him because he had accepted what she had so freely given. He was not an emotional man, but even he longed for some turn of life in which for her sake he might do something above the dead level of that commonplace heroism which begins in hard work and ends in the attainment of ordinary necessities. He felt his strength in him and about him, and he wished that he could let it loose upon some adversary in the physical satisfaction of fighting for what he loved. It was not a high aspiration, but it was a manly one.

He drew upon his resources to the utmost, in order to make her comfortable in Subiaco when they should get there. He was not a dreamer, though he dreamed when he had time. It was his nature to take all the things which came to him to be done and to do them one after another with untiring energy. He worked at his correspondence, and got additional articles to write for periodicals, though it was no easy matter in that day when the modern periodical was in its infancy.

Gloria, acting her part, complained sadly that he worked too hard. Work as he might, he had no such stress to fear as was wearing out her life. She hated him, she feared him, and she envied him. Sometimes she pitied him, and then it was easier for her to act the play. As for Griggs, he laughed and told her for the hundredth time that he was indestructible and defied fate.

So far as he could see what he had to deal with, he could defy anything. But there was that beyond of which he could not dream, and destiny, with leaden hands, was already upon him, on the day when a great, old-fashioned carriage, loaded with boxes and belongings, brought him and his to the door of Stefanone's house in Subiaco.

Sora Nanna, grey-haired, and withered as a brown apple, but tough as leather still, stood on the threshold to receive them. She no longer wore the embroidered napkin on her hair, for civilization had advanced a generation in Subiaco, and a coloured handkerchief flapped about her head, and she had caught one corner of it in her teeth to keep it out of her eyes, as the afternoon breeze blew it across her leathery face.

First at the door of the carriage she saw the baby, held up by its nurse, and the old woman threw up her hands and clapped them, and crowed to the child till it laughed. Then Griggs got out. And then, out of the dark shadow of the coach, a face looked at Sora Nanna, and it was a face she had known long ago, with dark eyes, beautiful and deadly pale, and very fateful.

She turned white herself, and her teeth chattered.

"Madonna Santissima!" she cried, shrinking back.

She crossed herself, and did not dare to meet Gloria's eyes again for some time.

CHAPTER XXXVIII

Sora Nanna showed her new lodgers their rooms. They were the ones Dalrymple had occupied long ago, together with a third, opening separately from the same landing. In what had been the Scotchman's laboratory, and which was now turned into a small bedroom, a large chest stood in a corner, of the sort used by the peasant women to this day for their wedding outfits.

"If it is not in your way, I will leave it here," said Sora Nanna. "There are certain things in it."

"What things?" asked Gloria, idly, and for the sake of making acquaintance with the woman, rather than out of curiosity.

"Things, things," answered Nanna. "Things of that poor girl's. We had a daughter, Signora."

"Did she die long ago?" inquired Gloria, in a tone of sympathy.

"We lost her, Signora," said Nanna, simply. "Look at these beds! They are new, new! No one has ever slept in them. And linen there is, as much as you can ask for. We are country people, Signora, but we are good people. I do not say that we are rich. One knows—in Rome everything is beautiful. Even the chestnuts are of gold. Here, we are in the country, Signora. You will excuse, if anything is wanting."

But Gloria was by no means inclined to find fault. She breathed more freely in the mountain air, she was tired with the long drive from Tivoli, where they had spent the previous night, and she was more hungry than she had been for a long time.

It was not dark when they sat down to supper in the old guest chamber which opened upon the street. Nanna was anxious and willing to bring them their supper upstairs, but Gloria preferred the common room. She said it would amuse her, and in reality it was easier for her not to be alone with Griggs, and by going downstairs on the first evening she meant to establish a precedent for the whole summer. He had told her that he must go back to Rome for his work on the next day but one, and she counted the hours before her up to the minute when she should be free and alone.

They sat down at the old table at which Dalrymple had eaten his solitary meals so often, more than twenty years earlier. There was no change. There were the same solid, old-fashioned silver forks and spoons, there were plates of the same coarse china, tumblers of the same heavy pressed glass. Had Dalrymple been there, he would have recognized the old brass lamp with its three beaks which poor Annetta had so often brought in lighted when he sat there at dusk. On the shelf in the corner were the selfsame decanters full of transparent aniseed and pink alchermes and coarse brown brandy. Stefanone came in, laid his hat upon the bench, and put his stick in the corner just as he had always done. There was no change, except that Annetta was not there, and the husband and wife had grown almost old since those days.

"How often does the post go to Rome?" Gloria asked of Sora Nanna, while they were at supper.

"Every evening, at one of the night, Signora. There are also many occasions of sending by the carters."

"I can write to you every day when you are away," said Gloria in English to Griggs.

She was thinking of those letters which she wrote to Reanda almost in spite of herself, but the loving smile did not play her false, and Griggs believed her.

In her, the duality of her being had created two distinct lives. For him, the two elements of consciousness and perception were merged in one by his love. All that he felt he saw in her, and all that he saw in her he felt. The perfection of love, while it lasts, is in that double certainty from within and from without, which, if once disturbed, can never be restored again. Singly, the one part or the other may remain as of old, but the wholeness of the two has but one chance of life.

On that first night Gloria had an evil dream. She had fallen asleep, tired from the journey and worn out with the endless weariness of her secret suffering. She awoke in the small hours, and moonlight was streaming into the room. She was startled to find herself in a strange place, at first, and then she realized where she was, and gazed at the clouded panes of common glass as her head lay on the pillow, and she marked the moonlight on the brick floor by the joints of the bricks, and watched how it crept silently away. For the moon was waning, and had not long risen above the black line of the hills.

Her eyelids drooped, but she saw it all distinctly still—more distinctly than before, she thought. The level light rose slowly from the floor; very, very slowly, stiff and straight as a stark, shrouded corpse, and stood upright between her and the window. She felt the heavy hair rising on her scalp, and an intense horror took possession of her body, and thrilled through her from head to foot and from her feet to her head. But she could not move. She felt that something held her and pressed on her, as though the air were moulded about her like cast iron.

The thing stood between her and the window, stiff and white. It showed its face, and the face was white, too. It was Angelo Reanda. She knew it, though there seemed to be no eyes in the white thing. She felt its dead voice speaking to her.

"An evil death on you and all your house," it said.

The face was gone again, but the thing was still there. Very, very slowly, stiff and white, it lay back, straight from the heel upwards, unbending as it sank, till it laid itself upon the floor, and she was staring at the joints of the bricks in the moonlight.

Then she shrieked aloud and awoke. The moonlight had moved a foot or more, and she knew that she had been asleep.

"It was only a dream," she said to Griggs in the morning. "I thought I saw you dead, dear. It frightened me."

"I am not dead yet," he laughed. "It was that salad—there were potatoes in it."

She turned away; for the contrast between the triviality of what he said and the horror of what she had felt brought an expression to her face which even her consummate art could not have concealed.

The impression lasted all day, and when she went to bed she carefully closed the shutters so that the moonlight should not fall upon the floor. The dream did not return.

"It must have been the salad," said Griggs, when she told him that she had not been disturbed again.

But Gloria was thinking of death, and his words jarred upon her horribly, as a trivial jest would jar on a condemned man walking from his cell to the scaffold. In the evening Griggs went by the diligence to Rome, and Gloria was left alone with her child and the nurse.

Then she sat down and wrote to Reanda with a full heart and a trembling hand. She told him of her dream, and how the fear of his death had broken her nerves. She implored him to come out and see her when Griggs was in Rome. She could let him know when to start, if he would write one word. It was but a little journey, she said, and the cool mountain air would do him good. But if he would not come, she besought him to write to her, if it were only a line, to say that he was alive. She could not forget the dream until she should know that he was safe.

She was not critical of her writing any more, for she was no longer in fear of being misunderstood, and she wrote desperately. It seemed to her that she was writing with her blood. She had sent him many letters without hope of answer, but something told her that she could not appeal in vain forever, and that he would at last reply to her.

Two days passed, and she spent much of her time with the child. She felt that in time she might love it, if Griggs were not beside her. Then he came back, and in the great joy of seeing her again after that first short separation, the stern voice grew as soft as a woman's, and the still face was moved. She had looked forward with dread to his return, and she shivered when he touched her; she would have given all she had if only he would not kiss her. Then, when she felt that he might have found her cold to him at the first moment, that he might guess, that he might find out her secret, she shivered again from head to heel, in fear of him, and she forced the smile upon her face with all her will.

"I am so glad, that I am almost frightened!" she cried, and lest the smile should be imperfect, she hid it against his shoulder.

She could have bitten the cloth and the tough arm under it, as she felt him kiss the back of her neck just at the roots of the hair; as it was, she grasped his arm convulsively.

"How strong you are!" he laughed, as he felt the pressure of her fingers.

"Yes," she answered. "It is the mountain air—and you," she added.

And, as ever, it seemed to him true. The days he spent with her were heavenly to him as they were days of living earthly hell to her. He did not even leave her alone for an hour or two, as he had done in the city, for when he was in Rome without her he did double work and shortened his sleep by half, that he might lengthen the time he was to have with her. The heat of the capital and the late hours brought out dark shadows under his eyes, and gave her another excuse for saying that he was overworking for her sake, and that she was a burden upon him—she and the child.

On the morning before he next went to Rome, she received a letter from Reanda. The blood rushed scarlet to her face, but Griggs was busy with his own letters and did not see it.

She went to the baby's room. The child had been taken out by the nurse, and she sat down in the nurse's chair by the empty cradle and broke the seal of the note. There was a big sheet of paper inside, on which were written these lines in the artist's small, nervous handwriting:—

"I am perfectly well, but I understand your anxiety about my health. I do not wish to see you, but as human life is uncertain I have given instructions that you may be at once informed of the good news of my death, if you outlive me."

Gloria's hand closed upon the sheet of paper, and she reeled forward and sideways in the chair, as though she had received a stunning blow. She heard heavy footsteps on the brick floor in the next room and with a desperate effort at consciousness she hid the crumpled letter in her bosom before the door opened. But the room swam with her as she grasped the straw cradle and tried to steady herself.

In an agony of terror she heard the footsteps coming nearer and nearer, then retreating again, then turning back towards her. She prayed to God at that moment that Griggs might not open the door. To gain strength, she forced herself to rise to her feet and stand upright, but with the first step she took, she stumbled against the chest that contained Annetta's belongings. The physical pain roused her. She drew breath more freely, and listened. Griggs was moving about in the other room, probably putting together some few things which he meant to take to Rome with him that evening. It seemed an hour before she heard him go away, and the echo of his footsteps came more and more faintly as he went down the stairs. He evidently had not guessed that she was in the little room which served as a nursery—the room which had once been Dalrymple's laboratory.

She did not read the letter again, but she found a match and set fire to it, and watched it as it burned to black, gossamer-like ashes on the brick floor. It was long before she had the courage to go down and face Griggs and say that she was ready for the daily walk together before the midday meal. And all that day she went about dreamily, scarcely knowing what she did or said, though she was sure that she did not fail in acting her part, for the habit was so strong that the acting was natural to her, except when something waked her to herself too suddenly.

He went away at last in the evening, and she was free to do what she pleased with herself, to close the deadly wound she had received, if that were possible, to forget it even for an hour, if she could.

But she could not. She felt that it was her death-wound, for it had killed a hope which she had tended and fostered into an inner life for herself. She felt that her husband hated her, as she hated Paul Griggs.

She was impelled to fall upon her knees and pray to Something, somewhere, though she knew not what, but she was ashamed to do it when she thought of her life. That Something would turn upon her and curse her, as Reanda had cursed her in her dream—and in the cruel words he had written.

She hardly slept that night, and she rose in the morning heavy-eyed and weary. Going out into the old garden behind the house she met Sora Nanna with a basket of clothes on her head, just starting to go up to the convent, followed by two of her women.

"Signora," said the old woman, with her leathern smile, "you are consuming yourself because the husband is in Rome. You are doing wrong."

Gloria started, stared at her, and then understood, and nodded.

"Come up to the convent with us," said Nanna. "You will divert yourself, and while they take in the clothes, I will show you the church. It is beautiful. I think that even in Rome it would be a beautiful church. I will show you where the sisters are buried and I will tell you how Sister Maria Addolorata was burned in her cell. But she was not buried with the rest. When you come back, you will eat with a double appetite, and I will make gnocchi of polenta for dinner. Do you like gnocchi, Signora? There is much resistance in them."

Gloria went with the washerwomen. She was strong and kept pace with them, burdened as they were with their baskets. It was good to be with them, common creatures with common, human hearts, knowing nothing of her strange trouble. Sora Nanna took her into the church and showed her the sights, explaining them in her strident, nasal voice without the slightest respect for the place so long as no religious service was going on. The woman showed her the little tablet erected in memory of Maria Addolorata, and she told the story as she had heard it, and dwelt upon the funeral services and the masses which had been said.

"At least, she is in peace," said Gloria, in a low voice, staring at the tablet.

"Poor Annetta used to say that Sister Maria Addolorata sinned in her throat," said Nanna. "But you see. God can do everything. She went straight from her cell to heaven. Eh, she is in peace, Signora, as you say. Requiesca'. Come, Signora, it takes at least three-quarters of an hour to make gnocchi."

And they did not know. She was standing on her daughter's grave, and the tablet was a memorial of the mother of the woman beside her.

"You make me think of her, Signora," said the peasant. "You have her face. If you had her voice, to sing, I should think that you were she, returned from the dead."

"Could she sing?" asked Gloria, dreamily, as they left the church.

"Like the angels in Paradise," answered Nanna. "I think that now, when she sings, they are ashamed and stand silent to listen to her. If God wills that I make a good death, I shall hear her again."

She glanced at her companion's dreamy, fateful face.

"Let us not speak of the dead!" she concluded. "To-day we will make gnocchi of polenta."

CHAPTER XXXIX

In the afternoon Gloria called Sora Nanna to move the chest against which she had stumbled in the morning. It would be more convenient, she said, to put it under the bed, if it could not be taken away altogether. It was a big, old-fashioned chest of unpainted, unvarnished wood, brown with age, and fastened by a hasp, through which a splinter of white chestnut wood had been stuck instead of a padlock. Gloria saw that it was heavy, as Sora Nanna dragged it and pushed it across the room. She remarked that, if it held only clothes, it must be packed very full.

Sora Nanna, glad to rest from her efforts, stood upright with her hand on her hip and took breath.

"Signora," she said, "who knows what is in it? Things, certain things! There are the clothes of that poor girl. This I know. And then, certain other things. Who knows what is in it? It may be a thousand years since I looked. Signora, shall we open it? But I think there are certain things that belonged to the Englishman."

"The Englishman?" asked Gloria, with some curiosity.

She was glad of anything which could interest her a little. For the moment she had not yet the courage to begin to write again after Reanda's message. Anything which had power to turn the current of her thoughts was a relief. She was sitting in the same chair beside the cradle in which she had sat in the morning, for she had called Nanna to move the box at a time when the child had been taken out for its second airing. She leaned back, resting her auburn hair against the bare wall, the waxen whiteness of her face contrasting with the bluish whitewash.

"What Englishman?" she asked again, wearily, but with a show of interest in her half-closed eyes.

"Who knows? An Englishman. They called him Sor Angoscia." Nanna sat down on the heavy box, and dropped her skinny hands far apart upon her knees. "We have cursed him much. He took our daughter. It was a night of evil. In that night the abbess died, and Sister Maria Addolorata was burned in her cell, and the Englishman took our daughter. He took our one daughter, Signora. We have not seen her more, not even her little finger. It will be twenty-two years on the eve of the feast of St. Luke. That is in October, Signora. He took our daughter. Poor little one! She was young, young—perhaps she did not know what she did."

Gloria leaned forward, resting her chin in her hand and her elbow on her knee, gazing at the old woman.

"She was a flower," said Nanna, simply. "He tore her from us with the roots. Who knows what he did with her? She will be dead by this time. May the Madonna obtain grace for her! Signora, she seemed one of those flowers that grow on the hillside, just as God wills. Rain, sun, she was always fresh. Then came the storm. Who could find her any more? Poor little one!"

"Poor child!" exclaimed Gloria.

And she made Nanna tell all she knew, and how they had found the girl's peasant dress in a corner of that very room.

"Signora, if you wish to see, I will content you," said Nanna, rising at last.

She opened the box. It exhaled the peculiar odour of heavy cloth which has been worn and has then been kept closely shut up for years. On the top lay Annetta's carpet apron. Nanna held it up, and there were tears in her eyes, glistening on her dry skin like water in a crevice of brown rock.

"Signora, there are moths in it, see! Who cares for these things? They are a memory. And this is her skirt, and this is her bodice. Eh, it was beautiful once. The shoes, Signora, I wore them, for we had the same feet. What would you? It seemed a sin to let them mould, because they were hers. The apron, too, I might have worn it. Who knows why I did not wear it? It was the affection. We are all so, we women. And now there are moths in it. I might have worn it. At least it would not have been lost."

Gloria peered into the box, and saw under the clothes a number of books packed neatly with a box made of English oak. She stretched down her hand and took one of the volumes. It was an English medical treatise. She looked at the fly-leaf.

A loud cry from Gloria startled the old woman.

"Angus Dalrymple—but—" Gloria read the name and stared at Nanna.

"Eh, eh!" assented Nanna, nodding violently and smiling a little as she at last recognized the Scotchman's name which she had never been able to pronounce. "Yes—that is it. That was the name of the Englishman. An evil death on him and all his house! Stefanone says it always. I also may say it once. It was he. He took our daughter. Stefanone went after them, but they had the beast of the convent gardener. It was a good beast, and they made it run. Stefanone heard of them all the way to the sea, but the twenty-four hours had passed, and the war-ship was far out. He could see it. Could he go to the war-ship? It had cannons. They would have killed him. Then I should have had neither daughter nor husband. So he came back."

The long habit of acting had made Gloria strong, but her hands shook on the closed volume. She had known that her mother had been an Italian, that they had left Italy suddenly and had been married on board an English man-of-war by the captain, that same Walter Crowdie, a relative of Dalrymple's, after whom Gloria and Griggs had named the child. More than that Dalrymple had never been willing to tell her. She remembered, too, that though she had once or twice begged him to take her to Tivoli and Subiaco, he had refused rather abruptly. It was clear enough now. Her mother had been this Annetta whom Dalrymple had stolen away in the night.

And the wrinkled, leathery old hag, with her damp, coarse mouth, her skinny hands, and her cunning, ignorant eyes, was her grandmother—Stefanone was her grandfather—her mother had been a peasant, like them, beautified by one of nature's mad miracles.

There could be no doubt about it. That was the truth, and it fell upon her with its cruel, massive weight, striking her where many other truths had struck her before this one, in her vanity.

She grasped the book tightly with both hands and set her teeth. After that, she did not know what Nanna said, and the old woman, thinking Gloria was not paying a proper attention to her remarks, pushed and heaved the box across the room rather discontentedly. It would not go under the bed, being too high, so she wedged it in between the foot of the bedstead and the wall. There was just room for it there.

"Signora, if ever your one child leaves you without a word, you will understand," said Nanna, a little offended at finding no sympathy.

"I understand too well," answered Gloria.

Then she suddenly realized what the woman wanted, and with great self-control she held out her hand kindly. Nanna took it and smiled, and pressed it in her horny fingers.

"You are young, Signora. When you are old, you will understand many things, when evils have pounded your heart in a mortar. Oil is sweet, vinegar is sour; with both one makes salad. This is our life. Rest yourself, Signora, for you walked well this morning. I go."

Gloria felt the pressure of the rough fingers on hers, after Nanna had left her. The acrid odour of peeled vegetables clung to her own hand, and she rose and washed it carefully, though she was scarcely conscious of what she was doing. Suddenly she dropped the towel and went back to the box. It had crossed her mind that the single book she had opened might have been borrowed from her father and that she might find another name in the others—that Nanna might have been mistaken in thinking that she recognized the English name—that it might all be a mistake, after all.

With violent hands she dragged out the moth-eaten clothes and threw them behind her upon the floor, and seized the books, opening them desperately one after the other. In each there was the name, 'Angus Dalrymple,' in her father's firm young handwriting of twenty years ago. She threw them down and lifted out the oak box. A little brass plate was let into the lid, and bore the initials, 'A. D.' There was no doubt left. The books all bore dates prior to 1844, the year in which, as she knew, her father had been married. It was impossible to hesitate, for the case was terribly clear.

She rose to her feet and carried the box to the window and set it upon a chair, sitting down upon another before it. It was not locked. She raised the lid, and saw that it was a medicine chest. There was a drawer, or little tray, on the top, full of small boxes and very minute vials, lying on their sides. Lifting this out, she saw a number of little stoppered bottles set in holes made in a thin piece of board for a frame. One was missing, and there were eleven left. She counted them mechanically, not knowing why she did so. Then she took them out and looked at the labels. The first she touched contained spirits of camphor. It chanced to be the only one of which the contents were harmless. The others were strong tinctures and acids, vegetable poisons, belladonna, aconite, and the like, sulphuric acid, nitric acid, hydrochloric acid, and others.

Gloria looked at them curiously and set them back, one by one, put in the little tray and closed the lid. Then she sat still a long time and gazed out of the window at the rugged line of the hills.

Between her and the pale sky she saw her own life, and the hideous failure of it all, culminating in the certainty that she was of the blood of the old peasant couple to whose house a seeming chance had brought her to die. She felt that she could not live, and would not live if she could. It was all too wildly horrible, too utterly desolate.

The only human being that clung to her was the one of all others whom she most feared and hated, whose very touch sent a cold shiver through her. She and fate together had pounded her heart in a mortar, as the old woman had said. With a bitterness that sickened her she thought of her brief married life, of her poor social ambition, of her hopeless efforts to be some one amongst the great. What could she be, the daughter of peasants, what could she have ever been? Probably some one knew the truth about her, in all that great society. Such things might be known. Francesca Campodonico's delicate noble face rose faintly between her and the sky, and she realized with excruciating suddenness the distance that separated her from the woman she hated, the woman who perhaps knew that Gloria Dalrymple was the daughter of a peasant and a fit wife by her birth for Angelo Reanda, the steward's son.

The ruin of her life spread behind her and before her. She could not face it. The confusion of it all seemed to blind her, and the confusion was pierced by the terrible thought that on the next day but one Griggs would return again, the one being who would not leave her, who believed in her, who worshipped her, and whom she hated for himself and for the destruction of her existence which had come by him.

In the box before her was death, painful perhaps, but sure as the grave itself. She was not a coward, except when she was afraid of Paul Griggs, and the fear lest he, too, should find out the truth was worse than the fear of mortal pain.

She sat still in her place, staring out of the window. After a long time, the nurse came in, carrying the child asleep in her arms, covered with a thin gauze veil. Gloria started, and then smiled mechanically as she had trained herself to smile whenever the child was brought to her. The nurse laid the small thing in its cradle, and Gloria, as in a dream, put the books and the clothes back into the box, and was glad that the nurse asked no questions. When she had shut down the lid, she rose to her feet and saw that she had left the medicine chest on the chair. She took it into the bedroom and set it upon the table.

Then she sat down and wrote to Reanda. There was no haste in the writing, and her head was clear and cool, for she was not afraid. Griggs could not return for two days, and she had plenty of time. She went over her story, as she had gone over it many times before in her letters. She told him all, but not the discovery she had just made. That should die with her, if it could. It would be easy enough, on the next day, when the nurse was out, to open the box again, and to tear out the fly-leaf from each book and so destroy the name. As for the medicine chest, Griggs might see that it had belonged to her father, but he would suppose that she had brought it amongst her belongings. He would never guess that it had lain hidden in the old box for more than twenty years. That was her plan, and it was simple enough. But she should have to wait until the next day. It was better so. She could think of what she was going to do, and nobody would disturb her. She finished her letter.

"You have killed me," she wrote at the end. "If I had not loved you to the very end, I would tell you that my death is on your soul. But it is not all your fault, if I have loved you to death. I would not die if I could be free in any other way, but I cannot live to be touched and caressed again by this man whom I loathe with all my soul. I tell you that when he kisses me it is as though I were stung by a serpent of ice. It is for your sake that I hate him as I do. For your sake I have suffered hell on earth for more than a whole year. For your sake I die. I cannot live without you. I have told you so again and a hundred times again, and you have not believed me. You write to-day and you tell me that I shall be free, when you die, to marry Paul Griggs. I would rather marry Satan in hell. But I shall be free to-morrow, for I shall be dead. God will forgive me, for God knows what I suffer. Good-bye. I love you, Angelo. I shall love you to-morrow, when the hour comes, and after that I shall love you always. This is the end. Good-bye. I love you; I kiss your soul with my soul. Good-bye, good-bye.
"GLORIA."

She cut a lock from her auburn hair and twisted it round and round her wedding ring, and thrust it into the envelope.

CHAPTER XL

Two days later, Paul Griggs stood beside Gloria. She was not dead yet, but no earthly power could save her. She lay white and motionless on the high trestle bed, unconscious of his presence. They had sent a messenger for him, and he had come. The door was locked. Stefanone and his wife whispered together on the landing. In the third room, beyond, the nurse was shedding hysterical tears over the sleeping child.

The strong man stood stone still with shadowy, unblinking eyes, gazing into the dying face. Not a muscle moved, not a feature was distorted, his breath was regular and slow, for his grief had taken hold upon his soul, and his body was unconscious of time, as though it were already dead.

She had suffered horrible agonies for two nights and one day, and now the end was very near, for the wracked nerves could no longer feel. She lay on her back, lightly covered, one white arm and hand above the coverlet, the other hidden beneath it.

The room was very hot, and the sun streamed through the narrow aperture of the nearly closed shutters, and made a bright streak on the red bricks, for it was morning still.

The purple lids opened, and Gloria looked up. There was no shiver now, as she recognized the man she feared, for the nerves were almost dead. Perhaps there was less fear, for she knew that it was almost over. The dark eyes were fixed on his with a mysterious, wondering look.

He tried to speak, and his lips moved, but he could make no sound, and his chest heaved convulsively, once. He knew what she had done, for they had told him. He knew, now that he tried to speak and could not, that he was half killed by grief. She saw the effort and understood, and faintly smiled.

"Why?"

He wrenched the single broken word out of himself by an enormous effort, and his throat swelled and was dry. Suddenly a single great drop of sweat rolled down his pale forehead.

"I could not live," she answered, in a cool, far voice beyond suffering, and still she smiled.

"Why? Why?"

The repeated word broke out twice like two sobs, but not a feature moved. The dying woman's eyelids quivered.

"I was a burden to you," she said faintly and distinctly. "You are free now, you have—only the child."

His calm broke.

"Gloria, Gloria! In the name of God Almighty, do not leave me so!"

He clasped her in his arms and lifted her a little, pressing his lips to her face. She was inert as a statue. She feared him still, and she felt the shiver of horror at his touch, but it could not move her limbs any more. Her eyes opened and looked into his, very close, but his were shut. The mask was gone. The man's whole soul was in his agonized face, and his arm shook with her. Her mind was clear and she understood. She was still herself, acting her play out in the teeth of death.

"I could not live," she said. "I could not be a millstone, dragging you down, watching you as you killed yourself in working for me. It was to be one of us. It was better so."

In his agony he laid his head beside hers on the pillow.

"Gloria—for Christ's sake—don't leave me—" The deep moan came from his tortured heart.

"Bring—the child—Walter—" she said very faintly.

Even in death she could not bear to be alone with him. He straightened himself, stood up, and saw the light fading in her eyes. Then, indeed, a shiver ran through her and shook her. Then the lids opened wide, and she cried out loudly.

"Quick—I am going—"

Rather than that she should not have what she wished, he tore himself away and wrenched the door open, forgetting that it was locked.

"Bring the child!" he cried, into the face of old Nanna, who was standing there, and he pushed her towards the door of the other room with one hand, while he already turned back to Gloria.

He started, for she was sitting up, with wide eyes and outstretched hands, gazing at the patch of sunlight on the floor. Dying, she saw the awful vision of her dream again, rising stiff and stark from the bricks to its upright horror between her and the light. Her hands pointed at it and shook, and her jaw dropped, but she was motionless as she sat.

Nanna, sobbing, came in suddenly, holding up the little child straight before her, that it might see its mother before she was gone forever. The baby hands feebly beat its little sides, and it gasped for breath.

Words came from Gloria's open mouth, articulate, clear, but very far in sound.

"An evil death on you and all your house!" the words said, as though spoken by another.

The outstretched hands sank slowly, as the vision laid itself down before her, straight and corpse-like. The beautiful head fell back upon Griggs's arm, and the eyes met his.

Nanna prayed aloud, holding up the child mechanically, and the small eyes were fixed, horrorstruck, upon the bed. A low cry trembled in the air. Stefanone, his hat in his hand, stood against the door, bowed a little, as though he were in church. The cry came again. Then there was a sort of struggle.

In an instant Gloria was standing up on the bed to her full height. And the hot, still room rang with a burst of desperate, ear-breaking song, in majestic, passionate, ascending intervals.

"Calpesta il mio cadavere, ma salva il Trovator!"

The last great, true note died away. For one instant she stood up still, with outstretched hands, white, motionless. Then the flame in the dark eyes broke and went out, and Gloria fell down dead.

"Maria Addolorata! Maria Addolorata!" Nanna screamed in deadly terror, as she heard the transcendent voice that one time, like a voice from the grave.

She sank down, fainting upon the floor, and the little child rolled from her slackened arms upon the coarse bricks and lay on its face, moaning tremulously. No one heeded it.

Stefanone, with instinctive horror of death, turned and went blindly down the steps, not knowing what he had seen, the death notes still ringing in his ears.

On the bed, the man lay dumb upon the dead woman. Only the poor little child seemed to be alive, and clutched feebly at the coarse red bricks, and moaned and bruised its small face. It bore the slender inheritance of fatal life, the inheritance of vows broken and of faith outraged, and with it, perhaps, the implanted seed of a lifelong terror, not remembered, but felt throughout life, as real and as deadly as an inheritance of mortal disease. Better, perhaps, if death had taken it, too, to the lonely grave of the outcast and suicide woman, among the rocks, out of earshot of humanity. Death makes strange oversights and leaves strange gleanings for life, when he has reaped his field and housed his harvest.

They would not give Gloria Christian burial, for it was known throughout Subiaco that she had poisoned herself, and those were still the old days, when the Church's rules were the law of the people.

Paul Griggs took the body of the woman he had loved, and loved beyond death, and he laid her in a deep grave in a hollow of the hillside. Such words as he had to speak to those who helped him, he spoke quietly, and none could say that they had seen the still face moved by sorrow. But as they watched him, a human sort of fear took hold of them, at his great quiet, and they knew that his grief was beyond anything which could be shown or understood. It was night, and they filled the grave after he had thrown earth into it with his hands. He sent them away, and they left him alone with the dead, leaving also one of their lanterns upon a stone near by.

All that night he lay on the grave, dumb. Then, when the dawn came upon him, he kissed the loose earth and stones, and got upon his feet and went slowly down the hillside to the town beyond the torrent. He went into the house noiselessly, and lay down upon the bed on which she had died. And so he did for two nights and two days. On the third, a great carriage came from Rome, bringing twelve men, singers of the Sistine Chapel and of the choir of Saint Peter's and of Saint John Lateran, twelve men having very beautiful voices, as sweet as any in the world. He had sent for them when he had been told that she could not have Christian burial.

They were talking and laughing together when they came, but when they saw his face they grew very quiet, and followed him in silence where he led them. Two little boys followed them, too, wondering what was to happen, and what the thirteen men were going to do, all dressed in black, walking so steadily together.

When they all came to the hollow in the hillside, they saw a mound, as of a grave, amidst the stones, and on it there lay a cross of black wood. The singers looked at one another in silence, and they understood that whoever lay in the grave had been refused a place in the churchyard, for some great sin. But they said nothing. The man who led them stood still at the head of the cross and took off his hat, and looked at his twelve companions, who uncovered their heads. They had sheets of written music with them, and they passed them quietly about from one to another and looked towards one who was their leader.

Overhead, the summer sky was pale, and there were twin mountains of great clouds in the northwest, hiding the sun, and in the southeast, whence the parching wind was blowing in fierce gusts. It blew the dry dust from the clods of earth on the grave, and the dust settled on the black clothes of the men as they stood near.

The voices struck the first chord softly together, and the music for the dead went up to heaven, and was borne far across the torrent to the distance in the arms of the hot wind. And one voice climbed above the others, sweet and clear, as though to reach heaven itself; and another sank deep and true and soft in the full close of the stave, as though it would touch and comfort the heart that was quite still at last in the deep earth.

Then one who was young stood a little before the rest, a strong, pale singer, with an angel's voice. And he sang alone to the sky and the dusty rocks and the solemn grave. He sang the 'Cujus animam gementem pertransivit gladius' of the Stabat Mater, as none had sung it before him, nor perhaps has ever sung it since that day—he alone, without other music.

They came also to the words 'Fac ut animæ donetur Paradisi gloria,' and the word was a name to him who listened silently in their midst.

Besides these they sang also a 'Miserere,' and last of all, 'Requiem eternam dona eis.'

Then there was silence, and they looked at the still face, as though asking what they should do. The mysterious eyes met theirs with shadows. The pale head bent itself in thanks, twice or thrice, but there were no words.

So they turned and left him there on the hillside, and went back to the town, awestruck by the vastness of the man's sorrow. And afterwards, for many years, when any of them heard of a great grief, he shook his head and said that he and those who had sung with him over a lonely grave in the mountains, alone knew what a man could feel and yet live.

And Paul Griggs lived through those days, and is still alive. His grief could not spend itself, but his stern strength took hold of life again, and he took the child with him and went back to Rome, to work for it from that time forward, and to shield it from evil if he could, and to bring it up to be a man, ignorant of what had happened in Subiaco in those summer days, ignorant of the tie that made it his, to be a man free from the burden of past fates and sins and broken vows and trampled faith, and of the death his dead mother had died, having a clean name of his own, with which there could be no memories of misery and fear and horror.

He wrote a few short words to Angus Dalrymple, now Lord Redin at last, to tell him the truth as far as he knew it. The hand that had laboured so bravely for Gloria could hardly trace the words that told of her death.

Then, when the summer heat was passed, he took little Walter Crowdie with him, hiring an Englishwoman to tend the child, and he crossed the ocean and gave it to certain kinsfolk of his in America, telling them that it was the child of one who had been very dear to him, that he had taken it as his own, and would provide for it and take it back when it should be older. And so he did, and little Walter Crowdie grew up with an angel's voice, and other gifts which made him famous in his day. But many things happened before that time came.

He could do no better than that. For a time he strove to earn money with his pen in his own country. But the land was still trembling from the convulsion of a great war, and there were many before him, and he was little known. After a year had passed, he saw that he could not then succeed, and very heavy at heart he set his face eastward again, to toil at his old calling as a correspondent for a great London paper, to earn bread for himself and for the one living being that he loved.

PART III

DONNA FRANCESCA CAMPODONICO

Not long after this Dalrymple returned to Rome, after an absence of several years. Family affairs had kept him in England and Scotland during his daughter's married life with Reanda; and after she had left the latter, it was natural that he should not wish to be in the same city with her, considering the view he took of her actions. Then, after he had learned from Griggs's brief note that she was dead, he felt that he could not return at once, hard and unforgiving as he was. But at last the power that attracted him was too strong to be resisted any longer, and he yielded to it and came back.

He took up his abode in a hotel in the Piazza di Spagna, not far from his old lodgings. Long as he had lived in Rome, he was a foreigner there and liked the foreigners' quarter of the city. He intended once more to get a lodging and a servant, and to live in his morose solitude as of old, but on his first arrival he naturally went to the hotel. He did not know whether Griggs were in Rome. Reanda was alive, and living at the Palazzetto Borgia; for the two had exchanged letters twice a year, written in the constrained tone of mutual civility which suited the circumstances in which they were placed towards each other.

In Dalrymple's opinion, Reanda had been to blame to a certain extent, in having maintained his intimacy with Francesca when he was aware that it displeased his wife. At the same time, the burden of the fault was undoubtedly the woman's, and her father felt in a measure responsible for it. Whether he felt much more than that it would be hard to say. His gloomy nature had spent itself in secret sorrow for his wife, with a faithfulness of grief which might well atone for many shortcomings. It is certain that he was not in any way outwardly affected by the news of Gloria's death. He had never loved her, she had disgraced him, and now she was dead. There was nothing more to be said about it.

He was not altogether indifferent to the inheritance of title and fortune which had fallen to him in his advanced middle age. But if either influenced his character, the result was rather an increased tendency to live his own life in scorn and defiance of society, for it made him conscious that he should find even less opposition to his eccentricities than in former days, when he had been relatively a poor man without any especial claim to consideration.

Two or three days after he had arrived in Rome, he went to the Palazzetto Borgia and sent in his card, asking to see Francesca Campodonico. In order that she might know who he was, he wrote his name in pencil, as she would probably not have recognized him as Lord Redin. In this he was mistaken, for Reanda, who had heard the news, had told her of it. She received him in the drawing-room. She looked very ill, he thought, and was much thinner than in former times, but her manner was not changed. They talked upon indifferent subjects, and there was a constraint between them. Dalrymple broke through it roughly at last.

"Did you ever see my daughter after she left her husband?" he asked, as though he were inquiring about a mere acquaintance.

Francesca started a little.

"No," she answered. "It would not have been easy."

She remembered her interview with Griggs, but resolved not to speak of it. She would have changed the subject abruptly if he had given her time.

"It certainly was not to be expected that you should," said Lord Redin, thoughtfully. "When a woman chooses to break with society, she knows perfectly well what she is doing, and one may as well leave her to herself."

Francesca was shocked by the cynicism of the speech. The colour rose faintly in her cheeks.

"She was your daughter," she said, reproachfully. "Since she is dead, you should speak less cruelly of her."

"I did not speak cruelly. I merely stated a fact. She disgraced herself and me, and her husband. The circumstance that she is dead does not change the case, so far as I can see."

"Do you know how she died?" asked Francesca, moved to righteous anger, and willing to pain him if she could.

He looked up suddenly, and bent his shaggy brows.

"No," he answered. "That man Griggs wrote me that she had died suddenly. That was all I heard."

"She did not die a natural death."

"Indeed?"

"She poisoned herself. She could not bear the life. It was very dreadful." Francesca's voice sank to a low tone.

Lord Redin was silent for a few moments, and his bony face had a grim look. Perhaps something in the dead woman's last act appealed to him, as nothing in her life had done.

"Tell me, please. I should like to know. After all, she was my daughter."

"Yes," said Francesca, gravely. "She was your daughter. She was very unhappy with Paul Griggs, and she found out very soon that she had made a dreadful mistake. She loved her husband, after all."

"Like a woman!" interjected Lord Redin, half unconsciously.

Francesca paid no attention to the remark, except, perhaps, that she raised her eyebrows a little.

"They went out to spend the summer at Subiaco—"

"At Subiaco?" Dalrymple's steely blue eyes fixed themselves in a look of extreme attention.

"Yes, during the heat. They lodged in the house of a man called Stefanone—a wine-seller—a very respectable place."

Lord Redin had started nervously at the name, but he recovered himself.

"Very respectable," he said, in an odd tone.

"You know the house?" asked Francesca, in surprise.

"Very well indeed. I was there nearly five and twenty years ago. I supposed that Stefanone was dead by this time."

"No. He and his wife are alive, and take lodgers."

"Excuse me, but how do you know all this?" asked Lord Redin, with sudden curiosity.

"I have been there," answered Francesca. "I have often been to the convent. You know that one of our family is generally abbess. A Cardinal Braccio was archbishop, too, a good many years ago. Casa Braccio owns a good deal of property there."

"Yes. I know that you are of the family."

"My name was Francesca Braccio," said Francesca, quietly. "Of course I have always known Subiaco, and every one there knows Stefanone, and the story of his daughter who ran away with an Englishman many years ago, and never was heard of again."

Lord Redin grew a trifle paler.

"Oh!" he exclaimed. "Does every one know that story?"

There was something so constrained in his tone that Francesca looked at him curiously.

"Yes—in Subiaco," she answered. "But Gloria—" she lingered a little sadly on the name—"Gloria wrote letters to her husband from there and begged him to go and see her."

"He could hardly be expected to do that," said Lord Redin, his hard tone returning. "Did you advise him to go?"

"He consulted me," answered Francesca, rather coldly. "I told him to follow his own impulse. He did not go. He did not believe that she was sincere."

"I do not blame him. When a woman has done that sort of thing, there is no reason for believing her."

"He should have gone. I should have influenced him, I think, and I did wrong. She wrote him one more letter and then killed herself. She suffered horribly and only died two days afterwards. Shall I tell you more?"

"If there is more to tell," said Lord Redin, less hardly.

"There is not much. I went out there last year. They had refused her Christian burial. Paul Griggs bought a piece of land amongst the rock, on the other side of the torrent, and buried her there. It is surrounded by a wall, and there is a plain slab without a name. There are flowers. He pays Stefanone to have it cared for. They told me all they knew—it is too terrible. She died singing—she was out of her mind. It must have been dreadful. Old Nanna, Stefanone's wife, was in the room, and fainted with terror. It seems that poor Gloria, oddly enough, had an extraordinary resemblance to that unfortunate nun of our family who was burned to death in the convent, and whom Nanna had often seen. She sang like her, too—at the last minute Nanna thought she saw poor sister Maria Addolorata standing up dead and singing. It was rather strange."

Lord Redin said nothing. He had bowed his head so that Francesca could not see his face, but she saw that his hands were trembling violently. She thought that she had misjudged the man, and that he was really very deeply moved by the story of his daughter's death. Doubtless, his emotion had made him wish to control himself, and he had overshot the mark and spoken cruelly only in order to seem calm. No one had ever spoken to him of his wife, and even now he could hardly bear to hear her name. It was long before he looked up. Then he rose almost immediately.

"Will you allow me to come and see you occasionally?" he asked, with a gentleness not at all like his usual manner.

Francesca was touched at last, misunderstanding the cause of the change. She told him to come as often as he pleased. As he was going, he remembered that he had not asked after his son-in-law. Reanda had always seemed to belong to Francesca, and it was natural enough that he should inquire of her.

"Where is Reanda to be found?" he asked.

"He is very ill," said Francesca, in a low voice. "I am afraid you cannot see him."

"Where does he live? I will at least inquire. I am sorry to hear that he is ill."

"He lives here," she answered with a little hesitation. "He is in his old rooms upstairs."

"Oh! Yes—thank you." Their eyes met for a moment. Lord Redin's glittered, but Francesca's were clear and true. "I am sure you take good care of him," he added. "Good-bye."

He left her alone, and when he was gone, she sat down wearily and laid her head back against a cushion, with half-closed eyes. Her lips were almost colourless, and her mouth had grown ten years older.

Reanda was dying, and she knew it, and with him the light was going out of her life, as it had gone out long ago from Dalrymple's, as it had gone out of the life of Paul Griggs. The idea crossed her mind that these two men, with herself, were linked and bound together by some strange fatality which she could not understand, but from which there was no escape, and which was bringing them slowly and surely to the blank horror of lonely old age.

The same thought occurred to Lord Redin as he slowly threaded the streets, going back to his hotel, to his lonely dinner, his lonely evening, his lonely, sleepless night. He alone of the three now knew all that there was to know, and in the chronicle of his far memories all led back to that day at Subiaco, long ago, when he had first knocked at the convent gate—beyond that, to the evening when poor Annetta had told him of the beautiful nun with the angel's voice. Many lives had been wrecked since that first day, and every one of them owed its ruin to him. He felt strangely drawn to Francesca Campodonico. There was something in her face that very faintly reminded him of his dead wife, her kinswoman, and of his dead daughter, another of her race. His gloomy northern nature felt the fatality of it all. He never could repent of what he had done. The golden light of his one short happiness shone through the shrouding veil of fatal time. In his own eyes, with his beliefs, he had not even sinned in taking what he had loved so well. But all the sorrow he saw, came from that deed. Francesca Campodonico's eyes were as clear and true as her heart. But he knew that Reanda's life was everything on earth to her, and he guessed that she was to lose that, too, before long. He would willingly have parted with his own, but through all his being there was a rough, manly courage that forbade the last act of fear, and there was a stern old Scottish belief that it was wrong—plainly wrong.

He did not wish to see Paul Griggs any more than he had wished to see his daughter after she had left her husband. But no thought of vengeance crossed his mind. It seemed to him fruitless to think of avenging himself upon fate; for, after all, it was fate that had done the dire mischief. Possibly, he thought, as he walked slowly towards his hotel, fate had brought him back to Rome now, to deal with him as she had dealt with his. He should be glad of it, for he found little in life that was not gloomy and lonely beyond any words. He did not know why he had come. He had acted upon an impulse in going to see Francesca that day.

When he reached the Corso, instead of going to his hotel he walked down the street in the direction of the Piazza del Popolo. He wished to see the house in which Gloria had lived with Griggs, and he remembered the street and the number from her having written to him when she wanted money. He reached the corner of the Via della Frezza, and turned down, looking up at the numbers as he went along. He glanced at the little wine shop on the left, with its bush, its red glass lantern, and its rush-bottomed stools set out by the door. In the shadow within he saw the gleam of silver buttons on a dark blue jacket. There was nothing uncommon in the sight.

He found the house, paused, looked up at the windows, and looked twice at the number.

"Do you seek some one?" inquired the one-eyed cobbler, resting his black hands on his knees.

"Did Mr. Paul Griggs ever live here?" asked Lord Redin.

"Many years," answered the cobbler, laconically.

"Where does he live now?"

"Always here, except when he is not here. Third floor, on the left. You can ring the bell. Who knows? Perhaps he will open. I do not wish to tell lies."

The old man grunted, bent down over the shoe, and ran his awl through the sole. He was profoundly attached to Paul Griggs, who had always been kind to him, and since Gloria's death he defended him from visitors with more determination than ever.

Lord Redin stood still and said nothing. In ten seconds the cobbler looked up with a surly frown.

"If you wish to go up, go up," he growled. "If not, favour me by getting out of my light."

The Scotchman looked at him.

"You do not remember me," he observed. "I used to come here with the Signore."

"Well? I have told you. If you want him, there is the staircase."

"No. I do not want him," said Lord Redin, and he turned away abruptly.

"As you please," growled the cobbler without looking up again.

CHAPTER XLII

Paul Griggs had gone back to the house in the Via della Frezza after his return from America, and lived alone in the little apartment in which the happy days of his life had been spent. He was a man able to live two lives,—the one in the past, the other in the active present. It was his instinct to be alone in his sorrow, and alone in the struggle which lay before him, for himself and his child. But he would have with him all that could make the memory of Gloria real. The reality of such things softened with their contrast the hardness of life.

He had taken the same rooms again. Out of boxes and trunks stored in a garret of the house, he had taken many things which had belonged to Gloria. Alone, he had arranged the rooms as they used to be. His writing-table stood in the same place, and near it was Gloria's chair; beside it, the little stand with her needlework, her silks, her scissors, and her thimble, all as it used to be. A novel she had once read when sitting there lay upon the chair. Many little objects which had belonged to her were all in their accustomed places. On the mantelpiece the cheap American clock ticked loudly as in old days.

Day after day, as of old, he sat in his place at work. He had made the room so alive with her that sometimes, looking up from a long spell of writing, he forgot, and stared an instant at the bedroom door, and listened for her footstep. Those were his happiest moments, though each was killed in turn by the vision of a lonely grave among rocks.

With intensest longing he called her back to him. In his sleep, the last words he had spoken to her were spoken again by his unconscious lips in the still, dark night. Everything in him called her, his living soul and his strong bodily self. There were times when he knew that if he opened his eyes, shut to see her, he should see her really, there in her chair. He looked, trembling, and there was nothing. In dreams he sought her and could not find her, though he wandered in dark places, across endless wastes of broken clods of earth and broken stone. It was as though her grave covered the whole world round, and his path lay on the shadowed arms of an infinite great cross. And again the grey dawn awoke him from the search, to feel that, for pity's sake, she must be alive and near him. But he was always alone.

Silent, iron-browed, iron-handed, he faced the world alone, doing all that was required of him, and more also. As he had said to Gloria in that very room, he was building up a superiority for himself, since genius was not his. He had in the rough ore of his strength the metal which some few men receive as a birth-gift from nature, ready smelted and refined, ready for them to coin at a single stroke, and throw broadcast to the applauding world. He had not much, perhaps, but he had something of the true ore, and in the furnace of his untiring energy he would burn out the dross and find the precious gold at last. It could not be for her, now. It was not for himself, but it was to be for the little child, growing up in a far country with a clean name—to be his father's friend, and nothing more, but to be happy, for the dead woman's sake who bore him.

As in all that made a part of Paul Griggs, there was in his memory of Gloria and in his sorrow for her that element of endurance which was the foundation of his nature. That portion of his life was finished, and there could never be anything like it again; but it was to be always present with him, so long as he lived. He was sure of that. It would always be in his power to close his eyes and believe that she was near him. If it were possible, he loved her more dead than he had loved her living.

And she had loved him to the last, and had given her life in the mad thought of lightening his burden. Her last words to him had told him so. Her last wish had been to see the child. And the greatest sacrifice he could now make to her was to separate himself from the child, and let him grow up to look upon the man who provided for him as his friend, but as nothing more. It was an exaggerated idea, perhaps, though it was by far the wisest course. Yet in doing what he did, Griggs deprived himself for months at a time of something that was of her, and he did it for her sake. He knew that in her heart there had been the unspoken shame of her ruined life. Shame should never come near little Walter Crowdie. The secret could be kept, and Paul Griggs meant to keep it, as he kept many things from the world.

All his lonely life grew in the perfect memory, cut short though it was by fate's cruel scythe-stroke. Even that one fearful day held no shadow of unfaithfulness. She had been mad, but she had loved him. She had done a deed of horror upon herself, but she had loved him, and madly had done it for his sake. She had laid down her life for him. All that he could do would be nothing compared with that. All that he could tear from the world and lay tenderly as an offering at her feet would be but a handful of dust in comparison with what she had done in the madness of love.

His heart strings wound themselves about their treasure, closer and closer, stronger and stronger. The two natures that strove together in him, the natures of body and soul, were at one with her, and drew life from her though she was gone. It seemed impossible that they could ever again part and smite one another for the mastery, as of old, for one sorrow had overwhelmed them both, and together they knew the depths of one grief.

Again, as of old, he defied fate. Death could take the child from him, but could not separate the three in death or life. So long as the child lived, to do or die for him was the question, while life should last. But Paul Griggs defied fate, for fate's grim hand could not uproot his heart from the strong place of his great dead love, to buffet it and tear it again. He was alone, bodily, but he was safe forever.

Out of the dimness of twilight shadows the pale face came to him, and the sweet lips kissed his; in a light not earthly the dark eyes lightened, and the red auburn hair gleamed and fell about him. In the darkness, a tender hand stole softly upon his, and words yet more tender stirred the stillness. He knew that she was near him, close to him, with him. The truth of what had been made the half dream all true. Only in his sleep he could not find her, and was wandering ever over a dreary grave that covered the whole world.

So his life went on with little change, inwardly or outwardly, from day to day, in the absolute security from danger which the dead give us of themselves. The faith that had gone beyond her death could go beyond his own life, too. He defied fate.

Then fate, silent, relentless, awful, knocked at his door.

He was at work as usual. It was a bright winter's day, and the high sun of the late morning streamed across one corner of his writing-table. He was thinking of nothing but his writing, and upon that his thoughts were closely intent in that everlasting struggle to do better which had nearly driven poor Gloria mad.

The little jingling bell rang and thumped against the outer door to which it was fastened. He paid no attention to it, till it rang again, an instant later. Then he looked up and waited, listening. Again, again, and again he heard it, at equal intervals, five times in all. That was the old cobbler's signal, and the only one to which Griggs ever responded. He laid down his pen and went to the door. The one-eyed man, his shoemaker's apron twisted round his waist, stood on the landing, and gave him a small, thick package, tied with a black string, under which was thrust a note. Griggs took it without a word, and the bandy-legged old cobbler swung away from the door with a satisfied grunt.

Griggs took the parcel back to his work-room, and stood by the window looking at the address on the note. He recognized Francesca Campodonico's handwriting, though he had rarely seen it, and he broke the seal with considerable curiosity, for he could not imagine why Donna Francesca should write to him. He even wondered at her knowing that he was in Rome. He had never spoken with her since that day long ago, when she had sent for him and begged him to take Gloria back to her father. He read the note slowly. It was in Italian, and the language was rather formal.

"SIGNORE:—My old and dear friend, Signor Angelo Reanda, died the day before yesterday after a long illness. During the last hours of his life he asked me to do him a service, and I gave him the solemn promise which I fulfil in sending you the accompanying package. You will see that it was sealed by him and addressed to you by himself, probably before he was taken ill, and he saw it before he died and said that it was the one he meant me to send. That was all he told me regarding it, and I am wholly ignorant of the contents. I have ascertained that you are in Rome, and are living, as formerly, in the Via della Frezza, and to that address I send the parcel. Pray inform me that you have received it.

"Believe me, Signore, with perfect esteem,
"FRANCESCA CAMPODONICO."

Griggs read the note twice through to the end, and laid it upon the table. Then he thrust his hands into his pockets, and turned thoughtfully to the window without touching the parcel, of which he had not even untied the black string.

So Reanda was dead at last. It was nothing to him, now, though it might have meant much if the man had died two years earlier. Living people were very little to Paul Griggs. They might as well be dead, he thought. Nevertheless, the bald fact that Reanda was gone, made him thoughtful. Another figure had disappeared out of his life, though it had not meant very much. He believed, and had always believed, that Reanda had loved Francesca in secret, though she had treated him as a mere friend, as a protectress should treat one who needs her protection.

Griggs turned and took up the note to look at it keenly, for he believed himself a judge of handwriting, and he thought that he might detect in hers the indications of any great suffering. The lines ran down a little at the end, but otherwise the large, careful hand was the same as ever, learned in a convent and little changed since, even as the woman herself had changed little. She was the same always, simple, honest, strangely maidenlike, thoroughly good.

He turned to the window again. So Reanda was dead. He would not find Gloria, to whatsoever place he was gone. The shadow of a smile wreathed itself about the mouth of the lonely man—the last that was there for a long time after that day. Gloria was dead, but Gloria was his, and he hers, for ever and ever. Neither heaven nor hell could tear up his heart nor loosen the strong hold of all of him that clung to her and had grown about her and through her, till he and she were quite one.

Then, all at once, he wondered what it could be that Reanda had wished to send him from beyond the grave. He turned, took the parcel, and snapped the black string with his fingers, and took off the paper. Within was the parcel, wrapped in a second paper and firmly tied with broad tape. A few words were written on the outside.

"To be given to Paul Griggs when I am dead. A. R."

The superscription told nothing, but he looked at it curiously as one does at such things, when the sender is beyond answer. He cut the white tape, for it was tied so tightly that he could not slip a finger under it to break it. There was something of hard determination in the way it was tied.

It contained letters in their envelopes, as they had reached Reanda through the post, all of the same size, laid neatly one upon the other—a score or more of them.

Griggs felt his hand shake, for he recognized Gloria's writing. His first impulse was to burn the whole package, as it was, reverently, as something which had belonged to Gloria, in which he had no part, or share, or right. He laid his hand upon the pile of letters, and looked at the small fire to see whether it were burning well. Under his hand he felt something hard inside the uppermost envelope. His fate was upon him—the fate he had so often defied to do its worst, since all that he had was dead and was his forever.

Without another thought, he took from the envelope the letter it contained, and the hard thing which was inside the letter. He held it a moment in his hand, and it flamed in the beam of sunlight that fell across the end of the table, and dazzled him. Then he realized what it was. It was Gloria's wedding ring, and twisted round and round it and in and out of it was a lock of her red auburn hair, serpent-like, flaming in the sunshine, with a hundred little tongues that waved and moved softly under his breath.

An icy chill smote him in the neck, and his strong limbs shook to his feet as he laid the thing down upon the corner of the table. There was a fearful fascination in it. The red gold hairs stirred and moved in the sunlight still, even when he no longer breathed upon them. It was her hair, and it seemed alive.

In his other hand he still held the letter. Fate had him now, and would not let him go while he could feel. Again and again the cruel chill smote him in the back. He opened the doubled sheet, and saw the date and the name of the place,—Subiaco,—and the first words—'Heart of my heart, this is my last cry to you'—and it was to Angelo Reanda.

Rigid and feeling as though great icy hands were drawing him up by the neck from the ground, he stood still and read every word, with all the message of loathing and abject fear and horror of his touch, which every word brought him, from the dead, through the other dead.

Slowly, regularly, without wavering, moved by a power not his own, his hands took the other letters and opened them, and his eyes read all the words, from the last to the first. One by one the sheets fell upon the table, and all alone in the midst the lock of red auburn hair sent up its little lambent flame in the sunshine.

Paul Griggs stood upright, stark with the stress of rending soul and breaking heart.

As he stood there, he was aware of a man in black beside him, like himself, ghastly to see, with shadows and fires for eyes, and thin, parted lips that showed wolfish teeth, strong, stern, with iron hands.

"You are dead," said his own voice out of the other's mouth. "You are dead, and I am Gorlias."

Then the strong teeth were set and the lips closed, and the gladiator's unmatched arms wound themselves upon the other's strength, with grip and clutch and strain not of earthly men.

Silent and terrible, they wrestled in fight, arm to arm, bone to bone, breath to breath. Hour after hour they strove in the still room. The sun went westering away, the shadows deepened. The night came stealing black and lonely through the window. Foot to foot, breast to breast, in the dark, they bowed themselves one upon the other, dumb in the agony of their reeling strife.

Late in the night, in the cold room, Paul Griggs felt the carpet under his hands as he lay upon his back.

His heart was broken.

CHAPTER XLIII

Lord Redin had barely glanced at the man in the blue jacket with silver buttons, whom he had seen in the deep shadow of the little wine shop as he strolled down the Via della Frezza. But Stefanone had seen him and had gone to the door as he passed, watching him when he stood talking to the one-eyed cobbler, and keeping his keen eyes on him as he passed again on his homeward way. And all the way to the hotel in the Piazza di Spagna Stefanone had followed him at a distance, watching the great loose-jointed frame and the slightly stooping head, till the Scotchman disappeared under the archway, past the porter, who stood aside, his gold-laced cap in his hand, bowing low to the 'English lord.'

Stefanone waited a few moments and then accosted the porter civilly.

"Do you know if the proprietor wishes to buy some good wine of last year, at a cheap rate?" he asked. "You understand. I am of the country. I cannot go in and look for the proprietor. But you are doubtless the director and you manage these things for him. That is why I ask you."

The porter smiled at the flattery, but said that he believed wine had been bought for the whole year.

"The hotel is doubtless full of rich foreigners," observed Stefanone. "It is indeed beautiful. I should prefer it to the Palazzo Borghese. Is it not full?"

"Quite full," answered the porter, proud of the establishment.

"For instance," said Stefanone, "I saw a great signore going in, just before I took the liberty of speaking with you. I am sure that he is a great English signore. Not perhaps a mylord. But a great signore, having much money."

"What makes you think that?" inquired the porter, with a superior smile.

"Eh, the reasons are two. First, you bowed to him, as though he were some personage, and you of course know who he is. Secondly, he lifted his hat to you. He is therefore a real signore, as good perhaps as a Roman prince. We say a proverb in the country—'to salute is courtesy, to answer is duty.' Therefore when any one salutes a real signore, he answers and lifts his hat. These are the reasons why I say this one must be a great one."

"For that matter, you are right," laughed the porter. "That signore is an English lord. What a combination! You have guessed it. His name is Lord Redin."

Stefanone's sharp eyes fixed themselves vacantly, for he did not wish to betray his surprise at not hearing the name he had expected.

"Eh!" he exclaimed. "Names? What are they, when one is a prince. Prince of this. Duke of that. Our Romans are full of names. I daresay this signore has four or five."

But the porter knew of no other, and presently Stefanone departed, wondering whether he had made a mistake, after all, and recalling the features of the man he had followed to compare them with those younger ones he remembered so distinctly. He went back to the Via della Frezza and drank a glass of wine. Then he filled the glass again and carried it carefully across the street to his friend the cobbler.

"Drink," he said. "It will do you good. A drop of wine at sunset gives force to the stomach."

The one-eyed man looked up, and smiled at his friend, a phenomenon rarely observed on his wrinkled and bearded face. He shrugged one round shoulder, by way of assent, held his head a little on one side and stretched out his black hand with the glass in it, to the light. He tasted it, smelt it, and looked up at Stefanone before he drank in earnest.

"Black soul!" he exclaimed by way of an approving asseveration. "This is indeed wine!"

"He took it for vinegar!" observed Stefanone, speaking to the air.

"It is wine," answered the cobbler when he had drained the glass. "It is a consolation."

Then they began to talk together, and Stefanone questioned him about his interview with the tall gentleman an hour earlier. The cobbler really knew nothing about him, though he remembered having seen him several times, years ago, before Gloria had come.

"You know nothing," said Stefanone. "That signore is the father of Sor Paolo's signora, who died in my house."

"You are joking," returned the cobbler, gravely. "He would have come to see his daughter while she lived—requiescat!"

"And I say that I am not joking. Do you wish to hear the truth? Well. You have much confidence with Sor Paolo. Tell him that the father of the poor Signora Gloria came to the door and asked questions. You shall hear what he will say. He will say that it is possible. Then he will ask you about him. You will tell him, so and so—a very tall signore, all made of pieces that swing loosely when he walks, with a beard like the Moses of the fountain, and hard blue eyes that strike you like two balls from a gun, and hair that is neither red nor white, and a bony face like an old horse."

"It is true," said the cobbler, reflectively. "It is he. It is his picture."

"You will also say that he is now an English lord, but that formerly they called him Sor Angoscia. You, who are friends with Sor Paolo, you should tell him this. It may be that Sor Angoscia wishes him evil. Who knows? In this world the combinations are so many!"

It was long before the cobbler got an opportunity of speaking with Griggs, and when he had the chance, he forgot all about it, though Stefanone reminded him of it from time to time. But when he at last spoke of the matter he was surprised to find that Stefanone had been quite right, as Griggs admitted without the least hesitation. He told Stefanone so, and the peasant was satisfied, though he had long been positive that he had found his man at last, and recognized him in spite of his beard and his age.

After that Stefanone haunted the Piazza di Spagna in the morning, talking a little with the models who used to stand there in their mountain costumes to be hired by painters in the days when pictures of them were the fashion. Many of them came from the neighbourhood of Subiaco, and knew Stefanone by sight. When Lord Redin came out of the hotel, as he generally did between eleven and twelve if the day were fine, Stefanone put his pipe out, stuck it into his breeches' pocket with his brass-handled clasp-knife, and strolled away a hundred yards behind his enemy.

If Lord Redin noticed him once or twice, it was merely to observe that men still came to Rome wearing the old-fashioned dress of the respectable peasants. Being naturally fearless, and at present wholly unsuspicious, it never struck him that any one could be dogging his footsteps whenever he went out of his hotel. In the evening he went out very little and then generally in a carriage. Two or three times, on a Sunday, he walked over to Saint Peter's and listened to the music at Vespers, as many foreigners used to do. Stefanone followed him into the church and watched him from a distance. Once the peasant saw Donna Francesca, whom he knew by sight as a member of the Braccio family, sitting within the great gate of the Chapel of the Choir, where the service was held. Lord Redin always followed the frequented streets, which led in an almost direct line from the Piazza di Spagna by the Via Condotti to the bridge of Saint Angelo. It was the nearest way. He never went back to the Via della Frezza, for he had no desire to see Paul Griggs, and his curiosity had been satisfied by once looking at the house in which his daughter had lived. He spent his evenings alone in his rooms with a bottle of wine and a book. Luxury had become a habit with him, and he now preferred a draught of Château Lafitte to the rough Roman wine barely a year old, while three or four glasses of a certain brandy, twenty years in bottle, which he had discovered in the hotel, were a necessary condition of his comfort. He had the intention of going out one evening, in cloak and soft hat, as of old, to dine in his old corner at the Falcone, but he put it off from day to day, feeling no taste for the coarser fare and the rougher drink when the hour came.

He often went to see Francesca Campodonico in the middle of the day, at which hour the Roman ladies used to be visible to their more intimate friends. An odd sort of sympathy had grown up between the two, though they scarcely ever alluded to past events, and then only by an accident which both regretted. Francesca exercised a refining influence upon the gloomy Scotchman, and as he knew her better, he even took the trouble to be less rough and cynical when he was with her. In character she was utterly different from his dead wife, but there was something of family resemblance between the two which called up memories very dear to him.

Her influence softened him. In his wandering life he had more than once formed acquaintances with men of tastes more or less similar to his own, which might have ripened into friendships for a man of less morose character. But in that, he and Paul Griggs were very much alike. They found an element in every acquaintance which roused their distrust, and as men to men they were both equally incapable of making a confidence. Dalrymple's life had not brought him into close relations with any woman except his wife. For her sake he had kept all others at a distance in a strange jealousy of his own heart which had made her for him the only woman in the world. Then, too, he had hated, for her, the curiosity of those who had evidently wished to know her story. That had been always a secret. He had told it to his father, and his father had died with it. No one else had ever known whence Maria had come, nor what her name had been. If Captain Crowdie had ever guessed the truth, which was doubtful, he had held his tongue.

But Angus Dalrymple was no longer the man he had been in those days. He had changed very much in the past two or three years; for though he had almost outlived the excesses into which he had fallen in his first sorrow, his hardy constitution had been shaken, if not weakened, by them. Physically his nerves were almost as good as ever, but morally he was not the same man. He felt the need of sympathy and confidence, which with such natures is the first sign of breaking down, and of the degeneration of pride.

That was probably the secret of what he felt when he was with Francesca. She had that rarest quality in women, too, which commands men without inspiring love. It is very hard to explain what that quality is, but most men who have lived much and seen much have met with it at least once in their lives.

There is a sort of manifested goodness for which the average man of the world has a profound and unreasonable contempt. And there is another sort which most wholly commands the respect of that man who has lived hardest. From a religious point of view, both may be equally real and conducive to salvation. The cynic, the worn out man of the world, the man whose heart is broken, all look upon the one as a weakness and the other as a strength. Perhaps there is more humanity in the one than in the other. A hundred women may rebuke a man for something he has done, and he will smile at the reproach, though he may smile sadly. The one will say to him the same words, and he will be gravely silent and will feel that she is right and will like her the better for it ever afterwards. And she is not, as a rule, the woman whom such men would love.

"I have never before met a woman whom I should wish to have for my friend," said Lord Redin, one day when he was alone with Francesca. "I daresay I am not at all the kind of man you would select for purposes of friendship," he added, with a short laugh.

Francesca smiled a little at the frankness of the words, and shook her head.

"Perhaps not," she said. "Who knows? Life brings strange changes when one thinks that one knows it best."

"It has brought strange things to me," answered Lord Redin.

Then he was silent for a time. He felt the strong desire to speak out, for no good reason or purpose, and to tell her the story of his life. She would be horrorstruck at first. He fancied he could see the expression which would come to her face. But he held his peace, for she had not met him half-way, and he was ashamed of the weakness that was upon him.

"Yes," she said thoughtfully, after a little pause. "You must have had a strange life, and a very unhappy one. You speak of friendship as men speak who are in earnest, because there is no other hope for them. I know something of that."

She ceased, and her clear eyes turned sadly away from him.

"I know you do," he answered softly.

She looked at him again, and she liked him better than ever before, and pitied him sincerely. She had discovered that with all his faults he was not a bad man, as men go, for she did not know of that one deed of his youth which to her would have seemed a monstrous crime of sacrilege, beyond all forgiveness on earth or in heaven.

Then she began to speak of other things, for her own words, and his, had gone too near her heart, and presently he left her and strolled homeward through the sunny streets. He walked slowly and thoughtfully, unconscious of the man in a blue jacket with silver buttons, who followed him and watched him with keen, unwinking eyes set under heavy brows.

But Stefanone was growing impatient, and his knife was every day a little sharper as he whetted it thoughtfully upon a bit of smooth oilstone which he carried in his pocket. Would the Englishman ever turn down into some quiet street or lane where no one would be looking? And Stefanone's square face grew thinner and his aquiline features more and more eagle-like, till the one-eyed cobbler noticed the change, and spoke of it.

"You are consuming yourself for some female," he said. "You have white hair. This is a shameful thing."

But Stefanone laughed, instead of resenting the speech—a curiously nervous laugh.

"What would you have?" he replied. "We are men, and the devil is everywhere."

As he sat on the doorstep by the cobbler's bench, which was pushed far forward to get the afternoon light, he took up the short sharp shoemaker's knife, looked at it, held it in his hands and pared his coarse nails with it, whistling a little tune.

"That is a good knife," he observed carelessly.

The cobbler looked up and saw what he was doing.

"Black soul!" he cried out angrily. "That is my welt-knife, like a razor, and he pares his hoofs with it!"

But Stefanone dropped it into the little box of tools on the front of the bench, and whistled softly.

"You seem to me a silly boy!" said the cobbler, still wrathful.

"Apoplexy, how you talk!" answered Stefanone. "But I seem so to myself, sometimes."

CHAPTER XLIV

The life of Paul Griggs was not less lonely than it had been before the day on which he had received and read Gloria's letters to Reanda, but it was changed. Everything which had belonged to the dead woman was gone from the room in which he sat and worked as usual. Even the position of the furniture was changed. But he worked on as steadily as before.

Outwardly he was very much the same man as ever. Any one who knew him well—if such a person had existed—would have seen that there was a little difference in the expression of his impassive face. The jaw was, if possible, more firmly set than ever, but there was a line in the forehead which had not been there formerly, and which softened the iron front, as it were, with something more human. It had come suddenly, and had remained. That was all.

But within, the difference was great and deep. He felt that the man who sat all day long at the writing-table doing his work was not himself any longer, but another being, his double and shadow, and in all respects his slave, except in one.

That other man sometimes paused in his work, fingering the pen unconsciously, as men do who hold it all day long, and thinking of Gloria with an expression of horror and suffering in his eyes. But he, the real Paul Griggs, never thought of her. The link was broken, the thread that had carried the message of dead love between him and the lonely grave beyond Subiaco was definitely broken. Stefanone came to receive the small sum which Griggs paid him monthly for his care of the place, and Griggs paid him as he would have paid his tailor, mechanically, and made a note of the payment in his pocket-book. When the man was gone, Griggs felt that his double was staring at the wall as a man stares at the dark surface of the pool in which the thing he loves has sunk for the last time.

It was always the other self that felt at such moments. He could abstract himself from it, and feel that he was watching it; he could direct it and make it do what he pleased; but he could neither control its thoughts nor feel any sympathy for them. Until the fatal day, the world had all been black to him; only by closing his eyes could he bring into it the light that hovered about a dead woman's face.

But now the black was changed to a flat and toneless white in which there was never the least variation. Life was to him a vast blank, in which, without interest or sensation, he moved in any direction he pleased, and he pleased that it should be always the same direction, from the remembrance of a previous intention and abiding principle. But it might as well have been any other, backwards, or to right or left. It was all precisely the same, and it was perfectly inconceivable to him that he should ever care whether in the endless journey he ever came upon a spot or point in the blank waste which should prove to him that he had moved at all. Nothing could make any difference. He was beyond that state in which any difference was apprehensible between one thing and another.

His double had material wants, and was ruled by material circumstances. His double was a broken-hearted creature, toiling to make money for a little child to which it felt itself bound by every responsibility which can bind father to son; acknowledging the indebtedness in every act of its laborious life, denying itself every luxury, and almost every comfort, that there might be a little more for the child, now and in time to come; weary beyond earthly weariness, but untiring in the mechanical performance of its set task; fatally strong and destined, perhaps, to live on through sixty or seventy years of the same unceasing toil; fatally weak in its one deep wound, and horribly sensitive within itself, but outwardly expressionless, strong, merely a little more pale and haggard than Paul Griggs had been.

This was the being whom Paul Griggs employed, as it were, to work for him, which he thoroughly understood and could control in every part except in its thoughts, and they were its own. But he himself existed in another sphere, in which there were neither interests nor responsibilities, nor landmarks, nor touches of human feeling, neither memories for the dead nor hopes for the living; in which everything was the same, because there was nothing but a sort of universal impersonal consciousness, no more attached to himself than to the beings he saw about him, or to that particular being which was his former self,—in which he chose to reside, merely because he required a bodily evidence of some sort in order to be alive—and there was no particular reason why he should not be alive. He therefore did not cease to live, but a straw might have turned the balance to the side of death.

It was certainly true that, so far as it could be said that there was any link between him and humanity, it lay in the existence of the little boy beyond the water. But it would have been precisely the same if little Walter Crowdie had died. He did not wish to see the child, for he had no wishes at all. Life being what it was, it would be very much better if the child were to die at once. Since it happened to be alive, he forced his double to work for it. It was no longer any particular child so far as he himself was concerned. It belonged to his double, which seemed to be attached to it in an unaccountable way and did not complain at being driven to labour for it.

At certain moments, when he seemed to have got rid of his double altogether for a time, a question presented itself to his real self. The question was the great and old one—What was it for? And to what was it tending? Then the people he saw in the streets appeared to him to be very small, like ants, running hither and thither upon the ant-hill and about it, moved by something which they could not understand, but which made them do certain things with an appearance of logical sequence, just as he forced his double to work for little Walter Crowdie from morning till night. So the people ran about anxiously, or strolled lazily through the hours, careful or careless, as the case might be, but quite unconscious that they were of no consequence and of no use, and that it was quite immaterial whether they were alive or dead. Most of them thought that they cared a good deal for life on the whole, and that it held a multitude of pleasant and interesting things to be liked and sought, and an equal number of unpleasant and dangerous things to be avoided; all of which things had no real existence whatever, as the impersonal consciousness of Paul Griggs was well aware. He watched the people curiously, as though they merely existed to perform tricks for his benefit. But they did not amuse him, for nothing could amuse him, nor interest him when he had momentarily got rid of his double, as sometimes happened when he was out of doors.

One day, the month having passed again, Stefanone came for his money. It was very little, and the old peasant would willingly have undertaken that the work should be done for nothing. But he was interested in Paul Griggs, and he was growing very impatient because he could not get an opportunity of falling upon Lord Redin in a quiet place. He had formed a new plan of almost childlike simplicity. When Griggs had paid him the money, he lingered a moment and looked about the room.

"Signore, you have changed the furniture," he observed. "That chair was formerly here. This table used to be there. There are a thousand changes."

"Yes," said Griggs, taking up his pen to go on with his work. "You have good eyes," he added good-naturedly.

"Two," assented Stefanone; "each better than the other. For instance, I will tell you. When that chair was by the window, there was a little table beside it. On the table was the work-basket of your poor Signora, whom may the Lord preserve in glory! Is it truth?"

"Yes," answered Griggs, with perfect indifference. "It is quite true."

The allusion did not pain him, the man who was talking with Stefanone. It would perhaps hurt the other man when he thought of it later.

"Signore," said Stefanone, who evidently had something in his mind, "I was thinking in the night, and this thought came to me. The dead are dead. Requiescant! It is better for the living to live in holy peace. You never see the father of the Signora. There is bad blood between you. This was my thought—let them be reconciled, and spend an evening together. They will speak of the dead one. They will shed tears. They will embrace. Let the enmity be finished. In this way they will enjoy life more."

"You are crazy, Stefanone," answered Griggs, impatiently. "But how do you know who is the father of the Signora?"

"Every one knows it, Signore!" replied the peasant, with well-feigned sincerity. "Every one knows that it is the great English lord who lives at the hotel in the Piazza di Spagna this year. Signore, I have said a word. You must not take it ill. Enmity is bad. Friendship is a good thing. And then it is simple. With maccaroni one makes acquaintance again. There is the Falcone, but it would be better here. We will cook the maccaroni in the kitchen; you will eat on this table. What are all these papers for? Study, study! A dish of good paste is better, with cheese. I will bring a certain wine—two flasks. Then you will be friends, for you will drink together. And if the English lord drinks too much, I will go home with him to the hotel in the Piazza di Spagna. But you will only have to go to bed. Once in a year, what is it to be a little gay with good wine? At least you will be good friends. Then things will end well."

Griggs looked at Stefanone curiously, while the old peasant was speaking, for he knew the people well, and he suspected something though he did not know what to think.

"Perhaps some day we may take your advice," he said coldly. "Good morning, Stefanone; I have much to write."

"I remove the inconvenience," answered Stefanone, in the stock Italian phrase for taking leave.

"No inconvenience," replied Griggs, civilly, as is the custom. "But I have to work."

"Study, study!" grumbled Stefanone, going towards the door. "What does it all conclude, this great study? Headache. For a flask of wine you have the same thing, and the pleasure besides. It is enough. Signore," he added, reluctantly turning the handle, "I go. Think of what I have said to you. Sometimes an old man says a wise word."

He went away very much discontented with the result of the conversation. His mind was a medley of cunning and simplicity backed by an absolutely unforgiving temper and great caution. His plan had seemed exceedingly good. Lord Redin and Griggs would have supped together, and the former would very naturally have gone home alone. Stefanone was oddly surprised that Griggs should not have acceded to the proposition at once, though in reality there was not the slightest of small reasons for his doing so.

It was long since anything had happened to rouse Griggs into thinking about any individual human being as anything more than a bit of the world's furniture, to be worn out and thrown away in the course of time, out of sight. But something in the absolutely gratuitous nature of Stefanone's advice moved his suspicions. He saw, with his intimate knowledge of the Roman peasant's character, the whole process of the old wine-seller's mind, if only, in the first place, the fellow had the desire to harass Dalrymple. That being granted, the rest was plain enough. Dalrymple, if he really came to supper with Griggs, would stay late into the night and finish all the wine there might be. On his way home through the deserted streets, Stefanone could kill him at his leisure and convenience, and nobody would be the wiser. The only difficulty lay in establishing some sufficient reason why Stefanone should wish to kill him at all, and in this Griggs signally failed, which was not surprising.

All at once, as generally happened now, he lost all interest in the matter and returned to his work; or rather, to speak as he might have spoken, he set his mechanical self to work for him, while his own being disappeared in blank indifference and unconsciousness. But on the following day, which chanced to be a Sunday, he went out in the morning for a walk. He rarely worked on Sundays, having long ago convinced himself that a day of rest was necessary in the long run.

As he was coming home, he saw Lord Redin walking far in front of him down the Corso, easily recognizable by his height and his loose, swinging gait. Griggs had not proceeded many steps further when Stefanone passed him, walking at a swinging stride. The peasant had probably seen him, but chose to take no notice of him. Griggs allowed him to get a fair start and then quickened his own pace, so as to keep him in view. Lord Redin swung along steadily and turned up the Via Condotti. Stefanone almost ran, till he, too, had turned the corner of the street. Griggs, without running, nearly overtook him as he took the same turn a moment later.

It was perfectly clear that Stefanone was dogging the Scotchman's steps. The latter crossed the Piazza di Spagna, and entered the deep archway of his hotel. The peasant slackened his speed at once and lounged across the square towards the foot of the great stairway which leads up to the Trinità de' Monti. Griggs followed him, and came up with him just as he sat down upon a step beside one of the big stone posts, to take breath and light his pipe. The man looked up, touched his hat, smiled, and struck a sulphur match, which he applied to the tobacco in the red clay bowl before the sulphur was half burned out, after the manner of his kind.

"You have taken a walk, Signore," he observed, puffing away at the willow stem and watching the match.

"You walk fast, Stefanone," answered Griggs. "You can walk as fast as Lord Redin."

Stefanone did not show the least surprise. He pressed down the burning tobacco with one horny finger, and carefully laid the last glowing bit of the burnt-out wooden match upon it.

"For this, we are people of the mountains," he answered slowly. "We can walk."

"Why do you wish to kill that signore?" inquired Griggs, calmly.

Stefanone looked up, and the pale lids of his keen eyes were contracted as he stared hard and long at the other's face.

"What are you saying?" he asked, with a short, harsh laugh. "What is passing through your head? What have I to do with the Englishman? Nothing. These are follies!"

And still he gazed keenly at Griggs, awaiting the latter's reply. Griggs answered him contemptuously in the dialect.

"You take me for a foreigner! You might know better."

"I do not know what you mean," answered Stefanone, doggedly. "It is Sunday. I am at leisure. I walk to take a little air. It is my affair. Besides, at this hour, who would follow a man to kill him? It is about to ring midday. There are a thousand people in the street. Those who kill wait at the corners of streets when it is night. You say that I take you for a foreigner. You have taken me for an assassin. At your pleasure. So much the worse for me. An assassin! Only this was wanting. It is better that I go back to Subiaco. At least they know me there. Here in Rome—not even dogs would stay here. Beautiful town! Where one is called assassin for breakfast, without counting one, nor two."

By this time Griggs was convinced that he was right. He knew the man well, and all his kind. The long speech of complaint, with its peculiar tone, half insolent, half of injured innocence, was to cover the fellow's embarrassment. Griggs answered him in his own strain.

"A man is not an assassin who kills his enemy for a good reason, Stefanone," he observed. "How do I know what he may have done to you?"

"To me? Nothing." The peasant shrugged his sturdy shoulders.

"Then I have made a mistake," said Griggs.

"You have made a mistake," assented Stefanone. "Let us not talk about it any more."

"Very well."

Griggs turned away and walked slowly towards the hotel, well aware that Stefanone was watching him and would think that he was going to warn Lord Redin of his danger. That, indeed, was Griggs's first impulse, and it was probably his wisest course, whatever might come of the meeting. But the Scotchman had made up his mind that he would not see Griggs under any circumstances, and though the latter had seen him enter the hotel less than ten minutes earlier, the servant returned almost immediately and said that Lord Redin was not at home. Griggs understood and turned away, thoughtfully.

Before he went down the Via Condotti again, he looked over his shoulder towards the steps, and he saw that Stefanone was gone. As he walked along the street, the whole incident began to fade away in his mind, as all real matters so often did, nowadays. All at once he stopped short, and roused himself by an effort—directing his double, as he would have said, perhaps. There was no denying the fact that a man's life was hanging in the balance of a chance, and to the man, if not to Griggs, that life was worth something. If it had been any other man in the world, even that fact would have left him indifferent enough. Why should he care who lived or died? But Dalrymple was a man he had injured, and he was under an obligation of honour to save him, if he could.

There was only one person in Rome who could help him—Francesca Campodonico. She knew much of what had happened; she might perhaps understand the present case. At all events, even if she had not seen Lord Redin of late, she could not be supposed to have broken relations with him; she could send for him and warn him. The case was urgent, as Griggs knew. After what he had said to Stefanone, the latter, if he meant to kill his man, would not lose a day.

CHAPTER XLV

It was past midday when Paul Griggs reached the Palazzetto Borgia and inquired for Donna Francesca. He was told that she was out. It was her custom, the porter said, always to breakfast on Sundays with her relatives, the Prince and Princess of Gerano. Griggs asked at what time she might be expected to return. The porter put on a vague look and said that it was impossible to tell. Sometimes she went to Saint Peter's on Sunday afternoon, to hear Vespers. Vespers began at twenty-two o'clock, or half-past twenty-two—between half-past three and four by French time, at that season of the year.

Griggs turned away, and wandered about for half an hour in the vicinity of the palace, uncertain as to what he should do, and yet determined not to lose sight of the necessity for immediate action of some sort. At last he went back to the Piazza di Spagna, intending to write a word of warning to Lord Redin, though he knew that the latter would pay very little attention to anything of such a nature. Like most foreigners, he would laugh at the idea of being attacked in the streets. Even in an interview it would not be easy to persuade him of the truth which Griggs had discovered more by intuition and through his profound knowledge of the Roman character than by any chain of evidence.

Lord Redin had gone out, he was told. It was impossible to say with any certainty whether this were true or not, and Griggs wrote a few words on his card, sealed the latter in an envelope, and left it to be delivered to the Scotchman. Then he went back to the Via della Frezza, determined to renew his attempt to see Francesca Campodonico, at a later hour.

At the door of the little wine shop Stefanone was seated on one of the rush stools, his hat tilted over his eyes, and his white-stockinged legs crossed. He was smoking and looking down, but he recognized Griggs's step at some distance, and raised his eyes. Griggs nodded to him familiarly, passing along on the other side of the narrow street, and he saw Stefanone's expression. There was a look of cunning and amusement in the contraction of the pale lids, which the younger man did not like. Stefanone spoke to him across the street.

"You are well returned, Signore," he said, in the common phrase of greeting after an absence.

The words were civil enough, but there was something of mockery in the tone. Griggs might not have noticed it at any other time, but his thoughts had been occupied with Stefanone during the last two hours, and he resented what sounded like insolence. The tone implied that he had been on a fool's errand, and that Stefanone knew it. He said nothing, but stood still and scrutinized the man's face. There was an unwonted colour about the cheek bones, and the keen eyes sparkled under the brim of the soft hat. Stefanone had a solid head, and was not given to drinking, especially in the morning; but Griggs guessed that to-day he had drunk more than usual. The man's next words convinced him of the fact.

"Signore," he said, slowly rising, "will you favour us by tasting the wine I brought last week? There is no one in the shop yet, for it is early. If you will, we can drink a glass."

"Thank you," answered Griggs. "I have not eaten yet."

"Then Sor Angoscia did not ask you to breakfast!" laughed Stefanone, insolently. "At midday, too! It was just the hour! But perhaps he invited you to his supper, for it is ordered."

And he laughed again. Griggs glanced at him once more, and then went quietly on towards his own door. He saw that the man had drunk too much, and the idea of bandying words in the attempt to rebuke him was distasteful. Griggs had very rarely lost his temper, so far as to strike a man, even in former days, and it had seemed to him of late that he could never be really angry again. Nothing could ever again be of enough importance to make it worth while. If a man of his own class had insulted him, he would have directed his double, as it were, to resent the offence, but he himself would have remained utterly indifferent.

The one-eyed cobbler was not in his place, as it was Sunday. If he had been there, Griggs would very possibly have told him to watch Stefanone and to try and keep him in the wine shop until he should grow heavy over his wine and fall asleep. In that state he would at least be harmless. But the cobbler was not there. Griggs went up to his rooms to wait until a later hour, when he might hope to find Francesca.

Stefanone, being left alone, sat down again, pulled his hat over his eyes once more and felt in his pocket for his clasp-knife. His mind was by no means clear, for he had eaten nothing, he had swallowed a good deal of strong wine, and he had made up his mind that he must kill his enemy on that day or never. The intention was well-defined, but that was all. He had put off his vengeance too long. It was true that he had not yet caught Dalrymple alone in a quiet street at night, that is to say, under the most favourable circumstances imaginable; but more than once he might have fallen upon him suddenly from a doorway in a narrow lane, in which there had been but a few women and children to see the deed, if they saw it at all. He knew well enough that in Rome the fear of being in any way implicated in a murder, even as a witness, would have made women, and probably men, too, run indoors or out of the way, rather than interfere or pursue him. He told himself therefore that he had been unreasonably cautious, and that unless he acted quickly Lord Redin, being warned by Griggs, would take measures of self-defence which might put him beyond the reach of the clasp-knife forever. Stefanone's ideas about the power of an 'English lord' were vague in the extreme.

He had not been exactly frightened by Griggs's sudden accusation that morning, but he had been made nervous and vicious by the certainty that his intentions had been discovered. Peasant-like, not being able to hit on a plan for immediate success, he had excited himself and stimulated his courage with drink. His eyes were already a little bloodshot, and the flush on his high cheek bones showed that he was in the first stage of drunkenness, which under present circumstances was the most dangerous and might last all day with a man of his age and constitution, provided that he did not drink too fast. And there was little fear of that, for the Roman is cautious in his cups, and drinks slowly, never wishing to lose his head, and indeed very much ashamed of ever being seen in a helpless condition.

By this time he was well acquainted with Lord Redin's habits; and though Griggs had been told that the Scotchman was out, Stefanone knew very well that he was at home and would not leave the hotel for another hour or more.

Leaning back against the wall and tipping the stool, he swung his white-stockinged legs thoughtfully.

"One must eat," he remarked aloud, to himself.

He held his head a little on one side, thoughtfully considering the question of food. Then he turned his face slowly towards the low door of the shop and sniffed the air. Something was cooking in the back regions within. Stefanone nodded to himself, rose, pulled out a blue and red cotton handkerchief, and proceeded to dust his well-blacked low shoes and steel buckles with considerable care, setting first one foot and then the other upon the stool.

"Let us eat," he said aloud, folding his handkerchief again and returning it to his pocket.

He went in and sat down at one of the trestle tables,—a heavy board, black with age. The host was nodding on a chair in the corner, a fat man in a clean white apron, with a round red face and fat red prominences over his eyes, with thin eyebrows that were scarcely perceptible.

Stefanone rapped on the board with his knuckles; the host awoke, looked at him with a pleased smile, made an interrogatory gesture, and having received an affirmative nod for an answer retired into the dark kitchen. In a moment he returned with a huge earthenware plate of soup in which a couple of large pieces of fat meat bobbed lazily as he set the dish on the table. Then he brought bread, a measure of wine, an iron spoon, and a two-pronged fork.

Stefanone eat the soup without a word, breaking great pieces of bread into it. Then he pulled out his clasp-knife and opened it; the long blade, keen as a razor and slightly curved, but dark and dull in colour, snapped to its place, as the ring at the back fell into the corresponding sharp notch. With affected delicacy, Stefanone held it between his thumb and one finger and drew the edge across the fat boiled meat, which fell into pieces almost at a touch, though it was tough and stringy. The host watched the operation approvingly. At that time it was forbidden to carry such knives in Rome, unless the point were round and blunt. The Roman always stabs; he never cuts his man's throat in a fight or in a murder.

"It is a prohibited weapon," observed the fat man, smiling, "but it is very beautiful. Poor Christian, if he finds it between his ribs! He would soon be cold. It is a consolation at night to have such a toy."

"Truly, it is the consolation of my soul," answered Stefanone.

"Say a little, dear friend," said the fat man, sitting down and resting his bare elbows upon the table, "that arm, has it ever sent any one to Paradise?"

"And then I should tell you!" exclaimed Stefanone, laughing, and he sipped some wine and smacked his lips. "But no," he added presently. "I am a pacific man. If they touch me—woe! But I, to touch any one? Not even a fly."

"Thus I like men," said the host, "serious, full of scruples, people who drink well, quiet, quiet, and pay better."

"So we are at Subiaco," answered Stefanone.

He cleaned his knife on a piece of bread very carefully, laid it open beside him, and threw the crust to a lean dog that appeared suddenly from beneath the table, as though it had come up through a trap-door; the half-famished creature bolted the bread with a snap and a gulp and disappeared again as suddenly and silently, just in time to avoid the fat man's slow, heavy hand.

When he had finished eating, Stefanone produced his little piece of oilstone, which he carried wrapped in dingy paper, and having greased it proceeded to draw the blade over it slowly and smoothly.

"Apoplexy!" ejaculated the host. "Are you not contented? Or perhaps you wish to shave with it?"

"Thus I keep it," answered the peasant, smiling. "A minute here, a minute there. The time costs nothing. What am I doing? Nothing. I digest. To pass the time I sharpen the knife. I am like this. I say it is a sin to waste time."

Every now and then he sipped his wine, but there was no perceptible change in his manner, for he was careful to keep himself just at the same level of excitement, neither more nor less.

Half an hour later he was smoking his pipe in the Piazza di Spagna, lounging near the great fountain in the sunshine, his eyes generally turned towards the door of the hotel. He waited a long time, and replenished his pipe more than once.

"This would be the only thing wanting," he said impatiently and half aloud. "That just to-day he should not go out."

But Lord Redin appeared at last, dressed as though he were going to make a visit. He looked about the square, standing still on the threshold for a moment, and a couple of small open cabs drove up. But he shook his head, consulted his watch, and strode away in the direction of the Propaganda.

Stefanone guessed that he was going to the Palazzetto Borgia, and followed him as usual at a safe distance, threading the winding ways towards the Piazza di Venezia. There used to be a small café then under the corner of that part of the Palazzo Torlonia which has now been pulled down. Lord Redin entered it, and Stefanone lingered on the other side of the street. A man passed him who sold melon seeds and aquavitæ, and Stefanone drank a glass of the one and bought a measure of the other. The Romans are fond of the taste of the tiny dry kernel which is found inside the broad white shell of the seed. Presently Lord Redin came out, wiping his mouth with his handkerchief, and went on. Stefanone followed him again, walking fast when his enemy had turned a corner and slackening his speed as soon as he caught sight of him again.

Francesca was out. He saw Lord Redin's look of annoyance as the latter turned away after speaking with the porter, and he fell back into the shadow of a doorway, expecting that the Scotchman would take the street by which he had come. But Dalrymple turned down the narrow lane beside the palace, in the direction of the Tiber. Stefanone's bloodshot eyes opened suddenly as he sprang after him; with a quick movement he got his knife out, opened it, and thrust his hand with it open into the wide pocket of his jacket. Lord Redin had never gone down that lane before, to Stefanone's knowledge, and it was a hundred to one that at that hour no one would be about. Stefanone himself did not know the place.

Dalrymple must have heard the quick and heavy footsteps of the peasant behind him, but it would not have been at all like him to turn his head. With loose, swinging gait he strode along, and his heavy stick made high little echoes as it struck the dry cobble-stones.

Stefanone was very near him. His eyes glared redly, and his hand with the knife in it was half out of his pocket. In ten steps more he would spring and strike upwards, as Romans do. He chose the spot on the dark overcoat where his knife should go through, below the shoulder-blade, at the height of the small ribs on the left side. His lips were parted and dry.

There was a loud scream of anger, a tremendous clattering noise, and a sound of feet. Stefanone turned suddenly pale, and his hand went to the bottom of his pocket again.

On an open doorstep lay a copper 'conca'—the Roman water jar—a wretched dog was rushing down the street with something in its mouth, in front of Lord Redin, a woman was pursuing it with yells, swinging a small wooden stool in her right hand, to throw it at the dog, and the neighbours were on their doorsteps in a moment. Stefanone slunk under the shadow of the wall, grinding his teeth. The chance was gone. The streets beyond were broader and more populous.

Lord Redin went steadily onward, evidently familiar with every turn of the way, down to the Tiber, across the Bridge of Quattro Capi, and over the island of Saint Bartholomew to Trastevere, turning then to the right through the straight Lungaretta, past Santa Maria and under the heights of San Pietro in Montorio, and so to the Lungara and by Santo Spirito to the Piazza of Saint Peter's. He walked fast, and Stefanone twice wiped the perspiration from his forehead on the way, for he was nervous from the tension and the disappointment, and felt suddenly weak.

The Scotchman never paused, but crossed the vast square and went up the steps of the basilica. He was evidently going to hear the Vespers. Then Stefanone, instead of following him into the church, sat down outside the wine shop on the right, just opposite the end of the Colonnade. He ordered a measure of wine and prepared to wait, for he guessed that Lord Redin would remain in the church at least an hour.

CHAPTER XLVI

Lord Redin lifted the heavy leathern curtain of the door on the right of the main entrance to the basilica, and went into the church. For some reason or other, the majority of people go in by that door rather than the other. It may be that the reason is a very simple one, after all. Most people are right handed, and of any two doors side by side leading into the same place, will instinctively take the one on the right. The practice of passing to the left in the street, in almost all old countries, was for the sake of safety, in order that a man might have his sword hand towards any one he met.

The air of the church was warm, and had a faint odour of incense in it. The temperature of the vast building varies but little with the seasons; going into it in winter, it seems warm, in summer it is very cold. On that day there were not many people in the nave, though a soft sound of unceasing footsteps broke the stillness. Very far away an occasional strain of music floated on the air from the Chapel of the Choir, the last on the left before the transept is reached. Lord Redin walked leisurely in the direction of the sound.

The chapel was full, and the canons were intoning the psalms of the office. At the conclusion of each one the choir sang the 'Gloria' from the great organ loft on the right. It chanced that there were a number of foreigners on that day, and they had filled all the available space within the gate, and there was a small crowd outside, pressing as close as possible in order to hear the voices more distinctly. Lord Redin was taller than most men, and looking over the heads of the others he saw Francesca Campodonico's pale profile in the thick of the press. She evidently wished to extricate herself, and she seemed to be suffering from the closeness, for she pressed her handkerchief nervously to her lips, and her eyes were half closed. Lord Redin forced his way to her without much consideration for the people who hindered him. A few minutes later he brought her out on the side towards the transept.

"Thank you," said Francesca. "I should like to sit down. I had almost fainted—there was a woman next to me who had musk about her."

They went round the pillar of the dome to the south transept where there are almost always a number of benches set along the edges of a huge green baize carpet. They sat down together on the end of one of the seats.

"We can go back, by and bye, and hear the music, if you like," said Francesca. "The psalms will last some time longer."

"I would rather sit here and talk, since I have had the good luck to meet you," answered Lord Redin, resting his elbows on his knees, and idly poking the green carpet with the end of his stick. "I went to your house, and they told me that you would very probably be here."

"Yes. I often come. But you know that, for we have met here before. I only stay at home on Sundays when it rains."

"Oh! Is that the rule?"

"Yes, if you call it a rule," answered Francesca.

"I like to know about the things you do, and how you spend your life," said the Scotchman, thoughtfully.

"Do you? Why? There is nothing very interesting about my existence, it seems to me."

"It interests me. It makes me feel less lonely to know about some one else—some one I like very much."

Francesca looked at her companion with an expression of pity. She was lonely, too, but in a different way. The little drama of her life had run sadly and smoothly. She was willing to give the man her friendship if it could help him, rather because he seemed to ask for it in a mute fashion than because she desired his.

"Lord Redin," she said, after a little pause, "do you always mean to live in this way?"

"Alone? Yes. It is the only way I can live, at my age."

"At your age—would it make any difference if you were younger?" asked Francesca. She dropped her voice to a low key. "You would never marry again, even if you were much younger."

"Marry!" His shoulders moved with a sort of little start. "You do not know what you are saying!" he added, almost under his breath, though she heard the words distinctly.

She looked at him again, in silence, during several seconds, and she saw how the colour sank away from his face, till the skin was like old parchment. The hand that held the heavy stick tightened round it and grew yellow at the knuckles.

"Forgive me," she said gently. "I am very thoughtless—it is the second time."

He did not speak for some moments, but she understood his silence and waited. The air was very quiet, and the enormous pillar of the dome almost completely shut off the echo of the distant music. The low afternoon sun streamed levelly through the great windows of the apse, for the basilica is built towards the west. There were very few people in the church that day. The sun made visible beams across the high shadows overhead.

Suddenly Lord Redin spoke again. There was something weak and tremulous in the tone of his rough voice.

"I am very much attached to you, for two reasons," he said. "We have known each other long, but not intimately."

"That is true. Not very intimately."

Francesca did not know exactly what to say. But for his manner and for his behaviour a few moments earlier, she might have fancied that he was about to offer himself to her, but such an idea was very far from her thoughts. Her woman's instinct told her that he was going to tell her something in the nature of a confidence.

"Precisely," he continued. "We have never been intimate. The reason why we have not been intimate is one of the reasons why I am more attached to you than you have ever guessed."

"That is complicated," said Francesca, with a smile. "Perhaps the other reason may be simpler."

"It is very simple, very simple indeed, though it will not seem natural to you. You are the only very good woman I ever knew, who made me feel that she was good instead of making me see it. Perhaps you think it unnatural that I should be attracted by goodness at all. But I am not very bad, as men go."

"No. I do not believe you are. And I am not so good as you think." She sighed softly.

"You are much better than I once thought," answered Lord Redin. "Once upon a time—well, I should only offend you, and I know better now. Forgive me for thinking of it. I wish to tell you something else."

"If it is something which has been your secret, it is better not told," said Francesca, quietly. "One rarely makes a confidence that one does not regret it."

"You are a wise woman." He looked at her thoughtfully. "And yet you must be very young."

"No. But though I have had my own life apart, I have lived outwardly very much in the world, although I am still young. Most of the secrets which have been told me have been repeated to me by the people in whom others had confided."

"All that is true," he answered. "Nevertheless—" He paused. "I am desperate!" he exclaimed, with sudden energy. "I cannot bear this any longer—I am alone, always, always. Sometimes I think I shall go mad! You do not know what a life I lead. I have not even a vice to comfort me!" He laughed low and savagely. "I tried to drink, but I am sick of it—it does no good! A man who has not even a vice is a very lonely man."

Francesca's clear eyes opened wide with a startled look, and gazed towards his averted face, trying to catch his glance. She felt that she was close to something very strong and dreadful which she could not understand.

"Do not speak like that!" she said. "No one is lonely who believes in God."

"God!" he exclaimed bitterly. "God has forgotten me, and the devil will not have me!" He looked at her at last, and saw her face. "Do not be shocked," he said, with a sorrowful smile. "If I were as bad as I seem to you just now, I should have cut my throat twenty years ago."

"Hush! Hush!" Francesca did not know what to say.

His manner changed a little, and he spoke more calmly.

"I am not eloquent," he said, looking into her eyes. "You may not understand. But I have suffered a great deal."

"Yes. I know that. I am very sorry for you."

"I think you are," he answered. "That is why I want to be honest and tell you the truth about myself. For that reason, and because I cannot bear it any longer. I cannot, I cannot!" he repeated in a low, despairing tone.

"If it will help you to tell me, then tell me," said Francesca, kindly. "But I do not ask you to. I do not see why we should not be the best of friends without my knowing this thing which weighs on your mind."

"You will understand when I have told you," answered Lord Redin. "Then you can judge whether you will have me for a friend or not. It will seem very bad to you. Perhaps it is. I never thought so. But you are a Roman Catholic, and that makes a difference."

"Not in a question of right and wrong."

"It makes the question what it is. You shall hear."

He paused a moment, and the lines and furrows deepened in his face. The sun was sinking fast, and the long beams had faded away out of the shadows. There was no one in sight now, but the music of the benediction service echoed faintly in the distance. Francesca felt her heart beating with a sort of excitement she could not understand, and though she did not look at her companion, her ears were strained to catch the first word he spoke.

"I married a nun," he said simply.

Francesca started.

"A Sister of Charity?" she asked, after a moment's dead silence. "They do not take vows—"

"No. A nun from the Carmelite Convent of Subiaco."

His words were very distinct. There was no mistaking what he said. Francesca shrank from him instinctively, and uttered a low exclamation of repugnance and horror.

"That is not all," continued Lord Redin, with a calm that seemed supernatural. "She was your kinswoman. She was Maria Braccio, whom every one believed was burned to death in her cell."

"But her body—they found it! It is impossible!" She thought he must be mad.

"No. They found another body. I put it into the bed and set fire to the mattress. It was burned beyond recognition, and they thought it was Maria. But it was the body of old Stefanone's daughter. I lived in his house. The girl poisoned herself with some of my chemicals—I was a young doctor in those days. Maria and I were married on board an English man-of-war, and we lived in Scotland after that. Gloria was the daughter of Maria Braccio, the Carmelite nun—your kinswoman."

Francesca pressed her handkerchief to her lips. She felt as though she were losing her senses. Minute after minute passed, and she could say nothing. From time to time, Lord Redin glanced sideways at her. He breathed hard once or twice, and his hands strained upon his stick as though they would break it in two.

"Then she died," he said. When he had spoken the three words, he shivered from head to foot, and was silent.

Still Francesca could not speak. The sacrilege of the deed was horrible in itself. To her, who had grown up to look upon Maria Braccio as a holy woman, cut off in her youth by a frightful death, the truth was overwhelmingly awful. She strove within herself to find something upon which she could throw the merest shadow of an extenuation, but she could find nothing.

"You understand now why, as an honourable man, I wished to tell you the truth about myself," he said, speaking almost coldly in the effort he was making at self-control. "I could not ask for your friendship until I had told you."

Francesca turned her white face slowly towards him in the dusk, and her lips moved, but she did not speak. She could not in that first moment find the words she wanted. She felt that she shrank from him, that she never wished to touch his hand again. Doubtless, in time, she might get over the first impression. She wished that he would leave her to think about it.

"Can you ever be my friend now?" he asked gravely.

"Your friend—" she stopped, and shook her head sadly. "I—I am afraid—" she could not go on.

Lord Redin rose slowly to his feet.

"No. I am afraid not," he said.

He waited a moment, but there was no reply.

"May I take you to your carriage?" he asked gently.

"No, thank you. No—that is—I am going home in a cab. I would rather be alone—please."

"Then good-bye."

The lonely man went away and left her there. His head was bent, and she thought that he walked unsteadily, as she watched him. Suddenly a great wave of pity filled her heart. He looked so very lonely. What right had she to judge him? Was she perfect, because he called her good? She called him before he turned the great pillar of the dome.

"Lord Redin! Lord Redin!"

But her voice was weak, and in the vast, dim place it did not reach him. He went on alone, past the high altar, round the pillar, down the nave. The benediction service was not quite over yet, but every one who was not listening to the music had left the church. He went towards the door by which he had entered. Before going out he paused, and looked towards the little chapel on the right of the entrance. He hesitated, and then went to it and stood leaning with his hands upon the heavy marble balustrade, that was low for his great height as he stood on the step.

A single silver lamp sent a faint light upwards that lingered upon the Pietà above the altar, upon the marble limbs of the dead Christ, upon the features of the Blessed Virgin, the Addolorata—the sorrowing mother.

Bending a little, as though very weary, the friendless, wifeless, childless man raised his furrowed face and looked up. There was no hope any more, and his despair was heavy upon him whose young love had blasted the lives of many.

His teeth were set—he could have bitten through iron. He trembled a little, and as he looked upward, two dreadful tears—the tears of the strong that are as blood—welled from his eyes and trickled down upon his cheeks.

"Maria Addolorata!" he whispered.

CHAPTER XLVII

Francesca had half risen from her seat when she had seen that Lord Redin did not hear her voice, calling to him. Then she realized that she could not overtake him without running, since he had got so far, and she kept her place, leaning back once more, and trying to collect her thoughts before going home. The music was still going on in the Chapel of the Choir, and though it was dusk in the vast church, it would not be dark for some time. The vergers did not make their rounds to give warning of the hour of closing until sunset. Francesca sat still and tried to understand what she had heard. She was nervous and shaken, and she wished that she were already at home. The great dimness of the lonely transept was strangely mysterious—and the tale of the dead girl, burned to take the place of the living, was grewsome, and made her shiver with disgust and horror. She started nervously at the sound of a distant footstep.

But the strongest impression she had, was that of abhorrence for the unholy deeds of the man who had just left her. To a woman for whom religion in its forms as well as in its meaning was the mainstay of life on earth and the hope of life to come, the sacrilege of the crime seemed supernatural. She felt as though it must be in some way her duty to help in expiating it, lest the punishment of it should fall upon all her race. And as she thought it over, trying to look at it as simply as she could, she surveyed at a glance the whole chain of the fatal story, and saw how many terrible things had followed upon that one great sin, and how very nearly she herself had been touched by its consequences. She had been involved in it and had become a part of it. She had felt it about her for years, in her friendship for Reanda. It had contributed to the causes of his death, if it had not actually caused it. She, in helping to bring about his marriage with the daughter of her sinning kinswoman, had unconsciously made a link in the chain. Her friendship for the artist no longer looked as innocent as formerly. Gloria had accused him of loving her, Francesca. Had she not loved him? Whether she had or not, she had done things which had wounded his innocent young wife. In a sudden and painful illumination of the past, she saw that she herself had not been sinless; that she had been selfish, if nothing worse; that she had craved Reanda's presence and devoted friendship, if nothing more; that death had taken from her more than a friend. She saw all at once the vanity of her own belief in her own innocence, and she accused herself very bitterly of many things which had been quite hidden from her until then.

She was roused by a footstep behind her, and she started at the sound of a voice she knew, but which had changed oddly since she had last heard it. It was stern, deep, and clear still, but the life was gone out of it. It had an automatic sound.

"I beg your pardon, Princess," said Paul Griggs, stopping close to her behind the bench. "May I speak to you for a moment?"

She turned her head. As the sun went down, the church grew lighter for a little while, as it often does. Yet she could hardly see the man's eyes at all, as she looked into his face. They were all in the shadow and had no light in them.

"Sit down," she said mechanically.

She could not refuse to speak to him, and, indeed, she would not have refused to receive him had she been at home when he had called that day. Socially speaking, according to the standards of those around her, he had done nothing which she could very severely blame. A woman he had dearly loved had come to him for protection, and he had not driven her away. That was the social value of what he had done. The moral view of it all was individual with herself. Society gave her no right to treat him rudely because she disapproved of his past life. For the rest, she had liked him in former times, and she believed that there was much more good in him than at first appeared.

She was almost glad that he had disturbed her solitude just then, for a nervous sense of loneliness was creeping upon her; and though there had been nothing to prevent her from rising and going away, she had felt that something was holding her in her seat, a shadowy something that was oppressive and not natural, that descended upon her out of the gloomy heights, and that rose around her from the secret depths below, where the great dead lay side by side in their leaden coffins.

"Sit down," she repeated, as Griggs came round the bench.

He sat down beside her. There was a little distance between them, and he sat rather stiffly, holding his hat on his knees.

"I should apologize for disturbing you," he began. "I have been twice to your house to-day, but you were out. What I wish to speak of is rather urgent. I heard that you might be here, and so I came."

"Yes," she said, and waited for him to say more.

"What is it?" she asked presently, as he did not speak at once.

"It is about Dalrymple—about Lord Redin," he said at last. "You used to know him. Do you ever see him now?"

Francesca looked at him with a little surprise, but she answered quietly, as though the question were quite a natural one.

"He was here five minutes ago. Yes, I often see him."

"Would you do him a service?" asked Griggs, in his calm and indifferent tone.

He was forcing himself to do what was plainly his duty, but he was utterly incapable of taking any interest in the matter. Francesca hesitated before she answered. An hour earlier she would have assented readily enough, but now the idea of doing anything which could tend to bring her into closer relations with Lord Redin was disagreeable.

"I do not think you will refuse," said Griggs, as she did not speak. "His life is in danger."

She turned quickly and scrutinized the expressionless features. In the glow of the sunset the church was quite light. The total unconcern of the man's manner contrasted strangely with the importance of what he said. Francesca felt that something must be wrong.

"You say that very coolly," she observed, and her tone showed that she was incredulous.

"And you do not believe me," answered Griggs, quite unmoved. "It is natural, I suppose. I will try to explain."

"Please do. I do not understand at all."

Nevertheless, she was startled, though she concealed her nervousness. She had not spoken with Griggs for a long time; and as he talked, she saw what a great change had taken place. He was very quiet, as he had always been, but he was almost too quiet. She could not make out his eyes. She knew of his superhuman strength, and his stillness seemed unnatural. What he said did not sound rational. An impression got hold of her that he had gone mad, and she was physically afraid of him. He began to explain. She felt a singing in her ears, and she could not follow what he said. It was like an evil dream, and it grew upon her second by second.

He talked on in the same even, monotonous tone. The words meant nothing to her. She crossed her feet nervously and tried to get a soothing sensation by stroking her sable muff. She made a great effort at concentration and failed to understand anything.

All at once it grew dark, as the sunset light faded out of the sky. Again she felt the desire to rise and the certainty that she could not, if she tried. He ceased speaking and seemed to expect her to say something, but she had not understood a word of his long explanation. He sat patiently waiting. She could hardly distinguish his face in the gloom.

The sound of irregular, shuffling footsteps and low voices moved the stillness. The vergers were making their last round in a hurried, perfunctory way. They passed across the transept to the high altar. It was so dark that Francesca could only just see their shadows moving in the blackness. She did not realize what they were doing, and her imagination made ghosts of them, rushing through the silence of the deserted place, from one tomb to another, waking the dead for the night. They did not even glance across, as they skirted the wall of the church. Even if they had looked, they might not have seen two persons in black, against the blackness, sitting silently side by side on the dark bench. They saw nothing and passed on, out of sight and out of hearing.

"May I ask whether you will give him the message?" inquired Griggs at last, moving in his seat, for he knew that it was time to be going.

Francesca started, at the sound of his voice.

"I—I am afraid—I have not understood," she said. "I beg your pardon—I was not paying attention. I am nervous."

"It is growing late," said Griggs. "We had better be going—I will tell you again as we walk to the door."

"Yes—no—Just a moment!" She made a strong effort over herself. "Tell me in three words," she said. "Who is it that threatens Lord Redin's life?"

"A peasant of Subiaco called Stefanone. Really, Princess, we must be going; it is quite dark—"

"Stefanone!" exclaimed Francesca, while he was speaking the last words, which she did not hear. "Stefanone of Subiaco—of course!"

"We must really be going," said Griggs, rising to his feet, and wondering indifferently why it was so hard to make her understand.

She rose to her feet slowly. Lord Redin's story was intricately confused in her mind with the few words which she had retained of what Griggs had said.

"Yes—yes—Stefanone," she said in a low voice, as though to herself, and she stood still, comprehending the whole situation in a flash, and imagining that Griggs knew the whole truth and had been telling it to her as though she had not known it. "But how did you know that Lord Redin took the girl's body and burnt it?" she asked, quite certain that he had mentioned the fact.

"What girl?" asked Griggs in wonder.

"Why, the body of Stefanone's daughter, which he managed to burn in the convent when he carried off my cousin! How did you know about it?"

"I did not know about it," said Griggs. "Your cousin? I do not understand."

"My cousin—yes—Maria Braccio—Gloria's mother! You have just been talking about her—"

"I?" asked Griggs, bewildered.

Francesca stepped back from him, suddenly guessing that she had revealed Lord Redin's secret.

"Is it possible?" she asked in a low voice. "Oh, it is all a mistake!" she cried suddenly. "I have told you his story—oh, I am losing my head!"

"Come," said Griggs, authoritatively. "We must get out of the church, at all events, or we shall be locked in."

"Oh no!" answered Francesca. "There is always somebody here—"

"There is not. You must really come."

"Yes—but there is no danger of being locked in. Yes—let us walk down the nave. There is more light."

They walked slowly, for she was too much confused to hasten her steps. Her inexplicable mistake troubled her terribly. She remembered how she had warned Lord Redin not to tell her any secrets, and how seriously she, the most discreet of women, had resolved never to reveal what he had said. But the impression of his story had been so much more direct and strong than even the first words Griggs had spoken, that so soon as she had realized that the latter was speaking approximately of the same subject, she had lost the thread of what he was saying and had seemed to hear Lord Redin's dreadful tale all over again. She thought that she was losing her head.

It was almost quite dark when they reached the other side of the high altar. Griggs walked beside her in silence, trying to understand the meaning of what she had said.

The gloom was terrible. The enormous statues loomed faintly like vast ghosts, high up, between the floor and the roof, their whiteness glimmering where there seemed to be nothing else but darkness below them and above them. A low, far sound that was a voice but not a word, trembled in the air. Francesca shuddered.

"They have not gone yet," said Griggs. "They are still talking. But we must hurry."

"No," said Francesca, "that was not any one talking." And her teeth chattered. "Give me your arm, please—I am frightened."

He held out his arm till she could feel it in the dark, and she took it. He pressed her hand to his side and drew her along, for he feared that the doors might be already shut.

"Not so fast! Oh, not so fast, please!" she cried. "I shall fall. They do not shut the doors—"

"Yes, they do! Let me carry you. I can run with you in the dark—there is no time to be lost!"

"No, no! I can walk faster—but there is really no danger—"

It is a very long way from the high altar to the main entrance of the church. Francesca was breathless when they reached the door and Griggs lifted the heavy leathern curtain. If the door had been still open, he would have seen the twilight from the porch at once. Instead, all was black and close and smelled of leather. Francesca was holding his sleeve, afraid of losing him.

"It is too late," he said quietly. "We are probably locked in. We will try the door of the Sacristy."

He seized her arm and hurried her along into the south aisle. He struck his shoulder violently against the base of the pillar he passed in the darkness, but he did not stop. Almost instinctively he found the door, for he could not see it. Even the hideous skeleton which supports a black marble drapery above it was not visible in the gloom. He found the bevelled edge of the smoothly polished panel and pushed. But it would not yield.

"We are locked in," he said, in the same quiet tone as before.

Francesca uttered a low cry of terror and then was silent.

"Cannot you break the door?" she asked suddenly.

"No," he answered. "Nothing short of a battering-ram could move it."

"Try," she said. "You are so strong—the lock might give way."

To satisfy her he braced himself and heaved against the panel with all his gigantic strength. In the dark she could hear his breath drawn through his nostrils.

"It will not move," he said, desisting. "We shall have to spend the night here. I am very sorry."

For some moments Francesca said nothing, overcome by her terror of the situation. Griggs stood still, with his back to the polished door, trying to see her in the gloom. Then he felt her closer to him and heard her small feet moving on the pavement.

"We must make the best of it," he said at last. "It is never quite dark near the high altar. I daresay, too, that there is still a little twilight where we were sitting. At least, there is a carpet there and there are benches. We can sit there until it is later. Then you can lie down upon the bench. I will make a pillow for you with my overcoat. It is warm, and I shall not need it."

He made a step forwards, and she heard him moving.

"Do not leave me!" she cried, in sudden terror.

He felt her grasp his arm convulsively in the dark, and he felt her hands shaking.

"Do not be frightened," he said, in his quiet voice. "Dead people do no harm, you know. It is only imagination."

She shuddered as he groped his way with her toward the nave. They passed the pillar and saw the soft light of the ninety little flames of the huge golden lamps around the central shrine below the high altar. Far beyond, the great windows showed faintly in the height of the blackness. They walked more freely, keeping in the middle of the church. In the distant chapels on each side a few little lamps glimmered like fireflies. Before the last chapel on the right, the Chapel of the Sacrament, Francesca paused, instinctively holding fast to Griggs's arm, and they both bent one knee, as all Catholics do, who pass before it. But when they reached the shrine, Francesca loosed her hold and sank upon her knees, resting her arms upon the broad marble of the balustrade. Griggs knelt a moment beside her, by force of habit, then rose and waited, looking about him into the depths of blackness, and reflecting upon the best spot in which to pass the night.

She remained kneeling a long time, praying more or less consciously, but aware that it was a relief to be near a little light after passing through the darkness. Her mind was as terribly confused as her companion's was utterly calm and indifferent. If he had been alone he would have sat down upon a step until he was sleepy and then he would have stretched himself upon one of the benches in the transept. But to Francesca it was unspeakably dreadful.

The strangeness of the whole situation forced itself upon her more and more, when she thought of rising from her knees and going back to the bench. She felt a womanly shyness about keeping close to her companion, her hand on his arm, for hours together, but she knew that the terror she should feel of being left alone, even for an instant, or of merely thinking that she was to be left alone, would more than overcome that if she went away from the lights. She would grasp his arm and hold it tightly.

Then she felt ashamed of herself. She had always been told that she came of a brave race. She had never been in danger, and there was really no danger now. It was absurd to remain on her knees for the sake of the lamps. She rose to her feet and turned. Griggs was not looking at her, but at the ornaments on the altar. The soft glimmer lighted up his dark face. A moment after she had risen he came forward. She meant to propose that they should go back to the transept, but just then she shuddered again.

"Let us sit down here, on the step," she said, suddenly.

"If you like," he answered. "Wait a minute," he added, and he pulled off his overcoat.

He spread a part of it on the step, and rolled the rest into a pillow against which she could lean, and he held it in place while she sat down. She thanked him, and he sat down beside her. At first, as she turned from the lamps, the nave was like a fathomless black wall. Neither spoke for some time. Griggs broke the silence when he supposed that she was sufficiently recovered to talk quietly, for he had been thinking of what she had said, and it was almost clear to him at last.

"I should like to speak to you quite frankly, if you will allow me," he said gravely. "May I?"

"Certainly."

"The few words you said about Lord Redin's story have explained a great many things which I never understood," said Griggs. "Is it too much to ask that you should tell me everything you know?"

"I would rather not say anything more," answered Francesca. "I am very much ashamed of having betrayed his secret. Besides, what is to be gained by your knowing a few more details? It is bad enough as it is."

"It is more or less the story of my life," he said, almost indifferently.

She turned her head slowly and tried to see his face. She could just distinguish the features, cold and impassive.

"I came to you to ask you to warn Dalrymple of a danger," he continued, as she did not speak. "I knew that fact, but not the reason why his life was and is threatened. Unless I have mistaken what you said, I understand it now. It is a much stronger one than I should ever have guessed. Lord Redin ran away with your cousin, and made it appear that he had carried off Stefanone's daughter. Stefanone has waited patiently for nearly a quarter of a century. He has found Dalrymple at last and means to kill him. He will succeed, unless you can make Dalrymple understand that the danger is real. I have no evidence on which I could have the man arrested, and I have no personal influence in Rome. You have. You would find no difficulty in having Stefanone kept out of the city. And you can make Dalrymple see the truth, since he has confided in you. Will you do that? He will not believe me, and you can save him. Besides, he will not see me. I have tried twice to-day. He has made up his mind that he will not see me."

"I will do my best," said Francesca, leaning her head back against the marble rail, and half closing her eyes. "How terrible it all is!"

"Yes. I suppose that is the word," said Griggs, indifferently. "Sacrilege, suicide, and probably murder to come."

She was shocked by the perfectly emotionless way in which he spoke of Gloria's death, so much shocked that she drew a short, quick breath between her teeth as though she had hurt herself. Griggs heard it.

"What is the matter?" he asked.

"Nothing," she said.

"I thought something hurt you."

"No—nothing."

She was silent again.

"Yes," he continued, in a tone of cold speculation, "I suppose that any one would call it terrible. At all events, it is curious, as a sequence of cause and effect, from one tragedy to another."

"Please—please do not speak of it all like that—" Francesca felt herself growing angry with him.

"How should I speak of it?" he asked. "It is an extraordinary concatenation of events. I look upon the whole thing as very curious, especially since you have given me the key to it all."

Francesca was moved to anger, taking the defence of the dead Gloria, as almost any woman would have done. At the moment Paul Griggs repelled her even more than Lord Redin. It seemed to her that there was something dastardly in his indifference.

"Have you no heart?" she asked suddenly.

"No, I am dead," he answered, in his clear, lifeless voice, that might have been a ghost's.

The words made her shiver, and she felt as though her hair were moving. From his face, as she had last seen it, and from his voice, he might almost have been dead, as he said he was, like the thousands of silent ones in the labyrinths under her feet, and she alone alive in the midst of so much death.

"What do you mean?" she asked, and her own voice trembled in spite of herself.

"It is very like being dead," he answered thoughtfully. "I cannot feel anything. I cannot understand why any one else should. Everything is the same to me. The world is a white blank to me, and one place is exactly like any other place."

"But why? What has happened to you?" asked Francesca.

"You know. You sent me those letters."

"What letters?"

"The package Reanda gave you before he died."

"Yes. What was in it? I told you that I did not know, when I wrote to you. I remember every word I wrote."

"I know. But I thought that you at least guessed. They were Gloria's letters to her husband."

"Her old letters, before—" Francesca stopped short.

"No," he answered, with the same unnatural quiet. "All the letters she wrote him afterwards—when we were together."

"All those letters?" cried Francesca, suddenly understanding. "Oh no—no! It is not possible! He could not, he would not, have done anything so horrible."

"He did," said Griggs, calmly. "I had supposed that she loved me. He had his vengeance. He proved to me that she did not. I hope he is satisfied with the result. Yes," he continued, after a moment's pause, "it was the cruelest thing that ever one man did to another. I spent a bad night, I remember. On the top of the package was the last letter she wrote him, just before she killed herself. She loathed me, she said, she hated me, she shivered at my touch. She feared me so that she acted a comedy of love, in terror of her life, after she had discovered that she hated me. She need not have been afraid. Why should I have hurt her? In that last letter, she put her wedding ring with a lock of her hair wound in and out of it. Reanda knew what he was doing when he sent it to me. Do you wonder that it has deadened me to everything?"

"Oh, how could he do it? How could he!" Francesca repeated, for the worst of it all to her was the unutterable cruelty of the man she had believed so gentle.

"I suppose it was natural," said Griggs. "I loved the woman, and he knew it. I fancy few men have loved much more sincerely than I loved her, even after she was dead. I was not always saying so. I am not that kind of man. Besides, men who live by stringing words together for money do not value them much in their own lives. But I worked for her. I did the best I could. Even she must have known that I loved her."

"I know you did. I cannot understand how you can speak of her at all." Francesca wondered at the man.

"She? She is no more to me than Queen Christina, over there in her tomb in the dark! For that matter, nothing else has any meaning, either."

For a long time Francesca said nothing. She sat quite still, resting the back of her head against the marble, in the awful silence under the faint lights that glimmered above the great tomb.

"You have told me the most dreadful thing I ever heard," she said at last, in a low tone. "Is she nothing to you? Really nothing? Can you never think kindly of her again?"

"No. Why should I? That is—" he hesitated. "I could not explain it," he said, and was silent.

"It does not seem human," said Francesca. "You would have a memory of her—something—some touch of sadness—I wonder whether you really loved her as much as you thought you did?"

Griggs turned upon Francesca slowly, his hands clasped upon one knee.

"You do not know what such love means," he said slowly. "It is God—faith—goodness—everything. It is heaven on earth, and earth in heaven, in one heart. When it is gone there is nothing left. It went hard. It will not come back now. The heart itself is gone. There is nothing for it to come to. You think me cold, you are shocked because I speak indifferently of her. She lied to me. She lied and acted in every word and deed of her life with me. She deceived herself a little at first, and she deceived me mortally afterwards. It was all an immense, loathsome, deadly lie. I lived through the truth. Why should I wish to go back to the lie again? She died, telling me that she died for me. She died, having written to Reanda that she died for him. I do not judge her. God will. But God Himself could not make me love the smallest shadow of her memory. It is impossible. I am beyond life. I am outside it. My eternity has begun."

"Is it not a little for her sake that you wish to save her father?" asked Francesca.

"No. It is a matter of honour, and nothing else, since I injured him, as the world would say, by taking his daughter from her husband. Do you understand? Can you put yourself a little in my position? It is not because I care whether he lives or dies, or dies a natural death or is stabbed in the back by a peasant. It is because I ought to care. I do many things because I ought to care to do them, though the things and their consequences are all one to me, now."

"It cannot last," said Francesca, sadly. "You will change as you grow older."

"No. That is a thing you can never understand," he answered. "I am two individuals. The one is what you see, a man more or less like other men, growing older—a man who has a certain mortal, earthly memory of that dead woman, when the real man is unconscious. But the real man is beyond growing old, because he is beyond feeling anything. He is stationary, outside of life. The world is a blank to him and always will be."

His voice grew more and more expressionless as he spoke. Francesca felt that she could not pity him as she had pitied poor Lord Redin when she had seen him going away alone. The man beside her was in earnest, and was as far beyond woman's pity as he was beyond woman's love. Yet she no longer felt repelled by him since she had understood what he had suffered. Perhaps she herself, suffering still in her heart, wished that she might be even as he was, beyond the possibility of pain, even though beyond the hope of happiness. He wanted nothing, he asked for nothing, and he was not afraid to be alone with his own soul, as she was sometimes. The other man had asked for her friendship. It could mean nothing to Paul Griggs. If love were nothing, what could friendship be?

Yet there was something lofty and grand about such loneliness as his. She could not but feel that, now that she knew all. She thought of him as she sat beside him in the monumental silence of the enormous sepulchre, and she guessed of depths in his soul like the deepness of the shadows above her and before her and around her.

"My suffering seems very small, compared with yours," she said softly, almost to herself.

Somehow she knew that he would understand her, though perhaps her knowledge was only hope.

"Why should you suffer at all?" he asked. "You have never done anything wrong. Nothing, of all this, is your fault. It was all fatal, from the first, and you cannot blame yourself for anything that has happened."

"I do," she answered, in a low voice. "Indeed I do."

"You are wrong. You are not to blame. Dalrymple was—Maria Braccio—I—Gloria—we four. But you! What have you done? Compared with us you are a saint on earth!"

She hesitated a moment before she spoke. Then her voice came in a broken way.

"I loved Angelo Reanda. I know it, now that I have lost him."

Griggs barely heard the last words, but he bent his head gravely, and said nothing in answer.

CHAPTER XLVIII

The stillness was all around them and seemed to fold them together as they sat side by side. A deep sigh quivered and paused and was drawn again almost with a gasp that stirred the air. Suddenly Francesca's face was hidden in her hands, and her head was bowed almost to her knees. A moment more, and she sobbed aloud, wordless, as though her soul were breaking from her heart.

In the great gloom there was something unearthly in the sound of her weeping. The man who could neither suffer any more himself nor feel human pity for another's suffering, turned and looked at her with shadowy eyes. He understood, though he could not feel, and he knew that she had borne more than any one had guessed.

She shed many tears, and it was long before her sobbing ceased to call down pitiful, heart-breaking echoes from the unseen heights of darkness. Her head was bent down upon her knees as she sat there, striving with herself.

He could do nothing, and there was nothing that he could say. He could not comfort her, he could not deny her grief. He only knew that there was one more being still alive and bearing the pain of sins done long ago. Truly the judgment upon that man by whom the offence had come, should be heavy and relentless and enduring.

At last all was still again. Francesca did not move, but sat bowed together, her hands pressing her face. Very softly, Griggs rose to his feet, and she did not see that he was no longer seated beside her. He stood up and leaned upon the broad marble of the balustrade. When she at last raised her head, she thought that he was gone.

"Where are you?" she asked, in a startled voice.

Then, looking round, she saw him standing by the rail. She understood why he had moved—that she might not feel that he was watching her and seeing her tears.

"I am not ashamed," she said. "At least you know me, now."

"Yes. I know."

She also rose and stood up, and leaned upon the balustrade and looked into his face.

"I am glad you know," she said, and he saw how pale she was, and that her cheeks were wet. "Now that it is over, I am glad that you know," she said again. "You are beyond sympathy, and beyond pitying any one, though you are not unkind. I am glad, that if any one was to know my secret, it should be you. I could not bear pity. It would hurt me. But you are not unkind."

"Nor kind—nor anything," he said.

"No. It is as though I had spoken to the grave—or to eternity. It is safe with you."

"Yes. Quite safe. Safer than with the dead."

"He never knew it. Thank God! He never knew it! To me he was always the same faithful friend. To you he was an enemy, and cruel. I thought him above cruelty, but he was human, after all. Was it not human, that he should be cruel to you?"

"Yes," answered Griggs, wondering a little at her speech and tone. "It was very human."

"And you forgive him for it?"

"I?" There was surprise in his tone.

"Yes," she answered. "I want your forgiveness for him. He died without your forgiveness. It is the only thing I ask of you—I have not the right to ask anything, I know, but is it so very much?"

"It is nothing," said Griggs. "There is no such thing as forgiveness in my world. How could there be? I resent nothing."

"But then, if you do not resent what he did, you have forgiven him. Have you not?"

"I suppose so." He was puzzled.

"Will you not say it?" she pleaded.

"Willingly," he answered. "I forgive him. I remember nothing against him."

"Thank you. You are a good man."

He shook his head gravely, but he took her outstretched hand and pressed it gently.

"Thank you," she repeated, withdrawing hers. "Do not think it strange that I should ask such a thing. It means a great deal to me. I could not bear to think that he had left an enemy in the world and was gone where he could not ask forgiveness for what he had done. So I asked it of you, for him. I know that he would have wished me to. Do you understand?"

"Yes," said Griggs, thoughtfully. "I understand."

Again there was silence for a long time as they stood there. The tears dried upon the woman's sweet pale face, and a soft light came where the tears had been.

"Will you come with me?" she asked at last, looking up.

He did not guess what she meant to do, but he left the step on which he was standing and stood ready.

"It must be late," he said. "Should you like to try and rest? I will arrange a place for you as well as I can."

"Not yet," she answered. "If you will come with me—" she hesitated.

"Yes?"

"I will say a prayer for the dead," she said, in a low voice. "I always do, every night, since he died."

Griggs bent his head, and she came down from the step. He walked beside her, down the silent nave into the darkness. Before the Chapel of the Sacrament they both paused and bent the knee. Then she hesitated.

"I should like to go to the Pietà," she said timidly. "It seems so far. Do you mind?"

He held out his arm silently. She felt it and laid her hand upon it, and they went on. It was very dark. They knew that they were passing the pillars when they could not see the little lights from the chapels in the distance on their left. Then by the echo of their own footsteps they knew that they were near the great door, and at last they saw the single tiny flame in the silver lamp hanging above the altar they sought.

Guided by it, they went forward, and the solitary ray showed them the marble rail. They knelt down side by side.

"Let us pray for them all," said Francesca, very softly.

She looked up to the marble face of Christ's mother, the Addolorata, the mother of sorrows, and she thought of that sinning nun, dead long ago, who had been called Addolorata.

"Let us pray for them all," she repeated. "For Maria Braccio, for Gloria—for Angelo Reanda."

She lowered her head upon her hands. Then, presently, she looked up again, and Griggs heard her sweet voice in the darkness repeating the ancient Commemoration for the Dead, from the Canon of the Mass.

"Remember also, O Lord, thy servants who are gone before us with the sign of faith, and sleep the sleep of peace. Give them, O Lord, and to all who rest in Christ, a place of refreshment, light, and peace, for that Christ's sake, who liveth and reigneth with Thee in the unity of the Holy Spirit. Amen."

Once more she bent her head and was silent for a time. Then as she knelt, her hands moved silently along the marble and pressed the two folded hands of the man beside her, and she looked at him.

"Let us be friends," she said simply.

"Such as I am, I am yours."

Then their hands clasped. They both started and looked down, for the fingers were cold and wet and dark.

It was the blood of Angus Dalrymple that had sealed their friendship.

The swift sure blade had struck him as he stood there, repeating the name of his dead wife. There had been no one near the door and none to see the quick, black deed. Strong hands had thrown his falling body within the marble balustrade, that was still wet with his heart's blood.

There Paul Griggs found him, lying on his back, stretched to his length in the dim shadow between the rail and the altar. He had paid the price at last, a loving, sinning, suffering, faithful, faultful man.

But the friendship that was so grimly consecrated on that night, was the truest that ever was between man and woman.

F. Marion Crawford – A Short Biography

Francis Marion Crawford was born in Bagni di Lucca, Italy on 2nd August, 1854, the only son of the American sculptor Thomas Crawford and Louisa Cutler Ward. His aunt was Julia Ward Howe, the American poet, most famous for the words to 'The Battle Hymn of the Republic'.

After his father's death in 1857, his mother remarried to Luther Terry, with whom she had Crawford's half-sister, Margaret Ward Terry.

Crawford's education began at St Paul's School, Concord, New Hampshire and then went on to Cambridge University, the University of Heidelberg and finally the University of Rome.

In 1879, Crawford went to India to study the ancient language of Sanskrit and to edit Allahabad, The Indian Herald.

Returning to America in February 1881, he enrolled at Harvard University for a year to continue his studies in Sanskrit. Crawford had no real career path at this time although for two years he contributed to various periodicals, mainly The Critic.

Early in 1882, Crawford established a close, lifelong friendship with Isabella Stewart Gardner, a noted and eccentric heiress from Boston who over the years built up a large and eclectic collection of art.

Crawford lived most of his time in Boston with his Aunt Julia and Uncle Sam. The family were concerned by his lack of ambition, prospects in general, and his financial ones in particular.

His mother had hoped he might train in Boston for a career as an operatic baritone based on his private renditions of Schubert lieder. With that in mind it was, in January 1882, that George Henschel, the conductor of the Boston Symphony Orchestra, was called in to assess young Crawford's talents. Henschel was direct and to the point. Crawford would 'never be able to sing in perfect tune'. His Uncle Sam, knowing that Crawford was keen on literary pursuits, proposed that his years in India might be good source material to write about. Crawford agreed. He set to work. Uncle Sam also set about developing contacts with a number of New York publishers.

Events moved very quickly. By December of that year Crawford had completed his first novel, 'Mr Isaacs', based on modern Anglo-Indian life flavoured with a touch of Oriental mystery. It was an immediate success. Crawford set about writing a second novel and the result was 'Dr Claudius' in 1883.

In October 1884 he married Elizabeth Berdan, the daughter of the Civil War Union General Hiram Berdan. The marriage would produce two sons; Harold and Bertram, and two daughters; Eleanor and Clara.

Crawford, buoyed by his excellent start, now decided to return to Italy and to live there permanently. The couple initially went to Sorrento and lived at the historic Hotel Cocumella during 1885 before moving permanently to Sant' Agnello, where the purchase of the Villa Renzi would now be rededicated as Villa Crawford.

As a writer Crawford had more than his fair share of detractors but, perhaps due to the physical distance between author and these detractors, they did not distract from his prolific output.

Each year seemed to bring a new F. Marion Crawford novel. His popularity was evident although some works, such as 1896's offering 'Adam Johnstone's Son', was described by his left-wing English contemporary, George Gissing, as "rubbish". Over half of his novels are set in Italy. He also wrote three long historical studies of Italy and was nearing completion on a history of Rome in the Middle Ages when he died.

His 'Saracinesca' series are considered his best works. The third in the series, 'Don Orsino' (1892) was told against the background of a real estate bubble and is especially effective. The volume immediately after was 'Corleone' (1897), and the first major treatment of the Mafia in literature.

Crawford himself was fondest of 'Khaled: A Tale of Arabia' (1891), a story of a genie who becomes human. 'A Cigarette-Maker's Romance' (1890) was dramatized, and had considerable popularity on the stage as well as in its novel form.

Towards the end of the 1890's Crawford ventured down another path with his writing. He began his historical works. 'Ave Roma Immortalis' was published in 1898, followed by 'Rulers of the South' (1900), and 'Gleanings from Venetian History' (1905). Most were re-titled with longer more explanatory titles for the American market. Within them all his careful and precise knowledge of the local Italian history together with his literary talents combined to great effect.

Whilst on an American Lecture tour in the winter of 1897-1898 Crawford was researching and gathering technical information for his historical work 'Marietta' (published 1901), that describes glass-making in late medieval Venice. Whilst visiting a glass-smelting plant in Colorado he suffered a severe lung injury when he inhaled toxic gasses. This would eventually contribute to his death a decade or so later.

Crawford's commercial popularity and appeal at the time was such that in 1901, the American Macmillan firm began a deluxe uniform edition of his novels as his works came up for re-printing. In 1904 the P. F. Collier Company in New York was authorized to publish a 25-volume edition (which was later expanded to 32 volumes).

In 1902 he wrote a stage play 'Francesca da Rimini', that was produced in Paris by his friend and legendary actress Sarah Bernhardt.

Towards the end of his life Hollywood had begun to realise that his works were a valuable source of stories and ideas and several were turned into movies and continued to be so for decades after his death.

Crawford also had a gift for pulling off excellent short stories. Several, such as 'The Upper Berth' (1886), 'For the Blood Is the Life' (1905, a vampiress tale), 'The Dead Smile' (1899), and 'The Screaming Skull' (1908), are among the most anthologized classics of the horror genre. After his death several collected volumes were published from various sources.

After most of his fictional works had been published, most had the view that he was a gifted narrator; and his books of fiction, were full of historic vitality and energy as well as dramatic characterization. He was widely popular among readers to whom literature was more for escapism than a confrontation with reality or pages of subjective analysis. In 'The Novel: What It Is' (1893), Crawford was both resolute and disarming in defending his literary approach, self-conceived as a combination of romanticism and realism, defining the art form in terms of its marketplace and audience. The novel, he wrote, is "a marketable commodity" and "intellectual artistic luxury" that "must amuse, indeed, but should amuse reasonably, from an intellectual point of view .... Its intention is to amuse and please, and certainly not to teach and preach; but in order to amuse well it must be a finely-balanced creation ...."

Francis Marion Crawford died at Sorrento on Good Friday 1909 at Villa Crawford of a heart attack.

F. Marion Crawford – A Concise Bibliography

Novels

Mr. Isaacs: A Tale of Modern India (1882)
Dr. Claudius (1883)
To Leeward (1884)
A Roman Singer (1884)
An American Politician (1884)
Zoroaster (1885)
A Tale of a Lonely Parish (1886)
Saracinesca (1887)
Marzio's Crucifix (1887)
Paul Patoff (1887)
With the Immortals (1888)
Greifenstein (1889)
Sant' Ilario (1889); sequel to Saracinesca
A Cigarette-Maker's Romance (1890)
Khaled: A Tale of Arabia (1891)
The Witch of Prague (1891)
The Three Fates (1892)
Don Orsino (1892); sequel to Sant' Ilario
The Children of the King (1893)
Pietro Ghisleri (1893)
Marion Darche (1893)

Katharine Lauderdale (1894)
The Upper Berth (1894); with "By the Waters of Paradise"
Love in Idleness (1894)
The Ralstons (1894); sequel to Katharine Lauderdale
Casa Braccio (1895); related to Katharine Lauderdale and The Ralstons.
Adam Johnstone's Son (1896)
Taquisara (1896)
A Rose of Yesterday (1897)
Corleone (1897)
Via Crucis (1899)
In the Palace of the King (1900)
Marietta (1901)
Cecilia (1902)
Man Overboard! (1903)
The Heart of Rome (1903)
Whosoever Shall Offend (1904)
Soprano (1905); U.S. title: Fair Margaret.
A Lady of Rome (1906)
Arethusa (1907)
The Little City of Hope (1907)
The Primadonna (1908); sequel to Soprano/Fair Margaret
The Diva's Ruby (1908); sequel to The Primadonna
The White Sister (1909)
Stradella (1909)
The Undesirable Governess (1910)
Wandering Ghosts; British title: Uncanny Tales.

Non-fiction

Our Silver (1881)
The Novel: What It Is (1893)
Constantinople (1895)
Bar Harbor (1896)
Ave Roma Immortalis (1898)
Rulers of the South (1900; 1905 in the U.S. as Southern Italy and Sicily and The Rulers of the South)
Gleanings from Venetian History (1905; in the U.S. as Salvae Venetia and in 1909 as Venice; the People and the Place)

Drama

In the Palace of the King (1900) with Lorrimer Stoddard.
Francesca da Rimini (1902) The piece was adapted into an opera by Franco Leoni in 1904.
Evelyn Hastings (1902) Unpublished typescript discovered in 2008.
The White Sister (1909) with Walter C. Hackett.

Filmography

A Cigarette-Maker's Romance, directed by Frank Wilson (UK, 1913, based on the novella)
The White Sister, directed by Fred E. Wright [it] (1915, based on the novel)
In the Palace of the King [it], directed by Fred E. Wright [it] (1915, based on the novel)
Whosoever Shall Offend, directed by Arrigo Bocchi (UK, 1919, based on the novel)
Il cuore di Roma, directed by Edoardo Bencivenga (Italy, 1919, based on the novel)
A Cigarette-Maker's Romance, directed by Tom Watts (UK, 1920, based on the novella)
Saracinesca [it], directed by Gaston Ravel (Italy, 1921, based on the novel)
Sant' Ilario [it], directed by Henry Kolker (Italy, 1923, based on the novel)
The White Sister, directed by Henry King (1923, based on the novel)
In the Palace of the King, directed by Emmett J. Flynn (1923, based on the novel)
Son of India, directed by Jacques Feyder (1931, based on the novel Mr. Isaacs)
The White Sister, directed by Victor Fleming (1933, based on the novel)
The Screaming Skull, directed by Alex Nicol (1958, named after the short story)
The White Sister, directed by Tito Davison (Mexico, 1960, based on the novel)

www.ingramcontent.com/pod-product-compliance
Lightning Source LLC
Chambersburg PA
CBHW030105260626
47156CB00008B/2526